Books by Eloisa James

ELOISA JAMES

The Taming of the Duke

AVON BOOKS

An Imprint of HarperCollinsPublishers

AVON BOOKS
An Imprint of HarperCollins*Publishers*
10 East 53rd Street
New York, New York 10022-5299

Copyright © 2006 by Eloisa James
ISBN-13: 978-0-06-078158-3
ISBN-10: 0-06-078158-0
www.avonromance.com

First Avon Books paperback printing: April 2006

Avon Trademark Reg. U.S. Pat. Off. and in Other Countries, Marca Registrada, Hecho en U.S.A.
HarperCollins® is a registered trademark of HarperCollins Publishers Inc.

Printed in the U.S.A.

10 9 8 7 6

*With my great thanks
to everyone who helped with this book,
from my wonderful editor, Lucia,
to my astute and learned research assistant, Franzeca,
to a friend of mine named Kim,
who understands Josie about as well as I do.*

1

In Which the Curiosities of Courtship are Reviewed

August 1817
Ardmore Castle, Scotland

"I wish I were a queen," Miss Josephine Essex said to two of her elder sisters. "I would simply command an appropriate man to marry me by special license."

"What if he refused?" Imogen, sometimes known as Lady Maitland, asked.

"I'd remove his head from his body," Josie said with dignity.

"Given that men make slim use of their heads," Annabel, the Countess of Ardmore said, "you don't have to threaten decapitation; simply allow the fellow to believe that he made up his own mind about marriage." She was tucked in Imogen's bed and appeared little more than a tousle of curls peeking from under the bedcovers.

"That is precisely the kind of advice I need." Josie snapped open a small book and poised her quill. "I am making a study of the skills required to succeed in the marriage market and since you two are both married, you are my primary sources of information."

"I'm a widow," Imogen said. "I know nothing of the marriage market." She was sorting silk stockings and didn't even look up from the dressing table.

"One should be able to dance," Annabel noted. "You really must practice harder, Josie. You were stomping on Mayne's toes the other night."

"I need better advice than that," Josie said to her. "You are the only one of us to have actually gone on the season, *and* you married into a title. You do remember that I'm to have a season next year, don't you?"

Annabel opened one eye. "Only because you mention it every other minute. Lord, but I'm sleepy!"

"I've heard that marriage rots the brain," her youngest sister told her cheerfully.

"In that case, I wonder that you're so interested in it."

Josie ignored that unhelpful comment. "There's more to gaining a husband than not tripping over his feet while waltzing. I want to understand the challenges beforehand. I can't rely on beauty, the way the two of you did."

"That's ridiculous. You are lovely," Annabel said.

"I was in London for the better part of April," Imogen said, "and I saw plenty of young ladies in your situation, Josie. It seemed to me that the primary requirement for a debutante is a smirk. An innocent simper," she clarified.

"Smirk," Josie noted in her book.

"And listen to everything your suitor says as if God Himself is speaking. Of course, sometimes it's difficult to stay awake."

"Men can be very boring," Annabel agreed. "They have such a penchant for discussing themselves. You have to learn to endure, which is not one of your best qualities, Josie."

"To this point, you have shown no ability to suffer fools gladly," Imogen said. "Yet fools have the deepest pockets. It's a proven fact that lack of brains and a large estate go hand in hand."

Josie had been writing busily in her book but she looked up at this. "So I smirk at the fool as he talks about himself? Essentially, toe-curling boredom buys a spouse?"

"I think Imogen is overstating the importance of a smirk," Annabel put in. "There are moments in courtship that can be rather interesting. In my view, for example, a prospective groom might prefer engaging in a mildly scandalous activity to a mutual smirk."

"Annabel has a point. I suppose you might occasionally engage in an impudent act," Imogen said, "but only if you found yourself in the company of a truly engaging young man."

"That's a bit steep coming from you," Josie said. "You devoted yourself to outrageous efforts from the very moment you saw Draven Maitland. Remember how he kissed you, *after* you arranged to fall out of a tree at his feet?"

Imogen's hands stilled for a moment. "Of course I do. It was spring and the apple tree was in bloom."

"And then you fell off a horse, and finally you fell into marriage. Your example seems to go against the model of the innocent simper," Josie said. "I intend to be practical about this business, and I have no particular disinclination to creating a scandal, if that is the most efficacious route to marriage."

"My foolishness is nothing to emulate," Imogen said, returning to her task and folding two pale blue stockings together. "You would do better to find a husband by a more conventional means."

Josie made a note in her book. "Employ an innocent look, no matter how imprudent one's private conduct may be. It sounds like that gentleman thief who is always getting described in the *Times*. One moment he appears as a fine gentleman and then with a twist of a dish clout, he's transformed into a beggar."

"In fact, the reverse of Imogen's style," Annabel pointed out, a hint of mischief in her tone. "Since Imogen specializes in appearing debauched, no matter how innocent her private activities may be. According to Griselda, all of London now believes you are carrying on an illicit amour with Mayne, whereas in truth the man has achieved slightly more intimacy than a footman."

"Every woman should have an occupation," Imogen said. "Mine is to provide interest to the old biddies." She tossed a few stockings over her shoulder. They gently drifted to the bed and fell on Annabel's legs.

"Well, as to that," Josie said thoughtfully, "you seem to be slightly behind the times, Annabel."

"She's more than behind the times. She's utterly out of style," Imogen said. "Last night she was flirting with her husband at supper. That kind of behavior is beyond unfashionable; it's practically indecent. No one is supposed to pay attention to her spouse in public. Or," she added, "in private either."

Annabel grinned and said nothing.

"I saw Ardmore kissing you in the breakfast parlor yesterday," Josie remarked. "Your husband has lost his head, which suggests that you should be able to help me. You must have better suggestions than improving my dancing."

"I hardly planned my course of action in a thoughtful manner," Annabel pointed out. "I was desperately unhappy with this marriage, remember? The only reason you two are in Scotland is to save me from my terrible fate."

"A slight miscalculation on our parts," Imogen said. "I could be in London at this very moment, surveying the dubious temptations of men interested only in my estate."

Annabel snorted. Imogen's hair was a glossy black, and smooth as a raven's feather unless she decided to curl it—whereupon it kept a perfect ringlet. Her eyes were wide apart and framed by brows in a flaring arch. Her mouth was just as wide and made for laughing, even though she'd done precious little of that since her husband died the previous year.

"There are more than enough besotted men throughout London to catalog your features for you," Josie said impatiently. "The really interesting point here is that Annabel doesn't seem to realize that you have been making a concerted effort to woo Mayne into far more intimate activities than are generally enjoyed by footmen."

She ducked as a stocking flew over her head.

"*Really*, Imogen?" Annabel asked.

"I told you in London that I intended to take a cicis-beo," Imogen said with a snap in her voice.

"But I thought you meant merely a gentleman escort, not a *cher ami*."

"It has been my distinct impression," Josie said, "that Imogen has demanded that Mayne prove his reputation as a Lothario is not exaggerated."

Imogen's scowl should have silenced Josie on the spot.

"And I regret to report," Josie continued, apparently unruffled by her sister's fiercest glare, "that to all appearances Mayne has refused the challenge and kept his virtue intact."

"How surprising," Annabel exclaimed, pushing herself up on the pillows and looking altogether more awake. "I was under the impression that he *had* no virtue."

"To the contrary," Josie said. "No matter how Imogen batted her eyelashes at him during the trip to Scotland, he kept to his own bedchamber."

"Josie," Annabel said. "You should not speak of bedchambers—no, or even contemplate such behavior. You sound positively hurly-burly. It would be disastrous for your marriage prospects if anyone heard you talking in this fashion."

"Don't be a goose, Annabel," Josie said unrepentantly. "It's not as if I intend to imitate that behavior. I know the difference between what's allowed a widow and an unmarried girl."

The color was rising in Imogen's cheeks under Annabel's interested gaze.

"I suppose the crucial point is not the position for which you considered Mayne," Annabel said to her, "but the position he has agreed to *take*."

"There's the rub," Josie said. "He managed to get all the way to Scotland with the unblemished virtue of a—a debutante."

Imogen threw a petticoat over her head but Josie just talked right through the frail lace. "There she was, batting her eyelashes, as I said—"

"I never bat my eyelashes!" Imogen put in.

"She batted them," Josie repeated, "and spent a great deal of time trying to convince Mayne that she was besotted with his dark eyes."

Imogen threw a whole heap of petticoats on top of her little sister. "Hurly-burly is too good a phrase for you."

Annabel was clearly fascinated. "Mayne is very handsome. I can certainly sympathize with the impulse."

"No, I—"

"I never said she was truly struck by his eyes," Josie said from under a heap of linens.

"Yes, you did—"

"No." Josie pulled the cloth off her head. "To call a spade a spade, Imogen, you may have tried to turn the earl into your *cher ami*. But you never, ever looked at him with that besotted expression with which you used to watch Draven." She turned to Annabel. "So I would deduce that Imogen was not entranced by his eyes. Perhaps by an arm, a leg, or some other . . . part of his anatomy?"

Annabel frowned at her. "Josie, you wanted advice about the marriage market; I have a serious piece of counsel. Do not indicate that you have the slightest notion what a *cher ami* is. And never make a joke about parts of the male anatomy that you do not feel comfortable naming."

"I have no reluctance to name—" Josie began readily, but Annabel cut her off.

"That's enough! I don't wish for any anatomy lessons from you."

"If Imogen wishes to forgo a life of celibacy, am I supposed to ignore her behavior?" Josie said plaintively. "It's not as if people ignored the fact that Mayne took up with the sister of a woman he jilted. You do remember that he jilted our eldest sister *at* the altar, don't you? Mayne's reputation was ruined the first time he danced with Imogen, given his behavior last year toward Tess."

"Nonsense," Imogen said, finally breaking into the conversation. "Mayne hasn't had a reputation in years. I had nothing to do with it. Any reputation he had left was shattered by his ill-mannered act of jilting Tess in the first place."

"I suppose your disrespectful tone reflects pique," Josie said. "It must be highly annoying to be refused by a man who has so generously spread his attentions around the *ton*."

"Mayne is an idler, and I have no wish to engage in any sort of intimacies with him."

"Excellent," Josie said heartily. "I shall follow your lead and thoroughly dislike all gentlemen who don't instantly succumb to my charms. Of course, given my girth, I just ruled out most of the available gentlemen in London."

"You are an extremely annoying person," Imogen said. "That alone may keep you unmarried."

"Could we return to that particular challenge for a moment?" Josie asked. "I am serious: I need to know how to attain a proposal of marriage, preferably within a few weeks of the season opening."

Annabel shook her head. "None of us has married in a conventional fashion, Josie. Tess married Felton only after Mayne jilted her. I married Ewan because I had to after that scandal broke."

"I eloped with Draven, but I did choose him in the normal way," Imogen said, "and Lord knows that didn't work out very well."

"It would have, if Draven had lived," Annabel pointed out. "You can hardly blame his death on your elopement."

"It's very annoying," Josie muttered. "How am I to do this? How am I to find a husband?"

"I'll be there," Imogen said consolingly. "And Griselda has already agreed to be your chaperone. You know that she knows all the ins and outs of the *ton*."

"She told me that her father arranged her marriage," Josie said, looking uncharacteristically helpless. "We don't have a father."

"We have Rafe," Annabel said.

Imogen shrugged. "When he's sober."

"You're just cross because he didn't like it when you took up with Mayne," Josie said.

"Rafe doesn't seem to understand that my marriage freed him from the need to act as my guardian."

"But you were only married a few weeks," Annabel said gently. "I can see why Rafe still feels responsible for your welfare."

"I have agreed to return to his house, haven't I? I had planned to set up my own establishment, but instead I'll be living with Rafe and trundling around with Griselda as my chaperone. I'm a widow. Why do I need a chaperone?"

"You seem to have left me out of that delectable picture," Josie said. "So, on that note, Annabel, would you consider allowing me to stay with you for the winter? Apparently, dancing is the only practical skill I need to polish before next spring, and I'm sure there must be a tutor somewhere in Scotland. It's so lovely to be back in the Highlands; I loathe the thought of returning to the south."

"Winter is coming," Imogen pointed out.

"I would love to have you stay with me, Josie," Annabel said.

"Will you be quite all right if I don't join you?" Imogen asked. "I doubt very much that Griselda would like to winter in the Highlands."

Annabel had snuggled back down in the covers. "Of course I will be. I'm married." There was a little smile in her eyes.

"I thought you might be nervous about the babe," Imogen said.

Josie gaped, and Annabel sat upright again. "How did you know?"

Imogen laughed. "For goodness sake, Annabel, you generally retire to bed for two days when your flux appears. We've been here since the end of May, and now it's August. You've spent no time whatsoever groaning about the unfairness of a female's condition. In fact, you look utterly pleased to be female."

"Oh, I am," Annabel said, the smile in her eyes growing.

"A baby!" Josie said. "When will it be born?"

"Not for ages yet," Annabel said. "Likely in January or February."

"I needn't return to England for the season until the end of March!"

"Your company would make me very happy," Annabel said, grinning at her little sister.

"Are you certain that you wouldn't like me to stay as well?" Imogen asked, feeling a tremendous reluctance to do so. It wasn't that she was bitter.

A surge of honesty corrected the thought. Of course she was bitter. Two of her sisters were happily married, and now Annabel was having a child. The memories of her two-week-long marriage with Draven were a cold comfort.

"I would love it if you wished to stay," Annabel said, holding out her hand to Imogen. "But I think you should go to London and drive the gentlemen mad by acting like the light widow you so emphatically are not."

"The season is over," Imogen said. "Griselda and I won't go to London. We'll stay with Rafe in the country."

"And Mayne?" Annabel asked.

Imogen shook her head. "A passing fancy," she said. "Luckily he was shrewd enough to see that before I did."

Annabel squeezed her hand.

"Perhaps over the winter you could occupy yourself by making me a list of appropriate *parti*," Josie suggested. "I don't want to waste my smirks on a man who is lacking in the necessary prerequisites. So many people drift through Rafe's house that you are sure to hear all the gossip."

"And those prerequisites are?" Imogen asked, amused.

"I've made a list, garnered from reading every single romantic novel published by Minerva Press." Josie consulted her book. "An estate is necessary, and a title would be nice. He should be able to read, but not too passionately. Unless he likes novels. And I don't want him to be overly fashionable."

"Don't you have any physical requirements?" Annabel asked.

Josie shrugged. "I would prefer that my husband be taller than I am. Since I am rather short, I foresee no difficulty there." She frowned. "Why are you both laughing? There's nothing ludicrous about my ambitions. My list is likely very close to yours, Imogen."

"My what?"

"Your list," Josie said. "Every woman has a list, even if she doesn't write it down."

"I don't," Imogen said, her lips tight.

"It's been almost a year since Draven died," Josie said, as usual wading in where any hardy soul would hesitate. "You'll have to think of marriage again at some point. You don't want to wither into nothing more than an aunt to Annabel's children."

She caught Imogen's sharp gaze but missed Annabel's.

"Well, for goodness sake, you certainly found it accept-able to contemplate intimacies with Mayne. From what I understand, marriage is merely a regularizing of that sort of relation."

"Josie!" Annabel moaned.

Imogen started laughing again. "Now there's a cold-hearted look at matrimony."

"Your list and mine are likely the same," Josie said. "You simply haven't clarified your demands and I have."

"Tell me again what qualities I am looking for?"

"An estate. A title, if possible. Intelligence, but not to an uncomfortable degree. The same goes with fashion. One would dislike being married to a man who always looked better than oneself."

"I think you should be a tad more specific," Imogen said. "Our own guardian would fit every category you mentioned—Rafe has an estate, a title, sufficient height, no sense of fashion whatsoever, and a reasonable amount of intelligence, if slightly pickled."

"You're right," Josie said. "I shall add an age limita-tion." She sat down, quill poised. "Shall I cut them off at thirty, or twenty-five?"

"My point was more that Rafe is a drunkard," Imo-gen said. "Your list overlooks every important character-istic that one would want in a husband."

"I suppose you are talking about steadiness of charac-ter," Josie said. "Rafe actually has that. He's attractive too, very. He's just too old for me."

Imogen suddenly noticed that both Annabel and Josie were watching her. "He's far too old *and* too drunk for me," she said quickly.

"You are over twenty-one," Josie said with her customary crushing truthfulness. "And you are a widow. I think it is an entirely inappropriate match, as far as age is concerned."

"Rafe may not be perfect for you, darling," Annabel said, taking Imogen's hand. "But someone will be."

A little wry smile turned the corner of Imogen's lips. "In truth," she said, "I'm one of those people who fall in love only once, Annabel."

"If we could all plan the moment when we would fall in love as easily as I am making this list," Josie said, "the world would be an altogether more tolerable place. For one thing, I would make certain to fall in love only *after* a man had sworn undying love."

"Good luck," Imogen said, hearing the disconsolate ring in her own voice.

Annabel squeezed her hand again.

2

A Conversation Being Heard Out of Order, as It Took Place Some Three Months Previous

May 1817
Holbrook Court, seat of the Duke of Holbrook

There was his nose and his jaw. Not his waistline, but definitely his eyes. Even as a man who had spent more time before the mirror at Bartholomew Fair than the glass in his own bedchamber, Rafe knew those eyes. Deeply shadowed, under straight brows. They were his.

And his father's.

It was as if one of the illusion mirrors from a fair had come to life and was standing before him. At Bartholomew Fair, for example, a person with tuppence to spend can view a man with two heads, or a chicken with three legs. For another tuppence, one can turn one-self into the sideshow: the Illusion Room features a mir-ror that endows one's stomach with the curve of a

Christmas pudding. Rafe had rather disliked the effect. Even pulling himself up and assuming a stature most suited to the Duke of Holbrook had no effect.

The Earl of Mayne had laughed at Rafe's sour expression. He was surveying his polished elegance in a mirror that made him as willowy as a nymph. "Try this one," he had said, "you'll prefer it."

Secretly, Rafe had. The image in the thinner mirror had no softness about the waist; all of a sudden he looked taut and fit, as if he never greeted the dawn with a full stomach and an aching head.

Now it was as if that second mirror image had come to life and was standing before him.

"You were born in 1781?" he asked, trying to pull his wits together.

"I'm thirty-six, having been born within a few days of yourself, as I always understood." There was just the faintest pause, and then he added, "Your Grace."

"May I offer you a whiskey?" Rafe said.

"Not at this hour."

Rafe walked over to the sideboard and poured himself a glass. Holding it in his hand made the next question easier. "So did you arrive in the world a few days before or after myself?" He didn't turn around, just stared through the mullioned windows of his library. He'd stood before them time and again, but now those little diamonds of shimmering Elizabethan glass seemed suddenly to frame the great sweep of front lawn with black-edged perfection.

Behind him, Mr. Spenser sounded amused. "I chased you into the world, Your Grace. But I can assure you, I have no wish for your estate, even if such a thing were possible."

Rafe turned about. "I had not assumed that you were expressing the desire; I merely wished to know our birth order for my own satisfaction."

There was a sardonic gleam in his half brother's eyes, and the fact that Rafe himself habitually greeted lame answers with the same look of disbelief was cold comfort. "My Christian name is Rafe," he said abruptly. "I dislike being addressed as Your Grace." And then, as if the two facts followed each other naturally, "I had a brother named Peter, but he died some years ago."

"I was under the impression that your given name was Raphael," the man said. He had seated himself while Rafe had his back turned, and he sat easily, with no sign of discomfort. As if they were equals, and as if he introduced himself to a brother or two every day.

"It is," Rafe said. "And your name?"

"We are tarred with the same brush," Mr. Spenser said rather obscurely.

Rafe found himself blinking like the village idiot. "What?"

"Gabriel."

"Raphael and Gabriel," Rafe said. "Bloody hell. I had no idea."

Suddenly the rather serious set of his brother's face shifted to a grin. "The discovery that you are named for an archangel drove you to curses?"

It was in his smile that Rafe found the difference between his brother's face and his own. For Gabriel

Spenser's grin had a charming seriousness to it that had never been part of Rafe's personality.

"What could our father have been thinking?" Rafe demanded. And then he caught, lightning quick, the shift in his brother's eyes that showed *he* knew perfectly well what the old duke had been thinking. "Next thing you'll be telling me that Holbrook dandled you on his knee," Rafe said resignedly.

"Only until age eight or so," Mr. Spenser said, adding with a touch of something like prudence, "Your Grace."

"Bloody hell," Rafe repeated. "And *don't* call me Your Grace. I've never taken to the title." There was a moment, and then: "My brother and I saw my—our—father on a biannual basis, just enough so that the duke could inform himself on how rapidly we were approaching the age of majority. We never appeared to be getting old fast enough."

He hated sympathy. Except from Peter, and it was an odd realization to find that he didn't mind seeing it in this new brother's eyes either.

"Would it be all right if I call you Gabriel?" Rafe asked, sipping his whiskey.

"Gabe."

"How many of there are you?" he asked, suddenly realizing that the countryside might well be littered with his kin. "Have I a sister?"

"Unfortunately, all the archangels were male."

"There are always the apocryphal gospels."

"I'm the only child of my mother. And the apocryphal gospels are unreliable. Your father would never have countenanced naming one of his children Uriel, although the name appears in the *Book of Enoch*."

"He's your father as well," Rafe observed. And: "You seem remarkably well informed about biblical matters."

"I'm a scholar," Gabe said with a faint smile. "Of biblical history, particularly the Old Testament."

Rafe's head was spinning. He had just discovered that he himself was named after an archangel and now it seemed that his brother was a scholar. A *biblical* scholar? For all Gabe looked like Beelzebub himself. "Damn me pink," he said. "Father didn't send you into that field because he named you with such ambition, did he?"

"The same nomenclature didn't turn you into a priest. No. Your father did pay for me to go to Cambridge, however. I am still there, at Emmanuel College."

"Is it bloody difficult to pass those exams?" Rafe said with ready sympathy. He'd been to Oxford himself, and although he found it easy enough, everyone knew that Cambridge was full of brilliant men who prided themselves on actually teaching something to their students.

"In fact, I did manage to pass the exams," his brother said gravely. "I am a professor of divinity."

Rafe blinked at him. Gabriel's hair was standing up at the back of his head, precisely as Rafe's was no doubt doing. "At Oxford, there are only twenty-four professors in the whole university."

"I suppose I haven't had the intrusions of rank and birth to hamper me," his brother said thoughtfully. "I can see that this house, for example, would be a terrible distraction."

Distraction? The seat of the Holbrooks since the 1300s . . . a distraction? But there was something Rafe had to ask. "Did my father have other children that you know about?" His lips felt stiff, even forming that question aloud. He was never fond of his father; indeed, he had hardly known the man. But he had thought him honorable if distant, interested in his reputation, if not his sons.

Gabe looked at him levelly, from under those black eyebrows that mimicked his own. "Your father and my mother were quite devoted to each other."

Rafe sat down, unable to imagine his father devoted to anyone.

"I do not think," Gabe added, "that you need worry about covetous siblings leaping from the woodwork."

"Ah," Rafe said. "Of course . . ." But he couldn't think what to say next. Only a fool would describe his mother as devoted to his father; they rarely saw each other. If one of his parents was in town, one was sure to find the other in the country.

A moment of silence fell between them. We're as alike as two peas in a pod, Rafe thought. Gabe had his large body, albeit with no softness in the waist. That was his unruly brown hair, and those were his large feet. The curve of his lip, the cleft in his chin, the square jaw were all familiar. Even the way Gabe was tapping his middle finger against the arm of his chair, which was precisely the kind of fidget that Rafe found himself doing when he had an unpleasant subject to broach.

"I expect this sounds preposterous," Gabe said. "But

my mother, in particular, was quite sorry to hear of your brother's death. She thought him a delightful man, and very like his father."

Rafe stared. "She *knew* Peter?"

"Yes. I met him as well. When your father's will was proved, there was a bequest for my mother and myself."

"But I was there when the will was read!" Rafe felt as if he were riding a nag, trying to catch a group on thoroughbreds. "I would surely have noticed when that bequest was mentioned."

Gabe shrugged. "A silent clause, as I understand it. One has to guess that they are quite common. I expect the solicitor informed your brother in private."

"He was your brother as well," Rafe corrected. "And so Peter sought you out." Of course Peter would have done that. He would have wanted to make sure that their father's mistress was well taken care of. His—no, their—elder brother had been the consummate gentleman.

"His Grace took tea with my mother. She quite enjoyed his company."

Rafe put his drink to the side. "Why did you wait so long to tell me of your existence? Peter died four years ago."

Instead of answering, Gabe looked at him quizzically. "You are quite different from your brother."

"It seems I have two brothers," Rafe said a bit sharply.

Gabe ignored that. "I would guess that your brother Peter would no more have asked an illegitimate brother to address him by his Christian name than he would have walked on water."

Rafe shrugged. "You likely know more about occurrences of the latter than I do."

After a moment, Gabe said, "I have seen no need to inform you of my existence. Your father was more than generous in his bequest."

"If there is any help that I can offer," Rafe said, "you must never hesitate to ask. You are my brother, for all you keep calling our father *mine*."

"Don't you wish to confirm my parentage with your solicitor?" There was a twist to Gabe's mouth that Rafe recognized with a drop of his stomach, because it wasn't his but Peter's. It seemed this new brother was a mixture of the two of them.

"There's no need." Rafe met his brother's eyes squarely. "I am only sorry that Peter did not see fit to share your existence earlier." Peter wouldn't have even thought of it, of course. His dearest brother had seen the world as a maze of distinct compartments, and illegitimate brothers did not belong in the same room—or compartment—with legitimate ones.

Then it was Gabe's turn to lunge from his chair and stare out the window. Only a faint stiffness about his shoulders betrayed tension. "It is a small thing that I ask," he said finally.

"Anything," Rafe said, wondering how many pounds he could raise in the next day or so without traveling to London.

"I need you to put on a play."

"*What?*"

"A play," Gabe repeated. "In the Holbrook Court theater." He swung about, those level eyebrows lowered now, tensed like a bull about to charge.

But Rafe couldn't help grinning. Just so would he have asked such an absurd question: hunched against the stupidity of it. "For God's sake. Never tell me *you*, a Cambridge doctor of divinity, have an ambition to tread the boards?"

He could feel laughter growing in the very edges of his soul. In fact, he hadn't felt this cheerful since—

"No!" Gabe said, looking disgusted.

"Damn," Rafe said. "I had a notion I could watch you tantalize the ladies while wearing my skin, so to speak."

"No such luck."

"It would have raised my countenance no end," Rafe said pensively. "Just think: the brother of the Duke of Holbrook as the ladies' favorite in *Romeo and Juliet*."

"I'm too old for the role. And that would be illegitimate brother, hardly a compliment to the family."

"I don't give a damn about your status. That's one thing you have yet to learn about me. I am not Peter. What about *Antony and Cleopatra*? Antony was over forty, wasn't he?"

"I'm too young for that. More to the point, I've no ambition to play a part."

"Then what do you want to use the theater for?" Rafe suddenly remembered his forgotten whiskey and took a mouthful.

"How can you drink that rotgut at nine in the morning?" Gabe asked, his eyebrows lowering again.

"It's the finest Scotch whiskey, not rotgut. It's been through an aging process," Rafe said, regarding his glass fondly. "This is from the Ardbeg stills, and not available in England yet. I had to send a man all the way to Aberdeen to fetch me some. It tastes . . ." Rafe paused and rolled the golden liquor on his tongue, "It tastes like burnt honey and kisses your throat like a strumpet."

Now *that* was Peter's look of disapproval. Just so had Rafe's elder brother signaled his ducal displeasure.

"It's not every day that one gains a brother," Rafe added. "You can remind me daily what I would look like if I were slimmer and more jovial and altogether a better person." He threw back the rest of the whiskey and then put down the glass with a click. It didn't taste very good, not with those eyes narrowed on him.

"I need you to put on an amateur theatrical," Gabe said. "Using a mixture of professional and amateur actors. I believe that is quite in fashion these days."

"I—"

"You'll have to open up the theater," Gabe continued. "By all accounts, the place hasn't been used since a performance of *Hamlet* in 1800. Unless you've been putting on private theatricals?"

Rafe shook his head.

"If you're not a drama enthusiast yourself," Gabe continued, "there appear to be any number of gentry about who are taken with the idea of amateur theatricals. Perhaps you could import one of them to do the business."

"I haven't even been to a theater in a year," Rafe said, "perhaps three or four years."

His brother scowled. "You'll have to find someone then."

His eyes were remarkably compelling under those eyebrows. Rafe felt as if he were expected to leap from his chair and begin ripping a copy of *King Lear* into players' parts. "Why?"

"Because if you can't get together a theatrical, we need someone who can."

"No, *why* am I putting on a play? And why here? I'd be happy to back the play of your choice in a London theater. But what possible value can there be to having such a performance here?"

Gabe paused.

"I'm waiting for an explanation," Rafe said, getting up and wandering over to pour himself another drink. The day would clearly have nothing productive about it. He might as well celebrate.

His brother appeared at his shoulder. "One glass," Gabe said, "may be attributed to the enthusiasm of discovering a sibling. Another smacks of something altogether different."

Rafe put down the decanter without pouring a drink. "How quickly one forgets the joys of living with family," he stated. "Now, do you care to tell me what this play business is all about?"

He could tell precisely how unpleasant the revelation, whatever it was, felt for his brother: by the rigidity of his jaw and the glower in his brows.

"I have a daughter," Gabe said abruptly.

"*What!*"

"Out of wedlock," he clarified. "Like father, like son,

it appears." That was no smile; more a widening of his lips.

"I have a niece," Rafe said to himself, knowing he was grinning like a fool. "Is she a very good actress?"

"God's sakes, no!" Gabe bellowed. "She's only two months old."

Rafe was thoroughly enjoying himself. He leaned against the sideboard, and crossed his arms. It was precisely the kind of pleasure he used to feel on the rare occasions when Peter betrayed some emotion unfitting to his dukedom. "And here I thought I'd gained myself a respectable biblical scholar as a brother. Perhaps I should check you for a cloven hoof."

"My daughter's mother is an actress."

Not a lady, then. Rafe sobered and tried to put the question delicately but it came out with all the finesse of a blunt weapon: "They say marriage is pressing to death, but sometimes it's acceptable."

"She's refused me. Several times."

"That's odd," Rafe said. In his experience, women used pregnancy as a battering ram to make their way into marriage. And that went equally for the kind of woman labeled *lady* and for her counterparts, those labeled by profession as actresses, singers and other less salubrious occupations.

"Loretta believes that a husband would hamper her career as an actress," Gabe said, his mouth a hard line.

"She let you warm her sheets, but she wouldn't take a ring? She must be stark, raving mad."

"Not mad, but young."

"How young?"

Gabe's mouth grew even tighter. "I had assumed she was at least three and twenty. It seems that she is only nineteen years of age."

Rafe gaped at him. "What the hell did you do? Steal her from under her father's roof?"

"Absolutely not. Her father was a wealthy burgher who left her his fortune. She was raised by an aunt, but the moment Loretta turned eighteen years of age and inherited control, she set up her own household."

"In Cambridge?"

"In London. She has a fierce passion for the stage."

It seemed his brother had fallen prey to a woman of little morals and less family. He tried to make the question delicate. "Are you quite certain that the child is . . ."

"She is mine. And she lives with me." Gabe swung around to face Rafe fully. "Loretta had no more wish to be a mother than to be a wife. Unfortunately, I am responsible for Loretta losing her place at the Royal Theater at Covent Garden. And a well-attended lead role in an amateur production might well result in a permanent position at one of the London theaters."

"That's where I come in," Rafe said, grinning.

Gabe didn't look amused. "Just because I'm named after an archangel doesn't mean that I couldn't clout Raphael to the ground if I wished."

Rafe laughed aloud. No one had offered to clout him since Peter died. Just so had Peter looked, about two minutes before he would make a concerted effort to pound him into the pavement. Not that a brother one has known for a mere twenty minutes would presumably lose control on such brief acquaintance, but the very thought of it made Rafe grin.

"We can have the theater in ready shape in a matter of a month or two."

Gabe's jaw was rigid. "I would never have approached you except this happened," he said fiercely. He stood in the middle of the room, his eyes shadowed, his face beautiful as that of an archangel himself, his body furious with rage.

Rafe couldn't seem to stop smiling. "I seem to remember the housekeeper nattering on about rain on the stage. The floor might have to be replaced."

"I regret putting you to the trouble." His eyes were bleak with distaste. Whoever Gabe's mother was—and she must have been quite a woman to inspire the former Duke of Holbrook's devotion—she had raised her son as a gentleman. Gabe had the pained look of every English gentleman caught in an untenable situation.

"You'll have to bring the baby here," Rafe said. "Believe it or not, I have a brand-new nursery upstairs. What's her name?"

"I most certainly will not!"

Rafe folded his arms over his chest. "You will. Unless you and my niece are here, I won't order work on the theater."

"I'm in the midst of the Easter Term."

"Don't tell me you're actually planning to talk to a student," Rafe scoffed. "Oxford can't be so different from Cambridge, and I think I only met a proper professor once in my years there."

"Why would you want us here?"

"You're my brother," he said, grinning. "My brother and his daughter will live at Holbrook Court."

"Your illegitimate brother and his illegitimate child," Gabe said grimly. "And I won't live here; I have a perfectly respectable house in Cambridge."

"Do I look as if I give a damn about your respectable house *or* my reputation?"

A grin quirked the corner of Gabe's mouth. "No. But I wouldn't wish to separate my daughter from her wet nurse, and the woman has children of her own in Cambridge."

"What is my niece's name? And don't tell me—" But he saw the truth of it in his brother's eyes. "You didn't!"

"I couldn't help it," Gabe said, and he was starting to laugh now as well.

"Poor child," Rafe said mournfully. "She has a crazed papa. Lucky for her, she will have me as a mitigating influence."

Gabe rolled his eyes.

"Poor little mite," Rafe repeated. "So she's Mary, is she?"

And, at Gabe's nod, "Heavenly. That's just heavenly."

3

Lessons in the Art of Widowhood

September 14, 1817
On the road from Scotland

There are people who travel well. They make long journeys with cheerfulness and fortitude, watching endless leagues spin by the window with equanimity. Imogen was not one of them. Sitting in a carriage gave her far too much time to think, and thinking tended to turn into brooding. Should she remarry? She'd spent so many years longing for Draven that she felt far more unmoored than one presumably should after the demise of a two-week marriage. It wasn't just a two-week marriage. It was the five years of adoration that preceded their marriage. It was the hundreds of times she'd traced the name Lady Imogen Maitland on a scrap of foolscap, and the thousands of times she'd assured her sisters that she would marry Draven ... someday.

It was a fact that she had designed her entire adult life around Draven Maitland. And now he was gone, sometimes she felt as if there was no Imogen without him.

Marry? Marry whom? And why?

Draven had been gone a year, and it was only now that such questions seemed to be leaping before her, unhampered by that burning grief that kept her in tears and anger for the past twelve months.

But the discomfort of being thrown on the mercy of her own thoughts was not a scrap on the discomfort suffered by her poor chaperone, Lady Griselda Willoughby.

Griselda had climbed into the carriage in Scotland with her crisped curls tucked under a beautiful little bonnet. She was starched, plump, and charming. Now, a fortnight later, she turned pale at the very sight of the carriage. She was no longer starched, much thinner, and charm was in short supply.

"I just don't understand what is wrong with your stomach," Imogen said, ringing the bell so that the coach could pull over for the second time that morning.

"I've always had these problems," Griselda said. She was leaning against the wall, her face a delicate green. The color of spring leaves that have just unfurled, Imogen decided. "How long have we left on this benighted road?"

"Just one more day," Imogen said, tucking a rug around Griselda's knees.

"Just look at me," Griselda moaned. "I've lost my shape entirely."

"Well," Imogen said tentatively, "there are a great many people who find a slim figure desirable given the current fashion in slender gowns."

"Naught more than female fools," Griselda moaned. "Men like curves and they always will. I do try to reduce sometimes, but not—not in this drastic fashion!"

"But Griselda," Imogen said, searching for a way to put her question delicately, "are you . . . *interested* in what men think?"

"I haven't been measured for a coffin yet," Griselda said, not opening her eyes.

"Of course not!" By Imogen's calculations, her chaperone was around thirty years old: not young, but not old either. And certainly not too old to remarry. "But you haven't shown any interest in marriage, to this point. Your husband has been gone for quite a while, hasn't he?"

"Over ten years," Griselda said. "And I am considering the possibility of marriage."

"Do you have anyone in mind?" Imogen inquired.

"No." She huddled in the corner looking as miserable as a sparrow with a broken wing. "I shall take the matter under consideration when the season begins."

Imogen thought for a while about the delights of marriage. Of course, she'd only been married two weeks, so it could be said that her experience was insignificant. "How long were you married?" she asked.

"A year. Did I have a small dog when you first arrived from Scotland?"

Imogen thought back to the days before she married Draven, when she, Tess, Annabel, and Josie had arrived at Rafe's house with little more than the clothes on their backs. "No," she said. "You didn't have a dog. I would remember that."

Griselda had walked into Rafe's drawing room wearing one of the most exquisite gowns that Imogen had ever seen. That night, Annabel had said dreamily that there could be nothing better than to be a rich widow with all the money in the world to spend, and no husband to share it with.

And here was Imogen, a rich widow with no husband. It was odd how unpleasant desirable states could be when one was experiencing them.

"I had a dog briefly," Griselda continued. "His name was Milo. He was one of those small brown dogs. But he started eating and eating and growing and growing." She opened her eyes and stared at Imogen. "Before I knew it, he was as high as my knee. *All* he thought about was food. A very nice dog, in his own way, but desperate to eat at any moment of the day."

"Hmmm," Imogen said, wondering if she should get a dog. At least it would provide companionship.

"Willoughby—my husband—was precisely like that dog," Griselda said, closing her eyes again. "Both of them thought about food before anything else. Both would get a painfully eager look in their eye and a little anticipatory wiggle in their bodies when it was time for a meal."

"Oh dear," Imogen said.

"The only difference was that I did not wait to find out whether Milo killed himself overeating, the way Willoughby did. I gave Milo away."

"So we have to find you a very slim man to marry."

"One who is uninterested in food," Griselda said firmly.

"Why have you decided to marry after so long?"

"I'm tired of being alone. Playing a chaperone to your sisters has been eye-opening in that respect."

Imogen thought about how much her sister Annabel was in love with her husband. And then there was Tess, whose eyes glowed at the very sight of her spouse. "I see what you mean," she said with a sigh. "My sisters are happy in their marriages."

"It gives one to think," Griselda said. She delicately wrapped a lacy scarf around her neck. "My marriage was not, you understand, of the same caliber."

"Nor mine," Imogen said, pushing away a tiny pulse of disloyalty.

But Griselda's eyes had no surprise in them. "Maitland was a very beautiful man," she said tranquilly. "In many years of being in society, I have found that beauty is a great drawback in a man. It seems frequently paired with petulance and an unfortunate degree of arrogance."

Imogen opened her mouth to defend her Draven . . . and shut it again. He had been arrogant. He had been petulant too, whining about his mother's tight control over her money. But worse than those, he had been reckless, throwing himself on the back of any horse in the pursuit of a bet. He simply couldn't bear not to win.

"Of course, Maitland may well have grown into an easier person over the years," Griselda offered.

A little smile curled Imogen's lips. "Or not."

"I find it helpful to regard the past optimistically. The important thing to remember is that there was little you could have done, either to make your marriage a success or to keep Maitland alive."

Imogen swallowed. She was finally coming to agree with Griselda. At first, she couldn't bear the pain of her own guilt. Then she began blaming herself. And now, finally, she was beginning to accept the fact that she couldn't have stopped Draven from racing to his death. He was like an unbroken colt, and she was by no means a strong enough woman to put him to bridle.

"I am not ready to remarry," she said suddenly. "I dreamed about marriage to Draven for most of my life. Now I would like to just be Imogen for a while."

"A laudable ambition," Griselda said. "Would that I did not have to be Griselda, at least until we get out of this carriage and my stomach calms."

"This may shock you," Imogen said, biting her lip.

"I doubt it," Griselda replied. "I have some difficulty working up to such excesses of emotion when in the throes of nausea. Besides I know perfectly well what you are planning."

Imogen raised an eyebrow.

"Last year," Griselda said, "you desired a little *affaire* for all the wrong reasons. You were angry at your husband for dying."

"I was angry at myself for failing him," Imogen said softly.

"Now you have decided on the same course of action, but for different reasons."

"You say it so calmly! Don't you mean to lecture me on the evils of illicit relationships?"

"No. I am quite certain you are aware of the disagreeable consequences if the *ton* were to discover your activities. But I have found that occasionally a small peccadillo that harms no one can be conducive to a cheerful disposition."

Imogen's eyes widened. "Are you saying that you have indulged in a peccadillo, Griselda? *You?*"

Griselda frowned. "As I said, I haven't been measured for a coffin yet. And the fact that I have not chosen to give myself in marriage does not mean that I haven't availed myself—very occasionally and very discreetly— of the pleasures of companionship."

Imogen stared with fascination at her chaperone, who was known far and wide in the *ton* for being one of the most chaste and virtuous widows in London. "Does Mayne know?"

"Why on earth would I share such a detail with a brother? Believe me, child, one learns quickly that making a confidant of a man can lead to nothing but trouble, and men who are actually in one's family are the worst choice of all."

Imogen thought about that.

"On that subject," Griselda said, "I would prefer that you did not choose my brother for your further adventures . . . I think it is time that he married."

"Do you?" Imogen found it extremely difficult to imagine the Earl of Mayne (who was riding beside the carriage) tied to anyone's apron strings.

"What's more, these little affairs are much better conducted out of the public eye. Everyone would take particular enjoyment in watching you and Mayne, given their delight in your so-public flirtation last year."

"Nothing came of it," Imogen said hastily.

"I know that. But if you and he are still seen together in the coming season, it will be a truly fascinating *on-dit*, given my brother's apparent inability to continue a relationship with a woman past a few weeks."

"Mayne is not a possibility," Imogen said. Never mind the fact that he showed no interest in her. Mayne was not what she had in mind. He was too volatile, too sophisticated and altogether too uncomfortable. "I thought to have a friendship with someone unknown to the *ton*."

"That is an excellent idea," Griselda approved. "A gentleman, naturally, but someone who keeps to himself. Perhaps Rafe has some particularly rustic friend who might interest you for a brief time. It is better to find someone who is absolutely *not* husband material."

Imogen shook her head. "I am amazed, Griselda. Truly, I am."

"If you will forgive me for saying so, my dear, you have been quite at the mercy of your emotions for several years. But emotion is an unreliable guide to men. I find it helpful to observe the male sex objectively whenever possible. They have great charms. Yet one should avail oneself of those charms only in situations in which one has the upper hand at all times."

She settled her rug around her more snugly. "Men are troublesome to one's dignity and one's peace of mind. Keep that firmly in mind, and choose a man with no wish to claim you in marriage."

"I am amazed," Imogen repeated. "Amazed."

Griselda raised an eyebrow. "Amazement is a necessary precursor to sophistication, my dear. Let me add that if you feel the inclination to befriend someone, do so for one night, or at the very most, two. If we females become overly intimate, we run every risk of falling in love. I have seen it happen to friends a hundred times."

Imogen opened her mouth but Griselda held up a delicate hand.

"I am well aware that you have already suffered a bout of love. While it undoubtedly cured you of a desire to repeat the experience, beware! Be very careful."

Imogen nodded. Griselda referred to love with all the horror that one might describe a bout of measles. It was eye-opening.

"One night, or perhaps two, if the gentleman in question is particularly amiable. Naturally, you must avoid having a child. I can give you some instruction on that matter."

"Nothing came of my marriage," Imogen said sadly. "I'm not certain that children are something I should worry about."

"You were only married for a few weeks. Now I was married for a year, but the truth of it was that poor Willoughby was rather too large to be comfortable in those circumstances. My dear friend, Lady Feddrington, tells me that her husband suffers a similar indisposition.

"End the affair briskly, and without allowing the slightest room for doubt," Griselda continued. "Tell the gentleman that while you are grateful for the lovely time that you spent in his company, you have seen the error of your ways and wish to lead a celibate existence. You can add some flummery about his having given you pleasure you never experienced before, if you wish."

Imogen nodded, wishing that she had Josie's little book to take notes in.

"On occasion, a hitherto rational man might act in a thoroughly distracted fashion when you inform him of your wish to end the relationship. I generally inform them that while I am not betraying poor Willoughby (he *is* dead, after all), I have decided, upon reflection, that I am betraying myself. They never have any adequate rebuttal, and you can part on the best of terms. If it weren't for this foolish stomach of mine, I could perhaps think of something else . . . oh, there is one more thing."

"Does every widow know these rules?" Imogen asked, fascinated by this glance into Griselda's life.

"Certainly not, or there wouldn't be so many foolish women throwing their reputations away. The most important rule is that you never look to the servants. I have to tell you, my dear, that there have been ladies who looked aside to footmen." She widened her eyes impressively. "Even gardeners!"

Imogen and her sisters had studied every London journal they could find during their childhood in Scotland, and they were well acquainted with the occasional shocked comment that the Countess of Such and Such had escaped to France in the company of a member of her household.

"Widowhood can be a long and a lonely state of affairs, Imogen. But only—" Griselda smiled—"if one chooses to experience it in that fashion."

Imogen nodded.

"I foresee a happy widowhood for you," Griselda observed. "Will you ring that bell again, my dear? I am afraid it is a matter of some urgency."

4

In Which it is Discovered That Marriage is the Greater of Many Evils

A house party, Wintersall Estate
Somerset

Gillian Pythian-Adams was bored. It wasn't an un-usual sensation, but it was certainly an unpleasant one. "Mr. Wintersall," she said, painstakingly remind-ing herself that in matters of grave importance, sincerity was not important. "I honor you enormously. I—"

"My mother is quite carried away by the boldness with which I affirmed to her that you were the spouse of my choice," Mr. Wintersall stated. "I think I hardly need tell you that, generally speaking, I take my mother's advice in all things. In fact, she asked particularly that I should assure you of that. I am not a man who refuses to take advice from a woman."

"I am touched by your—your boldness," Gillian said. "But—"

"Miss Pythian-Adams," Mr. Wintersall interrupted. It was likely a constitutional problem with him.

"Yes?"

"It seems to me that you may be laboring under a misapprehension . . ." And he was off again. Gillian caught sight of herself in the mirror on the opposite side of the room. There she was: green eyes, red hair, her mother's slender oval of a face. Her gown was, if she said so herself, exquisite. She was the picture of a perfect lady. So why was she so different from the other young ladies of her acquaintance?

Why was she the only one who found it a torment to listen to the insipidies and stupidities of men, to pompous, arrogant proposals given by half-baked men who expected her to respond with gratitude, if not slavish adulation? Her father laughed and said it was the penalty for reading too many plays. Her mother looked worried and said a man would come along who was not a fool.

For some years, Gillian had believed her. In the beginning she had punctiliously attended every ball to which she was invited, awaiting the moment when her less-than-foolish future husband would stroll into her presence. When that hope dwindled, she engaged herself to a fool, Draven Maitland, thinking that saving her family's fortunes was a passable alternative to loneliness. Then Draven had taken himself away, which left her prey to proposals.

The worst of it was that she was starting to dislike

everyone. She no longer met a strange gentleman with the hope that he would prove himself different; she merely watched, indifferent, as the creature sprouted his silly chatter, his foolish persiflage. From Gillian's point of view, all men, including Mr. William Wintersall, were primitive, direct and deadly (to borrow a phrase from a second-rate play) in their pursuit of one thing. She wished she could pretend it was pursuit of beautiful eyes, or even desire for her company in the bedchamber.

As far as she could tell, her dowry trumped the above.

Mr. Wintersall provided an excellent example of pure lust for lucre overcoming his obvious lack of interest in her person. He had (finally) dispensed with his mother's views of marriage and had launched into a genial hymn of self-praise. Gillian had no doubt that were she dull-witted enough to accept his hand in marriage, that particular hymn would grow into a daily chorus in which she would be compelled to join. The very thought of it made her shudder.

"Mr. Wintersall," she said firmly, "I cannot marry you."

"Oh, but—" he said, floundering into a sentence so full of platitudes that he couldn't see his way to the end.

"I never alter my opinion when it comes to things of this nature."

He blinked at her uncertainly. "In questions of marriage," she clarified. Then she patted the seat next to her. "You must tell your mama that you actually wish to marry Miss Hazeleigh."

Alarm filled his dull blue eyes. "But I don't! I wish to marry you." All the same, he stumbled off his knees—

all that weight around his middle must have been putting terrific pressure on them—and sank into the seat beside her.

"You do not wish to marry me," Gillian said calmly. "Your mother told you to marry me. You wish to marry Lettice Hazeleigh. And I think there is"—she paused for a moment—"a reasonable chance that she might return your affections."

"Oh, but I couldn't—I mean, I don't wish—"

"I recognize that her lack of dowry may be seen in some quarters as a problem. But *you*, Mr. Wintersall, do not seem to me a man whose soul is engaged in such material pursuits."

He gaped at her.

"While one naturally has confidence in the opinion of one's mother," she explained, "one does not wish to follow her lead in all things. In pursuit of the woman you love," Gillian said meditatively, "I can see that you, Mr. Wintersall, would be completely unlike all the silly men of the *ton*. No, you strike me as a man who would be primitive, direct, and deadly in your pursuit of the woman of your heart!"

Mr. Wintersall snapped his mouth shut. Gillian congratulated herself on the effectiveness of that particular line. Luckily, lines of dialogue were somewhat interchangeable.

"Tell your mama that you intend to marry Lettice," Gillian said.

Mr. Wintersall frowned.

"A man of your quality does not allow his mama to choose his wife."

"But my mama doesn't wish me to márry you," Mr. Wintersall blurted out. "She was of the opinion that you were long in the tooth and difficult to bring to the bridle."

Gillian recoiled for a second and then nodded. "She was right."

"I—I would like to marry you anyway," Mr. Wintersall said. He toppled off the sofa again and pressed his lips to Gillian's hand, painstakingly, moving his mouth up approximately two inches with each kiss.

At this rate, Gillian thought, he will reach my elbow by next Tuesday. Apparently it was wishful thinking when she decided that Mr. Wintersall had formed an attraction for Lettice. Lettice needed a husband, and Mr. Wintersall would have been just right for her.

He was reaching the edge of her glove and might actually touch her skin, so Gillian withdrew her hand. "Mr. Wintersall," she said, coming to her feet in a brisk movement, "I must make my regrets. I have an important appointment, and I can give you no further audience." She made up her mind on the moment. "Tomorrow morning my mother and I are leaving to attend a house party. You see, the Duke of Holbrook has requested my assistance in opening his private theater."

Mr. Wintersall's eyes narrowed slightly. "My mother feels that private theatricals are rather risqué, nay, even rash for a young lady."

Gillian thought about smiling and decided not to make the effort. "Your mother is slightly out-of-date," she said. "Everyone from Lady Hardwicke to the Duchess of Bedford are engaging in private theatricals these days. Why, before she died the Duchess of Holbrook herself was passionately interested in the theater. By all accounts, the theater at Holbrook Court is modeled on that of the Duchess of Marlborough, and you know hers is declared the most elegant outside London." Until this moment, Gillian had thought to reject the Duke of Holbrook's invitation, but she was feeling more interested by the second.

"If we were married," William pointed out, "no one would gainsay your interest in theatricals. No Mrs. Wintersall's virtue has ever been questioned." His chest swelled with pride.

Gillian thought of the sour, virtuous face of his mother and agreed.

William bounded to his feet with an ungainly enthusiasm. "You haven't given me time to argue my case!"

"There is no need to tax yourself. I—"

"Surely no theater can compete with my feeling for you." William enveloped her so suddenly that she didn't see it coming. His lips pushed down on hers, and she was pulled against a body that felt as softly rounded as her own. But strong.

"Mmmmfff!" Gillian said, struggling to free her mouth.

"Miss Pythian-Adams!" William said, panting a little as she managed to pull her head away. "You are *right* about me! Primitive and direct is precisely what I am!"

And before she could move, he pulled her against his body again. In the resulting fracas, Gillian inadvertently opened her mouth to scream at him, which led to some nauseating intimacies that incited her to violence.

"Ouch!" William shrieked, his voice rising to a level

that belied his dark, primitive directness. "You—you kicked me."

Gillian caught up the bodice of her gown. "Whereas you *mauled* me." She was so angry that she couldn't even speak clearly. "You—you impertinent buffoon!"

Mr. Wintersall's eyes narrowed. "There is no call for discourtesy between us."

"If you don't label your attack on my person discourtesy," Gillian snapped, "then you are precisely as caper-witted as you appear."

"My mother didn't just say that you would be hard to bridle!" William said. His face had turned so red that it matched the upholstery. "She said that your profile was undistinguished and your chin showed a sad lack of principle. She expressed grave misgivings about your character, given your evident addiction to theatricals."

Gillian's eyes narrowed. "Oh, so Mrs. Wintersall—"

He interrupted, naturally. "Obviously, your addiction to the stage shows a sad unsteadiness. One must wonder what other foolish notions you may be cherishing."

"If it is foolish not to wish to marry a man of your impoverished intelligence, then I am, indeed, foolish!"

"I am sorry to confirm, Miss Pythian-Adams, that I have come to agree with my mother," William said.

Gillian dropped the slightest of curtsies. "I shall be most—"

"No one in my household had the slightest hesitation as to why Lord Maitland was so eager to terminate your engagement that he fled to an impudent marriage. I braved the tide defending you, Miss Pythian-Adams. Indeed I did!"

"To speak ill of the dead is the mark of a particularly ill-bred person," Gillian snapped.

Mr. Wintersall pulled his heavily embroidered vest over his stomach. "In fact, I was merely applauding Lord Maitland's intelligence and forethought."

Touché.

Gillian chose the coward's way out and slammed the door behind her.

5

*In Which Imogen Meets a Man Unsuitable
for Marriage . . . if Eminently Suitable
for Other Pursuits*

Griselda and Imogen arrived at Holbrook Court late on a Thursday evening, after supper. After one look at them, Rafe's butler, Brinkley, began murmuring about fires, baths, and toddies, and two minutes later Imogen was walking into the so-called Queen's Bedchamber.

There was no call for Imogen to feel a rush of nostalgia on entering the room. It wasn't the same bedchamber in which she'd stayed when the four Essex sisters first arrived from Scotland. She wasn't sleeping in it the night that she first met Draven Maitland on English soil, nor yet did she elope from this house. Instead, she had ridden a matter of three miles to the west, deliberately fallen off her horse and in so doing, sprained her ankle, and then spent one night in the Maitland household before she and Draven eloped.

Before, she thought rather bleakly, she had talked Draven into eloping with her.

Her current bedchamber faced east, not west. She couldn't see anything of Maitland land. But she had looked that direction from the window of the carriage. Yellow leaves were tipping the willows between Draven's and Rafe's lands. There were blots of crimson low to the ground, probably rowan berries. Now those were her rowan berries, and her willows, and all the pretending in the world wouldn't erase the fact that her young husband had died, and his mother had died after him.

It is an odd truth that when grief wanes, other unpleasant emotions rush into the space left by mourning. Even the thought of Maitland House made her feel sick with guilt. Why should she own even a single Maitland rowan bush? She was practically a stranger to the family. The new baron lived in Dorset because Maitland House, unentailed, had passed to Imogen. She hadn't brought herself to enter the house since Draven's mother died. And yet she could feel it looming, full of ghosts, to the west.

She turned from the window impatiently. Her maid, Daisy, had unpacked her things and run a bath, so Imogen obediently sank into the pool of steaming water and tried to think of more cheerful subjects.

Of course it didn't work. She could hear Daisy talking to herself as she put away clothing, tut-tutting over the wear her clothing had taken on the journey from Scotland.

Draven's clothing was in that house. She couldn't let his cravats molder into silence and decay. She should parcel up Lady Clarice's things and give them to the poor, send her jewelry to female relatives, order the furniture muffled in Holland cloth. Perhaps she should sell the house.

It used to be that she would climb into the bath, and the very act of surrounding herself with water would bring on tears. But she hadn't cried in days. Her two-week marriage was starting to feel like a childhood memory, one of the vivid ones that slips from your fingers even as you try to remember it.

When she finally emerged, Daisy had left out a night-gown that was little more than a scrap of rosy silk, so pale that it resembled the inside of a baby's ear, which made Imogen remember that she did need to think about husbands. She was over twenty-one. Annabel was having a baby, and Tess would likely follow suit.

She whirled from the mirror, refusing to acknowledge the pain that had so agonized her after Draven's death, when it was clear that she hadn't managed to produce an heir. It had taken her days to gather the courage to tell Draven's mother that no heir was on the way, and sure enough, Lady Clarice had simply folded up and died after she was told that final bit of news. All her frivolities, her gossip, and her chatter faded after Draven's death. It was as if she relinquished her life as easily as one puts away a handkerchief, turned to the wall, and died.

Imogen caught sight of herself in the dressing table mirror and pulled up the sleeve of her nightgown. It was all very well to own a gown with the propensity to leave one's breasts open to the night air. There are undoubtedly situations in which such a nightgown might be useful, but the widow's blameless sleep is not one of them.

A baby, she thought, pulling up her sleeve again. A baby.

And then, as if it were an answer to her thought, she heard something. Surely that *was* a baby?

It was a chortle, a chuckle, a sound no one but a very small child could make. But that was impossible. Rafe's house was the quintessential bachelor establishment. Male friends drifted in and out on their way to the races in Silchester, or escaping from female companionship . . . but babies?

She must have misheard. But then it came again. A sound. A baby sound.

Imogen pulled open the door, walked outside, and promptly collided with a large body. She gaped up at him. In the dim light of the corridor, he looked rather like Rafe. Except . . .

It wasn't Rafe. He was slimmer than Rafe, and younger-looking, and not as sturdy. His eyes were the same gray-blue, and almond-shaped. She loved that about Rafe's eyes. Sometimes it was hard to look away from Rafe.

It was hard to look away from this man as well.

He was smiling politely at her, while she stood there rooted to the ground like an idiot. In his arms was a child, a bonny little girl who dimpled at Imogen, waved her right hand, and said "mamamam."

Imogen pulled her gaze away from the baby's father. "Well, aren't you a dear," she breathed, holding out a finger.

The baby curled a plump little hand around Imogen's finger and showed her dimples again.

"What an adorable child you have, sir. You must be—"

But her voice died as she became suddenly aware of two things. There was something in the stranger's eyes . . . an awareness of her as a woman that one did not generally encounter on a first meeting. For a moment she just blinked at him.

Then she suddenly realized that her nightgown had once again fallen from her shoulder. She looked down to find her breast gleaming in the dim light.

She jerked up her sleeve and her head at the same moment.

"I—" she said. And stopped. What could she say? There was a gleam of amusement in his eyes.

A second later she was behind the safety of a thick oaken door, cursing silently. That was Rafe's illegitimate brother, the one he only discovered he had last May. No question about it.

And his child, one had to assume. So the brother must be married.

That gave her a queer twist of disappointment. He was so beautiful, in the ways Rafe was beautiful, but without the faint wolfish air that Rafe had. Instead, this brother was a civilized version of their guardian, oddly enough, since he was illegitimate and Rafe quite legitimate.

He had Rafe's eyes; one had to admit that Rafe had fine eyes: gray-blue without a philandering tone to them. But Rafe had an ungentlemanly air, overlong hair, a care-for-naught attitude. And his eyes had a hint of sadness lurking in their depths.

She always thought that Rafe's lack of desire was constitutional; he'd drowned any desire in a pint of liquor. That wasn't the case with Rafe's brother. Surely that was interest in his eyes, along with amusement.

But of course, he was married. And making up one's mind to have a discreet *affaire* did not, to Imogen's mind, include the possibility of indulging with a man who had a wife.

Still, she leaned her head back against the door and grinned. It wasn't only from embarrassment. It was because she felt *alive* for the first time in months. He was tall and tautly built, this illegitimate brother.

Not that it mattered. But if her pulse could race over one man's amused glance, it would surely race over one thrown by another.

She pulled up the sleeve of her nightgown one final time.

6

In Which Illegitimacy Turns Out to Be Less of a Barrier Than One Might Think

The drawing room
On the following day

He *wasn't* married. At least, not anymore.

"He's a widower?" Imogen said. "That's—that's—" and caught herself on the verge of saying it was wonderful. Of course it wasn't wonderful that the poor man was widowed and left with a small child to raise. Of course not.

"There's something in your face that I don't like," Lady Griselda said. "He is the illegitimate—and therefore, Imogen, quite *ineligible*—son of the late Duke of Holbrook."

"I am not interested in marrying him," Imogen said, knowing full well that there was a smile on her mouth, and she was quite unable to restrain it. "I merely think that he's—he's delightful."

Griselda paid her no mind. "He may be Rafe's brother, but it does not make him a suitable subject for conversation, nor yet for our company. I shall be having a stern word with Rafe about—"

"About what?" Rafe said, strolling into the drawing room. "What a pleasure it is to see the two of you again. How was your little sojourn in Scotland? And where's Mayne? I should thank him for accompanying all of you on the journey."

"My brother went straight to London muttering about his clothing," Griselda informed him. "I'm afraid that the strain of wearing your garments for several months was too much for his disordered brain."

"And Annabel? I was under the impression that you were hell-bent on extracting her from her disordered marriage and bringing her back to England?"

"Didn't you receive my note?" Imogen asked. "I informed you that Annabel had changed her mind and decided to stay in Scotland."

Rafe straightened from kissing Griselda's hand and looked at Imogen. "Remarkable. I thought you succeeded in every endeavor."

"It's a pleasure to see you as well," she said, making a face at him. "Will Mr. Spenser join us for dinner?"

"Ah," Rafe said, heading to the sideboard. "My most beloved ward has come to greet me in her usual, charming style. I can see that you missed me while sojourning in the north country."

Imogen ignored that provocation. "Will your brother

join us for supper?" she said, making an effort to shape her voice into a pleasant tone.

"I imagine so," he said, rummaging through the brandy decanters on the sideboard. "He has been supervising restoration of the theater all day, and he's likely worn to the bone."

"Rafe," Griselda said, with a strain of deep uneasiness in her voice. "It is unsuitable for you to entertain your ward in the presence of this particular family relation."

"I can't see why. The Duke of Devonshire raised all of his children together, and if the stories are correct, they had three mothers among the seven. Not to mention Prinny's brother: how many children did Clarence have with Mrs. Jordon? Ten, wasn't it?"

"The Duke of Clarence is a *royal* duke," Griselda said painstakingly.

"Holbrook is the oldest title in these parts; my ancestors have been here since Domesday. I hope you are not suggesting that I should hesitate to commit any folly Devonshire or Clarence can commit."

"One would never know you were a duke from your appearance," Imogen remarked. "You look like a squirrel rummaging through your nut store. Why don't you just pour yourself something, for goodness sake?"

"Because I have a mind to drink the Tobermary this evening," Rafe said, showing no response to her insults.

"I suppose I should amend that to a *plump* squirrel sorting through its nuts," Imogen said, tapping a finger against her chin.

Rafe never bothered to appear ducal. He always looked precisely as he did at the moment: tall with a bit of gut hanging over his trousers and a lock of brown hair falling over his eyes. True, he did have those beautiful eyes. The same eyes, Imogen thought with a pulse of interest, as had his brother.

"Your title may be as old as Methuselah," Griselda said to him, "but that won't help Josie if her reputation is marred by having been known to have consorted with a man of this caliber. I am only thankful that she didn't accompany us home from Scotland. Imogen's reputation is, of course, entirely her own business."

At that Rafe turned around from the sideboard, and the look in his eye could have graced an offended king. "Josie is under my protection. Her reputation will be unmarred by meeting my brother who is, by the way, a professor of divinity at Emmanuel College, Cambridge."

"Oh," Griselda said, clearly taken aback by this information. "A professor. How remarkable. How on earth did he attain the rank, given his family . . . status?"

"It must be given out on the grounds of merit," Rafe said acidly. "A thoroughly unusual event, and not one generally observed among the *ton*."

That beautiful man was a scholar. Imogen's heart sped up at the very thought. He was a brilliant man. Still ineligible, of course—*if* someone were interested in marriage.

"I suppose the situation is not as bad as it might have been," Griselda decided.

"You're acting like an Almack's patroness," Rafe said, grinning. "In case you've forgotten, Grissie, you're no more than Mayne's baby sister, and younger than myself, so no putting on airs and graces."

"Don't fuss," Griselda said. "I must needs pay attention to propriety when both you and my brother are so ill acquainted with the notion. You did ask me to chaperone your wards, after all. I have a responsibility to Josephine."

To Imogen's mind Rafe's friendliness with Griselda was a bit vexing. It wasn't, of course, as if she herself wanted the friendship of such a great lummox. She didn't. Just to make that absolutely clear, she frowned at the glass of liquor he held.

"Have you found the miraculous whiskey you sought?" she asked. "You must be so pleased."

"The Tobermary," Rafe said, casting her a sardonic look that showed he had measured her gesture, and knew it for precisely the veiled insult it was. "May I pour you a glass?"

Imogen didn't drink spirituous liquors because when she did, she thought of Draven. And when she thought of Draven, she had an uncomfortable habit of crying. Rafe's eyes met hers, and she read amusement in them. He knew why she didn't drink. But had he any sympathy? Had he ever known grief?

Well, fairness led her to admit that he had. By all accounts Rafe's life had been shattered by the loss of his brother Peter. But whereas she turned away from drink when Draven died, Rafe had simply upended a barrel of brandy on his head and hadn't taken that hat off since.

Still, she didn't feel like crying today. Poor Draven died a year ago. And . . . there was the professor to think about. She cast a brilliant smile on Rafe. "I shall have a glass, thank you."

"Oh, darling," Griselda said with a frown. "It's so improper to drink whiskey. Rafe is quite ruining his disposition with this bad habit."

"I shall follow his lead," Imogen said with a delicately barbed precision. "He *was* my guardian, after all. I hasten to fashion myself to his every wish."

Rafe walked toward her, and suddenly there was something in his eyes that made her feel uncomfortable. "My every wish?" he murmured. "What a happy man I shall be."

"Your happiness," Imogen said hastily, "is found in the bottom of a bottle, and never at a woman's bequest." She took a sip of the drink and nearly choked. "How can you drink this? It tastes like fire!"

"That's just what I like about it," Rafe said, grinning at her.

She had to look away. Sometimes Rafe could be unsettling. Tess always said he was like a lone wolf. Of course, Tess tended to romanticize their drunken guardian, talking of him as being alone, like some figure from a tragedy. Imogen tended to see him more as an unkempt man, going to the dogs and drink as fast as he could take himself. But there were moments when—

When he could be quite disconcerting. It was his height, most like. She was a tall woman, and yet he loomed over her. His trousers were so old that they strained at the seams, and that, of course, was the fault of his gut. But even the gut didn't hide his muscled thighs.

Not that Imogen ever considered him in that light, other than noticing that he hadn't quite turned his entire body into a sagging mess. Somehow Rafe managed to do just enough exercise to make his old linen shirts stretch across muscled shoulders.

Of course, Imogen told herself, Rafe's brother has precisely the same attributes, but combined with something altogether more charming. Perhaps—Imogen felt herself turning a bit pink at the memory—it was because his eyes had been interested in her as a woman.

Rafe never looked at her that way, not that it was a personal affront to her. She'd never seen him regard any woman with desire. Eunuched by all that whiskey, most like.

But when Mr. Spenser had looked at her, the glow in his eyes had hinted at something—something delicious.

Herself.

Mr. Spenser had thought she was delicious.

Imogen only realized that a little smile was curling her lips when she caught Rafe's sardonic gaze. "Thinking of something?" he asked.

"Someone," she clarified, willing as always to bait her guardian.

"My goodness, I do believe you're blushing," Rafe said, touching her cheek with his finger.

She jerked back, surprised by his touch.

"Who knew that you were capable of such a thing?"

"A characteristically rude comment," Imogen said and collected herself for the attack. "I met your brother earlier last evening, and I was quite impressed."

Rafe's eyes narrowed. For a second she had the unnerving impression that he knew precisely what had happened in the corridor—but that was an impossibility.

"He's my brother," he said finally. His voice was always deep, but he said this so quietly that Griselda, who wasn't listening anyway, could not hear him.

"I am not a snob," Imogen informed him.

"That's not what I meant," Rafe said, his voice dropping even lower.

"Then what did you wish to say?"

"He has already had one unfortunate encounter with a willful woman. I would ask that you attempt not to throw yourself off a horse at his feet, at least until he has time to recover from the last Jezebel who crossed his path."

Imogen felt the shock of that word—Jezebel—to the bottom of her stomach, but she kept her smile steady. "I am shocked," she said, waving a hand in the air as she took a large gulp of that fiery liquor Rafe liked so much. She had to pause for a moment and gasp for air, but that gave her time to think of what to say. "As it happened, I have already fallen into your brother's arms. But I assure you that it was entirely fortuitous. Entirely," she clarified, feeling the rush of pleasure she always got when Rafe's eyes darkened, and his jaw tightened.

"You must, as always, please yourself," he said.

"Precisely," she said blithely. "Of course, if I had known that you would disapprove, I would have done my best not to—"

At that very moment, Mr. Spenser himself appeared in the doorway and paused with a becoming show of hesitation.

Rafe looked up and nodded with all the casualness of one brother to another. "Do come meet Lady Griselda

Willoughby," he called. "She has just returned from a brief trip to Scotland to visit Lady Ardmore, one of my wards. And here's another of those wards, Lady Imogen Maitland."

Imogen shook off the irritation of her conversation with Rafe by watching Mr. Spenser bow to Griselda. He was a beautiful, big man with all of Rafe's virtues and none of his faults. Rafe dressed like a peasant; his brother dressed with the quiet, controlled elegance of a duke.

Griselda's face was a perfect mixture of uncertainty and greeting. But Mr. Spenser bowed over her hand as if she were the queen herself, and Griselda visibly softened. Finally, he turned to Imogen.

"Lady Maitland," Rafe was saying, "is recently widowed."

"I am sorry to hear of your loss," Mr. Spenser said, showing, like a proper gentleman, no sign of remembering their encounter in the corridor.

"My first year of mourning is finished," Imogen said, rather awkwardly.

"In that case, I hope your grief is somewhat lessened by time." Mr. Spenser bowed and turned back to Griselda.

"Will Mayne be joining us in the near future?" Rafe asked Imogen, as he handed his brother a glass of whiskey.

"The earl?" Imogen said bemusedly. She was watching as Mr. Spenser touched the glass to his lips and then put it down barely tasted. His lower lip had beautiful definition.

"Last time we met, you informed me that Mayne was

your cicisbeo," Rafe said, his voice amused, but surely loud enough to be heard by his brother, who was talking to Griselda. "So naturally I thought that you were the proper person to inform me of his whereabouts."

Imogen's backbone straightened, and she frowned at him.

"You did tell me, did you not, that your relationship was unconsummated only due to Mayne's reluctance?" Rafe said. His voice was just low enough to be unheard by the others in the room.

"Be still," she hissed at him.

"One would have thought the trip to Scotland would have been such an intimate journey for the two of you." There was a wicked, wicked amusement in his eyes. Somehow, he obviously knew that Mayne and she had—had come to naught.

"I'm sure that Griselda wasn't much of a chaperone, especially at night," Rafe continued. "She suffers from an uneasy stomach during longish carriage rides, if I remember correctly."

"You will be happy to know that Griselda fulfilled all her chaperoning duties with unfailing attention to duty," Imogen informed him. He was trying to bait her, the way he always did.

"Frustrated you in your seduction plans, did she?" Rafe said sympathetically.

Imogen thought about whether she should snap at Rafe like an untamed dog . . . but no. She had changed. At some moments—like now—it seemed as if all the rage she felt at Draven's death was melting away. It was disconcerting, but very welcome.

The problem was that Rafe only came to know her *after* Draven died, and so he thought she was a snappy creature by nature. Lord knows, he'd stopped enough crying fits in their tracks by making insulting remarks; she had a fair notion that he used those comments as weapons for that very reason.

"You needn't tease me about Mayne," she said to Rafe, giving him a genuine smile. After all, he had done his best as a guardian, for all the two of them didn't see eye to eye. "We agreed to part ways. Well, not that we ever actually were together, if that makes sense."

"I am merely trying to instill in you a sense of moral responsibility," Rafe said. "It's a guardian's role. So naturally I am enchanted to hear that you have allowed Mayne to swim free. A fisherman should never keep an underweight fish, you know."

"Mayne is one of the most eligible men in the *ton*," Imogen said, growing nettled for all she had just promised herself that she'd stay calm. "He's hardly an underweight fish." She cast a little glance at Rafe's middle. "Now if you want to talk about *over*weight fish."

But Rafe just grinned. Of course, if he gave a damn about his belly or his drinking, for that matter, he wouldn't wander around looking like a ne'er-do-well.

Instead of answering her barb, he curled his hand around her glass, on top of her fingers. "Are you finding the whiskey potable?"

"Why? Do you wish to drink it yourself?" she demanded, feeling churlish about the fact that his fingers made her feel oddly shaky.

"Naturally," Rafe said without a touch of shame. "It's a glorious brew, and I'll be damned if I'll see it thrown away just because a chit with a grudge takes a glass to pique me."

"You'll have to drink your brother's as well," Imogen pointed out. "He shows no sign of liking it."

"Oh, Gabe will drink it eventually," Rafe said. "We've been living together for a few months, since you went to Scotland. He's abstemious by nature."

"What a charming trait," Imogen said, and she really meant it.

Rafe dropped his hand, and then tossed back his own glass. "It's a trait the two of us can only admire from afar."

"I don't drink," Imogen said. Now she could see that Mr. Spenser's hair had just the slightest curl.

"There's more than one kind of overindulgence," Rafe said sardonically.

"*I* mean to change," Imogen told him. "In fact, I should say as much to you. I'm sorry that I've behaved in such a churlish fashion in the past year."

Rafe blinked at her. Apparently she'd finally managed to take him by surprise. "I know I've been disagreeable," Imogen continued. "I don't contend with grief very well. It turned me into this . . . this odious person who was always angry and never laughing."

"And now you feel different?"

"Yes." She took another sip and nearly choked again. "Here, you take the rest of this."

He took the glass from her hands without comment.

"Don't you have anything to say?" she asked, just a bit tartly.

"I'm struck dumb. I was merely gathering my joy into an appropriate sentence."

"I shall wait for your wits to reassemble," she said. Brinkley was at the door, signaling that the meal was ready. "No, I won't take your arm," she said. "Do take Lady Griselda in to dinner, Rafe. You know precedence matters to her."

"But not to me," he said, although he went to Griselda willingly enough.

Which left Mr. Spenser holding out his arm to Imogen. She smiled up at him. He wasn't exactly like Rafe. Rafe's eyes were more deeply set, the shape of his mouth a bit wilder. Mr. Spenser was reserved. There was an odd sense about him, as if he were constantly stopping himself from leaving the room. Imogen put her fingers on his arm with the sense that she was holding a bird from flying away. But why should he dislike being here?

"How are you finding Holbrook Court?" she asked.

He looked down the corridor at Rafe's back as he turned into the dining room. "It is a charming establishment," he said.

"But—" Imogen couldn't think how to frame her questions appropriately.

He looked down at her. "Would you like to know how it feels to be an illegitimate brother in one's father's house?"

Mr. Spenser's voice was even, pleasant, not even a bit

chilly. Imogen glanced up at him uncertainly. "Not unless you'd like to tell me."

"I find it surprisingly tolerable," he said, guiding her into the dining room.

"I'm glad," Imogen said.

He moved around the table to sit on Griselda's left. Imogen's heart was beating quickly. She couldn't interpret his eyes at all. But the very sight of his closed face, the immense reserve, and those eyes made her bones turn to water.

She gave a sigh and turned to meet Rafe's sardonic glance.

"He's not for you," Rafe said, leaning close to her.

"I can't think what you mean," Imogen said loftily, accepting a glass of lemonade from Brinkley.

"You know precisely what I mean, you little witch," Rafe said, and there wasn't even a gleam of amusement in his eyes. "You mean to have him, don't you? I've seen that look in your eyes before. That look has had you in trouble before."

Imogen knew exactly what he meant, but she shook her head.

"It's that look that sent you falling off a horse in a deliberate ploy to enter Maitland's house," Rafe said. "It was that look that made Maitland discard his fiancée, Miss Pythian-Adams, to whisk you off to Gretna Green without more than a few pounds to his name."

Imogen gave him her fiercest scowl. "I don't know what you mean."

"You're looking at Gabe as if he wore a coronet of stars," Rafe said, his voice harsh in her ear.

"I am not!"

"Yes, you are. And since you never look at me in that fashion—"

"I should hope not!" Imogen said, and then for a heartbeat, wished she hadn't said it because there was a queer look in Rafe's eyes. But it must have been a trick of the candlelight, because the next second he laughed, and the jarring, sarcastic sound of his chuckle made it clear precisely what he thought of her.

"So should I," he said, "so should I. Because I prophesy a life of unease for the man who—"

"How dare you!" Imogen hissed at him.

"I dare," he said deliberately. "That's my brother over there, Imogen. A recent widower, as are you. I'm quite certain he doesn't wish to marry."

Anger was making her heart beat quickly. She smiled at him, the liquid cream smile of a happy cat. "You seem to be mistaken," she said softly, giving her voice the unmistakable ring of sincerity.

But Rafe's mouth just tightened slightly. "I doubt it."

"I have no wish to marry your brother."

"I am happy to—"

She raised her hand.

"There are so many other ways to enjoy a man of your brother's caliber, don't you think?"

For a moment she almost shivered. The rage in Rafe's eyes was so deep that it flared. She held her breath, waiting . . . for something she hardly visualized.

"You surprise me, Imogen: I thought you desirous, but not vulgar." He picked up his glass and drained it. "As with all things," he added indifferently, his mobile face expressing nothing more than a well-bred lack of interest, "you must please yourself."

7

Of Pump Handles, Privy Counselors,
and Other Bodily Necessities

By the fourth course, Rafe had drunk enough whiskey so that he was watching the scene through a golden haze, a haze that dulled his senses and made him something less than an active participant. He generally liked it that way; life was a great deal more palatable viewed through a slight fog.

Perhaps tonight was an exception. Griselda was clearly as charmed by his brother as was Imogen. As he watched Gabe turn courteously back and forth between Imogen and Griselda, bending his head occasionally to hear Imogen's little peppercorn remarks, Rafe began to feel overlooked. Neglected, even.

He never felt overlooked. Of course he could be as

much part of the conversation as anyone, if he wished to be so.

"So the theater is almost repaired," Griselda was saying.

"The dressing rooms are being papered on the morrow," Rafe put in, pleased to note that his voice didn't sound in the least blurred. "But the estate carpenter told me this morning that he thinks the floor of the green room may give way if we had a particularly burly group of actors milling about, so that will have to be replaced, delaying its readiness."

"How vexing," Griselda said, turning back to Gabe almost as if Rafe had said nothing.

Rafe wasn't so cast away that he didn't notice the coquettish way that Josie's chaperone was fluttering her eyelashes at Gabe. Nothing wrong with that. Griselda was a lovely little bundle of womanhood, with a hefty estate left by her late husband. She could raise little Mary.

What's more, I like her, Rafe thought to himself. She's a good-hearted woman. Look how she hared off to Scotland with Josie and Imogen, merely because Imogen got a bee in her bonnet about saving her sister Annabel from an undesirable marriage. A journey to Scotland is nothing much in itself, but when you're the sort of person whose stomach turns topsy-turvy during a half hour's carriage ride, the trip takes on different proportions. And yet she'd accompanied Imogen on her harebrained scheme without a complaint.

Griselda would make an altogether better spouse for

Gabe than would Imogen, who was also leaning toward his brother. Of course, Imogen didn't bother with fluttering her eyelashes: not for her, a female trait so pedestrian and obvious. No, Imogen was truly dangerous. At the moment she was looking at Gabe as if the sun and moon rose in his eyes.

I've seen that look before, Rafe thought to himself, fingering his glass. Poor Draven Maitland . . . the last time he saw Maitland alive was just down the table from where Gabe was sitting now. And now Imogen was regarding Gabe with the same intensity. Her dark eyes were sparkling with interest; Rafe could almost see the poor man melting.

Irritably he signaled for more whiskey. Griselda was delicately attempting to discover *why* Rafe and Gabe had spent the last months refitting Holbrook Court's private theater.

"You do remember how enamored my mother was of her theater," Rafe said.

"Of course I was aware of the duchess's interest in the stage," Griselda said, turning to him. "Yet I fail to see how your mother's passion for the theater she built has led to its refurbishing."

Rafe had found that people tended to forget he was there, for all he was sprawled at the head of the table. Not Miss Poisonous Imogen, never she. She made sure to cast him enough disapproving looks to keep him on his toes, no matter how much whiskey he swilled.

"We've found no end of amusing items in the lumber room of the theater," he said, ignoring the fact that even he could hear that his baritone had darkened to something altogether more rasping. "Eight small canoes. At least three chandeliers. A thunder barrel."

"What's a thunder barrel?" Imogen asked.

"A few old cannonballs trapped in a wine cask. It's quite loud; I tried it."

"Perhaps you should put on a performance of *Coriolanus*," Imogen said. "Just think how impressive it would be when the thunder roared from the sky."

"Is that a Shakespeare play?" Rafe said, hearing his voice slur slightly. "Whatever we produce has to have a female lead."

"What has the lead to do with it?" Griselda said, turning to him. "It's true that theatrical performance is acceptable these days. One cannot forget the dear Duchess of Marlborough's interest in the theater, nor Dowager Lady Townsend's passion for her private stage. But it would be entirely unacceptable for Imogen, for example, to appear on the stage in a lead role unless it was a performance for the family only."

"Oh no," Rafe said. Unfortunately, shaking his head made him feel dizzy. From Imogen's sardonic gaze, she had guessed that his head was spinning. "We're inviting somewhere around one hundred to one hundred and fifty guests."

Imogen's right eyebrow shot up. "So many? To this point you have concealed your passion to entertain the public very well, Rafe."

"Yes, haven't I?" Rafe said, recklessly finishing his drink even though he knew well enough that he would feel like death the next morning. In fact, his stomach was already beginning to feel unhappy. He had to cut back on the whiskey.

Griselda was chattering about a performance of Molière that the Margravine of Anspach had organized. "Now the war is over, one can certainly do a French play," she was saying, "and there can be no censure attached to a *private* performance. Of course, with French plays there is so often a French song, and that is highly unfortunate."

"Why?" Imogen asked. "What's the matter with French songs?"

"When a song is in French," Griselda said, turning to her, "people never understand it, even if they claim to speak fluently; that goes without saying. So either they think it is improper merely because of the language, and they look shocked, or they think it is humorous, and they laugh."

"Either way, one has to assume that they are amusing themselves," Imogen said. "Perhaps you ought to consider a play in the French language, Mr. Spenser."

"Absolutely not," Griselda said. "It is vulgar to look shocked, and tedious to laugh over songs that one merely assumes to be naughty. Invariably they aren't. I find French drama remarkably tiresome, in truth."

"Too much about adultery and not enough about courtship?" Rafe put in.

Griselda's smile was that of a widow who'd enjoyed the state for ten years without a drop of scandal attaching itself to her name. It was impossible to bait her. "Courtship is always so much more interesting than marriage," she pointed out. "The one is a comedy and the other, so frequently, a tragedy."

Her laughter went straight to Rafe's head and echoed about as if his brain were a vast empty storeroom and her laughter were the thunder barrel itself.

He pulled himself together, catching the sharp edge of Imogen's glance. She leaned over to him. "If you are going to be sick from overindulgence," she said, "I would be most grateful to be spared the sight. I'm afraid that our trip to and from Scotland was marked by the anguish of Griselda's delicate stomach."

Rafe growled at her. "That doesn't happen." It didn't sound very eloquent, but it was all he could muster. Damned if he didn't feel as if he were going to have to be dragged off, supported by the footmen. How embarrassing. An old wreck of a duke, half-dead before his time.

Imogen nodded. "I would find it embarrassing too."

"I said nothing of the sort!" he snapped at her.

"I'm showing you no sympathy," she said, unimpressed. "You certainly deserve every bit of humiliation that comes your way."

The very sharpness of it helped clear Rafe's head. "You're a virago, you know that? I thought you were turning over a new leaf."

"Oh, I am." There was a moment's pause as Imogen fiddled with her fork. "I suppose you could do the same."

Rafe drank a glass of barley water that his butler, Brinkley, thoughtfully brought him. "You'd like to declare a truce between us."

"No." She waved her hand. "Our encounters are trivial."

Of course, he agreed with her assessment. It was just perversity to feel a pang of disappointment.

"You could stop drinking," she said.

"Stop drinking?" Not that he hadn't thought of it himself. His stomach lurched again, and the idea was almost palatable. Still, he managed a sneer. "Why should I?"

She shrugged. "Why indeed?"

She had disturbing eyes. Even in a drunken haze, when his mind was vainly thrashing about for some sort of clarity, he could measure the effect of those eyes.

"I suppose the alternative is drinking yourself into an early death." So much for the new, kind Imogen. "It's a wonder that your nose isn't already bulbous and red, but that's acceptable given the glories of drinking Tobermary whiskey. You'll have to employ a particularly burly footman to tow you to your chambers every evening . . . perhaps that is already part of your nightly ritual?"

Rafe was rather stunned by just how much rage he felt. Generally, whiskey allowed him to listen to a number of insults with total equanimity. But not from Imogen. "I can make my way to my own bed," he said. With some approval, he noticed that his voice wasn't in the least thick anymore. Rage, it seemed, had mitigated his drunken slur. "*You*, on the other hand, seem to have a propensity for being escorted to your bedchamber by Mayne, if not by footmen."

"How fortunate that you show no signs of wishing an escort of the opposite sex. This way, you never have to worry about disappointing her," she said sweetly.

"Everyone knows that a drunkard can't get his rod to stand to attention."

Rafe felt his tongue swell in his mouth with pure rage. "Where did you learn to say such a thing?" he said, leaning over to her so that Griselda couldn't possibly hear him. "Who in the bloody hell taught you to say such a thing? Mayne?"

Imogen took a sip of her lemonade before she bothered to answer him. Then she swept him a sideways glance from under her eyelashes. "I *am* a widow," she noted.

"Your husband taught you to talk about his rod?" Rafe said. "I don't think so. Maitland was the sort to rootle about under the covers in the dark, with the least explanation the better."

He couldn't tell from Imogen's cool gaze whether that description was accurate or not. But fury drove him on. How dare she suggest that his rod was less than the reliable weapon it had always been? That, the whiskey, and her infernal composure drove him straight to the unsayable: "In my estimation, Maitland would have waved his rod about only when he'd hired the help, if you take my meaning."

Griselda was rising, fussing with her reticule and shawl, preparing to retire for tea. "It seems you have made it through dinner without swooning," Imogen said. "How fortunate. I take it you are suggesting that Draven would have waved his rod about in the open air when he was with a whore, but kept it in the dark in my presence."

"Something like that," Rafe said, feeling that

victory—in this conversation, at least—was surely slipping away from him. There was something about her gaze . . .

"You are likely right. We were, in retrospect, a remarkably prudish couple. But I expect that has something to do with the fact that we were married a mere two weeks. The one thing I can assure you, Rafe, since you seem so distressed about my marital memories, is that the instrument in question was in fine working order."

A smile touched her eyes but not her mouth. The very suggestion that she might be remembering Maitland with pleasure made Rafe feel half-blind with—with something.

"Now," she said softly, "can you assure me of the same?"

"Are you requesting *my* services?" he asked, dropping a note of acid sarcasm into his voice.

She didn't even flinch, just met his eyes square on. "Does that seem likely to you?"

"Who knows?" he asked. "You might get tired of haring after my brother. And Mayne seems to have fallen by the wayside." He narrowed his eyes. "It was Mayne who taught you this talk of rods, wasn't it?" And then, suddenly struck: "He only pretended not to have succumbed to your charms, as a sop to my conscience as your guardian!"

Again he couldn't tell what she was thinking. "Did he?" Rafe demanded.

Imogen leaned forward. "A man whose privy counselor means less to him than a glass of Tobermary will never be of interest."

"His privy—"

But she was gone, rustling after Griselda, leaving behind nothing but an infuriating whiff of perfume. She smelled like lemons.

Rafe sat for a moment, staring at the table. His heart was thumping with rage at the idea of Mayne lying to him. That was all there was to it, of course. He didn't really care if Imogen slept with half the known world. As she so frequently pointed out, he ceased to be her legal guardian the moment she married Maitland.

He was brought to himself by the solicitous tone of his butler, Brinkley, asking if he would care for a little port. He looked at the jewel red liquid with some loathing, and shook his head.

How dare Imogen suggest that his privy counselor wouldn't be up for any sort of engagement?

"You appeared to be having a lively conversation with Lady Maitland," Gabe said, moving to a seat next to Rafe since the ladies had left the room.

But Rafe was desperately trying to think when he last hired a whore. It wasn't last year because he'd been in London with his wards and of course he didn't do anything so debauched when they were about, and before that—before that—

"What did you say?" he asked.

Gabe shot him an amused glance. "Apparently Lady Maitland left you with much to think about." He took up an apple and began to peel it.

Rafe considered the apples but remembered that his hands generally shook too much to make a pretty job of it, at least after four glasses of whiskey. Or was it five? "She's demented," he said, which felt like a fair sum-up.

"She is a remarkably beautiful woman," Gabe said.

Rafe shot him a quick glance. Of course, his little brother (for so Gabe seemed, even given that they were born days apart)—his little brother would be capable of defending himself from Imogen about as well as straw touched by flame. He could do something about that later, when he felt more clearheaded. He searched about for something more civil and less complicated to talk about.

"When is Mary arriving?" he asked, gulping down another glass of barley water. "Didn't you say that she was finally weaned from that nurse of hers?"

"Actually, I found her a new wet nurse, since her first could not travel and the theater is taking so much longer to repair than we originally thought. I didn't care to have her living in Cambridge with merely servants to care for her any longer."

"Excellent," Rafe said heartily.

"I did tell you last night that Mary and her nanny had arrived," his brother said. "The new wet nurse is in residence as well."

Rafe felt a dull red flush mount his cheekbones. Dammit, he did remember that. Perhaps.

"They didn't arrive until after dinner," Gabe said, and there wasn't even a touch of reproach in his voice. "I'm afraid that I interrupted your studies."

"I wasn't studying," Rafe said, his voice dull and his insides rumbling with a volcanic upheaval. "I was drunken. Sodden drunk, although I do remember your coming to the study now you bring it up. After Griselda and the rest arrived from Scotland, Brinkley had my valet take me up the servants' stairs so that Imogen and Griselda wouldn't see me drunk."

There was a moment's silence and then: "They saw you tonight," Gabe said.

The words struck at Rafe's heart. "I'd better stop drinking," he said dully.

"Yes."

Rafe drank the glass of water that Brinkley had refilled, wondering at its pallid emptiness, its lack of pleasure. Drink nothing but water for the rest of his days?

"She'll never take you while you're drinking," Gabe said.

Rafe squinted at him. "What the devil are you talking about?"

"Lady Maitland. Imogen, if you prefer."

Rafe gave a short laugh. "She doesn't want me, you fool. She wants you. Couldn't you tell from the way she looked at you?"

"She looked at me with some desire," Gabe said with his usual scholarly objectivity.

Rafe considered fratricide.

"But she looks at you with rage, and I judge that the stronger emotion."

"You're a fool. She'd never take me."

"Why?"

"Worthless," Rafe said shortly. "If I were Peter, it might be different. You met Peter. You must have noticed what a great fellow he was. He kept the estate going, you know. Even when he was a mere boy, he negotiated between my parents. When they were fighting, which was often, he was the only one who could speak to both of them. He was . . . rather wonderful."

"Ah."

"Naturally, Peter never drank to excess."

"It must have been difficult to follow in his footsteps," Gabe said.

Rafe laughed shortly. "I think my father put it best. He said I'd make a dog's breakfast of the business, and he was right. I made the same of this guardianship." His fingers clenched on his glass. "Though that's less my fault. What the devil was Brydone doing, leaving his daughters in the care of a person he'd met only once? If he hadn't taken a ride on a half-broken stallion, all four of the Essexes would still be safely living in Scotland."

And if that were the case, he added silently to himself, Imogen would be sharpening her tongue on some poor Scotsman rather than flaying him as her daily pastime.

One had to suppose that if she were looking at Gabe with desire, she'd be interested in trying out his rod soon. Or the performance thereof.

Gabe had finished his apple. "I expect Brydone thought to live forever. It's a common human condition."

Rafe felt the opposite himself, but the subject didn't interest him, so he started brooding over Imogen again. Nothing along the lines of an ethical argument would stop her. She and Mayne had probably spent every free moment on the trip to Scotland in the bedchamber. Of course Mayne had lied to him when he swore that he was staying out of Imogen's bed. No sane man would do that.

What's more, Gabe was eminently sane. A touch of ice slid down his neck. Gabe would presumably see no reason not to avail himself of Imogen's eminently available charms.

"She's not as composed as she appears," he said abruptly. "She truly loved Maitland, you know. They weren't married long enough for disillusionment to set in."

"What sort of man was he?" Gabe said, beginning to peel another apple.

"A bounder. Passionate about his horseflesh and little else. A man for a wager. He lost his life when he rode a horse that his jockey had refused to mount. Thought he could win the race. Instead he smashed his head into a post before his wife's very eyes."

"Poor Lady Maitland."

"She chose him," Rafe said, knowing his voice was just a growl. "She came into this house already in love with that excuse for a man. She sat at this table and stared at him as if he were the Christ Child come straight from heaven. And that was *Maitland* she was staring at!"

He raised his head and stared unbelievingly at Gabe. "You wouldn't countenance it if you'd met him. A finer specimen of village idiot was hardly to be found throughout England. And he was engaged at the time. But Imogen didn't give a fig. She simply marched over to his house—well, rode, actually—and before we knew it, she'd eloped with the man."

"A decisive young woman," Gabe said, placing the apple before him.

Rafe blinked at it.

"Go on, I peeled it for you."

Their eyes met, and for a moment Rafe felt an embarrassing wave of emotion. "Thanks." And then: "Imogen flung herself from her horse on purpose, you see, and injured her ankle. That got her into Maitland's house, and of course the man had no chance, once she had him in close quarters."

Gabe didn't seem to take in the veiled warning Rafe was giving him. "And was Maitland relieved to be rid of his fiancée, or otherwise?"

"Didn't know what hit him," Rafe said, eating a piece of apple. He rarely ate after the first course, preferring not to complicate the taste of whiskey with that of food. But the apple tasted clean and good.

"Was it a happy marriage?"

"Can't have been," Rafe said. "She's—well, you've met Imogen. And he was a buffoon. Addicted to the track, most happy when he was mounting a horse, not a woman. One look at him and anyone could tell that he thought of his rod with about as much delicacy as a pump handle. Wouldn't have been capable of giving a woman pleasure."

Gabe placed the silver knife with which he had peeled the apple precisely in the middle of his plate. "If you want to stop drinking," he said, "I believe the best way to do so is simply to give it up altogether."

Rafe managed a grunt.

"I have heard that attempts to cut down one's consumption are doomed to failure."

"Oh, I don't know," Rafe said, responding to a nervous spasm at the thought. "I'm sure I could just reduce my consumption to a more suitable level."

"It's certainly worth a try," Gabe said.

It must be something about a scholar's exactitude. Rafe could tell without even thinking twice that his brother was correct about the inadvisability of cutting down as opposed to giving up spirits altogether. Gabriel Spenser was likely very often correct in his judgments.

"How *did* you get to be a professor, given as you're a by-blow of my father's?" he asked suddenly.

His brother had a sweet, crooked smile. "I'm quite good at what I do."

"I know that. I suppose you took a tripos in mathematics first?"

"Indeed. For a time I wasn't sure whether I would continue in mathematics, but I found the lure of ancient history to be strong."

"I don't care if you were bloody Peter and Paul come back to earth in one body," Rafe said. "Everything I know about Oxford—and I assume that Cambridge is much the same—implies that ability can only take one so far."

Gabe's crooked smile had a great deal of candor in it. Rafe found himself glad that Imogen had left the room. Who could resist a smile like that?

"Your father helped," Gabe said.

"Our father," Rafe corrected him. "I'm getting sick of correcting you on that point. What the hell did Holbrook do?" And found himself waiting with genuine curiosity. To the best of his knowledge, his father had never shown the slightest interest in how Rafe sent himself to the devil. He certainly would not have put himself out, had Rafe made a choice of career that required parental support.

"He endowed the college," Gabe said.

"What?"

"He gave Emmanuel College a sum of money." And then, responding to Rafe's lifted eyebrow, "something in the neighborhood of forty thousand pounds. The money undoubtedly came from your estate," he said, his eyes troubled. "I have long felt the guilt of having taken that money from you and yours."

Rafe snapped his mouth shut. At least the whiskey seemed to have retreated enough that he was understanding the conversation. "Damn me pink," he said.

"I'm afraid that the money cannot be—"

Rafe waved his hand. "Our father, for all he kept his real family in secret, would never have endangered the estate. We could endow three such colleges, and not feel more than a pinch."

"That is some consolation."

Rafe narrowed his eyes and saw precisely what the problem was. "Holbrook couldn't have bought you a place, if you hadn't been the very best there was," he said roughly.

Gabe nodded.

Rafe searched around for another topic. "What did Griselda say to the story of your dead wife?" he asked.

"She accepted it," Gabe said. "I told her that my wife's name was Mary and that she died in childbirth. I dislike telling lies."

"This is an important one," Rafe said. "There's no

amount of money that I could give as dowry for young Mary that could make her a marriageable *parti* if the truth were known. As it is, we'll have to throw the entire weight of the Holbrook name behind her. But that—" he added with a grin—"is quite formidable."

"Not," his brother responded, with no smile, "if the duke has succumbed to a liver complaint by the time Mary comes of age."

Rafe swallowed.

"You have no wife in the wings," Gabe said. "So who is the heir to the estate?"

He tried to remember.

"There must be an heir?"

"Of course there is! My cousin Roderick. Twice removed and a bit of a prig, but he'll make a decent duke."

"He may be the most estimable of men," Gabe said, turning his silver fruit knife over and over in his hand, "but he will not throw the weight of the Holbrook name behind an illegitimate niece's marriage. My Mary, in other words."

In his happiness at finding a brother, Rafe had forgotten that family entailed more than pleasure. But even when drunk, he had never failed to recognize the truth when it was presented to him.

"I'll give it up," he said grimly.

"I would be most grateful." Gabe looked at him, and it was like glimpsing himself in a mirror. "Not just for Mary and her future. For myself."

For a horrifying second Rafe felt as if tears might be coming to his eyes. He rose from the table so quickly that he had to catch the edge so as not to topple over. "You haven't introduced me to my niece. Shall we?"

"Lady Maitland expressed a wish to meet her as well."

"Then let's collect the ladies," Rafe said. He was on his feet with barely a wobble in his knees. Still, he made a mental note not to hold the child. The last thing he wanted to do was drop his niece to the floor.

8

In Which Miss Mary Spenser is Introduced
to the Party at Large

Gabriel Spenser was accustomed to making quick
and sure decisions. The moment he first saw Aramaic script, he knew that he wanted to read it. And the
moment he first saw his daughter Mary, he knew that he
would have moved a mountain—or married Loretta—in
order to be near her. She was his, from the top of her anxious little face to the bottom of her enchanting little toes.

"She is such a sweet baby," Imogen was saying. Mary
was smiling now, but when they entered the nursery, the
baby had been standing up, holding on to the bars of her
crib and crying for attention.

The fact that her nurse had been peacefully sitting by
the fire and paying no attention had been duly noted by

her father. Gabe meant to have a word with that nurse on the morrow, but now he just scooped up his daughter. She started dimpling and smiling at him. Obviously she was lonely. He had missed her sorely in the last few months. So much that he'd finally scooped her away from her wet nurse in Cambridge and brought her to Rafe's house.

He held her a little closer. So far he was ignoring Griselda's and Imogen's pleas to hold her.

"I've never seen such enchanting curls," Griselda said. "Did your wife have those red curls?"

Gabe spared a moment's thanks for the fact that Loretta had golden hair. With luck, no one would ever see a resemblance. "Mary is the image of her mother." Not that it was true. Loretta was pretty enough, but to him Mary was beautiful. She had a face like a tiny triangle, and cap of soft curls the color of new roses. Her mouth was a tiny, curved rosebud.

"Did your wife see her before she died?" Imogen said, looking up at him.

Gabe froze, unsure what to say. He and Rafe hadn't worked out the details of his supposed wife's death, merely hammered out the agreement that the solicitor put in front of Loretta, swearing her to secrecy about her motherhood. Not that Loretta had shown the faintest interest in acknowledging the role.

Luckily Rafe broke into the conversation. "Do you remember when I bought all these things for you?" he called to Imogen, gesturing at the heaps of toys on the nursery shelves.

"Who could forget?" Imogen turned to Gabe. "Your

brother believed that he had become guardian to four small children, so he bought these toys—as you can see—in quadruple. Four rocking horses, four dolls."

"There were four nursemaids," Rafe said rather owlishly.

After a few months of living in close proximity with Rafe, Gabe could judge his whiskey intake to the glass. At the moment, he would judge him more than half-seas over; he could only hope that his brother would remember his promise to stop drinking on the morrow. More likely, he'd have no memory of the whole evening.

Reluctantly Gabe allowed Imogen to hold the babe. He'd spent far too much time in the nursery as it was. That afternoon, the nurse had finally had to tell him to leave so that Mary could nap.

Mary smiled at Imogen with the same joy with which she greeted him. Gabe couldn't distinguish precisely why that was so infuriating. All he knew was that he wanted Mary to smile at *him*. She might even frown at a stranger or two instead of greeting all and sundry with the same welcome.

She was chuckling now, and pulling at the slippery strands of Imogen's hair. And Imogen was smiling at him over Mary's head with an expression that told him as clearly as if it had been written in ancient Aramaic that she thought he himself would make a very nice birthday present. She must have forgotten his illegitimacy.

Mary seemed to like Imogen. But so did Rafe, for all he snarled about her. It was an odd thing, to Gabe's mind, to discover that after thinking of oneself as an only child for half a lifetime, he had fallen so easily into the role of brother.

But fall he had. He was astounded by how much he cared for his greathearted drunkard of a brother. Rafe was as generous in his sins as he was in his affections.

Imogen was laughing now. Mary was patting her cheek with her little hand, and Gabe noticed that Rafe had stopped rearranging the cast-iron toys and was staring over his shoulder at Imogen. She was beautiful, but sharp-tongued. Still, there was no accounting for tastes, and Rafe clearly had a taste for his former ward.

"Mr. Spenser," Imogen said, turning to him, "anyone can see that Mary has received nothing but loving attention since her birth. You have done very well by your little motherless babe."

"I have done the best that I could," he said uncomfortably.

"I hope you don't mind if I ask again," she said. "Was her mother able to see little Mary before she died?"

"Of course she did," Gabe said, feeling himself sinking into a deeper pool of lies. "She—she did."

"That's lovely," Imogen said, kissing Mary on the forehead. "You must be sure to tell her so when she grows to the age of understanding. My father foolishly told Josie that our mother had not survived to hold her, and the idea has caused Josie an unnecessary amount of pain."

Gabe blinked down at Mary in Imogen's arms and tried to imagine himself weaving a complicated set of lies about a dead wife that he would, someday, tell his daughter. He couldn't imagine it.

Mary was starting to look a little tired. She was wearing a little dress that poofed out in all directions and made her look rather like a buttercup. She put her head back against Imogen's arm.

"Oh, she's a love," Imogen whispered.

Gabe nodded. Mary was looking around drowsily, probably searching for her nurse. But then her eyes caught on him and a little crooked smile hitched up one side of that rosebud mouth.

And she stretched out her arms. Gabe felt his heart fall into the bottom of his boots.

"Isn't that sweet," Imogen crooned. "Mary wants her papa, doesn't she? Here you are." And without further ado, she plopped the baby back into Gabe's arms.

Mary sighed, turned her head against his waistcoat, and went promptly to sleep.

9

Parched

Contrary to his brother's uncertain assessment, Rafe woke early the next morning, quite aware that he had promised to give up whiskey. Not just whiskey, but wine. Ale. Everything. He didn't feel ill this morning, as was his characteristic sensation in the morning; he was too gripped by fear.

It took over an hour for him to talk himself into getting out of bed and into the bath. Of course he could give up the liquor. He'd said a million times that he would, hadn't he? It wouldn't be so difficult. It wasn't as if he was the sort of man who fell over a bottle of ale on his way to breakfast and never looked up from it. This was simply a matter of accepting the logical judgment that whiskey, lovely though it was, has ill effects on his body and his health.

And now he had a niece and a brother. A family who wanted him to stop drinking. Commanded him to do so, in truth.

He walked down to the breakfast room to find that a lively discussion was afoot. Gabe looked up at him with the expression of pure relief.

A second later, Rafe understood why. Griselda had decided to tackle the whole project of the play. It didn't make sense to her. Hell, it didn't make sense to him either, and poor Gabe was making a sad hash of explaining himself while trying to avoid blatant untruths.

Having no disinclination whatsoever to lie, Rafe waded in before Gabe perjured himself. Leave that to those who were already beyond redemption.

"This is all Gabe's fault," he said, allowing the footman to heap coddled eggs on his plate. Normally, he didn't eat in the morning, but here he was, turning over a new leaf. "He knocked down a young woman in London last year. While in a hackney, you understand."

That struck a chord with Griselda. "There's nothing worse than a drunken hackney driver," she said, waving away all the dishes on offer. "And London is full of them. I should like dry toast only," she told the footman. "Very dry."

"Precisely," Rafe said. "The driver reeled off the box, he'd had so much gin. Of course, my brother felt responsible for the young woman's well-being. He's a very responsible sort of man."

"Of course," Griselda said, adding: "No, no, I said dry. Without butter, if you please."

"The young woman was slightly wounded in the accident, and unfortunately that caused her to lose her part in a play. So of course—"

"What theater was it?" Imogen asked.

"Covent Garden," Gabe said.

"So this young woman. . . ." Griselda stopped. "What does this young person have to do with our production? Never tell me that you gained an appreciation for the theater from this unfortunate incident, Mr. Spenser?" From the way she gazed at Gabe, Rafe could tell that visions of young men taken in by the reckless charms of immoral actresses were dancing before her eyes. Not so far off the mark, either.

"Of course not," Rafe said hastily. "But knowing of the fame of the Holbrook Court theater, Gabe offered her the chance to display her considerable talents before a large audience. We mean, of course, to invite the most important theater people from London."

"It seems to me well beyond the call of duty," Griselda said, a small frown creasing her brow. "A small gift to the Covent Garden would likely have ensured the woman a part in an upcoming production."

"She doesn't want just a part," Rafe said cheerfully, "she wants a lead. And no amount of money could have dislodged Eliza Vestris from the leading role at the Covent Garden, unless the owners caught glimpse of a future luminary."

"I trust she is a woman of moral repute?" Griselda

asked. "Because if I understand you, Rafe, you plan to proceed on your mother's theatrical model. The duchess employed professional actors for the lead parts, but she filled the extras with people of our own acquaintance. That makes the moral fiber of the hired help extremely important."

Rafe hastened to answer that before Gabe would commit himself to further untruths that would keep the poor fellow up at night. "Absolutely above reproach. Devoted to her craft, naturally. Passionate about it." To a fault, he added silently.

"Well," Griselda said, looking unsatisfied but resigned, "I still fail to see who precisely is going to run this production, Mr. Spenser. Unless you are quite remarkable for a doctor of divinity, no one among this company has the slightest idea how to mount a theatrical production, particularly one to which will be invited one hundred and fifty people. The duchess worked extraordinarily hard at the task, and she had a great deal of experience."

Rafe opened his mouth, but she held up her hand. "Make no mistake, if you go forward with this production *and* in conjunction with the fascinating revelation that you are not only in possession of a half brother, but that you have welcomed him into the household, every single person you invite will appear on your doorstep. In fact, your play will likely be the social event of the year."

"I suppose that's true," Rafe agreed.

"I would definitely like a part," Imogen put in. "If the lead is being given to an actress, perhaps I could play a villainess. I would enjoy that."

She was saying it to bait him. Definitely. Devilish woman.

"I wrote a letter to the only woman I can think of with a passion about the theater akin to my mother's . . . that young woman your husband used to be engaged to," he told Imogen.

Imogen's eyes hardened slightly. "Miss Pythian-Adams."

"A lovely young woman," Rafe said with satisfaction. "She had memorized the entirety of a Shakespeare play, as I recall. I was certain that she would be overjoyed to be involved in a theatrical party and in fact, she has accepted. She and her mother should be arriving any day."

"She's coming *here?*" Imogen asked.

"By a happy coincidence, Miss Pythian-Adams happens to be rusticating in Somerset," Rafe said. "I believe that her last season was considered rather disappointing. After she was . . . jilted."

Imogen's eyes flared at that. Miss Pythian-Adams was jilted when Draven Maitland trotted off to the altar with Imogen.

"I doubt she will wish to be in my company," she pointed out.

"To the contrary," Rafe said cheerfully, "she has told all and sundry that she considers herself to have escaped a terrible fate. Not," he added, "that her opinion of Maitland is in the least derogatory to his memory." He was feeling altogether better now. Even his head had stopped throbbing.

"You—" Imogen said, and stopped.

"Quite right," Griselda said, patting her hand. "Some

people have to wait for reform until the next world, my dear, and I expect Rafe is one of them."

"From what I've heard of the next world," Imogen said, "it might not be displeasing enough to effect a reform. Although"—she bared her teeth in some semblance of a smile—"by every account I've heard, Heaven is a remarkably abstemious location. Given the undoubted state of your liver, you will find yourself there sooner rather than later."

"I will blend into my surroundings," Rafe said helpfully. "Since I gave up alcohol this morning."

"You did *what*?"

Rafe felt a pulse of annoyance. He shrugged. "There's nothing so unusual about it. *You* rarely drink, for example."

"Are you giving up whiskey in emulation of me?" Imogen shot him a look of pure scorn.

"Just think how much I look forward to our growing similarities. I do hope that abstemiousness doesn't make me bad-tempered."

She glared at him.

"Or"—he shuddered delicately—"cause me to throw my moral scruples to the wind."

"I doubt that will happen," Griselda said, buttering a final piece of toast. "In my experience, people who reform become remarkably keen to replace sin with respectability. I expect you will marry within a year."

At that, Imogen grinned. "A life entirely of pleasure to be reformed into one of virtue. How very glad I am that Papa chose you as our guardian, Rafe. It will be so edifying to watch your transformation."

But Rafe wasn't going to be drawn by her again. "Griselda, if you are quite done with that marmalade, may I have some?"

"I never eat marmalade," Griselda said absently. "It's not at all good for the waist."

"In that case," Rafe said, "you might as well give me the toast you are holding as well."

"If Miss Pythian-Adams has accepted your invitation," Griselda said, keeping a firm grasp on her toast, "we shall need to arrange a house party in order to cover over the oddness of it all."

"It's a matter of semantics. Theatrical parties are all the rage. An old friend of mine from school, Yates, is quite obsessed with them and wrote me a remarkably tedious letter about some performance of *Lovers' Vow.* We have a house party already, with the two of you. I'll ask Mayne to join us, if you wish."

"*Mayne,*" Griselda scoffed. "It would be better if Tess joined us. Oh, but she's traveling on the Continent, isn't she? Well, perhaps Lady Finster or Mrs. Claiborne. Or Lady Olney. I know that she is quite enthralled by amateur theatricals. I could ask Mrs. Thurmon. Perhaps . . ." Her eyes lit up. "Lady Blechschmidt."

Imogen scowled at that. "I thought you and Lady Blechschmidt were no longer speaking. We never did ascertain why she was at Grillon's Hotel in the middle of the night, you know."

"Never make the mistake of confusing reputation with unsuitable behavior, my dear," Griselda said. "Lady Blechschmidt was certainly at Grillon's at an unsavory hour, but since no one knows of it but us, and we told no one, she and I are still the best of friends. More to the point, her reputation is unimpeachable. I shall write to her immediately."

"I think we should wait," Rafe said. "The preparations for my mother's plays used to take weeks. Lady Blechschmidt would hamper us, and it's not as if anyone would wish to see *her* marching about the stage. Why don't we invite people once we are almost ready for the performance?"

"Am I to understand that you will be taking a lead part?" Griselda asked.

Rafe opened his mouth to say no, but Gabe jumped in. "Yes, he will," he said. "He will play the male lead."

"Like h—" Rafe said and caught his brother's eye. "Oh for goodness sake," he said, "I suppose I will play a role, but does it have to be the lead, Gabe? Why don't you play the lead?"

"If you've given up whiskey, I suppose you'll be able to remember your lines," Imogen said cheerfully.

"That's enough to make a man drown himself in a barrel of malmsey like the old Duke of Clarence," Rafe said. "That and playing Benedict to your Beatrice."

"Mr. Spenser," Imogen said, leaning forward so that the world could see straight down inside her neckline. "What part will you play?"

"The villain," Rafe put in. "Gabe is playing the villain, aren't you?"

"I hadn't thought to play a part myself," Gabe said reluctantly.

"You are the villain," Rafe said firmly. "You shall

have to swirl a black cape and affix a mustache to your upper lip."

Gabe opened his mouth and then shut it again after a look from Rafe. Rafe would be damned if he was going to be jockeyed into having a role in a play—when he hadn't the faintest ambition to tread the boards—and let his brother off scot-free.

"When does your young actress join us?" Griselda asked. She clearly had some reluctance to find herself in such company. "And do you think that you ought to hire some other professional actors?"

"Not that we're worried about Rafe playing a convincing romantic hero," Imogen said, more than a touch of doubt in her voice.

Rafe glared at her.

"Miss Hawes will join us just before our performance is ready," Gabe said. "As a professional, she will quickly grasp her part. We will inform her of the play beforehand."

"I think that would be best," Griselda said. "Much though I appreciate the kindness of Mr. Spenser's gesture—although I do think it is overly kind given the situation—I have no particular wish to dine with a woman of that profession."

"You're turning into a regular stuffy Jane," Rafe told her. "Be careful: you'll get your comeuppance by falling in love with an actor."

Griselda didn't bother to respond.

10

Misery

Rafe was throwing up again. Imogen could hear him all the way down the corridor. She couldn't sleep. Of course, he deserved all the discomfort he got, but still . . .

Finally she got up and walked out of her room and down the hallway. It was the dead of night, and Holbrook Court was as quiet as a tomb.

Imogen stopped outside his door. He was retching again and again. He'd probably curse at her if she entered the room.

Naturally, she entered the room.

"Damn you!" he roared. "Get out!"

"At least you're not naked," she said. He had a towel around his waist, but he was an odd gray-green color, covered with sweat, and shivering. "Do you think you've taken a chill?"

"Out," Rafe said, bending over. "Get. Out. Do you hear me?"

But there was no way Imogen was going to leave him alone in this state. "You need a bath," she said.

He was doubled over at the waist, gasping because he was retching so hard. Imogen felt a germ of panic.

"Perhaps it's too much to give up liquor all at once?" she said. "You could try cutting back first."

"Gabe says I have to get it out of my system," he said, grunting as he straightened up. "Imogen. I'm asking you. May I suffer through this humiliation on my own? I'm sure it will be over in the morning."

"No," Imogen said. "Definitely not. You need a bath."

"I am *not* calling the servants at this hour—"

"You have no need," she said. "I can't imagine why you haven't brought this chamber up-to-date, but my bedroom has a proper bathroom. The water in the pipes should still be hot enough." She took his arm. It was chilly and covered with sweat. "You're a mess."

"So leave me alone," he growled. "You shouldn't be in here, in the middle of the night."

"You're not going to seduce me, are you?" she said. "Because I'm nothing more than a wee, frail female and I might be overcome by the sight of your belly."

"God damn—" But he was retching again.

As soon as he was done she took his arm again. "Come on," she said bracingly. "Just down the hallway." She got him down the hall and into her room, though he protested every inch of the way. Then she went into the bathroom and turned on the faucets.

"Isn't this wonderful?" she said, watching as the hot water poured into the tub.

"I—" Rafe grunted. "Oh God—"

"Pail's in the other room," Imogen said. She had decided that the last thing Rafe needed was sympathy.

He wavered in the door of the bathroom a moment later, looking about to faint. She grabbed his arm. "I'm not taking a bath with you in here," he said, but his voice was losing strength.

"Nonsense," she said. "You'll do just as I please." She pushed him down into the bath, taking some pleasure in the fact that a man who topped six feet and was a good many stones heavier than she was would collapse at the press of her hand. His white towel billowed a little as he settled into the water, but it still covered his privates.

He didn't even look to see if he were decent, just leaned his head against the back of the tub with a groan.

"God almighty!" he said. It didn't sound like a prayer.

Imogen perched on the side of the tub. He was white as a sheet and sweating unattractively. But he couldn't be more than thirty-five, for all he'd turned himself into a dissipated brandy bottle. "So did you start drinking when your brother died?" she asked, just to make conversation.

He rolled his head against the marble. "What if I have to vomit?"

"Here's the basin," Imogen said. "When did your brother die?"

"Six years ago now," he said. "Six years."

"What was he like?"

"Argumentative," Rafe said, not opening his eyes. "He would argue till the sun came up and back down again. He had a born lawyer's tongue. He would talk me into circles and then talk himself into such a state that neither of us knew what the point was anymore." He smiled faintly.

"Did he have a degree?"

"No. Our father didn't think it was appropriate for the future Duke of Holbrook to go to university. Peter . . ." His voice trailed off and he started to look a bit green again.

Imogen perched on the edge of the bathtub and threw a little water over his chest. It was broad and muscled, for all that he did little more than drink. It must be because when he wasn't drunk, he was down at the stables. "Was your brother's name Peter?" she asked. She was thinking that he needed to be distracted. It couldn't be good to be so sick, so many times.

But he threw up again anyway, into the basin she held under his chin.

"I can't believe you're doing this," he said weakly, leaning back. "Quite the fastidious maiden, are you?"

"I've been married," Imogen reminded him.

"More fool you," he said.

Imogen narrowed her eyes. "Don't speak ill of Draven."

"I didn't," he pointed out. "I spoke ill of you."

"You've no call to speak anything of me," she said haughtily, rinsing out the basin in the sink.

"You were a fool to marry that puppy," he said, still with his eyes closed.

Imogen filled up the basin with cold water and dumped it over his head.

"Argh!" He sat straight up and glared at her, water dripping down his face.

Imogen started laughing. All that messy, brown hair of his was dripping with cold water, hanging over his face. "You look like some sort of water monster," she said, gurgling with laughter. "Green and weedy. You could frighten children."

"Shut up and give me the basin again," he snapped.

Afterward she rinsed out the bowl, and he opened one eye. "Don't throw any more water on me."

"Warm this time," she said. She emptied it over his head and then poured a handful of liquid soap into her hand.

"What are you doing now?" he asked suspiciously.

"Making you smell like lemons rather than vomit," she said. She slapped it on top of his head and then started to massage it about.

"You can't do that," he said, sounding really shocked. "It's entirely too intimate."

"What? And holding a basin to your mouth isn't intimate?" She laughed at him. "Just think of me as your old nanny come to nurse you through an illness."

"My nanny never wore a nightgown that turned transparent in the light," he said.

Imogen looked down at her white nightgown. "Really?"

He nodded. "Every time you walk in front of a candle, I can see everything you have to offer."

"That's extremely coarse," she said. "Not that it matters because you don't care what I have to offer, and I certainly don't care about your offerings, *if* you have any—"

He growled, a deep masculine sound that almost made her giggle nervously, but instead she just kept rubbing the soap around his head. She had never washed anyone's hair. He had a beautifully shaped head with ears set back against his scalp. Bone-deep beauty. And his hair was long and surprisingly silky for a man. She wouldn't have thought men's hair felt soft.

Which made her think about Draven. Had his hair been soft? Draven had fine blond hair that he wore sleeked back in a style that accentuated his high cheekbones.

"What are you thinking about?" he demanded.

"Draven."

"What about him?"

"His hair." Then she added, "He had very soft hair."

"He was going to lose it," Rafe said dispassionately. "All those fair-headed men do. In a few years, he would have looked like one of those marble balls you find at the bottom of staircases."

"Whereas you will just get hairier and hairier," she said, sliding her fingers over his scalp again and again.

"God, that feels good," he said, leaning into her hands. "Did you do this for Draven?"

She and Draven had never been so intimate. He was bathed by his manservant, and she by her maid, and they only met under the covers. "Of course," she said without hesitation. "Draven loved the way I bathed him."

"Well, damned if there isn't something about which I

agree with that blighter." Rafe sighed. "Did he bathe you as well?"

"Naturally," Imogen said, turning her mind away from the awkward couplings that she and Draven had shared.

"Lucky man," Rafe said, sounding almost drowsy. "I suppose this is why you're so quick to talk about privy matters. Maybe I should get married. This is the part of marriage that you never hear about."

Because this part doesn't exist, Imogen thought to herself. In her experience, husbands and wives didn't find themselves alone in palatial marble bathrooms lit by candles. At least she and Draven hadn't. The thought made her irritated, and she didn't pour quite as warm water as she might have into the basin.

"Oof," Rafe said, shaking his head like a dog coming out of a lake.

Imogen stood over him, grinning as he ran his hands back through his hair. Then she noticed.

His towel had come undone and was floating on the surface of the water. He certainly had a little gut, but his legs were strong and muscular—the riding, she would guess.

And there between his legs—

She turned away to get more water and poured it over his head. He was looking less green. His eyes were closed. She peeked again.

He was definitely much larger than Draven had been.

Interesting.

11

Neighbors May Well Be the Nearest . . .
But Not the Dearest

October 1, 1817
Ardmore Castle, Scotland

The Countess of Ardmore was not pleased. "Every time I look at Crogan, I think about how he wished to plaster me with molasses and feathers," she told her husband. "How could you invite him for supper?"

Ewan tucked his wife closer under his arm. "The Crogans have always had a meal with us after the harvest fest; 'twould be paramount to a declaration of war to change the tradition. The Crogans and the Ardmores have marched along beside each other these hundred years now. And the present Crogan's grandda actually managed to feather my grandmother, if you remember."

"I can hardly believe it," Annabel said, thinking of

Ewan's fierce grandmother. "Are there any other un-pleasant family traditions I should know about?"

"Well, there is the one," Ewan said, rubbing his wife's stomach thoughtfully.

"She's kicking, can you feel it?" Annabel whispered, leaning into his shoulder.

"How could I not?" He laughed out loud. "For all you think this is a girl, darling, I think those thumps bespeak a son."

"Nonsense," Annabel said. "She's a high-spirited Scotswoman, that's all. And what is this other tradition I should know about?"

"Well, there is an ancient agreement between the Crogans and ourselves that when a daughter of this house marries a son of that house, a particularly large amount of gold travels to the Crogan household."

"My goodness, you should be happy that I married you. Your blood has likely been weakened by that little arrangement." Annabel's eyes widened. "If you think that a daughter of mine would *ever*—"

Ewan bent over and dropped a kiss on her tummy. "The arrangement is of long standing, but to this date, no Crogan has managed to talk a woman of this house into marrying him. Mind you, the Crogans have generally done some serious courting, so that is something our daughter will have to look forward to."

"She will kick them into the next county," Annabel said without hesitation.

Just then Josie entered the room and walked over to them.

"You look very lovely tonight," Annabel said, smiling

at her little sister. "That velvet makes your skin look utterly delectable."

Josie smoothed the peach-blossom skirt of her dinner gown. "Imogen had this made for me last spring." She made a face. "We had to let out the seams in the back so I could wear it tonight. I've started another reducing diet. I'm having cabbage for dinner."

Annabel frowned at her. "I don't think cabbage is particularly good for you. And look at you, Josie! Why should you go on a slimming diet? You're one of the prettiest girls in the Highlands."

"I agree with that," Ewan said, smiling at his sister-in-law. "You're a bonny lass, and I'm sure every man in Almack's will agree with me next spring."

"I doubt that," Josie replied. *"Item, two lips, indifferent red, item, two gray eyes, item, one face as round as a pumpkin."*

"You're distorting Shakespeare," Annabel said, but just then Ewan's butler, Warsop, entered the room. "Mr. Crogan and Mr. Hew Crogan."

"Oh joy, both of them," Annabel moaned under her breath, as she allowed her husband to haul her from the couch.

One of the surprising things about the Crogans was that they seemed to feel not the slightest embarrassment at meeting her, the woman whom they had attempted to cover with molasses and feathers just before she married Ewan.

"We can see what you've been doing recently, Lady Ardmore," said the elder Crogan with a veritable howl of laughter.

Annabel blinked at him.

"Stroking the sheets," he said cheerfully. "Just as a countess ought. Nice breeding stock, you are." He pulled his younger brother over to them. "Now think on this, young Crogan. Lady Ardmore has been married almost no time a-tall, and she's telling the world that she's the one to produce an heir. It's good breeding stock we see here. Good breeding stock."

Annabel was so dumbfounded by Crogan's deplorable freedom of conversation that she might have just stood there with her mouth open if Ewan hadn't caught the end of Crogan's speech and intervened. "I am a fortunate man," he said, smiling at them with a touch of steel in his eyes.

"I'm thinking to the future," Crogan said. "I've no doubt but what your lovely wife will give you a brace of bonny lasses, and you know that there's long been a wish to create closer bonds between our households. I've got four young lads growing up at home, you know. And if it weren't for the fact that the youngest is all of a week old, my wife would be here to offer her congratulations as well. Our son, your daughter: 'tis a perfect match."

"I'll have your guts for garters first" didn't seem a ladylike thing to say, so Annabel pleaded an aching back and fell into a chair.

"And who is this lovely young woman?" Crogan said, his eyes wandering to Josie in a manner that was just on this side of acceptable.

Ewan explained while Josie curtsied to the Crogans. "This is my youngest sister-in-law, Miss Josephine Essex. Her father was Charles Essex, the Viscount Brydone."

"Ah, and if he didn't take me for a Johnny flat by selling me a horse that was out at the knees," Crogan shouted. But he didn't seem to have taken an insult at it, but instead stood beaming at Josie.

"Was that True Confession?" she asked.

"Indeed it was!"

"I remember her," Josie said, nodding. "She was not only out at the knees, but she had a droopy eye as well, didn't she?"

"Right you are, young lady," Crogan said, looking rather less cheerful. "I'd forgotten that detail." He shrugged. "Ah, well, and I gave her as payment for a loan that I never meant to repay anyway, so it comes to the same thing, doesn't it?"

The two Crogans looked almost identical: beefy, red-haired, and red-necked. As if they routinely pinched ladies in any area of her physique they could lay hands on.

"Now if I'd picked a mare who looked like yourself," Crogan said, "things could have been different." He reached around and plucked his little brother closer. "Did you meet the young Crogan here, by the name of Hew?"

Josie curtsied again. Young Crogan had, if anything, a larger lower jaw than his brother. It was a miracle that his teeth met in order to chew his meat.

"This is Miss Essex," Crogan bawled at his brother. "She's the youngest of Viscount Brydone. Remember him? Now, Miss Essex, who has your father's stables these days?"

"My father's estate was inherited by his cousin," Josie said.

"Right you are. And I agree with that. Don't like the idea of property passing to a woman, and I reckon your father agreed with me. Your face can be your fortune, lass!" Crogan roared with laughter.

Josie looked at Annabel rather desperately, but her sister appeared to be taking a short sleep. From what Josie could see, a woman might as well stay in bed through pregnancy, given the way Annabel napped even in the midst of company.

Luckily, Ewan came to her rescue. "Josie's fortune is far more than her face," he said to Crogan. "Not only did her father leave her a prime piece of bloodstock as a dowry, but her sisters' husbands—myself included—have given her a dowry that any young woman can be proud of."

Josie smiled up at him rather grimly. It had been manifestly obvious to her, ever since she was told of this dowry, that her sisters had come up with the scheme simply because she was too large to make a success of it on the market. After all, Annabel went through the season last year without Tess' husband putting a ha'penny toward her dowry. No man would need a bribe to consider taking Annabel to wife.

Crogan stiffened all over, like a hound scenting a trail. "So, your lordship, would you say that Miss Essex is a *daughter of your house*?" he demanded. There was a challenge in his voice that Josie didn't understand.

But Ewan just smiled. "She is indeed a daughter of my house," he said, turning away and bringing Josie with him. "Now look at this, my lamentable wife has deserted her hostessing duties once again."

Behind them she could hear Crogan saying something urgent to his brother in an undertone.

"Precisely what was that about?" Josie asked.

"Nothing important," Ewan said. "I'll take Annabel upstairs and she can have supper in her chambers when she wakes."

Josie didn't have time to agree; Ewan already had his arms around Annabel and was lifting her from the chair. It was amazing to watch, given that Annabel had to have gained two stone while carrying the child. And yet Ewan carried her like a feather.

She turned to find the elder Crogan grinning at her, his hand clenched on his younger brother's arm. "Tell us about yourself, lass," he said ingratiatingly. "We'll wile the time away while Ardmore takes his wife upstairs for a bit of rest. My wife was just the same, I assure you. The nights I've carried her to her bed!"

Josie felt a moment of companionship with his younger brother as they both stared at Crogan in disbelief.

"So precisely what horse did your father leave to you, Miss Essex?" Crogan asked.

"Her name is Fancied Lady," Josie answered. "My guardian, the Duke of Holbrook, is breeding her this season, I believe." She couldn't figure out where Crogan's interest lay. Ewan came back into the room just as she was explaining that the terms of her father's will did not allow her to sell the horse he left her.

She discovered the answer to Crogan's interest later in the evening. She had run out the side door to check on the progress of a mare with a nasty boil on her hock, and was coming back down the path when she heard the

Crogan brothers arguing loudly. It sounded as if they were walking toward her. They must have decided to fetch their own horses from the stables, rather than wait for a groomsman to bring them.

The moon was shining brightly, and the woods were almost clear as day, so Josie didn't hesitate a moment. She slipped to a large oak by the side of the road and pressed herself against the far edge. Only a very foolish woman would risk encountering two Crogans, each of whom had undoubtedly imbibed a fair amount of whiskey after the meal. A kiss would be the least of it—and more the fool she, for having left her maid at home while she nipped down the path to the stables. Not but what she did that every night, but it wasn't a wise thing to do with the Crogans on Ardmore ground.

They were ambling along, arguing as they went, their voices echoing off of the quiet woods around them.

"She's a daughter of the house, you ass," Josie heard. *"A daughter of the house."* She strained to hear. Could they be talking about her? That was the same term that Ewan had used earlier.

"More like a sow of the house," one of them said sullenly.

Josie's heart dropped. They were definitely speaking of her. And by his sulky tone, that was the younger Crogan. It must be difficult to be the younger one when the estate wasn't all that large, and the Crogans not exactly celebrated for fine management.

"I don't give the devil's hind leg if you think the girl is a pug-nosed piglet," Crogan roared, his words coming clearly to Josie's ears. "She may be bit round in the face, but a proper man likes a bit of meat on the bone."

The younger Crogan muttered something Josie didn't hear. She felt as if she couldn't breathe, pressed up against the tree, praying they wouldn't glimpse her. Her fingers were gripping its rough surface so hard that she could feel every gnarly lump in the bark.

"Nay, and it's not as if your own stomach isn't a bit overpadded," Crogan said. To her horror, it sounded as if they had stopped walking almost directly in front of her.

"She's got three stone on me," the younger Crogan said flatly. "I ain't marrying a woman who might squash me in my sleep."

"You're a fool, that's what you are. She may be robust, but she's got a pretty look about her."

"And a sharp tongue!"

"But she's not ill shaped," Crogan said.

His brother spat on the ground. "You might as well tell me to poke a lard barrel."

I wouldn't squash you, Josie thought. *I'd kill you before we made it to the bed.*

"She's a bit on the chuffy side, perhaps," Crogan conceded. "But God's a-live man, where are you going to find a woman who comes along with a dowry like that? She's got a horse from her father, guineas from those sisters of hers, and if she's called a daughter of the Ardmore house, that brings into play the old agreements. It's a handsome package, Young Crogan. You'd be cracked not to take it."

Young Crogan muttered something that Josie couldn't

hear. Mostly, she could hear her own blood pounding in her veins.

"I don't give a twat if you don't want her," Crogan roared again, his voice echoing down the empty road. "She's a prime Scottish piglet, and I'd snuffle around her skirts any day. You should be grateful for a wife who will never cuckold you, and leave it at that, you feather-headed dunce. Now you either start courting that lass to-morrow, or you're out on your puddinglike ass to sing for your supper."

The younger Crogan used a few words that Josie had never heard before. But she heard the word "hog" clear as a bell.

"Shut your trap," his brother advised. "You keep the woman happy by feeding her enough bacon, and she'll give you no trouble. You can do whatever you want in your spare time, and you'll never have to worry about whether your children are your own. What could be better?"

Finally, he started to walk off again, his boots scuffing in the dirt and by the sound of it young Crogan followed.

Josie stayed there, fixed to the oak as if she'd been molded to the bark. The last thing she heard as they rounded the curve was a final outburst from Crogan: "You beef-witted fool!"

12

Of the Vulgarity of Greek Plays

Two weeks after his final drink Rafe was as dry as a bone, and the house felt like a rabbit hutch in April. Miss Pythian-Adams was expected in time for supper. The whole house resounded with the sound of pounding from the location of the theater. The ballroom was full of women sewing red velvet curtains. The great salon was full of spindly-legged chairs being re-covered and re-paired. Never mind the fact that the duke felt more like the inhabitant of a tomb than a hutch.

"Everyone wishes to come to our performance," Griselda said, waving another acceptance at him. "I'm receiving letters from people whom I haven't invited. Although I can hardly attribute it to my status. Your Mr. Spenser is quite the talk of the day. Did you know that he is considered to have been the most brilliant man to have taken a degree at Cambridge in years?"

"Humph," Rafe said. He was having trouble drumming up enthusiasm, which had something to do with the incessant, pounding headache he was trying to learn to live with.

"Quite unusual," Griselda said, with unnecessary emphasis, to Rafe's mind.

"Will your friends draw lots to see who marries him?" Rafe drawled, trying to achieve a tone beyond utter disinterest.

"Absolutely *not!*"

"Why not?" Rafe said, leaning his head against the back of the settee.

"You may be acting with the best of motives in welcoming your brother, but greater society will not be so unforgiving. He does have an awkward background."

At that moment the man himself strolled into the sitting room. In the crook of his arm was a red-haired urchin with a toothless grin.

Rafe looked at his brother blearily. To tell the truth, he felt worse sober than he had on the most terrible of mornings. For one thing, back when he could have a whiskey or two, he used to sleep at night. He never slept anymore. And he used to eat a decent first course or two. Now his stomach churned at the thought of food. Yesterday he'd managed to choke down a few bites of bread.

The only thing standing between him and a comfortable haze of brandy was the very baby waving a rattle at him. Well, that baby, and his brother. And the scorn that

Imogen would undoubtedly heap on his head. And perhaps at the very bottom of all that, the wish to show the world that he could do it.

In the meantime, he was pretending that everything was just fine. He sat at meals although he didn't eat, and he retired into his room at night to contemplate sleeping. He even carried on a conversation now and then.

"Where's her nanny?" he asked Gabe, making an attempt at discourse. Try as he might, he couldn't remember his niece's name at the moment.

"I released the woman from her employment," his brother replied. "She was incompetent and unkind."

"All right," Rafe said. And then he realized that perhaps further comment was called for. "What'd she do?"

"I found Mary crying again," Gabe said.

Rafe knew his brain was exceedingly slow these days, but there was something misguided about Gabe's household arrangements. "Then who," he said, painstakingly shaping the words between the hammerblows assaulting his brain, "is going to care for the child?"

"She still has a wet nurse," Gabe said. "And one of the upstairs housemaids is quite good with children."

"Oh." The very thought of a wet-nurse was distasteful and made Rafe's stomach reel, so he gave up on the conversation.

Brinkley opened the door with a crash that could have been heard in the next country. "Lady Ancilla Pythian-Adams," he announced. "And Miss Pythian-Adams."

Rafe lurched to his feet. Miss Pythian-Adams's mother, Lady Ancilla, had the air of being a woman who knew she was still beautiful and was, therefore, accepting middle age with amusement. You could tell with one glance that she took her own importance with a grain of salt and was conventional without being tedious.

Her daughter was altogether a different sort. Rafe remembered her quite clearly as a young woman who was not tedious—but certainly not conventional. It would be an extraordinarily foolish man who didn't look past Miss Pythian-Adams's delicate features and Cupid's bow mouth and realize that she was a true eccentric.

Of course, Griselda had rushed toward Lady Ancilla, so Rafe bowed to Miss Pythian-Adams. Luckily his head didn't topple to the floor and roll away.

Just then Imogen walked into the room. *That* was going to be a slightly tricky encounter: former fiancée meets widow. Miss Pythian-Adams was all very well in her own way, but there wasn't a woman in the *ton* who could hold a candle to Imogen. She had her hair piled on top of her head with just a few curls hanging down over her shoulders. Rafe wouldn't have known exactly how to describe what she was wearing—some sort of morning gown, but it looked different on her than on other women. His ward could wear a potato sack and make it look like a silk gown.

The women were curtsying to each other just as if they hadn't, once, shared a man called Draven Maitland, a man whom Imogen lured away, leaving Gillian Pythian-Adams without a husband.

Rafe felt sweat break out on his brow just watching them. How did people get through their days without drinking? And what was the point?

* * *

Gabriel Spenser had learned as a boy that there were many things in the world that he would want and that he could not have. Likely, every illegitimate child learned that lesson at his mother's knee. Thankfully, he had never longed for food; the old Holbrook duke, in his stubborn and unlikely affection for Gabriel's mother, had always provided for their material needs. But there were other things. From his earliest days he knew that the visits from the duke were events.

A messenger would arrive, announcing an impending visit, perhaps five days in advance. His mother's eyes would shine. Soon the house would be shining too. It was years before he understood the implications of his mother's preparation—the visits from the hairdresser, the new stockings, the flowers in her bedchamber.

He was six years old when Harry Hunks pointed out the obvious in the schoolyard. Gabe had promptly knocked Harry to the ground. He stood over him, knuckles stinging and his right knee bleeding, feeling rather triumphant because Harry had at least a stone's weight on him. Then Harry looked up at him through a rapidly swelling right eye, and said: "I don't care. Your mother's no better than a chipper. My da said so."

Gabe didn't know what a chipper was, but he could guess.

"My ma says that her own family won't have anything to do with her," Harry added. "You don't have a grandda."

Gabe pulled Harry to his feet and slugged him so hard that he knocked out one of Harry's front teeth.

But none of it made any difference. Harry might have been toothless, with a shrill voice, but his mother was the butcher's wife and they were fast married. Gabe's mother was beautiful and wellborn, the third daughter of a country squire, but she was a chipper. To Gabe's mind, Harry's lack of a front tooth was his own fault because it was pure stupidity to taunt him about his mother's situation.

Before that, he had never really noticed that he didn't seem to have any grandparents. He knew his mother was a squire's daughter, although he never wondered where the squire was. Of course, he had known that his father was a duke who had another wife, but he hadn't thought about the implications of that statement.

Not until Harry pointed it out.

Gabe formed his entire philosophy of life in one panting second in the dusty schoolyard. He could wish that his mother were married (and he did), but it wouldn't make any difference. He took the schoolmaster's whipping with stoic resignation because he deserved it. Not for beating Harry, but for fighting for something he could never have. That was *stupid,* as stupid as Harry losing a tooth over someone else's mother. It was worse to be stupid than to be the son of a chipper. It was stupid to get into fights, and it was even stupider to want what you could never have.

He never fought over the subject again. Occasionally boys called his mother a light-frigate or worse, a doxy or a drab. He just looked at them and walked away. There was something unpleasant in his eye, even without his fists behind it. Generally the words dried in their mouths.

And Gabe accustomed himself to making instantaneous decisions. If there was something—or someone—he desired, he decided whether it was possible. If it was not possible, he didn't spare it another thought. If it was possible, he fought for it tooth and nail, as long as he judged it an intelligent goal.

His philosophy held him in excellent stead until the Year of Our Lord 1817, on a morning in October, when he looked up and met the eyes of a certain Miss Pythian-Adams. It wasn't merely longing that flooded his body; it was pure, unmitigated desire: for this ladylike, contained, intelligent, exquisite person. For her.

He shouldn't spare her a glance.

He couldn't help looking at her again and again.

It went against all his most deeply held principles. She was unattainable. He shouldn't spare her a thought.

He would have to work on that one later.

For the meantime he settled on making himself as objectionable as possible. Because, after all, she undoubtedly shared the opinion of most gentlefolk, that irregular birth manifested itself in a disagreeable personality. And he had never felt more illegitimate in his life.

For her part, Gillian Pythian-Adams had just discovered that a simple theatrical party was in fact a serious production and that *she* was, by all accounts, the stage manager.

"None of us knows the faintest thing about these productions," the Duke of Holbrook was saying. "We depend on you for everything."

"Generally speaking, private theatricals are a quite private business," Gillian pointed out. "Did you say that you wished to invite over one hundred people, Your Grace?"

Holbrook nodded. "At least."

"Does that really sound like a *private* theatrical?" her mama asked.

The duke seemed to have a headache. He had covered his eyes with his hand and just mumbled something in reply.

"I quite agree," her mother said cheerfully. "Let's invite a mere fifty. Or—better yet—let's just invite the village and leave it at that."

"I'm afraid that this must be an altogether more public affair," Mr. Spenser said with quiet authority.

Gillian narrowed her eyes. The man holding the baby was in charge, for some reason. "May I ask why?" she inquired.

"We have a fancy to it," the duke said, his voice hollow. "My mother calculated that the theater could sit two hundred, if need be."

Gillian suddenly remembered how taken she was by the idea of putting on a play in the Duchess of Holbrook's famous little jewel box of a theater. "The first thing is to decide which play we would like to put on," she said. She picked up a stack of books to her right. "I took the liberty of bringing a few plays with me."

"Since you're holding a volume of Sophocles," the duke said, "I might as well tell you that my mother tried the Greek dramatists, but they failed on the stage. In fact, a few of them were viewed with true dislike."

"There is something uncommonly vulgar about some Greek plays," Gillian agreed.

The professor of divinity looked at her, and she felt herself flushing. "Ought one to enjoy tales such as *Oedipus*?" she inquired, feeling like a prude.

"The Bible has moments of great vulgarity," he said, "and yet it retains its rightful place in the canon of reading material."

"I would suggest George Etheridge," Gillian said, not feeling up to a skirmish over vulgar moments in sacred texts. "*The Man of Mode.*"

"Petty stuff," the professor said, his lip curling.

Gillian's mouth tightened. "*School for Scandal*?"

"Baroque in its pettiness."

"I am particularly fond of that play," Gillian commented.

"I haven't read either," Lady Griselda said. "Should I? Are these plays humorous or of the serious genre?"

"Humorous," Gillian said, at the same time that the professor said, "Trivial."

"And what would you suggest?" Gillian demanded.

"I shall ransack Rafe's library tonight," Mr. Spenser answered, "and find an appropriate play. It's not my field."

"We could always try a Shakespeare play, though I do think they're quite difficult for amateurs to do well," Gillian offered.

"Shakespeare was excluded from the early collections of the Bodleian Library, and for good reason," the professor remarked. "Dr. Johnson was the first to note the extraordinary bawdiness of those plays. The comedies, in particular, celebrate nothing so much as reckless behavior."

"Such as falling in love?" Lady Griselda asked. "My dear Mr. Spenser, what kind of plays would be left without human folly?"

Gillian was conceiving a strong dislike for the professor and his haughty opinions about art. "Perhaps Lady Maitland and Lady Griselda could glance at my suggestions tonight," she said. "Since Mr. Spenser does not seem to be suggesting a less trivial alternative."

"Oh no," Lady Griselda said hastily, "I have nothing to do with it. I couldn't possibly act. The professional actress can manage whatever play you choose, I am sure."

"I myself cannot play a part for such a large audience, as I am unmarried," Gillian said. "Since my mother has stalwartly refused to act since the time I've known her, we may be forced to beg you to play a female role, Lady Griselda."

"I'm most happy to help in other respects. Perhaps if the village were our only audience, but since people are being invited from London—"

"The invitations have already been accepted," the duke said from the couch where he had collapsed. His voice allowed no compromise.

"I don't understand," Gillian said. She looked from the expressionless eyes of the professor to the wan face of his half brother, the duke. Then she put down the stack of books she was holding with a gentle thud. "There is something about this production that I do not grasp."

"I understand your confusion," Imogen Maitland said. "It is unusual. Given that Rafe never troubles himself about anything."

"How can you say that?" the duke asked her, with a

distinct snap in his voice. "When there are four rocking horses upstairs at this very moment to disprove you?"

An odd comment, to Gillian's mind.

"Miss Pythian-Adams likely knows that you've never shown the slightest interest in amateur theatricals," Lady Maitland said to him.

"I've developed just such an interest," he said stubbornly.

"If you'll forgive me my skepticism, Your Grace, there's more to this than your sudden enthusiasm. Where is this professional actress coming from? Who is she?" Gillian looked directly at Mr. Spenser. It was he who was pulling the strings of this particular puppet show, or she'd miss her guess.

"Her name is Miss Loretta Hawes."

"And where did Miss Hawes come from?"

"Mr. Spenser accidentally hit her with his carriage," Imogen Maitland explained. "Due to her injury, she lost her place at the Covent Garden, so he promised her a lead role here. Thus Rafe's unwonted theatrical enthusiasm."

"As some sort of compensation?" Gillian said, her eyes searching Mr. Spenser's face.

"Precisely."

"So we have a professional actress in the main role," the duke said wearily. "Is there anything else we need to discuss?" He stood up, swaying slightly.

"He should be lying down," Lady Griselda said flatly, once the duke had left the room. "I have an idea for the performance."

"What do you suggest, Lady Griselda?" Mr. Spenser asked.

"What about a Christmas pantomime? Everyone loves a pantomime, and if the caliber of our acting isn't all that it could be, it certainly won't be noticed in a pantomime."

"You mean a proper pantomime, with a farce and—"

"Precisely! It suits us perfectly. All the parts are generally taken by men, but we can give one female role to this young person from London. She can play a princess or something. I'm sure she'll be happy if we find an ostentatious costume."

There was something fishy about the story of the actress knocked down by the carriage. Gillian was under the impression that Mr. Spenser had only just made himself known to his half brother. He looked like a man who would be much more comfortable tucked away in a dusty library in Cambridge. There was something faintly desperate in his eyes when he mentioned Miss Hawes that made her suspicious.

Lady Maitland came forward and put her hand on Mr. Spenser's arm. "I think it's a lovely thing you're doing for this young woman," she said, looking up at him.

Last time Gillian had seen Imogen look at a man with that intense interest, her name had been Imogen Essex, and her gaze had been directed at Gillian's own fiancé, Draven Maitland. Gillian had welcomed it with joy, as it signaled a possible release from her engagement. This time, her name was Imogen Maitland, and her gaze was directed at the duke's brother.

Gillian didn't like it this time.

Not at all.

13

A Council of War Involves a Division of
Battlegrounds Amongst Generals

I'm not afraid of a widow's cap, Imogen said to herself. She was dressing for dinner. When the season arrives, I'll travel to London and decide if I wish to remarry, and that will be that.

But the season doesn't start for months. Six months. And I . . .

Want something for myself. Her grief was gone, but there was a sort of emptiness in its place. Last spring, she'd thought to have an affair out of rage, humiliation, and guilt. Now she felt as if the last year had happened to someone else. Surely it was another woman who had turned on her dearest sister Tess like a viper and blamed her for Draven's death. And why?

Imogen's hands stilled. Because she and Tess had been arguing at the moment when Draven's horse flashed by the stand? She had apologized to Tess, of course. But she ought to apologize again. Surely she had been mad, maddened by grief.

She needed to scatter her apologies everywhere. She had to apologize to Miss Pythian-Adams as well. She put the thought away.

Mr. Spenser was *delicious*. She shivered even thinking of him.

Surely it wouldn't be too hard to seduce him. Imogen took a deep breath. She'd do it this very night. Tonight.

"Daisy," she said, turning about.

Imogen's maid looked up from straightening her cupboard. "Yes, my lady?"

"I'll wear the velvet evening gown that Madame Carême made for me."

"Of course, my lady," Daisy said, pulling forth a swath of glorious deep crimson, with a dipping neckline and small velvet sleeves that clung. It was trimmed in seed pearls and subtly shaped to follow Imogen's curves. "Would you like a ribbon in your hair?"

"No," Imogen said, "I'll wear the rubies." They would give her confidence.

I can seduce Mr. Spenser as easily as I fell from that apple tree at Draven's feet, Imogen told herself twenty minutes later, looking in the mirror.

There was a sound at the door. Daisy opened it and said: "Miss Pythian-Adams wonders if you might receive her."

"Do ask her to come in," Imogen said. "And Daisy, I shall finish dressing myself. Thank you."

The maid curtsied and shut the door behind her.

Gillian Pythian-Adams was dressed in a subdued striped silk, fashionable, certainly, but eminently suitable for a quiet dinner in the country. Her eyes widened when she saw Imogen.

"You look exquisite, Lady Maitland," she said. "I am put to shame."

"Thank you," Imogen said, leading her to a chair, "but the idea of shame is ridiculous. I remember despairing the moment I saw you for the first time, last year. I had been so hopeful that you would be a dreary bluestocking." She hesitated and then took the plunge. "I have wanted to apologize, Miss Pythian-Adams. I behaved in a truly despicable fashion when I ran away with your fiancé."

"The fact that you loved him is a mitigating influence," Miss Pythian-Adams said, dropping into a chair.

Imogen didn't sit down. "I have given a great deal of thought to my behavior over this past year, and I have no excuse for it. I was utterly single-minded about your— your former fiancé, Draven Maitland. I'd been in love with him for some years, and although that cannot excuse my behavior, it might explain it."

"Please sit down," Miss Pythian-Adams said, "*please*. And you must call me Gillian. As for explaining your behavior, I felt only admiration, I promise you. You felt so strongly for poor Draven."

"Yes, I did," Imogen said, sitting down.

"If you will forgive my plain speaking," Gillian said, leaning forward to touch Imogen's knee, "I was amazed. You see, I was engaged to Draven myself, and yet you managed to see such a better side to him than I had glimpsed."

"He was difficult," Imogen said. "But he was also— magnificent."

"I was fond of him," Gillian said. "And yet I was so glad when the two of you eloped. If poor Draven had to live such a short time, I am grateful that he didn't spend his days with such a sharp-tongued termagant as I am. I was terribly unpleasant to him, you know."

"I'm sure you weren't."

"Oh, I was," Gillian said cheerfully. "I tried any way I could to get him to cry off. I couldn't break the engagement myself as his mother held the mortgage to my father's estate. Luckily"—and she had the smile of a cat who'd found the cream—"she was kind enough to give it back to us when Draven married you. I believe she was afraid of a breach-of-promise suit. So you see, Lady Maitland, not only do you have nothing to apologize to me for, but I have every need to thank you."

"You were truly attempting to get Draven to call off your wedding?"

"Absolutely. I was desperate."

"How odd," Imogen said after a moment of silence. "I'm afraid I felt the same emotion, reversed. I was desperate to marry."

"What a lovely contrast you must have presented to me," Gillian said. "There I was, trying to bore him to death by reciting Shakespeare morning, noon, and night. But Draven was so affable . . . he simply refused to be annoyed by me." She opened her eyes wide. "I can promise you that I can be *very* annoying."

"I've no doubt," Imogen said wryly. "Perhaps Draven didn't listen very closely."

"By all accounts, such deafness was a formative part of his character," Gillian agreed. "I am quite envious of you for being able to overcome that fact and love him enough to elope with him."

Imogen shrugged. "At the time, I couldn't conceive that he wasn't perfect in any way."

The corner of Gillian's mouth quirked up but she said nothing.

"I know," Imogen said. "There was a great deal of Draven that I had to overlook in order to find him perfect. But I mastered it."

"How lovely for him," Gillian said. "Now if only I could manage to be hit by a kindred stroke of lightning, I might fall in love someday."

"I shall do my best to help you if I may," Imogen said earnestly. "Whether I overlooked Draven's faults or not, the truth is that I should never have overlooked *you*."

"I am most grateful for your offer of help, but I'm afraid that your kindness is likely unnecessary. I seem to be missing the necessary trait. I'm truly finding it difficult to imagine falling in love. I'm afraid—"she said it lightly—"that I am destined to marry for thoroughly practical reasons. I am schooling myself to view marriage like Chaucer's Wife of Bath: a thoroughly commercial exchange, with interesting benefits."

There was something so dry about her voice that Imogen found herself laughing out loud. "How can you be so elegant and yet so witty?" she asked. "It is taking all my intellect merely to dress myself with a modicum of grace, and though I read Chaucer with my sisters, I don't remember very much."

"There is more than elegance involved in the dress you wear tonight," Gillian said, with a twinkle in her eye.

Imogen grinned at her. "And what, pray, do you imply by that?" By all rights, Gillian's thick lashes should lend her eyes a limpid innocence. And yet somehow she managed to turn a mere glance at Imogen's shoulders into a laughing commentary.

"You appear to be in full battle regalia. I would have to be unobservant indeed not to notice. Should I take it that you mean to go a-courting, as the old song goes?"

"I am not a frog," Imogen said.

Gillian waited.

"Perhaps not courting . . ."

"In the sense of an endeavor aimed at the altar," Gillian finished for her.

"Precisely."

"You are surely thinking to bedazzle, if not marry. Your erstwhile guardian?"

"Absolutely not!"

"Then his brother," Gillian said. "The ineligible Mr. Spenser."

"He *is* ineligible."

"But?"

"Indeed," Imogen said. "I find him appealing."

"An interesting pursuit."

"Indecent by many standards," Imogen said.

"Yes," Miss Pythian-Adams sounded thoughtful and utterly unperturbed by the truth of Imogen's statement. "I shall watch you with interest, Lady Maitland."

"Oh, please, you must call me Imogen. I have been missing the presence of my sisters, and you and I have had such a frank conversation . . . don't you think that we are practically sisters, given that we almost married the same man?"

"And that fact gives us a claim to family?" Gillian asked, cocking her head to the side. "I am honored."

"We should go downstairs to the sitting room," Imogen said. "I have to be there before Rafe, if only to stop him from being alone with the whiskey decanters."

"My maid told me that he has recently stopped drinking. It seems a terrible process."

"Only if you were thoroughly pickled when you gave up spirits," Imogen said, glancing at the mirror. "Am I outrageously overdressed, or will it simply pass for eccentricity?"

Gillian looked at her. "You would not be out of place dressed for a formal dinner in Paris. If I were you, I would remove the rubies, as they are perhaps a trifle too anxious."

Imogen looked back at the mirror. "I see what you mean."

"There is a great charm in the obvious," Gillian said. "For example, if you hadn't been quite so forthright with Draven, I would likely be widowed at this moment. There are certain men with whom one has to be blunt."

"But Mr. Spenser—"

"I would judge him to be quite a different sort of gentleman," Gillian said. "There is his illegitimacy, for instance. That in itself makes him an altogether more complicated man than an average self-satisfied English gentleman."

"Yet he *is* a gentleman," Imogen said. "I find it fascinating that he looks every inch the aristocrat . . . in contrast to his lamentable brother, the duke."

"Indubitably," Gillian said. "But likely he is more sensitive than the typical Englishman."

"I'm not used to sensitivity in the male sex," Imogen said, thinking of her burly, shouting father.

"Since we were engaged to the same man," Gillian said wryly, "you'll understand that I can offer very few pointers in that direction myself. This promises to be a truly interesting evening," she added. "I am so happy that I came."

"Why *did* you come?"

"To put on the play, of course. And to escape a most unpleasant suitor."

Imogen looked at her and shook her head. "I am not sure I entirely believe you, Gillian Pythian-Adams. You, like Mr. Spenser, are a good deal more complex than the typical English nobleman."

Gillian smiled but said nothing.

Imogen looked at Gillian, at her gleaming copper curls, her slim white arms, and the discreet swell of her bosom. She looked delectable.

She was courting as well.

"It's Rafe," she said with a little gasp. "You're courting . . . *Rafe*."

Gillian smiled. "I had thought of it. He is such a tremendously kind man, isn't he? And"—her eyes were sparkling now—"I find him rather—"

"I know he's attractive," Imogen said hastily, "but have you thought about actually living with him? He is the opposite of fastidious, after all."

"He is untidy because he is unhappy, or so I thought when I last met him," Gillian said. "I would like to see him happy."

"Didn't you just remark that you would never fall in love?" Imogen said.

"Yes. Love seems to me a fatal mistake. Think of Lord Maitland versus the Duke of Holbrook, for example. Draven was—if you'll forgive me—rash, ill-tempered, and childish to the extreme. Rafe, to give him his Christian name, has been unfailingly polite on all occasions and has accepted his illegitimate brother into his family without a qualm. Moreover"—she smiled—"he is, as you say, attractive."

"He's plump," Imogen said, feeling as if she were standing in quicksand.

Gillian shrugged.

How could Imogen have thought she looked docile? Now she saw that Gillian's lips were dark cherry, and her eyelashes were tinged with black color, making the green sparkle. "I like a man to have heft about him," she remarked. "It is obvious that you do not care for him—"

"I don't," Imogen said quickly. "I dislike drunkards."

"It's my lamentable hardheadedness," Gillian replied. "Holbrook is not a fool. He may have been a drunkard, but he doesn't have the look of a cruel man. And he may have a bit of a tummy, although I must say that he appears to have lost weight since I saw him last."

"He hasn't eaten properly since he stopped drinking."

"Hopefully he will recover his good health in the near future," Gillian said.

"Do you have the sense that Rafe is interested in women?" Imogen asked rashly.

"In the way of craving a female, you mean?"

And, at Imogen's nod, "I didn't think that I had to put on a low-necked dress in order to interest him, no. He's lonely, though. I could feel it when I was here with Draven, last year."

"Oh," Imogen said, and then: "Of course, you're right. My sister Tess always said the same."

"There are many ways to catch a wedding ring," Gillian said composedly. "Shall we retire to the sitting room? Now that we are both party to our surreptitious plans, I might as well tell you that I would prefer that the duke not take up drinking again. It is much easier to handle a husband who is not soaked in liquor, although I would never wish to become a nagging wife."

"I nag him," Imogen said abruptly. "I can't bear it when he drinks."

"Well, I suppose given your connection to him, you have more latitude," Gillian said, opening the door. "There is nothing more objectionable, in my opinion, than a husband or wife always pointing out a spouse's shortcomings. I doubt I shall ever dabble in the subject; it's so horrid when a wife is plaguing her husband to death over that kind of thing."

"You must," Imogen said, walking out the door behind her. "He'll kill himself if he begins drinking again."

"I trust not," Gillian said. "At any rate, if he's given it up, I shan't have to think about it at all. I believe I shall try to bring about our engagement as soon as possible. Once the *ton* realizes that he's sober, the matchmaking mamas will be out in force. A sober Duke of Holbrook will be the most eligible *parti* in London."

"Yes," Imogen said, feeling oddly unsettled at the thought.

"So what with one thing and another," Gillian said, smiling at the footman who whisked open the door to the sitting room, "this project to put on Mr. Spenser's play is quite fortuitous."

"I see that," Imogen said slowly.

She looked over Gillian's shoulder and there was Rafe, standing by the window. As always, her gaze flew to his hand, but he wasn't nursing a golden glass of liquor. He was staring out the window. Gillian was right. His gut was definitely reduced. It looked almost flat.

"You see?" Gillian said, turning to her, her eyes dancing. "He's quite appealing, isn't he? I'm so tired of wispy English gentlemen in striped vests with buffed fingernails. Your Rafe is a *brute*. A great brute of a man."

Imogen tried to smile. Was she blind that she didn't see him as a brute of a man? When she looked at Rafe, all she saw was the way he stood alone, staring out the window, and hadn't even realized that they'd entered the room.

Then Gillian had marched up to him, and said something. And he was looking down at her, and then he was laughing.

He never used to laugh, back when he was drinking. Chuckle, definitely. But Gillian had him laughing.

Imogen turned away.

14

The Consequences of Dancing in the Sheets

Regency Theater, Charlotte Street
London

"You'll end up married to the duke," Jenny said wistfully. Jenny Collins and Loretta Hawes were preparing to go on the stage. Jenny was blackening her tights with shoe black so that the worn parts wouldn't show. Loretta was sitting rigidly upright, doing the facial exercises that she had been told would prevent wrinkles. Not that she had to worry at age nineteen but Loretta believed in thinking ahead.

"I have no wish to marry a duke," she said, massaging her cheekbones.

The wondrous thing, to Jenny's mind, was that Loretta probably actually meant it. Jenny would have loved to marry a duke. That is, if her dear Will had been a duke. She reached up to touch the sprig of rosemary she'd tucked behind the glass; Will had given it to her when she was last home.

"Why not?" she asked. "If I didn't love Will, I wouldn't think twice before marrying a duke. Why, you'd have all those things that dukes have, Loretta!"

"Such as?"

"Such as—as a footman, and a carriage, and butter, lots of butter!"

"I never eat butter. It makes a woman plump."

She didn't glance at Jenny's middle, but Jenny felt the rebuke. "You needn't be so high-and-mighty about it," she said sharply. "It's not as if I swill myself in butter. I haven't had a taste for months."

Loretta looked up in surprise, and Jenny sighed. Loretta was a different sort of person than anyone Jenny had ever met. As far she could tell, Loretta never thought about anything other than how to become a great actress. Even when she stepped on people's toes it was only because she had forgotten that they weren't privy to her thoughts.

"I didn't mean it that way," Loretta said penitently. "You know that I couldn't touch butter, not after that unfortunate episode last year."

Jenny was the only one who knew that the unfortunate episode was a baby. Loretta had lost her place at the Covent Garden (a small role, but it might have led to something), and now here she was, playing intervals at the Regency Theater. Jenny alone knew what had happened.

"No one would ever guess," Jenny said, eyeing her friend. Loretta's straw-colored curls bounced on her shoulders with all the silky energy of her trim little figure. Her skirts swirled around ankles that were as slim as they were visible in her short milkmaid's costume.

Loretta shuddered. "I'll never forget how plump I looked. It was truly awful."

"But why don't you wish to marry a duke?" Jenny persisted. "You're so pretty. I bet the man will fall in love with you at once. What's his name? Arphead, isn't it?"

"I never heard of a duchess who was a famous actress," Loretta said, clearly thinking that statement was explanation enough.

"You can't be an actress all your life. You have to marry someday."

"Perhaps," Loretta said with a stark lack of interest in her voice. "It seems a disagreeable state, and I don't want to think about it. Do you think there's any chance that Bluett will allow me to try for the understudy role for Queen Mab?"

"Of course he won't," Jenny said. "He never allows a junior member to try for an understudy role, Loretta, you know that."

"Bluett will beg me to try for an understudy after I play Mrs. Loveit. It's the Duke of Holbrook's theater, Jenny, not Arphead." There was nothing overly ambitious in her tone: it was calm and matter-of-fact. "But you're right. Bluett will give the role to Bess, and she'll mangle all the lines if she ever takes the house."

"Everyone is saying that she did him a *favor*." Jenny giggled. The stage manager, Bluett, was not a man for whom a woman would do favors unless there was a certain reward attached.

Loretta wrinkled her nose. "How disagreeable." Loretta did not like to dwell on disagreeable subjects. As she saw it, to think about unpleasant issues was to waste valuable time that could be spent in consideration of important issues, the most important of which was her future as a brilliant actress, dominating every stage in London.

She could hardly ignore the occasional events that threatened this rosy future. Being struck down by a carriage last year was one of those. The theater manager at Covent Garden had been most unsympathetic when she appeared, late for the performance, and limping. When Mr. Spenser's consoling sympathy had led to a most enjoyable evening—if a most unpleasant outcome—the manager had terminated her employment with little more than a grunt and a wave of his head. The very memory made Loretta narrow her eyes. He would be sorry later, when she was the star at Drury Lane. Of course, she would be gracious.

Loretta believed in being gracious unless absolutely necessary. She had cut her teeth in the Covent Garden Theater traveling company, and there had been one or two episodes in which another actress needed to be shown her place, and Loretta had done so. But, for the most part, she maintained a sunny ability to turn her back on unpleasant people as quickly as unpleasant events.

If she hadn't learned that skill, she wouldn't have survived her childhood, given her father's proclivities. But childhood was one of the things that she never, ever thought about. Some years ago, she had constructed in her mind a loving father, who had been so indulgent that he left his estate to his only daughter. There was nothing whatsoever to be gained by letting it be known that she was Jack Hawes's daughter.

There were only two good things that anyone could say about Hawes: the first was that he took his hanging with remarkable cheer, wearing a new suit of pea green and his hat bound with silver strings. Of course, the suit was stolen, but by the time the former owner heard of its fate, his garments had been buried a week. The second was that he left all his profits from thief-taking to his daughter.

Perhaps he didn't directly leave them to her, but since she was the only person who knew of her father's false-bottomed wig box, she entered the house the morning after his arrest and removed the box.

One could suppose it was payment for enduring her childhood. Even thinking of that made Loretta feel queer and hot, so she never did think of it. She had first came to her father's attention at age eight, and she perfected the art of not-thinking by the time she finally escaped the house at age fourteen.

By then she knew where the hatbox was. In fact, the hatbox served as a good example of what Loretta might have called her philosophy: when awful things happened—like that little episode with the baby last year—good things often resulted.

If she hadn't been knocked down by the hackney, Mr. Spenser wouldn't have escorted her home. And if he hadn't escorted her home, she wouldn't have decided that she would like to be comforted in an intimate fashion. Loretta did not begrudge herself entertainment now and then, although she did resent her own lapse of judgment when it came to preventing conception. But even that disaster had turned to good, because now she was going to play a role in the biggest amateur theatrical production of the year.

Bluett, who ran the Regency Theater, had raised an eyebrow when she said she needed time off from her current part for rehearsal at Holbrook Court. He not only let her off, but the news spread like wildfire, and soon all the girls were asking enviously how she got the place.

Since she could hardly say that it had to do with that unpleasant five-month respite she'd taken in the country, and the screaming little bundle she had thankfully handed over to Mr. Spenser, she made up a lovely tale about the Duke of Holbrook. Probably no one believed it, but Loretta had never seen the point of worrying about what people believed and what they didn't.

"I just don't see why you don't wish to be a duchess," Jenny said dreamily, taking down her rosemary and sniffing at it. "I would adore having a maid, and people calling me *Your Grace*. I would wear huge diamonds around my neck, morning and night. I would sleep in them."

Loretta laughed. "There's only one thing I would adore, and that's to have three thousand people shouting my name, the whole stage littered with flowers, and Mr. Edmund Kean eager to share the stage with me."

"Oh, you'll have that," Jenny said, with absolute faith. "You're the best actress of all of us by far, Loretta, and you're the only one who's memorized parts that aren't even your own. Do you suppose you could just step into the role of Queen Mab tomorrow?"

"I could do any role in the play," Loretta said without hesitation.

"You didn't memorize the whole script!"

"It's not hard to memorize, and how can you really know a play if you didn't? How could you know its bones, and its roots and—"

"You're daft," Jenny said. "*Daft*. We're opera dancers. We come out in the interval and sing a tune and kick up our heels. The only applause I ever hear is when my dress goes a little farther up than it was supposed to."

"I'll be on the stage proper someday," Loretta said. "You never know when it might happen."

Jenny couldn't help smiling. Loretta looked like a fragrant, yellow-haired miss, and underneath she was the most driven, determined woman whom Jenny had ever known. Had ever heard of. "I've no doubt but that people will be piling roses around your feet, and I'll be likely still waiting for Will to get off his father's land and find an acre of his own."

"I'll fund you," Loretta said with determination.

Bluett stuck his stubbly head in their doorway, heedless of whether they were dressed or stark naked. "Time!" he barked.

Loretta checked her lip color; Jenny tucked her little sprig of rosemary back behind the glass, and they both ran off as the first rollicking sound of "I went to an alehouse and what did I see?" came from the pit. The interval had begun.

Queen Mab lurched off the stage cursing and demanding her flagon of beer. She was sweaty and half-drunk, but a ghost of royalty still clung to her garments as she swept by with a flutter of gold lace. Loretta flattened herself against the wall to let her pass. The Queen was followed by her fairy consort, John Swinnerton, who stopped and winked at Loretta.

He was London's leading man at the moment. His black hair and white skin gave him such a romantic air that ladies fainted at the very sight of him. Not that he was in the least romantic off the stage. "Heard about the performance at Holbrook Court," he said. "Know the duke, do you?

Loretta smiled up at him. "I've never met him." She liked Swinnerton, who never leered at her. He never leered at any woman, and Loretta thought the better of him for that.

"Keep yourself away from the swells," he told her. "Those royal dukes have done us actors a great disservice. They all think to dally in the sheets with an actress is a rare treat."

Bluett hissed at Loretta but Swinnerton waved him silent. "The nobility's a queer lot," he added, "with a touching ability to think that they are of erotic interest. Which, invariably, they are not."

Loretta grinned at that and scampered after Jenny, who was waving at her from the stage entrance.

A second later they linked hands and pranced onto the stage, bobbing their curls and showing a touch of ankle. "*I went to an alehouse and what did I see . . .*" they sang.

From the outside, Loretta was all sparkling eyes, tossing curls, and dimples. But inside, she was thinking hard about the nobility. No duke would want to marry her: she knew that. But he might well want to sleep with her.

She wasn't going to do it. Mr. Spenser had been rather enticing, with his deep voice and beautiful cheekbones. It was probably the shock of the accident that made her collapse into his arms thinking he was even handsomer than Swinnerton. But look how that had ended: with her losing a part and a good five months in London. It was only the grace of God she had ended up without lines on her stomach for all to see the truth of it.

Swinnerton was right. She had to stay away from the occupants of Holbrook Court. She had no wish to find a duke between her sheets.

Nor yet to fall backwards into those sheets just to make herself a duchess.

15

In Memoriam for Good Whiskey and Crimson Skirts

They were having a game of whist, Imogen and Gabriel Spenser against Rafe and Gillian. The pairing was rather obvious, to Imogen's mind.

"I forgot to mention that the floor of the green room was finished today," Rafe said, looking up from his cards. "Once we choose a play, we can assemble the cast and begin rehearsals."

Gillian kept touching his arm every once in a while. Not that Imogen cared, but didn't Rafe notice? Perhaps he did notice, and it pleased him.

Griselda was sitting on a chair next to Gillian's mother and sorting through one of the three large cases of theatrical costumes, stage properties, and face paints that had arrived from London that afternoon. "I have read all the various plays," she said, "and I have to admit that I couldn't make head nor tail of *The School for Scandal*. It seemed rather ill spirited. But *The Man of Mode* was quite humorous. I suppose that Rafe would play Dorimant?"

"That *is* the leading role," Gillian said, smiling at Rafe.

"But that means I'm playing a lover," Rafe said, looking rather disgusted.

Imogen bit her tongue. There was a dangerous spark in his eye that dared her to say something. But it was one thing to taunt a pickled Rafe about the working of his pump handle. It was quite another now. There were a thousand changes to him . . . his skin had a healthy flush to it, and he looked eminently capable. The thought made Imogen feel rather tongue-tied.

"Dorimant is certainly a lover," Gillian was telling Rafe. "After all, there are three females in his life: Mrs. Loveit is a friend, Belinda is another, and finally there is Harriet, who has just arrived in London and is quite unaffected. She is Dorimant's new love interest."

"Look at this splendid mustache!" Griselda said, holding up something that looked like a bunch of black chicken feathers. "There's a wig here too . . ." She dug back into the box.

"Which part will Miss Hawes play?" Rafe inquired of Gabe.

"I would expect that Miss Hawes will prefer to play Mrs. Loveit, as there is more room for passion in the role. She strikes me as the sort of actress who would wish to play a tragic role, and Mrs. Loveit indulges in a certain amount of grief when Dorimant casts her off."

"We wouldn't be able to manage a true tragedy," Gillian said. "You need good actors to play a tragedy. I've noted it again and again."

"I doubt I am a good actor," Rafe said. He raised his heavy-lidded eyes. "And I imagine that Imogen has the same misgivings that I do. I presume she will play Harriet?"

"I am quite looking forward to it," Imogen said, laying down a card. "Trump called."

"You must not have understood that you will be playing my love interest," he said. "You must lure me away from two experienced women, Mrs. Loveit and Belinda. You will have to conceal your cordial dislike, and that may take more dramatic skill than you possess."

"I doubt it," Imogen said calmly. "I would say that the demands of your part are the more rigorous. I read the play last night. You, sir, are supposed to be a man with *something of the angel yet undefaced in him.* Perhaps you could employ the mustache that Griselda found."

"You don't think I'm angelic?" he demanded.

She almost laughed but stopped herself. "No! And you, Mr. Spenser, what part will you play?"

"Mr. Fopling Flutter," Rafe said wickedly. "My brother must needs shed all this gravity of his. 'Twill be good for him."

"If I must play a role," Gabe said, "I should prefer to be Mr. Medley."

"A friend of Dorimant's," Imogen said, smiling at him. "I had thought you in a larger role than that, Mr.

Spenser." She put a hand on his arm. After all, if Gillian were doing the same to Rafe . . .

He looked for a second at her hand and then smiled at her, and Imogen felt a flutter of excitement.

Rafe looked across the table and narrowed his eyes. She was doing it again, gazing at poor Gabe as if he were a Sunday treat she intended to gobble. The very sight of it sent a pulse of longing for whiskey through him. If he were drinking, he wouldn't care whether his poor brother were seduced.

And yet it was the first night in weeks that he'd had no headache. He felt better, there was no doubt about it.

He wrenched his eyes away from Imogen and looked at Miss Pythian-Adams instead. Now there was a sensible young woman. She was not only delectable, but she showed no signs of wanting to bite a man's head off at the least provocation.

"I would have thought that you couldn't play cards," he said to Gabe. "Or play the part in an adulterous comedy, for that matter." He took another huge swallow of water.

Imogen turned from her infernal gazing at Gabe. "Be careful," she said, "you'll make yourself retch."

Bitch, Rafe thought to himself.

"I am not ordained," Gabe replied. "I study the Bible, but I do not profess to have the mission to do more than learn about its intricacies."

"Acting doesn't seem a professor-like thing to do," Rafe said, wanting to poke at his brother, though he hardly knew why. Other than that he wanted a drink.

"*The Man of Mode* is not about adultery," Gabe returned, his eyes narrowing a trifle. "Dorimant and Medley are unmarried, as is Belinda."

"But Mrs. Loveit?"

"For all I know, she's a charming widow," Gabe said, giving Imogen a smile.

Rafe felt a surge of rage at the sight. If only he had a drink . . . the truth of it was that now that he finally felt better, he was grappling with a burning desire for liquor. He felt as if his throat were parched, no matter how much water he drank.

There was nothing to stop him walking over to the sideboard right now and pouring himself a glass of that exquisite golden whiskey they made in Scotland. The idea had hovered at the edge of his mind all day. He could see himself throwing down his cards and saying, "Enough is enough!" He was a duke, wasn't he? He could do as he wished.

Imogen looked at him sharply and then pushed away from her chair. *She* walked over to the sideboard while he watched hungrily.

"How is baby Mary today?" she asked over her shoulder, giving Gabe another one of her delicious smiles.

Gabe answered something, but Rafe was too busy watching to pay attention. If Imogen took a drink in front of him, that would be a sign. He'd been through enough agony. He could drink a little, and then keep his drinking more controlled, so he didn't have a headache every morning. It wasn't as if he ever neglected his estate . . . much. Perhaps he would only allow himself a drink three times a week. That sounded good. Or perhaps only when he had guests.

He started to his feet. "What the *devil* are you doing?"

Imogen had pushed open one of the windows that looked down over the courtyard before Holbrook Court. "I'm throwing out this liquor," she said simply, as if she were discarding a piece of broken glass.

Rafe wasn't even sure how he found himself on his feet, but there he was, grabbing her arm.

"Ow!" she said.

"That's whiskey," he snapped. "My God, you've tossed the Tobermary."

With her left hand she reached out and grabbed a crystal decanter. "Why not?" she said tauntingly. "You're not going to drink it again."

"That's no reason to destroy it!" He looked wildly back at the table. His brother was watching, eyebrows raised. Griselda had looked up and was actually smiling. "Tell her that she has no right to pitch my best whiskey into the courtyard," he snarled at Griselda.

"The only one who will care is *you*," Imogen said, still holding the decanter high in her left hand. "You can't stop thinking about it, can you? I've watched you look over here all evening. I wouldn't put it past you to sneak down after we've all gone to bed and drink the place dry!"

Rafe just stared at her. He had toyed with that idea . . . but—

Crash! The crystal decanter shattered against the dark cobblestones far below, and quick as the flash of an eye, Imogen snatched up another.

"Don't—" Rafe gasped, but this one didn't make it through the window. It caught on the frame and shattered, filling the room with the pungent, deep smell of the best whiskey made in the world. Rafe felt like a terrier scenting a fox.

"You're pathetic," Imogen said to him, tossing another decanter into the darkness outside the window.

By some miracle this one didn't smash; he heard it fall on its side with a dull clunk. He could just see jewel-colored port leaking onto the dusty cobblestones, far below.

"Will you please sit down so that I don't have to destroy any more of your crystal? Because I will," she added.

Rafe just blinked at her, a hairbreadth from doing her an injury. Then Gabe took him by the elbow and led him back to the table, and Imogen commenced, as happy as a housewife hanging out laundry, to empty all the decanters Rafe owned: whiskey from the Bowmore distillery, from Ardbeg, Glen Garioch, and Magnus Gunson. They weren't labeled. He knew which was which by the color and the weight of the liquor.

"I expect you have more of the same stored around the castle," she said. "Phew, what a stench!" She reached out and pulled the bell.

Brinkley appeared so promptly that he must have been just outside the door, likely wondering about all the crashing glass. "I've had to purge the duke's whiskey collection," Imogen said airily. "Now, is whiskey kept in another location as well?"

Brinkley nodded, eyeing the cracked decanter on the floor.

"Then why don't you lead me to it," Imogen said, her voice allowing no disagreement.

Brinkley looked at Rafe, who shot him a look of pure rage. But before he could open his mouth, Gabe said, "His Grace agrees with Lady Maitland, Brinkley." And Gabe put a hand on Rafe's arm.

It took everything Rafe had not to floor his brother. But he couldn't. Floor him, that is.

Imogen followed Brinkley from the room.

"I know why Draven Maitland jumped onto that horse," Rafe said hoarsely. "He was just trying to get away from his wife."

"Imogen has backbone," Griselda said. "She fought to keep that foolish young man alive."

Rafe didn't like the implicit comparison. "I'm not trying to kill myself."

"In that case, it's a good thing that you've given up the liquor," Gabe said, laying out the cards for another hand.

"We can't play without that she-devil," Rafe snarled.

"We'll play this hand as dummy whist," Gabe said.

A few minutes later Imogen returned, positively beaming with success.

"Well?" Rafe couldn't not ask. "Did you destroy the best whiskey to be found outside Scotland, then?"

"Just imagine," Imogen said, not meeting his eyes. "There were *barrels* of it in the basement. So rather than throw it all out, Brinkley is loading it onto carts. It'll be taken to Bramble Hill, Lucius's house, come daylight. Would you like to confirm that all your spirits are leaving the premises?" She nodded mockingly toward the windows that faced the courtyard. "I wouldn't want you to injure yourself wandering around the castle at night searching through the wine cellars."

He hated her. With every cell in his body, he hated her. He didn't move.

She didn't even shiver at the look in his eyes. "In that case, you'll have to take my word for it. Brinkley took all the whiskey and the port. He seemed to have some scruples about moving the port—something about it needing to remain still—but when I made it clear that it was either move or be smashed, he gave in. There are only a few bottles of wine left in the entire castle."

"You're a she-devil," Rafe said. He looked down at the cards. They seemed to be pulsating in his hand, growing larger and then shrinking. He lurched to his feet. "I have to get out of here. I'm going for a walk."

"I'll join you," Imogen said.

"Anyone but you!"

"What's the matter?" she taunted. "Are you afraid I'll say something you don't want to hear?"

Gabe gathered together the piles of cards. "Perhaps Miss Pythian-Adams will consent to play a two-handed *vingt-et-un*?"

Rafe strode out of the room after Imogen. He pushed open the great north door, and they walked into a patch of light cast from the entry at their backs. The tall firs that usually tossed their heads in the sun and the wind had merged into shapeless, dark crests, barely moving in the light of the moon. It was unseasonably warm for an

October evening. He walked down the steps, his feet crunching on the gravel sweep before the great door.

"It's rather gloomy out here," Imogen said.

Rafe heard with pleasure the shiver in her voice. It would do that termagant good to be unnerved. She generally acted as if nothing could frighten her. "Let's go," he said.

"Where? Into the dark?" But she trotted after him as he stepped out of the circle of light.

"To the stables." It really was dark, so he let her catch up and took her hand in his. It felt oddly intimate. He had walked arm in arm with ladies his whole life, but it was different to walk through the trees in the dark, feeling only the clutch of a woman's hand. She had a small, delicate hand for such a shrew.

"Why the stables?" she said. Then she stopped, pulling him to a halt. "You're not thinking of riding to the village to find a pub, are you?"

The scorn in her voice stiffened his backbone. "Actually, no." And he hadn't been. That was too demeaning, as if he were—indeed—in servitude. "I have a horse on the point of foaling."

They followed the path by avoiding the pitch black of the woods around them rather than by actually seeing their way. He could hear only little rustlings in the woods. For a moment his stomach roiled, and then quieted.

"It sounds as if we're walking through a huge abandoned house," Imogen said. He could hear the fear in her voice. She was holding his hand tightly.

"Amazing," he said laconically. "You're actually

showing an emotion that characterizes ladies. Afraid of the dark, are you?"

She didn't answer. They walked into the yard surrounding a long row of whitewashed stables. A boy started to his feet as they walked in the door, rubbing his eyes.

"You shouldn't sleep with the lamp lit," Rafe said, his voice harsh. "You could start a fire."

"Yes, sir," the boy stammered. "Yes, sir, I know that. I just dropped off for a moment, sir."

Rafe unhooked the lantern. "Why don't you go to your bed? We'll blow this out when we leave."

"I can't, sir," the boy said. "Mr. James said as how I was to stay because Lady Macbeth is expecting to foal, sir, and if she makes a sound, I'm to go wake Mr. James, sir."

"I looked at her this afternoon, and I doubt she'll foal tonight. But I'll bring the lantern back to you."

They walked down the alleyway between the stalls. None of the horses seemed to be sleeping. They were standing in their clean, spacious stalls, stamping their feet and whickering anxiously as Rafe and Imogen walked down the aisle. "It's the foal coming," Rafe said. "They can tell, and they don't sleep."

"I would guess this is Lady Macbeth," Imogen said, stopping.

The mare had glossy, swollen sides. She turned to look at them, a bit of hay stuck to her nose in a way that made her look comical, like a clown wearing cat's whiskers.

"She won't have the babe tonight," Rafe said.

Imogen had her hand out, and the mare began snuffling, licking her palm for the salt. "She's lovely," Imogen breathed. "Oh, you're a beauty, aren't you?"

Rafe walked on, carrying the lantern, and after a moment she ran to catch up. "You could have waited while I greeted that mare," she said crossly.

"I haven't time for a girl's palaver with ponies," he said.

"Oh? Because you have important things to do, do you? Out here in the middle of the night?"

Rafe thought about how much he disliked Imogen. "I'm thinking of taking a ride."

"A ride? In the *dark*?"

He liked the idea more and more. "You needn't join me. You're not dressed for it."

"I can ride in anything!" she said, just as he knew she would. "But where will you go?"

"You look awake," he said to a cheerful-looking gelding with an arching nose and sweet eyes.

"He's not heavy enough for you!" Imogen exclaimed.

He liked that she knew horses so well. "For you," he said. Then he turned and bellowed down the stables. "A side saddle, if you please."

Imogen's eyes were huge in the light of the lantern. "I'll take my own mare. Where is Posy?"

"You can't. I sent her to the north pasture yesterday."

"I'm not going sidesaddle in the dark on a strange horse," she said. "It's unsafe. I'll ride him astride."

"In that dress?" he flicked a glance down at her dress. Of course it had practically no bodice; none of her garments did.

"I'm sure I can manage," she snapped.

The boy came, puzzled, and then swung an ordinary saddle, rather than the sidesaddle, onto the gelding. "He's called Luna," he told her. "In a foreign language, that means sun. Or maybe moon."

Rafe took his own thoroughbred, a huge animal with a barrel chest.

"Well, *he* should be able to manage your weight," Imogen said. He felt another surge of dislike. Maybe she wouldn't be so cocky riding down a strange road in the dark.

"Let's go," he said, leading out his horse and allowing her to take her own. He had sent the boy back to the far end of the stables, with the lantern. Now the stables were lit only by the chilly light of the moon.

"I hope movement makes you throw up," she said suddenly. She had figured out why he wanted to go for a ride in the dark. Rafe grinned, his first real smile in days. Too bad she couldn't see it.

Outside he swung onto his horse without offering to assist her. A woman who thought to ride astride in an evening gown had no need of his help. But he did look around. She had deftly backed Luna to a mounting post, and a second later she was on the horse. Luna stood quietly enough, his ears flicking back and forth, while Imogen rustled about with her skirts.

"Right," she said. "Let's go, then."

Rafe couldn't see how she'd arranged herself. In fact, he'd never seen a woman ride astride. If she hadn't been the shrew that she was, he would have found it incredibly arousing. Presumably her legs were hugging the back of the steed—

"Are those your undergarments?" he asked. Her legs seemed to be clothed in white.

"Yes," Imogen said casually. "French pantaloons. Quite useful for riding, if only Papa had been able to afford such a thing back when we used to ride without saddles."

He grunted and moved off toward the road. The last thing he needed to do was stare at her legs. He had enough problems.

At first they both minced their way down the road. The moon slipped in and out of clouds, and when it was hidden the road would suddenly disappear. Rafe guessed she must be frightened. Once he thought he heard a gasp. But he kept his horse ahead of hers, relishing the idea of Imogen with wide-open, terrified eyes. It would do her good.

There was a ripping noise behind him.

"Imogen!" he said sharply, swinging about. He didn't want her so terrified that she fell from her horse.

At that moment the moon sprang from behind a cloud, covering the road and the trees with a silvery trembling light. Imogen held up a stretch of cloth. She was laughing, with not a sign of terror on her face. Then she let it go.

"It was in my way. Isn't this brilliant? I love riding at night!"

He watched her skirt fly into a ditch. Now all she wore was the low-necked top of her gown and those white pantaloons.

"Isn't that uncomfortable?" he asked.

"Nope." She grinned at him. "Want to have a race?"

"A race? In the *dark*?"

"Yes!"

"No! You're risking your horse's fetlocks. There might be a hole in the road, and he'd have no time to adjust."

She pouted. Her hair was falling down all over her shoulders. He looked back at the road. It shimmered in front of them, looking as straight and clean as an English toll road.

"The clouds have blown away for the moment," she pointed out.

He hesitated. "You're not drunk," she said acidly. "I'm sure you'll have much steadier hands with your mount than you are accustomed to."

"Fine!" he snapped, backing his horse next to hers. He glanced at her and frowned. "Why are you riding like that?"

She was poised above her saddle, bottom tilted slightly in the air, legs gripping her horse.

"It's more comfortable," she said cheerfully. "I'm afraid I don't have a great deal of padding where it most counts." She looked down fleetingly.

He felt a surge of lust such as he hadn't felt in years. He swallowed. It must be the effect of giving up liquor.

Actually, he couldn't remember the last time he felt desire for a woman. One advantage, to put against all the disadvantages of not drinking. Even if he did have to recover his desire in the presence of his least desirable ward.

"Your choice," he said, shrugging.

"The jockeys ride this way," she said, clearly unconcerned by the fact he was seeing every curve of her bottom, clad only in the lightest cotton. A lady she wasn't. "That means I shall win."

"No, you won't," he growled. "We'll go to that bend. On my mark."

He won. But only by a hairbreadth, and only in a terrific gallop at the end of the road and a wild scream of laughter from her.

"Oh, that was marvelous!" she cried when it was over. "Luna, you're a beauty, a true beauty! We would have had you if you weren't riding such a monster of a horse," she said to Rafe.

Rafe grinned back. But he noticed how she winced as she sat back on her horse. "Perhaps we should walk them now," he suggested. "After all, it's the middle of the night, and they must be tired."

"All right," she agreed, too quickly. So he jumped off his horse and then came to the side of hers and held up his hands.

He hadn't done such a thing in years, and so he bungled it; somehow his hands caught on her bottom rather than her hips. And where she should have been covered by layers and layers of cloth, of course there was only fragile French cotton, tied with little bows, he noticed now. His hands were sliding down a curve that had him harder than—

Harder than he'd been in years.

Perhaps there was something to giving up the tipple. He could take a mistress . . . a lush, welcoming woman who would greet him with a smile and a hot look of desire. Who would never scold.

He saw something in Imogen's eyes when he put her on the ground. She had felt his hands too. And it had quieted her, at least. So that was good. She didn't rail at him on the way home. That would teach her not to rip off her skirt and throw it in a ditch when there was no one around but a man. She was lucky he was a gentleman. And, for that matter, her guardian, for he still considered himself such, whether she was widowed or no.

They walked their horses back down the moonlit road. Imogen's hair spilled around her shoulders, making her look witchlike.

He felt completely alive, his hair blowing from his brow, his legs warm from the exercise, his horse snuffling cheerfully in his ear. They walked farther, and it occurred to Rafe that he couldn't remember having such a vivid experience in years.

Oh, he remembered the headaches in the morning. And the golden, burning pleasure of his first drink in the evening. And the lullaby sweetness of finishing a glass and feeling calm steal over him.

But now he felt alive, raging with desire, if unfortunately directed to absolutely the wrong place. But still, it was back. His head didn't hurt. He felt alive, every inch of him, alive.

He knew without thinking that he wouldn't drink again.

Ever.

16

In Which Imogen Issues an Invitation

Gabe woke up at one in the morning with a peculiar feeling. He pulled on a dressing gown and walked out of his room. Sure enough, by the time he reached the end of the corridor he could hear her furious little squall. A second later he pushed open the door of the nursery and snatched Mary from her bed.

She gulped when she saw him and kept wailing, so Gabe dropped into the rocking chair and tried to soothe her against his shoulder. Her eyes were all small from crying, and she was obviously exhausted. Not to mention wet. Gabe's nose twitched.

Where the devil was the maid? Or her wet nurse? There was no one in the room at all. But he could hardly carry her about the dark house in this state. So he took her over to the low table where her supplies were set up and carefully peeled off all the wet layers.

She had fat little legs. The moment all that cold wool was removed she stopped crying and gave a few snuffling gasps.

"That's my Mary," he heard himself saying to her, rather idiotically. Which made her smile at him, and he had the heart-wrenching realization that he would jump out the window for her. Which might be easier than fixing her clothing.

He found a clean cloth without a problem. All the material around her waist was supposed to tie, he could see that. But whenever he tried to pull the ties, the cloth just fell off her legs. Finally, he just pulled all of it around her waist and put on one of her little shirts. Then he wrapped her in a blanket and picked her up.

He had started down the hallway when Mary decided that now she was awake, she might as well test her voice.

"Mamamamama!" she shouted cheerfully.

"Shhhh," he said. He had made up his mind to go down to the kitchens and see if Mary's wet nurse was to be found there.

She apparently took that as encouragement. "Mamamamam!" she shouted. And then, just for a change: "Ammmmmmm. Ammmmmm."

Sure enough a door opened in front of Gabe. He had one second to wonder whether it would be Imogen, when out stepped not a flagrant seductress in a nightrail but a neatly wrapped Miss Pythian-Adams.

"Are you and Mary going for a stroll?" she asked, smiling up at him.

She was very small, no higher than his breastbone.

"Mamama!" Mary said, by way of greeting.

"I can't find her nurse," Gabe said, feeling ridiculously embarrassed. "And I couldn't manage to fix her undergarments together."

"Oh dear," Miss Pythian-Adams said. She paused. "That would likely explain the puddle on the floor."

Gabe looked down. "Mary!" Now he felt an unpleasantly warm liquid dripping from his forearm.

Miss Pythian-Adams stepped neatly around the puddle, put a hand on his arm, and turned him about. "I'm sure I can figure out how to fix her underclothing," she said. "Why not ring for help? I have found that someone generally comes if one rings long enough."

Gabe could feel his face growing hot. He hadn't thought of ringing for help—because in his own house, and the house he grew up in, there hadn't been as many servants as Rafe maintained. Of course, in this house someone would be up at all times. It seemed Brinkley never slept.

A second later they were back in the warm nursery and put Mary on the table again. She kicked joyously when the newly wet fabric was taken off her.

"She's so active!" Miss Pythian-Adams said, laughing a little. "Here's a cloth. I'm sure it just goes on . . ."

A minute later Miss Pythian-Adams had the cloth wound around Mary's legs . . . and a second after that it fell off. She frowned and tried again.

Gabe watched in the flickering light of the fire. She was an alarmingly beautiful woman who either didn't realize how lovely she was, or didn't care. She had a straight nose and such thick eyelashes that he couldn't see her eyes as she struggled with Mary's nappy. He should have been helping her, but instead he just drank her in.

She was the quintessential English gentlewoman. She was everything that he could never have, given his illegitimacy: delicate, refined, bred through generations of gentlefolk into a perfect bundle of femininity.

"Bloody hell," muttered the delicate bundle of femininity. "How on earth does anyone get these things fastened?"

A laugh wrenched its way out of Gabe's chest.

She looked up at him, blinking through those eyelashes, one hand protectively keeping Mary from rolling off the table. "I'm sorry if my language offended you. I know you're a man of the church—"

"No," he said quickly. "I am a professor, but never a priest."

"Well," she said, and he watched the emotions dance over her face. "Mr. Not-a-priest, do you think that you could give that bell a good tug? Because we don't seem to be able to clothe little Mary. Not that she minds much."

Mary was pinwheeling her legs joyfully.

"She wears so many clothes normally," Gabe said.

"The curse of womanhood," Miss Pythian-Adams replied.

"Why so?" Gabe asked.

"Haven't you ever noticed how difficult it is for a woman to be properly dressed?" And, when he shook his head, she continued, "As a man, you wear simple yet comfortable attire at all times, occasionally changing in the evening. Ladies must change their dress for every period of the day: morning gowns, riding costumes, evening gowns, opera gowns, ball gowns—even the greatest folly of all, presentation gowns sewn with pearls and other fripperies, and worn with hoops!"

"I thought women liked changing clothes," Gabe said. His mother certainly had.

Miss Pythian-Adams sighed. "Some indubitably do. And there are times when I quite relish it. But it's a sad way to spend one's life."

Gabe was quite aware that he would be happy to spend his life and time taking Miss Pythian-Adams's clothes *off*. That was a ridiculous thought. He had sworn off women forever after the debacle with Loretta.

And Miss Pythian-Adams was a *lady*. His face started to burn a little with embarrassment. Should she be here with him, in the middle of the night? What if someone came and her reputation was damaged? What if—

The door swung sharply open. "Oh, so there's my lovey," said a blowsy, sleepy-looking woman.

"We have had some trouble fixing her nappy," Gabe said. "She was wet through when I arrived here and had been crying for some time."

There was a touch of steely cold in his voice that sent the woman jittering with apologies: she was downstairs, it was that warm by the fire, she had fallen off for a moment. The ribbons on her cap danced as she hurriedly tied the strings on Mary's garments.

A second later Mary had been wrapped into a snug, warm bundle. Gabe ushered Miss Pythian-Adams out the door before him, and they stood for a moment in the hallway. He knew he was acting like a great lummox, staring down at her without saying a word.

The color rising in her cheeks made him ache for things he could never have: the clean, sweet smell of a good woman. The kind of woman who would never be called a chipper, who would never be overtaken by female hunger. You could see that in Miss Pythian-Adams's face. She would never be led astray by her emotions, the way his mother had been.

It was perverse, the way her very coolness, her lack of interest in him as a man, was kindling his body like dry timber. Quite rightly, she had put him in a category marked "illegitimate" and never thought twice about him.

Even now her eyes were thoughtful, meeting his, obviously wondering what on earth was the matter with him. "We must say good night," he said, his voice rough.

"Yes," she said. "Do you know, I think Mary's maid might have spent a great part of the evening in the kitchen?"

She apparently didn't feel the tension in the air, even though he was standing before her vibrating like a tree in a high gale.

"Mary needs a nanny, but I haven't found a replacement yet."

Her lips had perfect definition: the mouth of a woman who would never succumb to animal passions. He was bowing when yet another door opened in the hallway. He snapped up, cursing himself, wondering whether a woman could be compromised simply by being seen in the corridor with a man.

Imogen Maitland peered around the door, her eyes curious. "What on earth is going on?" she said, walking into the corridor. To Gabe's relief, she was wearing a dressing gown, and her bosom seemed to be covered.

"Mr. Spenser's child has been crying," Miss Pythian-Adams said. "Good night, Imogen." And then without even a look at him, she vanished through the door into her bedchamber.

Lady Maitland turned to him. If there was no recognition of him as a man in Miss Pythian-Adams's eyes, there was abundant appreciation in Lady Maitland's. She drifted toward him, and her intentions were unmistakable. In the moonlight coming through the high windows at the end of the corridor, her features looked slightly exotic. Her hair was loosely braided and curled around her face as if she were some sort of night witch, come to bewitch men from their senses. And yet . . . and yet to Gabe, Lady Maitland's crimson lips and secret smile didn't move him at all.

Well, perhaps a little.

She was one who would know precisely what she wanted: *him*, on a limited lease. Illegitimacy worked in the proper way, for her. It would make him the perfect *parti*, not likely to infringe on her fashionable life.

Yet there was something slightly uncertain in her eyes that belied the bold way she was standing before him, asking in a husky voice whether he would accompany her to the library to find a book.

Of course she was the sort of woman he could have. Exquisite and yet available. Approaching him, rather than the other way around. It was oddly mortifying. Her eyes were dark and interested, even with that bit of uncertainty in the back of them. She was no whore. Perhaps this was her very first seduction of an appropriate man.

The thought was sour in his stomach.

"I—" he cleared his throat. "I'm rather tired."

Her face fell and then instantaneously smoothed to a sophisticated smile. And his heart lurched. What was he doing? Who was *he* to make her feel less than entrancing? Shouldn't he be kissing her hand for even looking his direction?

"I quite understand," she said. "In fact, this is not the first time—that is, I should go to bed at once as well. I have much to do tomorrow and—"

Gabe felt a surge of protective anger against whoever it was who had dared to refuse such a beautiful young woman in the past. And a strong inclination to inform her that her lack of parents need not transform to a lack of morality. Obviously, he couldn't refuse her.

"Would you possibly like to—to—" he searched his memory. Where did illicit relationships happen when people were at a house party? One had to suppose they just tiptoed from room to room. The last thing he wished to do was ask her to his room. He took Mary there sometimes. "Would you like to accompany me to Silchester tomorrow evening?" he asked.

"Someone might see us," she said, a little light dawning in her eyes. Of course, she couldn't be seen with someone like himself. "I say that only because Rafe is quite nervous about my being chaperoned," she added, putting a hand on his arm again. "I would not want you to think that I did not wish to go."

"Why don't we go in disguise?" He heard himself say it, as if another person were speaking. And her face lit up.

"What fun that would be! Perhaps we could go to a rather out-of-the-way spot." Her eyes were glowing, clearly picturing all kinds of debauched environments about which he knew nothing.

Gabe suddenly remembered that he'd seen a broadside nailed to a tree in Silchester. "There's a singer from London performing at the Black Swan."

"This would be wonderful!" she whispered, looking more like a child anticipating a treat than a young woman fixing up an illicit liaison.

He bowed. "In that case, tomorrow night."

Her eyes were melting, with exquisite hints of laughter deep in them. Gabe knew with a bone-deep knowledge that to make love to Imogen Maitland—nay, even to spend an evening with her—would be the kind of pleasure that a man is lucky to have once in his life.

She disappeared into her bedchamber, presumably to drop her dressing gown and climb into bed in a swish of delicate silk.

And Gabe stayed there in the chilly hallway, staring at the two doors. It was like the old medieval mystery plays where a man was offered the choice of good and evil. Except as life always is, the doors were so much more complicated than that.

Gillian Pythian-Adams was coolly uninterested in him. Perhaps in all men, but certainly in him. And yet she had that old-fashioned quality, decency, that his very soul yearned for.

Imogen Maitland was a woman so beautiful that a

smile from her, laced with desire, was as potent as sin it-self. She was not indecent, nor yet sinful. She was . . . just Imogen, and she wanted him, the son of a chipper, who was only good for a liaison.

Never for marriage.

17

A Mustache and a West Wind

Rafe was not sleeping. It was such a new experience for him, to be up in the middle of the night and yet not inebriated, that he was bent on exploring it. He found himself hanging out of his own window, for all the world like a second housemaid with a blushing acquaintance with a groomsman. There was a soft west wind blowing: a night wind. His old nurse used to say that a night wind from the west made men tumble into love.

Night smelled different from the day. Leaves were drifting gently to the courtyard, blown inside out by the wind. They littered the ground, darker splotches on the soft gray of the cobblestones. Those cobblestones, Rafe thought, have been here since the 1300s. My ancestors walked those very stones.

It should have been a profoundly moving thought, but Rafe couldn't quite manage the proper emotion. All he could think about was his great-uncle Woodward, who used to prance about in pumps with high red heels, his hair powdered and his face carefully painted. He had been a quintessential Georgian rake, according to servants' gossip when Rafe was growing up.

It must have been difficult to negotiate cobblestones in such high heels, Rafe thought idly.

Just then there was a sound at his door, and he turned.

"Gabe!" And: "I'd offer you a drink, but water is so tedious." For some reason his brother looked as burnt to the socket as Rafe used to feel after a fourth brandy. "Is Mary all right?"

"She was crying again," Gabe said, throwing himself in a chair. "I apologize for bothering you, but I saw the light under your door."

"Isn't crying normal for children?" Rafe asked. "My understanding is that they are irksome at their best and pestilent at their worst."

"That has a faintly poetic quality."

"Trying to impress you," Rafe said honestly. "I find myself wishing that I'd paid more attention to books. Perhaps the two of us could discuss philosophy if I'd had."

"I'd rather discuss women," Gabe said, drumming his fingers against the chair.

Rafe's eyebrows rose. "A subject about which I know slightly more than I know about ancient philosophers. Only slightly, mind you."

"I've made an assignation for tomorrow night."

Rafe's heart sank so quickly that he almost imagined it was visible outside his body. In fact, it took a moment for him to gain control of his voice, and then he heard it as if he stood outside his body, oddly calm. "Ah, my ward, I presume. Much though I deplore her behavior, I have every belief that the invitation came from Imogen and not from you."

"No, I did issue the invitation," Gabe said.

"Ah."

"But only after she invited me to the library to help her find a book," he added.

The ice in Rafe's veins was replaced by fury. "Imogen is a remarkably light-heeled young woman. I don't know why I feel surprised."

Gabe waved a hand in the air. "I don't wish to meet your ward tomorrow evening."

"That is, of course, something the two of you must decide between yourselves," Rafe said rigidly. Then he couldn't help it and added: "I will note, Gabe, that Imogen is newly widowed. She is rather desperate."

Gabe nodded. "It surprises me that she seems to have suffered some sort of rejection in the past."

"Lord Mayne," Rafe said. "He understood that she didn't truly wish for the sort of scandal she was courting."

There was a veiled rage in his voice that made the hair on Gabe's neck stand on end. And told him, without words, that his instincts were correct. He would have to play this just right.

"We agreed to go in disguise to see a concert in Silchester tomorrow night. So that we wouldn't be recognized. She seems to be of the opinion that you would prefer her to be chaperoned."

"I would," Rafe said grimly.

"Yet she's a widow, of course, and on her own, is she not?"

Rafe's eyes were chilly. "She is not on her own. She has me, and make no mistake, I shall watch out for her interests."

Gabe opened his mouth, but Rafe held up his hand. "I may not be able to protect her from issuing inadvisable invitations to all and sundry but"—he leaned forward— "I can make damn sure that anyone who toys with her is tied to her. So make very certain, brother, that you wish for the parson's mousetrap before you take Imogen to Silchester tomorrow."

There was an odd, pulsating moment of silence in the room. "I don't," Gabe said.

"You don't what?"

"I don't wish to marry Lady Maitland."

"Then," Rafe said, leaning back in his chair and speaking very softly, "you might want to rethink the advisability of meeting her tomorrow night."

"It is my impression that Lady Maitland would be disappointed if I withdrew my invitation."

"Perhaps her disappointment will make her rethink her current ambition to become a vulgar lightskirt."

"Lady Maitland is no lightskirt," Gabe said. And then: "I should know."

"I would gather that you are implying that your mother should be known by that label," Rafe said. "I would never think such a thing. The family solicitor has recently told me of my father's devotion to your mother, as have you."

"I am only saying that Lady Maitland has turned to me in an effort to stop grieving for her husband."

"And because she desires you," Rafe said with a faint, twisted smile.

"I am certain that you are as aware as I am of the inadvisability of acting on such an emotion."

"And I assure you that if I lectured Imogen on the subject, it would make no difference to her determination to seduce you," Rafe said. Even he could hear the raw raggedness in his voice. "Dammit!"

"Yes," his brother said, his eyes amused.

"Don't look at me like that. I'm not quite brokenhearted."

"Just a bit touched," Gabe said after a moment's consideration.

"Not even."

"Overcome by bashfulness, are we?" Gabe said, suddenly finding that he was enormously enjoying the role of younger brother.

Rafe glared at him balefully from beneath lowered brows.

"You'll have to go in my stead."

"*What?*"

"Tomorrow night. Stick on the mustache, cloak, etc."

"Don't be an ass!"

"Would you rather that she is humiliated by my rejection? Because while I would not want to spurn her, I am not—"

"Not what?" Rafe said fiercely.

"Not interested."

"Rubbish. There's no man alive that wouldn't be *interested* in Imogen."

"I don't wish to marry her."

Rafe's eyes visibly darkened. "Then—" he stopped.

Gabe stood up. "Bring a carriage to the orchard gate at nine o'clock tomorrow night."

"I won't."

Gabe paused at the door. "If you don't," he said gently, "Imogen will wait for me. I imagine that she will be humiliated by my nonappearance. I suppose you could comfort her."

Rafe just stared at him, eyes narrowed and chilly. He was remembering all those stories of Cain and Abel and just how much sense they made.

"Oh," Gabe said, reaching into his pocket. "I forgot this." A long black mustache flew through the air and landed on Rafe's bed like a limp mouse skin. "Just in case you decide to spare your ward the humiliation. Nine o'clock at the orchard gate. You are taking her to Silchester to see a singer from London, by the way. I think her name is Cristobel."

"*Cristobel*?" Rafe said, his eyes narrowing. "Are you quite certain?"

Gabe shrugged. "I saw something nailed to a tree. The woman likely has all the skill of a caterwauling cat."

"You're a professor of divinity, and you promised to take my ward to see *Cristobel*?"

"Imogen is not a child," Gabe said, opening the door.

"If you allowed yourself to see Imogen as a woman rather than someone fit to play with toys, she might truly surprise you."

The door closed quietly behind him.

18

A Chapter of Intelligent Conversation
About Intelligent Subjects

Gillian Pythian-Adams had been seated in the library for two hours, painstakingly copying out actors' parts from *The Man of Mode*. At the moment she was copying out Mrs. Loveit's part so that it could be sent to Miss Loretta Hawes. As she wrote, Gillian was trying to memorize the part; surely the stage manager of a theatrical event should know all the lines better than the actors.

"*I know he is a devil,*" Gillian murmured to herself. What a stupid line that was. If the man was a devil—and every indication was that Dorimant was just that—then Mrs. Loveit should spurn him, not waft around the stage sighing that she *must love him, be he never so wicked.*

Wicked men were to be detested. Especially the wicked kind like Dorimant, who had obviously dallied with half the women in London.

Dorimant was rather like Mr. Spenser, to tell the truth. Mr. Spenser looked innocent as an angel—a divinity professor!—while in truth he was importing his mistress into the household. Because that was the conclusion Gillian had drawn about Mr. Spenser's suspicious interest in Miss Hawes's welfare. At the same time, there was Imogen, and her ambitions for Mr. Spenser's further acquaintance. Yes, perhaps she should switch Mr. Spenser to Dorimant and make the duke play Medley.

It was all rather depressing, for some reason. Of course Imogen was so beautiful that Mr. Spenser would succumb to her wiles.

Mrs. Loveit was complaining about all the odious fools in London. Well, she, Gillian, knew about fools. After all, she'd been engaged to Draven Maitland, hadn't she?

"Excuse me," came a deep voice.

She jerked her head up. "Oh!"

"I merely wondered if you would like some assistance." How could he be so devilish when he looked so blameless?

"That is very kind of you," she said. "But as you can see, I have only one copy of *The Man of Mode*, and I am afraid that only one person can use the book at a time."

Mr. Spenser moved closer to the table and looked down at her. He had a lovely square jaw. Not that Gillian was noticing in particular. "If I sat next to you," he suggested, "I could copy out a part at the same time."

"Oh, no—" Gillian said, but he was already pulling a chair close to her and drawing a scroll toward him.

"Where are you?"

"I'm in Act Two," she said weakly. "Mrs. Loveit."

"Shall I do Dorimant's part?" he asked, glancing over her sheet. "We can add his earlier lines at another time."

"I won't be able to write with you so close to my arm, Mr. Spenser," she protested. He smelled like soap and the outdoors.

He politely moved his chair to the right. "In that case, why don't you read Mrs. Loveit's lines aloud, and I'll write down the lines?"

Gillian smiled weakly at him. "All right. I'll start with Dorimant's entrance. *Is this the constancy you vowed?*"

"Is that Mrs. Loveit?" His eyebrows were delicious when they pulled together with that little pang of bewilderment.

"Yes," Gillian said with a gulp. "Of course it is. And then Dorimant says: *Constancy at my years! 'tis not a virtue in season; you might as well expect the fruit the autumn ripens i' the spring.*"

"A charming fellow," Gabe said as his pen scratched across the foolscap.

"Like all men," Gillian said before she thought.

"You think that constancy is in short supply in my sex? That an honorable man is, in fact, as rare as autumn fruit in the spring?"

Gillian hesitated a moment and then nodded. Normally she didn't share her opinions with males, but surely Mr. Spenser was the exception. He could have no interest in her, what with his Loretta and Imogen, and Lord only knows who else.

"A harsh judgment," Mr. Spenser said, sounding genuinely perplexed.

"I hardly think so," Gillian said. "This play and its hero is only one of many celebrations of the rakish hero. Is a rake, a man like Dorimant, anything to venerate or to adore? Dorimant abandons Mrs. Loveit, flirts with Belinda, and courts Harriet. What sort of man is he to admire?"

"Why on earth did you chose the play? I have always found it a paltry bit of entertainment, as I said at the time."

"But the only suggestion you came up with was translated from ancient Greek," Gillian said, nettled. "We have no skills for solemn tragedy; this company will be hard put to perform a comedy."

"A play should correct vices, not celebrate them. We might as well be putting on one of those foolish bits of fluff called *Love in a Hollow Tree*."

"*Man of Mode* does not precisely celebrate vice. It laughs at the vanities of men like Dorimant," Gillian pointed out. "One never truly admires the person who is the subject of humor."

"But the author gives him excellent lines," Mr. Spenser said. He took the book from her hands and turned back a few pages. "Here he defends himself: *Should I have set up my rest at the first inn I lodged at, I should never have arrived at the happiness I now enjoy!*"

"That proves my point!" Gillian said triumphantly. "No one could be expected to admire such a man. He's treating women as little more than a rest at an inn. Why, he might as well say that Mrs. Loveit is nothing more than a bed to him." Gillian colored.

Mr. Spenser looked down at her, his gray-blue eyes amused. "A descriptive turn of phrase, Miss Pythian-Adams."

But Gillian could feel her backbone stiffening. She was not going to be condescended to by this man, who was practically worse than Dorimant himself. For all Dorimant was a rake, he didn't claim to be a divinity professor. "And yet," she said, looking him straight in the eyes, "when is a woman truly more than a mere temporary inn for a man? Your sex decides to marry with as much prudence as if they had decided to visit a spa and take the waters: in fact, with precisely the same combination of disenchantment and carelessness."

He had a small crooked smile that might soften a woman who was more inclined to be softened. "We see marriage quite differently, Miss Pythian-Adams. Marriage seems to me the most fascinating of states."

"Why on earth would you say that?" Gillian asked with genuine surprise.

"Love can be a fleeting thing. But once married, a man and woman are bound to live for each other, not for pleasure."

"Dorimant, married, will continue to live for pleasure," Gillian said. For some reason her heart was beating extremely quickly.

"That may, of course, be true," Mr. Spenser said

thoughtfully. "But I think that Harriet will tame him, don't you?"

"I think she will learn to tolerate him. And that is quite different from taming."

"In fact, she says that she will learn to *endure* her husband."

"The fate of many women." For some reason, all Gillian could think about was how empty the library was, and how silent the large house felt around them. It was as if there were only the two of them in the whole building. Mr. Spenser's eyes were so—so thoughtful. It was enthralling to have his fixed attention.

"Do you believe that?" He looked genuinely curious.

"How can one love such a creature?" Gillian asked, speaking the truth as she never had before. "You must forgive me the libel to your sex, sir, but men are dictatorial, frequently tedious, and almost always inconstant, as we noted when this conversation began. They—" And then she suddenly had the horrified thought that he was the child of an adulterous union and would likely feel quite mortified by the topic.

He didn't look mortified.

"They?" he prompted.

"This is an unseemly subject for conversation," Gillian said. "You must forgive me." She turned back to her foolscap, noticing with irritation that her fingers were trembling slightly.

"Why don't I read?" Mr. Spenser asked. "While I do not care particularly for the play, there is an enchanting scene between Harriet and Young Bellair."

"When she instructs him in how to woo?"

"You have dimples when you smile," Mr. Spenser said, and a look of near horror crossed his face.

For goodness sake, Gillian thought to herself rather crossly. He needn't act as if she were unavailable, given that no other woman in the house seemed to be.

He cleared his throat. "Forgive me for not having thought of this before, but is there a chance that your reputation will be dented by being alone with me? Shall we ring for your maid, or your mother, or some other person to join us?"

"I very much doubt it," she said.

"I was under the impression that young ladies were not to entertain gentlemen in private."

"My mother is an extremely sensible woman," she said. "In my experience, claims of compromised female reputations follow young women who are ardently interested in the state of marriage. I assure you that I have not the least wish nor need to force a man into marriage."

"In that case, why don't I read aloud from this scene, and you write down Harriet's words?" His voice was as even as ever.

She poised her pen obediently.

"This is Young Bellair," he said. "*Now for a look and gestures that may persuade them I am saying all the passionate things imaginable.*"

"Oh, I know this part," Gillian said. "Harriet tells him to put his head to one side and tap his toes."

"*Your head a little more on one side, ease yourself on your left leg, and play with your right hand.*"

Gabe was furious. Absolutely furious. The more he

thought about it, watching Miss Pythian-Adams's pen move across the page, the angrier he felt. True, he was illegitimate. But that didn't make him a eunuch. She *should* be worried about being in a room alone with him. Perhaps not because her mother would consider them compromised, given that he was apparently about as marriageable as a spoiled chicken. But because—

"The next line?" she asked. And then when he looked at her, "Harriet's next line?"

"Now set your right leg firm on the ground, adjust your belt, then look about you." She had beautiful hands, slim hands that looked as intelligent and ladylike as she was.

"Turn your face to me, smile, and look to me," he said, watching her hands. They were like her lips, sweet, innocent and clean. Ladylike.

"Oh, but I don't think that line—"

But he caught her face, that ladylike sweet triangle in his hands, and pressed his lips to hers. She tasted startled, but not outraged, although of course in a moment she'd be beating him about the head and screaming. But she was startled into silence, and he meant to make the moment last as long as he could.

Gillian tasted like everything he'd ever wanted in his life. She smelled clean, and sweet, with just the faintest hint of something—a perfume that smelled like peaches, not like the lush heavy scent of roses. There was no oily red color on her lips either. He ran his tongue over her plump lower lip, and she made a startled little noise in the back of her throat.

The little bird he'd caught had never been kissed, perhaps. Gabe was having the oddest sensations. As if he were Dorimant himself, the rake called *the worst man breathing*. Dorimant wouldn't hesitate to kiss an innocent in the library, and take advantage of her inexperience . . . The thought slipped away because Gillian hadn't fled yet. She must be so startled that she'd gone into shock, like a rabbit afraid to move. He'd be a fool to waste time.

So he nibbled on her full lower lip, but of course she wasn't like Loretta, or the other women he'd bedded—not that there'd been that many. Gillian had no idea what he wanted, he could tell that. So he just slid into her mouth between one breath and another, a sweet, deep stroke into her mouth.

He felt her astonishment as if it were his own body. And yet . . . still she didn't begin to scream for help.

Gabe was having a rakish feeling that he had literally never had before. It was as if Dorimant had leaped off the page and was whispering in his ear. Before he knew it, he scooped Gillian's sweet little body off her chair and plumped her down on his lap, and without ever stopping the kiss—that same slow kiss that couldn't end.

She gasped again when she settled on his lap, but her arms went around his neck, and so he dared to wander from her lips and run his mouth across her smooth cheek. No powder, no color, no bitter taste of strange potions designed to make a woman's skin white, or red, or smooth. Just Gillian's pure, sweet skin, and the tiny sound of her breath and the way her breath hitched when he pulled her closer.

He could feel her corset, and it was one of those kinds that held a woman upright and encased as if in steel. Paradoxically, it made him wild with desire. She clearly had three or four layers of clothing on, and his fingers trembled as they soothed the layers and he couldn't help it, he dipped back into her mouth.

Now her fingers curled into his hair.

He delved into her sweet mouth as if he were on the edge of death, which he was because any moment now she'd come to her senses and realize whom she was kissing. But for the moment he was Dorimant, strutting down the London street with all the bravado and the beauty of an angel.

"Kiss me back, sweetheart," he said, and his voice came out as dark and liquid gold as any actor's.

"I—I—"

He shifted her just a little so that he could rub a thumb up her neck. "You taste like peaches," he said into her mouth. "Gillian."

And then, all of a sudden, she *was* kissing him back. All that sweetness turned wild, and the little hoarse sounds he heard were his as well as hers. Stunned, he pulled back and looked at her.

Her hair was falling around her shoulders. Her eyes weren't bewildered anymore. She raised her eyelashes as if they were too heavy. Her lips were as deep crimson as if she'd painted them. He froze, hands in the silky sweep of her hair.

What had he done?

"I shouldn't—" he said hoarsely.

And just like that, all the passion disappeared from her eyes and she looked at him with all the cool calculation of an aristocrat. "You," she whispered.

"It's all right," he said uneasily, picking up a hairpin and handing it to her.

She leaped from his lap as if he had poked her with the pin. "You're a man of no principles."

"You're quoting from the play," he said, making a grimace that might count as a smile.

"It seemed a useful line."

Strangely enough, she didn't begin screaming, just looked at him as she briskly wound her hair back up into a chignon that hid all that glowing color as if it didn't exist. "Well, I suppose I should thank you," she said briskly.

She really was one of the oddest women he'd ever met. In fact, he couldn't even think of a repost to that.

"This has taught me sympathy for the women of the play. I previously thought Mrs. Loveit and Belinda were rather foolish women, negligible in intelligence and prey to their passions."

Gabe felt queerly distant, as if he were watching the scene from another room, or even from the audience of a theater.

"She's your mistress, isn't she?" Gillian asked.

"Who?" he asked. "I don't think Medley has a mistress."

"This Loretta. Miss Hawes."

"No!" But she read his eyes; she knew it, and he saw it, and she didn't bother to acknowledge his protest. "As the manager of this production, I should perhaps insist that you play Dorimant. As far as I know, the Duke of Holbrook is as pure as the driven snow. And yet you . . ."

"I assure you that my reputation—"

"Of course, Emilia's mother is the one who really understands Dorimant," Gillian said, almost to herself. "She says that *if he does but speak to a woman she's undone.* I never credited the line before."

He noticed with extreme irritation that there wasn't a trace of passion in her voice or face now, only a kind of inquiring curiosity.

"You would go a long way to changing my mind about rakes, Mr. Spenser, I assure you."

"You make me feel like an animal on exhibit," he said.

She ignored him. "Merely a little conversation and a few minutes copying out parts, and you quite diverted my attention. It was a masterful performance." She gathered up her scrolls. "Good afternoon, sir."

And without further ado, she tucked herself through the door.

19

Love's Mistress

It was one of those evenings when the sky is a clear, dark blue, almost as if it is lighted from the inside. He was wearing the mustache. And a black opera cloak.

It felt rather dashing, as if he were a spy. Or an illicit lover. But he'd given a great deal of thought to the evening, and he knew precisely how it would unfold. Imogen didn't really wish to engage in surreptitious intimacies with Gabe. This was merely a wild flight, akin to when she tried so desperately to entice Mayne into improprieties. He'd wager half his estate that she would change her mind when it came to the point. Then he could bring her back to the house without her ever knowing that Gabe had backed out of the evening.

The moon was just bright enough so that the acacia

leaves kept a faint golden glow, as if they'd kept a trace of sunshine. He had arrived early and taken up a place leaning against the rounded, mossy stones of the orchard wall. The old acacia kept flinging its leaves at him: beautiful golden ovals that tumbled through the air as if they were waltzing a particularly vigorous, solitary measure.

He straightened when he heard the sweep of a cloak in the leaves. He couldn't quite believe that Imogen wouldn't recognize him. Surely she would take one look at his face and know it was he. They'd exchanged enough hard glances.

He would certainly pick her from a hundred women. No other woman had such a deep bottom lip, and those flaring eyebrows. No, or the cracking wit she constantly broke over his head either.

A moment later he took that back. To say she looked like a romp would be a compliment: a night-walker would be the common assumption. He would never have recognized her.

"Imogen!" he said, forgetting for a moment that he was Gabe, and Gabe would address Imogen as Lady Maitland.

"May I call you Gabriel?" she said, dimpling up at him and putting a hand on his arm.

"You—you look—"

"I look positively decadent," she said with satisfaction. "Once I was completely costumed, my maid had what she called a Very Nasty Spasm at the thought of my being seen in public like this. But I assured her that no one could possibly guess who I am."

Rafe stared down at her, speechless. Imogen's lips were shining crimson, and her eyes were lined in black.

She'd covered her face in some sort of powder, and a great quantity of flaxen ringlets spiraled out of her hood in all directions. "I believe you are correct in your assumption," he said. Of course, she was the most beautiful night-walker he'd ever seen.

"Shall we go?" Imogen asked.

"Where did you find the wig?" Rafe said, pulling himself together and taking her arm to lead her through the orchard door.

"It was in one of the boxes of theatrical properties sent from London, of course," she said, glancing up at him. "Didn't you help Griselda catalog the contents?"

"Of course!" Rafe said hastily. "I didn't recognize it on your head."

"I do believe it's meant for a queen," Imogen said, laughing. "It has alarming height in the back. I thought Daisy would have another spasm when we finally got it fixed in place. Is this your carriage?"

"No," Rafe said gravely—for now he was keeping in mind Gabe's customary solemn demeanor—"I hired a vehicle, thinking that we would be less likely to be recognized."

"What a good idea! I can see that you know precisely how to handle this kind of arrangement."

Rafe raised an eyebrow at this evidence of Imogen's opinion of his brother's expertise in arranging illicit liaisons, but climbed into the carriage after her.

Once they were seated opposite each other, she took a deep breath. "There is bound to be some sense of discomfiture in the beginning of an excursion such as this," she said.

Rafe thought that was likely true, but he had never taken an illicit trip to Silchester in his life. And he was beginning to enjoy himself exceedingly. "What are you wearing under your cloak?" he asked.

"Mrs. Loveit's costume. It's a trifle gaudy, of yellow spangled satin, embroidered in silver. I can only suppose that it will look well on the stage, because I assure you that it is far too vulgar for a drawing room."

Rafe couldn't see anything glittering in the dark carriage, but he could picture it.

"But I do wish to speak to you, Mr. Spenser," Imogen said. "Perhaps this is not an uncomfortable moment for you, since you have such experience. But—"

"You said you would address me as Gabriel," Rafe interrupted.

"Yes, of course." Imogen was fidgeting with her handkerchief, and Rafe was aware of a deep, abiding sense of enjoyment. He was always one to love moments of exquisite ridiculousness, and unless he missed his guess, his ward was about to confess to the man she had coerced into this excursion that she wished their friendship to be platonic.

"You see," Imogen said haltingly.

Rafe smiled to himself. He *could* put her out of her misery—but why bother? Of course Imogen didn't really mean to sleep with Gabe. She was far too much of a lady for that.

"I have limited experience with the male sex," Imogen said.

And I mean to keep it that way, Rafe thought with a touch of grim humor.

She leaned forward and touched him lightly on the knee. "You will likely laugh, but I assure you that it is quite a new sensation for me to be embarking on an *affaire* of this nature."

Suddenly Rafe didn't feel the slightest inclination to laugh. His eyes narrowed. The script was not going precisely as he had predicted.

"You must think me very bold," Imogen was saying. "Indeed, I *am* being bold, if not immoral. But my husband died over a year ago now, and we were only married for two weeks." She looked at him appealingly.

Rafe managed to nod.

"I am truly not an immoral woman," she continued. "That is, I suppose I *am* an immoral woman because—because I am here. And yet, Mr. Spenser—Gabriel—I don't wish to marry again. Not until I understand something of men."

"Of men?" Rafe said hollowly.

"I really don't know any of your sex. That is, I knew my father, and I loved him, but he was rather irresponsible. Then I married Draven, and I'm afraid he was quite similar to my father. In fact, in retrospect, they behaved in precisely the same ways. And now—now I should like to . . ."

Her voice trailed away.

"You do know Rafe," Rafe said over the promptings of his better self.

"Well, of course." But she closed her lips and didn't say anything further.

"You could be ruined if anyone discovers this little excursion," Rafe said, carefully schooling his voice so that it had the solemn depth of his brother's.

"Oh, we won't be discovered. I'm not afraid of that. But I have been rather discomforted all afternoon by—"

Here it came. Of course Imogen wouldn't be able to go through with an illicit assignation with a man she scarcely knew. True, Gabe was a handsome man. But she was a lady of taste and . . .

And passion.

"I have thought over our conversation in the hallway, you understand, many times. And I cannot get it out of my head that you did not, in fact, wish to accompany me to the library, nor to Silchester either, Mr. Spenser."

"Gabe," Rafe said shortly. "Of course I wished to accompany you, or I wouldn't be here."

A sudden gleam of moonlight entered the carriage and flashed past Imogen's hands in her lap, twisting a handkerchief.

"I shall be absolutely honest with you," she said, her voice low but steady. "I am haunted by the idea that my husband was not as—as enthusiastic about our elopement as I was."

Rafe remembered just in time that his brother had never met Imogen's dead husband and so could hardly say something scathing about Maitland's limp manhood. "I am absolutely certain that could not have been the case."

Moonlight began pouring in the window as the carriage lurched onto the open road leading to Silchester. Imogen's little rueful smile made Rafe long to pull Maitland back to life, just long enough so he could kill him for ever making Imogen feel undesirable.

"You didn't know Lord Maitland," she said, looking down and concentrating on folding her handkerchief into a small square. "My husband was far more devoted to his horses than to any one person. I loved him"—she paused—"far more than he loved me. Naturally, that understanding was rather grievous to me at first, but I have come to understand that life is not always equally balanced in these matters."

"In general, you may be right," Rafe said in a harsh tone. "But I find it inconceivable that Lord Maitland did not value you exactly as you are worth."

"I take it you mean to say that I am worth more than a horse?" Imogen asked, looking at him with a sly humor that made Rafe want to grin back. But Gabe was not the sort to grin, not when it came to serious subjects.

"Far more than a horse, or indeed, other women," he said.

"Thank you," Imogen said. And then: "This is rather difficult to say."

"Anything you tell me will never leave this carriage," Rafe said, achieving Gabe's solemn tone without even thinking about it.

"The truth is that I thought to have an *affaire* last year, when poor Draven had only been gone six months. You'll think I'm the variest drab. I believe I was rather crazed with sorrow."

"I can understand that," Rafe said, thinking of himself after his brother Peter died.

"Well," Imogen said with a little gulp, "most people

manage their misery a great deal better than I have done. I was so . . . I can't say it."

Rafe leaned forward, regardless of the moonlight and the fact that she might recognize him, and wound his fingers through hers. "You may tell me," he said firmly.

"I tried very hard to take a lover," Imogen said with a rush. "Lord Mayne. Of course, you don't know him, but he is a veritable rake, I assure you. Though he did not—"

"He did not take advantage of your grieving state," Rafe said, promising himself that he would apologize to Mayne for ever doubting him.

"I would like to imagine that he suffered a sudden attack of virtue, but I'm afraid it isn't true. He simply wasn't attracted to me," Imogen said flatly.

"I do not believe it."

"You haven't met him," Imogen said with a little sigh that went straight to Rafe's heart. "But I assure you that he told me directly that he was not interested. Which returns us to my original subject. You see, Mr. Spenser, the more I thought about our meeting in the corridor, the more certain I became that you are here in this carriage out of some sort of reluctant chivalry. Like a true knight, you did not allow me to suffer embarrassment, but that does not mean that you actually wish to be *here*."

Imogen thought that Gabe didn't want to be with her—and he didn't. Rafe knew deep in his bones that he would do whatever it took to keep her from knowing that Gabe was indeed in the ranks of Draven and Mayne: men who were inexplicably blind to her charms and couldn't tell a diamond from a river rock.

"I gather you are worried that I don't desire you," he said, his voice coming out in a low growl.

She flinched a bit, and said, "I suppose you could put it that way."

He pulled the curtains shut. Without moonlight, the carriage became a dark and cozy place, a room hardly big enough for the two of them. He could just see the slanting beauty of her eyes, shadowed black by all that kohl she was wearing.

Without further ado, he reached over and hauled her into his lap. The first thing he did was rub her handkerchief across her lips, holding her startled eyes with his own. He only meant to rub off the greasy ointment. But he rubbed once and found himself riveted by the deep curve of her lower lip. She was watching him, not fighting, just watching.

Well, if she were trying to find signs of desire, she was sitting directly on a fairly potent one. But the next moment that thought fled. Because she licked her lip after he rubbed it. He took the cloth and rubbed across her lip again. And, watching him, that small pink tongue touched her bottom lip.

He threw the handkerchief to the ground, and tilted up her face. Her eyes were only just visible in the shadowy carriage. Slowly he rubbed a thumb across that plump lower lip.

And without saying a word, and looking him straight in the eyes, her tongue touched his thumb.

That was it. He took her mouth with all the hunger that had been building in him for weeks, watching her flit about his house, flicking seductive glances at Gabe under her lashes, flicking him glances that were nothing if not indifferent.

She didn't open her mouth so he nipped her lip, and then swept into her mouth with all the searing hunger that had fueled him during the week. Of course he would never do such a thing to his ward.

But she wasn't *his* ward, because he was Gabe, and she was a minx bound on adventure, and he—he couldn't stop kissing her lips, that lower lip that fired his belly with a wish to devour her.

The carriage was rocking to a stop.

"We must—" Rafe said, horrified by the thickness in his voice. He thrust her back onto the bench.

Sophisticated Imogen, the young woman who had astonished—and delighted—the *ton* by flaunting her supposed affair with Mayne, sat on the other seat with the look of someone who had been struck by a bolt of lightning.

The hackney driver pulled open the door. Rafe bundled her out and turned back to the driver. "Meet us here in an hour," he said, giving the man a sovereign.

"Yes, sir," the driver said, eyeing the man in the cloak with new respect. He had more than tuppence to throw away, clearly. Of course, that light piece he was with would burn it soon enough. There was nothing like a yellow-haired lass when it came to burning through the ready, at least in his opinion.

She stepped from the carriage and Snug's eyes widened. Now that was a nice bit of buttered bun, if he said so himself. She even looked clean. Perhaps she was one of those that cost two hundred pounds a night. His cousin Burt had sworn there were such in Londontown.

They were going to an inn, the Black Swan. Could be they were only hoping to hear Cristobel, though 'twas a queer thing to bring a woman to see her. Or . . . could be they were making use of those beds. But if so, the gentleman had picked the wrong inn, because Hynde, the innkeeper, didn't hold with buns taking their wares into such a place.

With a sigh Snug climbed onto the box and clucked to the horses.

Carriages were drawing up every which way under the spreading oak trees in front of the door. Every moment another carriage would draw up, and cloaked gentlemen would jump out, shouting at their drivers. Imogen and Rafe threaded their way between the vehicles, heading for the open inn door.

"There are so many people," Imogen said, watching as four more men shouldered their way into the inn, light spilling out with a swell of noise from the inn.

"It's due to Cristobel," her escort said. There was a faint tone of amusement in his voice.

"Have you seen her before?"

"Once. She is a notable attraction. I expect that men have come from several counties."

Imogen registered that word *men* with a small frisson of surprise. But she wanted an interesting evening, didn't she? This was much better than sitting about hemming a seam and listening to Griselda complain about the play's inconvenience. So Cristobel was likely not a proper woman. In fact, Imogen thought, perhaps she's a bird of paradise. That seemed the right kind of label for someone called Cristobel.

She walked into the Black Swan inn clutching her escort's arm because, to tell the truth, her knees were trembling. So far, although she kept stealing looks at Gabriel, he hadn't looked down at her since they left the carriage. It must be the kiss that made him look so entirely different to her. She thought he was handsome before; now the lights of the tavern played over the planes of his cheekbones and his shadowed eyes and made him look far more than handsome: dangerous. Her eyes kept catching on his lips; they were deep and full, pure seduction. And the line from the play describing Dorimant kept running through her mind; Gabriel Spenser, this evening, seemed to have *something of the angel yet undefaced in him*.

"I'd like you to keep your hood on," he said, cutting her a slanting glance.

Imogen nodded, aware that her cheeks were burning rose under all the powder she had on her face. They walked into a very large room, lit by a number of lanterns precariously attached to nails stuck in the wall. At one end was a fireplace that was likely lit during the day but was now blocked by a makeshift stage. The rest of the room was crowded with male bodies shouting at each other and hoisting tankards of ale.

"I fail to see how any singer is going to make herself heard in here," Imogen said in a faint shriek.

Her escort glanced down at her. "Oh, they'll shut their mouths for Cristobel."

It seemed that Cristobel was a woman of many talents, Imogen thought, feeling a sudden possessive pang. Just how frequently did a divinity professor travel to London to indulge in such unsavory entertainments?

The innkeeper was a short man with a pockmarked face who scuttled sideways toward them through his crowded room. "What may I help you with?" he hollered, over the noise of the crowded room. Then he added, after looking sharply at Imogen's yellow curls, "No chambers available for the night. Women are allowed but"—he jerked his head toward the room—"as you can see, there aren't many females with a taste for Cristobel."

Rafe restrained an urge to knock the man to the ground. "A bottle of wine," he said. And then lowered his face to the level of the rotund little innkeeper. "I would greatly dislike it if my companion and I found ourselves in any sort of scuffle, innkeeper."

"My name's Joseph Hynde," the innkeeper said, falling back a step. "There's no call for a fine gentleman like yourself to worry about scuffles, not in Hynde's Black Swan."

"In that case," Rafe said agreeably enough, "I'd like a table in the back next to the wall, with a view of the stage."

"You want everything, you do," Hynde replied. "I'll have you know that the inn's been crowded for the whole day with people waiting for this very performance. They was outside my door while I washed my face this morning. And you wants a good view of the stage, do you? Well, so does everyone else!"

Rafe didn't bother to answer, just dropped two sovereigns in Hynde's waiting hand.

Hynde turned around. "This way," he said over his shoulder. "You're lucky to be here, sir. Cristobel has been the biggest attraction in Whitefriars for the last months, and this is the first time she's been outside London in over a year." Hynde cleared a way through the crowd by the simple process of cuffing anyone who happened to have a chair in his way.

A moment later Imogen was tucked behind a round table, with her back to the wall. Her companion pulled forward a chair in such a way as to shield her from the crowds. She saw now that it was an interesting room, lined with maps, mirrors, and old portraits, with the air of a chamber designed for a more elegant fate than had befallen it. There was even a dusty old harp in one corner. Everything showed its age: cracks in the mirror glinted brightly in the light from two candles recklessly screwed to its frame; one of the lanterns to their right had fallen from its hook on the wall and lay in a cluster of glass, unheeded by the innkeeper.

At first Imogen thought the crowd was entirely male. But once her eyes were accustomed to the gloom, she saw there was a sprinkling of women throughout the room. The men were not so different than those she'd known in her father's stable, if rather less sober. But the women . . . she'd never seen their like.

She pulled Gabriel close. "What is that woman on the stage doing?" she whispered, just as Hynde slapped a bottle of wine and two glasses onto the table.

Rafe looked over his shoulder. A chair had been

placed on the stage, and an extremely well endowed woman had frozen into a pose as if she were in the act of pulling up her stockings. Her chemise was falling from her breast, and she had a gown tossed next to her, as if she were in the very act of dressing. Or—perhaps—undressing. Most of the men in the room were far more interested in their conversations or cards to pay her any mind.

"She's posturing," Rafe explained. "She's the prologue to Cristobel." He had just made an uncomfortable discovery. There was wine—and only wine—to drink. And while he could probably drink a small quantity of wine, or so he told himself, he had no inclination to try his fortitude with Hynde's rotgut. Yet surely Imogen would notice if he didn't drink. And if she did, she would instantly guess that the man behind the mustache was Rafe and not Gabe.

Rafe shuddered at that thought. It was Gabe she had been kissing so passionately, not himself. Without thinking twice, he accidentally knocked his glass off the table.

Imogen didn't even notice; she was watching the posturing woman, who was pushing her petticoats higher and higher on her thighs. "Are those beauty marks on her breast?" she asked.

Rafe glanced over his shoulder again. The woman had an admirable white breast, marked by a delicately placed beauty spot just on the inside curve. It almost made up for the fact that she was clutching a bottle of gin behind her skirts and occasionally took a swig when she wasn't frozen in place. Imogen was leaning her chin in her hand and gazing at the prostitute with rapt attention.

"They wear beauty spots to cover the effects of disease," he said. "You see that she has four on her cheek?"

"Fascinating," Imogen said, not taking her eyes from the actress.

Rafe signaled the innkeeper. "What have you for supper?"

"Calf's heart stuffed," the innkeeper said, "fried liver, pigeon pie—here, you!" He turned around and cuffed a young man behind him. "Sheathe that sword or you'll be taking your ale in the alleyway, or my name's not John Hynde. If you aren't here, you lose your chance with Cristobel, *may* I remind you?"

The young man sullenly returned his sword to his sheath, and Hynde didn't even pause for breath before continuing, "leg of mutton, green peas."

"We'll have pigeon pie," Rafe said, "and lemonade for my companion."

"Here!" Hyde roared, not bothering to reply, "do you think this is a flash house?" And a second later he had cracked two heads together and thrown one of the men clear across the room.

"My goodness," Imogen said, sipping her wine. "He's very strong for someone so small."

"Throwing people across the room is excellent exercise."

"Do you think that our actress may have made a friend?"

Rafe pushed his chair back so that he was shoulder to shoulder to Imogen. "Why, so she has," he said, watching as the actress hopped off the stage straight into the waiting arms of a young man who lifted her high in the air and then triumphantly out of the front door.

"Where are they—" Imogen asked, and then stopped.

"They are retiring for the night." He couldn't tell if she were blushing because of all the theatrical color on her face. "Of course," he added, "I wouldn't say such a thing to a proper lady such as Griselda."

Imogen giggled. She glanced sideways at him and then she laughed outright.

"What?" Rafe said, bending close, so that his mouth was just beside all those unnatural yellow curls of hers.

"I said nothing."

Her voice was impudent, but Rafe's attention was caught by the curve of her ear. He could just see it in the midst of a froth of yellow curls. "You're a different sort of woman than Griselda," he said into that ear, hearing the throbbing tone in his own voice with some wonder. And then he touched his tongue to that delicate pink.

She jumped.

"You taste good," he said. "Sweet and womanly, for all you have apparent ambitions to the experience of a lightskirt."

"You *do* sound like Rafe!" Imogen said, pulling back and frowning at him. "I have no wish to become any man's kept mistress. Do you know what that poor woman likely has to do to support herself?"

"Yes," Rafe murmured, bending toward her again.

But her eyes were flashing as only Imogen's eyes could flash. "Women all over this country are forced into unsavory practices due to a wish for their daily bread," she informed him.

There was only one way to shut her up.

Even that didn't work for a moment. She tried to say something, and thumped him on the shoulder with a slender fist. But Rafe didn't give a damn.

He hadn't kissed a woman—really kissed a woman—since before his brother died, and he started drinking, and all the pleasure in life just dried up and blew away with the whiskey. Now he could feel every tremble of her soft, sulky lower lip. It was too full to be in beautiful symmetry, and too soft to be anything other than perfect.

She wasn't fighting anymore. Slim white arms circled his neck, and now he couldn't smell the spilled gin and pipe smoke of the inn: merely the innocent woman smell of Imogen who hadn't—though she had her ambitions—taken a lover. Not yet.

A plate slapped on the table next to them. "I pay for me posturings," Hynde said. "You two are looking too impatient to behave in the way that I requires amongst my patrons."

Rafe put Imogen away and slowly rose, his eyes burning down into Hynde's. "Did you make an impolite remark that included this young lady?" he asked. His voice wasn't loud, but silence fell over their part of the room like a pool of water. "Mr. Hynde, did I hear you make an impertinent remark?"

"No," Hynde stammered, looking quite unlike the burly wrestler who had tossed one of his patrons straight out the door. "I said nothing. Nothing!"

"Good," Rafe said, sitting down again. Hynde scuttled away.

"Oh my," Imogen whispered. "Gabriel, everyone is staring at us!"

"Drink your wine," Rafe said. "They'll turn back to their sport soon enough." He looked at Imogen. "I expect they're just fascinated by your hair. That wig looks like a cross between a corkscrew and a lightning stroke."

Her curls had abandoned all their moorings and bounded in every direction. "A flaxen Medusa," Rafe said, amused.

Imogen's eyes were shining and not from excitement. That was desire. The look in her eyes made Rafe shudder like an adolescent in the hands of his first lass. He could feel his heart thumping in his chest. She's craving Gabe, not me, he told himself. She was pulling off her gloves.

"What are you doing?" he asked hoarsely.

"Taking off my gloves so that I can eat some of this excellent pigeon pie you ordered." The men around them had gone back to hoisting tankards of ale to their mouth, quarreling, pinching, and generally carrying on like the near lunatics they were. She had her gloves off now and was looking around for tableware. Rafe handed her a fork.

"Where did you find that?"

"In a place like this, you bring your own."

Luckily, at that moment there was a squeal of a solitary trumpet, because Rafe wasn't quite sure he could watch her eat without pulling her into his lap and feeding her himself. "That should be Cristobel," he said, unnecessarily.

"Actually, according to the sign on the door, it should

be *Love's Mistress*," Imogen said, a smile playing around her mouth.

Rafe took her ungloved hand in his and brought it to his lips. "Surely you can give her a run for her money?" he said, slow and deep.

She was blushing. He could see it through the face powder.

The audience was howling. They had surged to their feet, and each man was straining forward, trying frantically to push enough people out of the way so that he had a clear view of the stage.

An escalation in the general howl seemed to indicate that Cristobel had arrived.

"If they all stand throughout, we shan't be able to see," Imogen said.

"I doubt they'll sit down." But he bellowed, "Down in front!" The ocean of men in front of him hadn't the slightest intention of sitting. They were surging at the stage, held back only by five or six burly men guarding the edge.

Imogen was on her tiptoes. "What does she look like? Didn't you say that you'd seen her before?"

"Cristobel? Her hair is even higher than yours, if you'll credit it." Never mind that Imogen was fifty times more beautiful than Cristobel. Imogen didn't need him to praise her features.

"Does she wear a beauty spot?"

But Rafe didn't answer because Cristobel had begun to sing. "*Come all wanton wenches,*" she sang, "*who long to be in trading.*" She had the kind of rich, dark voice that rolled over the room like barley beer. It was husky and erotic, a promise made in song, a mermaid's call. Instantly the men before them stopped shouting and shoving, and simply gazed at her.

"She has a lovely voice," Imogen said breathlessly. "Oh, Gabriel, I have to see her. This is so frustrating!"

"*Come learn from me, Love's Mistress, to keep yourself from jading,*" Cristobel sang.

"What's jading?" Imogen asked. "Do you think anyone would notice if I climbed on my chair?"

In Rafe's opinion, they wouldn't notice unless Imogen threw off her clothing. Cristobel had them in her throaty spell. "*Be not at first too nice or coy, when Gamesters you are courting.*"

With a swift grab, Rafe pushed a wine cask against the wall. "Here," he said. "No one will notice you."

"What?" Imogen said, looking around.

He had his hands on her waist to lift her onto the cask, but she looked up at him with an adorably confused expression and before he knew what was happening he lowered his mouth to hers again. Cristobel's voice rolled over them like rough honey. "*Let not your outward gesture, betray your inward passion.*"

Rafe had just enough conscious thought left to think that he was certainly betraying inward passion. But there was no time to consider the fact because Imogen was trembling, and now she was holding his face in her hands. He had her pressed against the rough wood of the wall, protecting her from the gaze of strangers. But of course he hadn't allowed their bodies to touch.

Of course.

But he couldn't help it: there in the swelter and the

smell of gin and the coiled sensual tone of Cristobel's voice, he brought their bodies together, shuddering at the softness of her.

"Gabe," she said, her voice half-caught in a rough sound.

It was enough to chill him. He picked her up without a word and put her on the wine cask.

She gasped and clutched his shoulder. Rafe turned around so that he was in front of her and she could hold his shoulders if she lost her balance. No one had noticed them at all. Even though Imogen was on a wine cask and visible to the whole room, who could look otherwise than at Cristobel?

Now that he was standing up he could see straight to the stage. He had only seen Cristobel once before, a year or so ago, but she wasn't a woman one forgot. The intervening year had done nothing but give her a slightly exotic patina. She was sitting on the same old chair used by the posturer, holding nothing more than a small stringed instrument, and yet she had every man in the room mesmerized. Last time he saw her she had dark red curls piled on the top of her head. Now her hair was free, curling wildly down her back as if she had just stepped out of bed.

Which was undoubtedly what every man was thinking about. She was the kind of woman who made you think about sweet butter and sweeter cream: there were no angular bones poking through a gauzy dress, the look beloved by the *ton*, but curves so sweet that they seemed to beg to be stroked. She was on to another song now, about a man and a young maid that were "taken in a frenzy in the midsummer prime." And she wasn't singing it, she was purring it. She didn't even seem to have bothered much with face paint, contenting herself with one beauty patch high on a cheekbone and lip rouge in a crimson shade.

She stood up now, putting her instrument to the side, and swaying, dancing a little dance. Her gaze drifted around the room as she sang, licking at the bodies of the men. Rafe watched her with some amusement as she effortlessly bewitched them.

Still her eyes drifted from man to man, making certain every man felt that he and he alone was the one whom she'd singled from the crowd. She reached the heart of the song. *"He landed in a hole ere he was aware. The lane it was straight, he had not gone far . . ."* when she finally looked to the back of the room.

She recognized him. There was a lush little smile in the back of her eyes, a warm greeting that made most of the heads in the room turn in their direction. But she was a consummate performer, and her eyes drifted on instantly, flicking over Imogen and her yellow corkscrew curls, the knot of laboring men standing to their right, breathing heavily as they watched Cristobel's hips sway.

"Gabriel," Imogen said, bending down so that she could speak in his ear, "I do believe that Cristobel knows you."

"Absolutely not," he said.

"Why not? You have met her, haven't you?"

Rafe looked up, and her amused eyes went through his system like lightning. Would he ever understand Imogen? She was amused by the fact he had been recognized by a prostitute—nay, by *Cristobel*. There wasn't a woman in a thousand who would think it humorous if Cristobel hailed their escort. "She couldn't possibly recognize me," he said, remembering to school his voice to his brother's scholarly tones. "I'm wearing a mustache, remember?"

"How could I not," Imogen whispered back. "I think my cheek is rubbed raw by that same mustache."

He smiled up at her, a little crooked smile, and then caught her chin, surveying her face. "I don't see anything." His lips were almost touching hers.

"Everyone can see us," she whispered.

"No one's interested," he said, rubbing his lips across that deep lower lip of hers.

Imogen pulled back and shoved at him. "Turn around," she ordered.

So he did. He turned around, waiting with arms crossed until Imogen had seen enough so that he could lift her from the wine cask. In fact, he was planning that very move. He'd lift her down, and let her drop against his body, slowly—very slowly . . .

Suddenly he noticed that Cristobel was dancing toward the steps leading to the stage. All around them the men were shifting, pushing toward her. She came down the stairs like the promise of a succubus, like a man's wickedest, wildest fantasy come true. Each man in the room strained toward her. And all that protected her were the bodies of five burly men who cleared a little path before her. Down that path danced Cristobel, coming face-to-face with this man, quickly touching that one on the neck, blowing a kiss to a third.

Cristobel was wanton: genuinely wanton. Her eyes warmed every man in the room, told him a secret story that promised he was the one.

Every inch of Rafe's body was conscious that Imogen's warm body was just above his on the wine barrel. But he wasn't exactly unaware that Cristobel kept stealing looks in his direction. And she wasn't drifting around the room aimlessly either. Soon she had visited all areas of the room—except theirs. A table had overturned when a young stripling leaped forward in the hopes she would smile at him; she gave him a night of happy dreams by kissing her finger and placing it on his lips.

But still she was moving steadily toward Rafe. Damnation.

"What is she *doing*?" Imogen asked, above him.

"Singing," Rafe said, watching Cristobel the way one watches a curious bear cub to make sure it doesn't come too close.

Cristobel had started a new song about a phoenix who rose, and rose again. Imogen was laughing. "She's astounding. But why is she—"

She stopped. Rafe guessed that Imogen had just realized why Cristobel was drifting around the room. He turned his head. "She chooses one man."

Imogen's mouth fell open inelegantly.

"One man, a different man?"

He nodded.

"Every night?"

"Only one."

"No wonder men come from three counties," Imogen

breathed, looking, to his relief, more interested than scandalized. But then her eyes narrowed.

"She's coming in this direction," Imogen pointed out.

Rafe was quite aware of that. What's more, he had the distinct impression that every man in the room thought that Cristobel was about to take away that yellow-haired little crumpet's customer.

"*Our Grandam Eve before the Fall,*" sang Cristobel, "*Went naked, and shamed not a whit.*"

"I'm getting down from here," Imogen said suddenly.

"Wait!" he said, but at that moment Cristobel and her escort of former pugilists swept up to them. Her guards formed a little circle around them. And Cristobel was staring at Rafe, a little liquorish smile playing around her mouth.

Rafe suddenly realized that if Cristobel had, indeed, looked past his mustache—and it certainly looked that way—she was about to blurt out his name. But instead she drifted up to him as if she was about to give him one of the little kisses she'd handed out so liberally.

Except that he was suddenly pulled back, away against the cask of wine.

"Oh, I don't *think* so," Imogen said. She was smiling, but there was a little edge there.

She had draped a slender arm around Rafe's neck and she was resting her cheek against his hair. "You see," she said to Cristobel with a sweet persuasiveness that was at utter odds with her costuming, "my friend is occupied for the night."

The crowd was absolutely silent. Cristobel didn't seem to have even heard Imogen. She came a step closer, and now he could see that though she was still beautiful, she was tired. She was lovely—likely would always be lovely, if she didn't catch the pox and lose a nose. But what struck you, up close, was not the fact that Cristobel had an attractive face. It was the force of her languorous sexuality. The fact that whatever else was in her eyes when it rested on the faces of the men around them, there was a genuine invitation there.

At the moment that invitation was clearly directed at Rafe.

"I remember you," she said, her voice husky.

"That's all right then," Rafe heard a young farmer say to the right. "She never takes the same one twice."

"I don't think so," he said evenly.

"Ah, but I do. You and your friend—he was a lovely man. What was his name?"

He met her eyes with a secret warning.

"He was an earl," she said. "What a night I had with him! Your friend is a man among men." She gave him a dewy-eyed smile. "A man worth returning to."

"We shall surely let him know," Imogen said.

Cristobel's eyes raised to Imogen, and this time they didn't flick away. "Aha," she said sweetly, "what have we here? A little canary-bird, are you? Because you look far too delicate to be common ware, my dear."

Rafe was thinking frantically about what to do. They were surrounded by five of the biggest, burliest men he'd seen outside a boxing match. Moreover, the path between the door and their corner was blocked by at least fifty customers. At any moment Imogen might faint. She was being insulted by a prostitute, for goodness sake.

That was not the kind of thing that happened to gently bred young ladies. Wards. Wards of *dukes*.

"And you look too common to be Bartholomew-ware," Imogen said sweetly. "But appearances are *so* deceiving, and now that we're closer I can see . . ." She let her voice trail away.

Cristobel's eyes narrowed. "I'm no Bartholomew-ware, child, though I doubt you know the meaning of the word."

"Oh dear. Perhaps I meant some other word. Did I, Gabriel?" She turned to Rafe and he realized with a pang of deep surprise that Imogen was thoroughly enjoying herself. Her eyes were shining, and even with those tumbled, frowsy curls around her head, no one in his right mind could think she was a chipper. Not with those laughing eyes, laughing even now at Cristobel who—Rafe noticed with a similar shock of surprise—was laughing back.

"Try *très coquette*," Cristobel said in a ravishing French accent. She turned to one of her guards. "Now, darling, if you would just do me a favor?" Before Rafe knew what was happening, one of the burly men had hoisted Cristobel directly onto the wine barrel next to Imogen.

Who gasped and straightened, automatically giving Cristobel more space on the top of the cask.

Cristobel laughed down at the crowd. "Aren't we the prettiest ladies for leagues around?"

They roared their approval.

Rafe looked up at Imogen, judging how quickly he could pull her down and bust their way out of the room.

He could take those bodyguards if he had to. If Cristobel said one indecent thing—

"Now my young friend isn't as ripe in the business as I am," Cristobel was saying. The whole room was listening, of course.

Rafe cursed under his breath. Imogen didn't look scared. She had a hand on her hip and a little smile on her lips. But even though she was wearing a wig, and a satin dress as gaudy as a parrot's feather, there was no real comparison between the two women.

Imogen was bone-deep beautiful and glowing with the kind of laughter and sensuality that would take a man a whole lifetime to get tired of.

Cristobel's laughter was of a harder sort, still laughter, but deeper, more calculated, jaded by life.

"In honor of my young friend!" Cristobel shouted. The room quieted instantly. She wrapped an arm around Imogen's shoulder, took up a saucy pose, and began to sing. *"A Puritan of late, and also a Holy Sister . . ."*

And that's when Rafe had the greatest shock of the evening. Because Imogen shook out her skirts and with an impudent smile for him, joined Cristobel's husky alto with a clear soprano: *"She, a Babe of Grace, A child of the Reformation, Thought kissing a disgrace!"*

The men watching were beside themselves. The two women stood next to each other on the cask, both of them with one hand on a hip and the other curled over each other's shoulder, both of them laughing as they sang. As soon as this song is over, Rafe thought, she comes down and we leave. Before someone in the room decides to challenge me for my night's companion.

Imogen and Cristobel were trading every other line now.

"*He laid her on the ground.*" Imogen's clear soprano sang. "*His spirits fell a-ferking.*"

She doesn't know what ferking is, Rafe thought. But damn, every man in the place certainly did, and every man of them was longing to play Puritan to her Holy Sister. The women were swaying in unison as they launched into the last verse. Rafe saw Hynde fighting his way across the room, frowning. At this rate, they'd be lucky if the night watch didn't get called. He turned around to grab Imogen the very moment the last word left her lips.

But just as they rounded into a rousing last line, there was a sharp crack, like a mast breaking at sea.

He caught a glimpse of Imogen's face, her mouth forming a perfect little O, like a child seeing a birthday pony for the first time.

Then a tide of red wine reared out of the barrel as the top cracked and flipped to the side and with simultaneous—and very loud—screams, Cristobel and Imogen plunged down in the wine barrel up to their waists.

There was a moment of astounded silence in the room. Soaked to the skin, Rafe reached out to pull Imogen from the rocking barrel. She was laughing, gasping, and smelled like rotgut red wine. He pulled her up in the air, droplets of red wine flinging in a semicircle, and then against his chest, if only to stop every man in the room from ogling her breasts. The wet, gold satin gown appeared to have been made for a small child.

He felt like licking all the wine off Imogen's body, and it wasn't even for the alcohol.

Cristobel was still inside the barrel, leaning against the side and laughing. She was surrounded by strong arms, leaning in to rescue her. With sudden decisiveness she leaned forward and chose a sturdy young man in a weather-beaten white shirt.

He looked clean, muscled, and his eyes, Imogen noticed, were a beautiful green color. "I choose you," Cristobel said, drawing his head toward hers.

Imogen's mouth nearly fell open. She'd never seen a kiss like that. The young farmer was devouring Cristobel, pulling her against his strong chest, heedless of the splashes of red wine that instantly stained his shirt. She leaned back against his arm, her long red hair almost trailing the surface of the wine. Without another word, he plucked her from the wine and carried her from the room.

The men fell back as he strode toward the door. Cristobel had a sleepy, languorous smile that promised the young man would have a night such as he never knew before.

Imogen suddenly shivered.

"Shall we retire to our carriage?" Rafe asked. The men were laughing now, slapping each other and talking about how next time they would be the one chosen by Cristobel. Without waiting for her reply, he began drawing her toward the door. The comments echoing on all sides were enough to make a nun faint, but naturally Imogen showed no signs of such ladylike behavior.

Hynde was holding the door open with a look on his face that signaled a wish to be paid for a barrel of wine.

"Who was the man whom Cristobel chose?" Imogen asked suddenly. "He was no simple farmer, was he?"

There was a clink as Rafe's hand met Hynde's and then he pulled her out into the velvet black night, looking for their carriage. Finally, he saw it, backed against a stand of trees.

"Who was he?"

"I believe he's her husband. At any rate, he has an actor's way with costumes. When I saw her perform in London, he was dressed in the garb of a student at the Inns of Court."

"Are you certain of that? What happened?"

Rafe yanked open the door of his hackney carriage and shook the driver awake. "What do you think happened?"

Imogen smiled at him. "Unless she was blind, she chose you."

"Wouldn't that bother you?" he asked.

Her smile didn't waver. "Why should it?"

Why should it indeed? Theirs was merely a passing affair, after all.

20

The Kind of Thing Rafe Would Say

The carriage was bright with moonlight because Rafe opened a window to let the smell of wine blow away. He had a rug wound around Imogen, but she was still shivering, so finally he pulled her onto his lap.

Her only response was a small gasp.

"I have to ask myself," he said after a time, "whether you've had what you came for, Lady Maitland."

She didn't say anything.

"I expect I offer all the charms of forbidden pleasure to a young widow. Here I am . . . illegitimate, almost invisible in society."

"Don't say that!" Imogen said.

"Why not?" Rafe realized he'd forgotten to lower his voice and brought it down to a professor-like timbre.

"The illegitimate children of great men are invisible to the *ton*. We exist in the shadows, sometimes remembered in wills, often forgotten."

"Very poetic," Imogen remarked. "I must say that I find it hard to regard a Doctor of Divinity as living in the shadows. Rafe told me that only eight men hold the title in the whole of Cambridge University."

"But I still represent those shadows to you."

"Not really. I have very little interest in the *ton* and its opinions." There was a ring of genuine disinterest in her voice. "I will say, though, that it is remarkably easy to speak to a man who is both a member of the *ton* and yet not."

"In no way am I a member of the *ton*."

"You are the beloved brother of the Duke of Holbrook," Imogen said flatly. "Whether you wish to be or not, you are now a member of society. And unless I misunderstand Rafe, your daughter will be raised firmly within the *ton*. So we are your fate, Gabriel, wish it or no."

"Surely you might call me Gabe, after we shared a wine barrel?" Rafe asked.

"We did not share that wine barrel; I shared it with the lovely Cristobel."

"Gabe," Rafe said. Though why he was insisting that she call him by another man's name, he would never know. But he wanted the intimacy between them. He had kissed her, for God's sake.

"What do you think of Rafe?" he asked, telling himself it was only to hear the sound of his own name on her tongue.

"Rafe?" she repeated. And then no more.

"Do you wish to see me again?" he asked, schooling his voice to a slow darkness. "May I escort you to your chambers?"

There it was: the question out in the open.

"No." She moved, a little rustle that he first heard in the dark and then felt with a shock all the way down his legs. "I am drenched in wine and rather uncomfortable. But perhaps we might go to Silchester again. This evening has been so different from my normal life . . . I realize that I am bored."

"Tomorrow night?" he asked lightly, as if her refusal had meant nothing. How did he think he could keep his real identity from her once in her chamber? The mustache would presumably have to go with his trousers.

"Will you ask again tomorrow to escort me to my chamber?" she asked. "Because I feel I should be honest with you, Gabe. I am not certain that I am as ready to be a depraved woman as I had thought."

And there were the words he thought she'd say earlier, but she hadn't. Yet now that she had said them, the only thing he wanted was to sweep her off to that bedchamber. Even the rounded shape of her bottom—through a blanket, and a cloak, and all those undergarments—was driving him mad.

"I think that I may have been wishing to hear that I was desirable," she said.

"You are," he growled. And cleared his throat. "Why don't we allow that part of tomorrow evening to take care of itself?"

She laughed. "That's just the kind of thing that Rafe would say."

"What do you mean?" he asked, scowling because she couldn't see him in the dark anyway.

"You know Rafe." She gave a little shrug that sent her bottom in a small but delicious slide across his lap. "He thinks that foreplanning is a waste of time."

Unjust, he thought, but bit his tongue. Foreplanning, foreplay, it was all the same.

It was only at that moment that Raphael Jourdain, Duke of Holbrook, realized that he was playing for keeps. That he meant to seduce his own ward, whether under another man's name or not. And he meant to keep her for life.

Not only did he like foreplanning, he had been indulging in a form of it without bothering with forethought.

It was such a shocking realization that he lapsed into total silence and didn't even notice until he got home that wine had soaked through Imogen's gown, her cloak, and her blanket and was dampening his crotch.

21

In Which Holbrook Court Welcomes an Unexpected Visitor

The following day
Around noon

Imogen sat straight up in bed. "Josie! What on earth are you doing here?"

"I arrived an hour ago," Imogen's youngest sister said. "I was tired of the Highlands. It's a boring place, so full of snow and stupid Scotsmen."

Josie loved the Highlands. "Is Annabel all right?" Imogen asked. "How is the baby?"

Josie plopped down on the end of her bed. "Annabel is as round as a smallish lighthouse. Ewan spends most of his time rubbing her shoulders and her back and her toes. And she sleeps so much! It was like watching ice melt. I grew tired of it."

Josie didn't sound like . . . Josie. She sounded deflated, somehow. "What's the matter?" Imogen demanded. "What happened?"

Josie shot her an annoyed look. "Absolutely nothing. Am I not allowed to grow tired of watching lovebirds coo?"

"When I left Scotland, you were quite determined to return to England only for the season."

"Spend the winter in the Highlands? What would I do in a godforsaken castle with no one for company but a pair of lovebirds, a few old monks and—"

"Josie," Imogen said, cutting into this miserable tirade. "You have a letter for me from Annabel, I trust. May I have it, please?"

"I haven't concealed it from you," Josie said irritably. She pulled open her reticule and handed over an envelope.

"She says you're unhappy," Imogen said a moment later, putting the note to the side. "Why doesn't she know the reason?"

Josie chewed on her lower lip.

"*Josie.*"

"I didn't like it there!" she burst out. "I ceased to enjoy the company."

"What company in particular?"

Josie waved her hand. "The—the whole lot of them."

"Come here," Imogen said, holding out her arm. Josie came, but unwillingly.

"You smell like wine," she said, her voice quivering a little.

"You smell like tears. What happened? Was it something terrible?"

"No," Josie said wanly. "Not at all. I shouldn't be bothered. I keep telling myself not to be bothered."

Imogen gave her a squeeze. "Tell me."

"It's too humiliating."

Josie tried to move away, but she had forgotten that Imogen had very strong arms, due to restraining twitchy horses.

"Where do you think you're going?" Imogen asked. And then, when Josie showed no signs of revealing all: "So shall I tell you what happened to me last night?" She asked it casually, as if she didn't have Josie in a strangle grip.

Josie sighed. "I suppose this will be some sort of morality lesson, like at church?"

"Not precisely. In fact, definitely not."

"I had about all the morality I could take from the monks who live with Ewan."

"You mean the monk who won all my bawbees playing cards and left me without tuppence to my name?" Imogen said, trying to tease her into a better mood. "So there I was up on the wine cask," she said a while later, "and Cristobel hopped up right beside me."

"Next to you?" Josie asked, clearly fascinated.

"Very much so. The cask did not have a large circumference. Do you remember Peterkin's favorite song?"

"Do you mean Peterkin who was in charge of cleaning the stables when we were growing up?"

"Yes."

"Of course." Josie giggled. "If you sang that song, Imogen, I hope that your disguise was an excellent one."

"The disguise *was* excellent—at least until it washed off."

"Washed off?"

"In the wine," Imogen said.

"*What!*"

Imogen explained.

"And then Mr. Spenser brought you right back here? Not—" Josie added—"that he would take you anywhere else."

"I should hope not," Imogen said. "It was very kind of him to offer to take me to hear her in the first place."

Josie looked at her, unconvinced. "Are you setting up Rafe's illegitimate brother as your cicisbeo? Like Mayne?"

"Absolutely not!" Imogen said with dignity. "It's an entirely different situation."

"What's different about it?" Josie said, looking intently interested.

Josie had such expressive eyes and lovely eyebrows; like a stroke of lightning, Imogen knew what had happened.

"Someone said something unkind about your figure, didn't they?"

Josie had been laughing, but the joy drained right out of her eyes. "Certainly not!" But she said it too hastily.

"I'll travel to the Highlands and send whoever it was on a long carriage ride with Griselda."

Josie managed a wobbly smile. "That was one wonderful thing about my return trip. Miss Flecknoe's stomach is made of iron. She sat opposite me and read improving tracts aloud for hours without turning the faintest shade of green."

"Tell me," Imogen said.

"I don't want to."

"If you don't, I'll write a note to Tess and ask her to come for a visit. And you know that Tess will have the truth in five minutes."

Tess was their eldest sister, and since she had practically raised them, she had perfected all kinds of examination techniques. "I would be worried, if I didn't know that Tess was traveling on the Continent with her husband," Josie pointed out. But then she relented. "It wasn't so bad. Really, it was almost a compliment."

"You disliked this compliment so much that you fled Scotland?"

"Yes," Josie whispered.

Imogen tightened her arms around her little sister. "Humiliation is a universal condition. My only consolation is that I will likely never again make such an ass of myself as I made over Draven."

"I'll never have the chance to make a fool of myself over a man."

"Yes, you will."

"Men will never even consider me, so I shan't have to worry about embarrassing myself."

"Who said what?" Imogen asked. "A carriage trip with Griselda may be too good for them."

"They didn't say anything *to* me," Josie said wearily. "It was people who live next to Ewan. The Crogans."

"You mean the men who tried to feather Annabel? Why in heaven's name would you pay any attention to what those fools said?"

"Because they were saying what everyone else thinks," Josie said. "I didn't mean to overhear them."

"Perhaps they meant you to overhear."

"No. I was hidden behind an oak tree." Josie sniffed. Imogen kissed her on the forehead.

Then it all rushed out. "The older one tried to get his brother to marry me. Except he didn't want to, because he said I was a prime Scottish hoglet. And then the older one said he'd love to snuffle around my skirts. But the younger one said that his brother could snuffle all he wanted, but when a girl is as fat as—as I am, she's going to turn into a proper sow. A—a *sow*!"

"They're cruel drunkards," Imogen said, stroking Josie's hair and wishing that she had the Crogans within the sights of a hunting rifle. "I think you're right in that the older one might have been attempting a compliment. I wish that men didn't think that snuffling was a compliment, but they do think that way."

"They spoke about me as if I were disgusting, as if—as if I was incontinent or something. That's how they talked about it. The older one said that at least I would never cuckold my husband, because—" Her voice broke again.

"You could cuckold anyone you pleased," Imogen

said, resting her chin on Josie's soft hair and stroking her shaking back, "although I hope you never do."

"He said I would never cuckold anyone because all my husband would have to do is give me enough bacon and I'd be happy." She lost her voice for a few moments.

"That was cruel, and they are both horrible, horrible people," Imogen said with conviction.

"The worst of it was that the next morning the younger Crogan showed up and started to court me!" Josie said in a wail. "He brought me flowers, and he smiled at me, just as if he didn't think I was a great fat sow. It was—it was awful!"

Imogen narrowed her eyes. "You should have spoken to Annabel. Ewan would have killed him for the impudence of it."

"What would be the point? They knew he was courting me for my dowry. She and Ewan thought it was funny that the Crogans were so hopeful."

"So what did you do?"

Josie sniffed.

"I know you," Imogen observed. "I've known you for your whole life. I don't believe for a moment that you simply allowed this Crogan to court you, without saying a word to him about his true intentions."

"I didn't do anything the first time he came. I was so shocked that he would attempt it, after those things he said about me. But he acted as if he'd never said them."

"Horrible."

"A few days later he asked if I wished to attend an assembly. Annabel told him immediately that an assembly was out of the question because I hadn't been formally introduced to society. So he showed up the next evening with some sort of musical instrument."

"Oh, no!"

"Apparently he sang for hours before anyone noticed him. He had hoisted himself up onto the tree outside Annabel's chambers, rather than mine, and it's impossible to wake her up these days."

Imogen was laughing so hard that she was clutching her stomach.

"When Ewan came to bed, at first he had no idea what the noise was, and then he realized that it was a scratchy version of 'Will Ye Go Lassie, Go.'"

"Were you being courted by the short, roundish Crogan or the tall, thin one?"

"The short one. The tall one is the older brother, and he's already married."

"What happened next?" Imogen asked, catching her breath.

"Well, a few days after that he came bringing a poem he'd written about my eyes. It was rather short."

"You *did* keep a copy, didn't you?" Imogen implored, starting to laugh again.

"Naturally," Josie said with dignity. "It might be my only love poem, so naturally I entered it in my book. But I have it memorized. Wait a minute . . ." She struck a declamatory pose.

> *Her eyes they shone like diamonds,*
> *You'd think she was queen of the land*
> *And her hair it hung over her shoulders*
> *Tied up with a black velvet band.*

"What next?" Imogen said after a moment.

"That was all."

"When did you tie up your hair with a black velvet band?"

"I think," Josie said thoughtfully, "that he might have run out of room on his sheet of paper."

"It's surprisingly good."

"Yes, Ewan said it's a well-known song that his grandmother loves."

"So a borrowed love song . . ."

"And an enforced suitor. It just made me so angry. What if I had believed him? What if I had thought that poem was his, and his feelings were genuine?"

"And now we come to the heart of it. What did you do to that man?"

"I dosed him," Josie said. There was satisfaction in her voice and her eyes were—indeed—gleaming like diamonds.

"You dosed him?" Imogen asked, bewildered.

"With one of Papa's horse medicines. Actually it's one I developed myself to treat colic caused by green apples. But I know that it doesn't agree very well with humans, because Peterkin gave it to one of the stablemen when he had a stomachache, and the poor man was sick for a week."

"Oh, Josie!" Imogen said, laughing again. "That's so cruel."

"I wouldn't have done it," Josie said, "but I told him to go away, and he wouldn't. So finally I said that I knew perfectly well that he thought I was a hog-faced sow."

"What did he do?"

"He just stared at me for a moment, and then he said that I wasn't going to have any other chance at marriage, and it was best that we were clear amongst ourselves. And then he said that he could make me happy, and I would never do as well. He couldn't see anyone wanting to marry me, especially in England."

"What an ass," Imogen said dispassionately.

"He said they have standards in England." Josie looked a little teary again, but she took a deep breath. "I still wouldn't have done something as mean as dose him, except that he said he'd watched me eat and he could tell that I liked my food better than any man. And then— and then I made up my mind."

"Good. He deserved it."

"But it didn't stop what he said from being true. I do love Scottish food. I ate and ate while I was there, and Miss Flecknoe kept talking about how I should go on a vinegar diet, and I kept not doing it, because Ewan's chef would make fresh bannocks in the morning. Every night I decided to start with vinegar and cucumbers in the morning. And then every morning, there would be bannocks and kippers and ham in the breakfast room, and before I knew it, I would have eaten."

"You can't eat vinegar and cucumbers!" Imogen said. "Where did she get such a ridiculous idea?"

"She says that the Duchess of Surrey's daughter lost three stone doing that. And she says that I am lacking in determination, and unless I stop eating, I'll never be able to marry."

Imogen rubbed her sister's back some more and decided to talk to Rafe about Miss Flecknoe. "If you drank nothing more than vinegar during the day, darling, you would probably die. Waste away."

Josie looked unconvinced. "I have a long way to go before I waste away. I could just stop somewhere between here and the grave."

"It's not safe. Besides, you'll get spots."

That was a better argument, she could see at once. Josie had been through a rather spotty spell last year, but these days her skin was as flawless and smooth as Irish cream.

"All over your face," she added. "The red, sticking-out kind."

"Perhaps I should just stop eating altogether," Josie said, sniffling a bit. "I can't have a season when people are calling me a Scottish piglet behind my back. I just can't. I'd rather be a spinster, like Miss Flecknoe."

Imogen laughed at that. "Miss Flecknoe is like a long drink of the vinegar she's trying to get you to take. No one would want to be with her."

"Nor yet with me."

"That is not true. You are a beautiful young woman. You are curvaceous and beautiful, as well as being funny and loving."

"I wish that was true," Josie said heavily. "But the truth is that I curve out and out. And after being in Scotland, those curves just got bigger. I had to leave. And I simply couldn't bear to tell Annabel why I was leaving. I don't know why I have no will power, and everyone else in the world seems to have it. Even the disgusting Crogan brother isn't as round as I am."

"We'll write Annabel and say something. She's obviously worried."

"I doubt it. She lies around and sleeps all the time, when she's not eating. But she's carrying a child. I have no excuses."

"Annabel has never been as slim as those women pictured in *La Belle Assemblée*. And yet she has never failed to make a man desire her."

"Well, I'm plumper than she is. Her curves are in different places. And I haven't the faintest idea how to make anyone desire me!" Josie wailed.

"Have you had breakfast this morning?"

"I'm never eating again. I quit last night."

Imogen sighed and put her feet over the edge of the bed.

"Euw," Josie said. "You really do smell like wine."

"That happens if you fall into a wine barrel. I bathed last night, but I didn't want to go to bed with wet hair. Let me have a quick scrub and then we'll both have breakfast. The world is always tragic if you haven't eaten. I swear all those Greek dramatists must have been writing in the midst of a hundred-year famine."

"Sophocles was at war for years," Josie said, looking marginally more cheerful. "He probably had to eat soldiers' rations."

Imogen shuddered. "Mrs. Redfern may not make bannocks as well as Ewan's chef, but we can do better than soldiers' rations."

"So what is Mr. Spenser like?" Josie asked. "Annabel and I are utterly fascinated by the subject and talked about it endlessly after we got your letter about the play. We must write her today and describe every detail."

"He's quite gentlemanly."

"Does he have any sign of his birth? Say, a hunch-back?"

"Josie! How can you be so unkind, especially after the story you just told me?"

"I suppose you're right," Josie said, after a moment. "That was unjust. I just find it interesting, that's all. I've never known anyone to be illegitimate except for Auld Michael in the village. Do you remember him?"

"The old man who used to sit on the well and charge ha'pence to draw up the water? And if you refused, he'd spit tobacco juice down the well?"

Josie nodded. "I have only that charming example to go on."

"Well, expecting every man born out of wedlock to be like Auld Michael is like expecting every woman to be as slim as Lady Jersey herself." Imogen pulled on her dressing gown and headed for her bathroom.

Josie's voice stopped her. "Could it be that you've taken a true liking to Rafe's brother, Imogen?"

She stopped, hand on the door, and didn't turn around. "He's a very likeable person."

Josie said: "Oh, but—" and then stopped.

Imogen went into the bathroom and closed the door.

22

In Which a Seducer is Brought Up-to-Date on His Private Activities

Rafe had to suppose that there would be many a gentleman among his acquaintances who might feel awkward after almost seducing his ward. Alternatively, there were other gentlemen who might feel a certain amount of self-reproach at the idea that they had almost seduced a young widow. Even the most hardened reprobate would presumably feel awkward about encountering the said ward at the breakfast table.

Which only went to show that people should wear false mustaches far more often. True, he had barely restrained himself from dragging Imogen into his bedroom the previous night and stripping her down to the dregs of wine. But, mustache-free, he could eat an egg opposite her with total impunity. And likely Gabe could as well, since he enjoyed a blameless sleep in his own chamber.

"Your Grace," Trevick said. "May I ask you to stand still? I am having some trouble with your cuffs."

"Do you think I ought to have some new clothes?" Rafe asked, idly surveying himself in the mirror. His shirt was spotless, but even he had noticed lately that it seemed all his shirts were fraying.

Trevick's eyes lit up. "A wonderful decision, Your Grace. Wonderful!"

The poor man was almost babbling. "You could have just ordered a few shirts," Rafe said, turning to the side. Damned if his gut wasn't just fading away. At this rate, he'd be as thin as Gabe soon.

"You gave me a direct command not to do so," Trevick said reluctantly.

"I did?" Then, after a moment, "I must have been cup-shot."

Trevick's silence was confirmation enough.

"Get someone out here from London," Rafe said, tying his neckcloth. "One of those people Mayne uses. I can't look like a castaway when I'm bringing my wards into society."

His man said nothing, but Rafe knew his thoughts. "Not that I didn't look like that and worse, last year," he said resignedly.

"Only very occasionally," Trevick said reassuringly, pulling the shoulders of his coat straight. "Will you ride after breakfast, Your Grace?"

Rafe nodded. "Do you know what's amazing about

not drinking, Trevick?" He didn't wait for a reply: the curse of a manservant was that they had to listen to all their master's trivialities. "The day is long. Endless, in fact. I'll go riding, and then I'm meeting the bailiff, although I just met him four days ago. I used to go a month or two before I would find the time to see him."

Trevick said nothing but Rafe caught his eye in the mirror. "More than a month, eh? Ah well, months and months, then. The house hasn't fallen down about our ears."

But now he looked around, his room wasn't looking much better than his frayed shirt sleeves. "We could use a bit of plaster in here."

"Mr. Brinkley will be very glad to know if you have plans for restoration, Your Grace."

Rafe was silent as he tied his neckcloth with swift movements.

"I'll speak to Brinkley after eating," he said, leaving.

Sure enough, Imogen looked up at him with a cheerful smile. "Good morning!" she said. "Josie has returned to us; isn't that wonderful?"

"Young Josephine," Rafe said, going over to ruffle her hair. "You're looking blooming."

Without saying a word, Imogen's face told him to drop the subject, so he sat down and allowed the footman to pile his plate high.

On second thought, he wasn't quite sure he liked the whole cloak-and-dagger aspect of last night's adventures. If he and Imogen were engaged in a normal, if illicit, affair (not that he actually knew much about them), presumably he could catch her up against the wall on the way out of the room and steal one of those slow, hot kisses they'd shared last night.

But under the circumstances Imogen's eyes slid over him as easily as if he were her brother, whereas his kept getting stuck on her, like molasses. The morning dress she was wearing was practically akin to sackcloth. In fact, it looked like a dress that any lady might wear on a morning in the country, kind of a bluish color with little ribbons here and there. Rafe had never spent any time examining women's finery. But it didn't take sartorial sense to notice the way her skin glowed creamily against the gathered part of her bodice. And the bodice was low, low enough that a man could scoop a woman into a kiss and then when she wasn't noticing, slide _his_ hand down her neck and her shoulder—

"Have you really stopped drinking?" Josie asked.

Rafe blinked at her. "Yes, I have."

"You're quite oddly flushed," she pronounced. "Perhaps it's because you're up so early. I don't believe I ever saw you in the breakfast room before."

"I'm going riding," he said abruptly. "Would either of you like to accompany me?"

"I shall not," Josie said.

"I'm sure Rafe has a gentle pony you can ride," Imogen said.

"No."

Rafe turned to Imogen, eyebrow raised. "Posy needs exercise, I'm sure."

"All right." She barely glanced at him. "Directly after breakfast?"

Dammit, if he had met her at the orchard wall without that mustache—if she knew who had really kissed her the night before—she wouldn't look so apathetic about riding with him. But the worst was yet to come. Because a moment later, in strolled Gabe.

Frankly, Rafe was amazed that Imogen didn't fly out of her seat and embrace the man. Her whole face changed when she looked up at Gabe.

Didn't she have any understanding of how people conducted affairs? For God's sake, you don't look at a man as if you wanted to eat him alive, not at a house party. She asked, in a high, clear voice, if Gabe would go riding. Well, Rafe would be damned if Gabe was going riding with them. For one thing, he clearly needed to give his ward a lecture on how to conduct an illicit affair.

The only merciful thing was that Gabe seemed oblivious. Really it was a miracle that he managed to seduce that actress from London, given that his interest in women seemed so muted. He calmly replied no, he would be interviewing nannies directly after the meal, and after that he thought to help Miss Pythian-Adams in copying out actors' roles.

"I can stay and help you as well," Imogen said quickly.

But Miss Pythian-Adams, who had just seated herself next to her mother, wasn't nearly as oblivious as Gabe. She had taken one look at the wild rose flush in Imogen's cheeks and grown stiffer than an oak tree. Perhaps she had ethical qualms about people having affairs at country house parties; if that was the case, she should stick to London and Almack's.

"I shall not recommence copying parts until this afternoon," Miss Pythian-Adams said. "My mother plans to spend the morning with Lady Griselda, and I shall accompany them on a visit to one of your neighbors, Your Grace."

Well, at least someone remembered he was alive and well at the end of the table. He felt about as much a part of the conversation as when he sprawled drunk and silent in the same chair.

But suddenly he was part of the conversation. Because Miss Pythian-Adams was leaning toward him with a distinctly welcoming light in her eyes. "Perhaps you might join us copying out the parts, Your Grace?" she asked. "After all, you will be playing Dorimant. If you wished to copy out his part, for example, I'm sure it would be of help in memorization."

She was a lovely young woman. He glanced sideways at Imogen, who was talking with utter absorption to Gabe. Perhaps he should have stopped by Gabe's room the previous night and told him precisely what had happened.

But a gentleman didn't tell tales. Particularly when they involved a gentlewoman, a barrel of wine, and those long kisses of Imogen's.

"I'd be happy to join you, for as much time as I can manage," he said heartily, looking into Miss Pythian-Adams's eyes. They were lovely eyes too: calm and sweet and not at all like Imogen's exhausting passion.

Imogen was finally glancing at them.

"I might need some tutoring," Rafe told Miss Pythian-Adams. "This is my first thespian encounter. I haven't the faintest idea how to play a role."

It wasn't Imogen who was paying attention to his flummery, so much as Gabe. And he was scowling.

"I'd be happy to drill you," he said curtly.

"As would I," Miss Pythian-Adams said, dimpling. There seemed to be a slight constraint between herself and Gabe; at any rate, she didn't even look at him when he spoke.

"And I would be happy to interview nannies with you, Mr. Spenser," Imogen said to Gabe.

"There's no need for that," Gabe said, adding, "although I am, of course, grateful for your interest, Lady Maitland." He didn't just sound indifferent; he looked indifferent.

Despite himself, Rafe felt a pang, watching Imogen's face. She reached out rather blindly for her cup of tea and drank it. That bastard Gabe. Wasn't he in the least interested in what he was supposed to have done the previous night while wearing a mustache?

Which is just what Rafe asked his brother a few minutes later, by the subtle ploy of grabbing his arm and pulling him back into the now-empty breakfast room. "What the hell were you doing acting so coolly toward Imogen?" he hissed. "You're in a bloody affair now, you idiot. You can't act as if she is nothing more than a lady collecting for the parish. You hurt her feelings."

Gabe's mouth fell open. "You went to Silchester?"

"What do you mean? You told me to!"

"I never thought you'd go through with it. I gather you wore the mustache."

"Of course I went through with it." Rafe snarled.

"And now you have to play your part. She thinks you bloody well—" he didn't want to say.

"What did I do?" Gabe asked with some fascination.

Rafe just stopped himself from snapping that it was none of Gabe's business. "You kissed her," he said finally.

"Oh, did I?" Gabe raised his eyebrow. "Was that all I did?"

"Yes," Rafe snapped. "And now you've left Imogen feeling terrible."

"Was it *I?*"

"Of course it was you."

"Then I shall immediately make it clear to her. I'll make her feel much better."

"Good," Rafe muttered.

"Obviously, I should kiss her surreptitiously."

"What?" Rafe bellowed.

His little brother grinned. "How else am I to make her feel better about my apparent desertion? Beast that I am."

"Go to hell!" Rafe said, pushing past him in the corridor.

Which left Gabe in the corridor, grinning madly at the angry sound of boots on the marble stairs.

23

The Lucky Piece

Imogen did not really wish to go riding. But Gabriel had shown no particular desire to see her, more the opposite. It was so shocking that she couldn't quite fathom it.

"I misjudged you," Josie said to her, on the way back upstairs. "I thought you were taking Mr. Spenser as a cicisbeo. But I can see that isn't the case. I think I've read too many novels. Perhaps I should turn to something improving. More of Plutarch's essays."

"A common mistake," Imogen said airily. "You know all those ballads about wanton widows."

"I suppose," Josie said dubiously. "If you don't mind my saying so, Imogen, you didn't seem to be greeted with the same enthusiasm as the widows in those songs."

Imogen thought of several unpleasant replies and choked them back.

Josie patted her arm. "I have known you for years and years, Imogen. I'm sure no one else could tell how taken you are by Mr. Spenser."

"Although he's not taken with me, is that what you're saying?" Imogen's throat felt a little choked.

Josie suddenly realized that she had strayed onto dangerous territory. "Well," she said cautiously, closing the door to Imogen's bedchamber behind them, "he might be the sort of gentleman who doesn't wear his heart on his sleeve."

Because he has no heart, Imogen thought to herself. He'd been friendly with Cristobel, and with herself, and with Lord knows how many other women. Divinity professor indeed!

And yet she felt a terrible yearning to slip out to the orchard gate that very evening.

He wouldn't be there. He hadn't shown by a flicker of an eyelash that they had shared kisses. Or laughter. That was even more perplexing, in a way. Of course, Draven and she had kissed during their brief marriage, but they'd never laughed as hard as she and Gabriel had laughed on the way home, when she was drenched in wine, and he almost as wet. He laughed so hard that at one point his mustache started to fall off.

On the other hand, perhaps Gabe's behavior was precisely like Draven's. Her husband had been intimate with her under certain conditions: in the dark. But the rest of the time she hardly existed.

"I'm going riding with Rafe," she said, ringing the

bell for Daisy. "Are you certain that you wouldn't like to come, Josie?"

"Absolutely not. I've discovered two more Minerva Press novels that were published since we left for Scotland last summer. I need to read them and compile the results in my guide to marriage. Where will you ride?"

"I mean to ask Rafe to accompany me to Maitland House," Imogen said.

Daisy entered the room and pulled out a riding costume.

"No, not that one," Imogen said.

"Why not?" Josie asked. "It's lovely. I adore the imperial braid effect down the front."

"That's my favorite riding costume. I don't want to waste it on Rafe, and besides we're going to open Draven's house. It may well be dusty."

"You needn't speak of Rafe quite so slightingly," Josie said, climbing into Imogen's bed as if she belonged there. "*I* think he's much more handsome than Mr. Spenser."

"I don't agree at all," Imogen said curtly.

"Yes, he is. Mr. Spenser is very nice-looking, but there's something about Rafe's eyes that makes one— oh—all shivery."

"Don't even think about marrying him, Josie. He's far too old for you."

"He'll be married by the time I have my season," Josie said, opening one of her books. "Oh, lovely! It's by Teresa Middlethorpe. She writes the most thrilling books. You can't imagine."

"I know her work. I read *The Rake's Last Lament*. But what do you mean by saying that Rafe will marry?"

"Miss Pythian-Adams," Josie said absently. "She's going to give him private tutoring of his part. She deserves someone as nice as Rafe, after what you did to her."

Imogen raised her chin and looked in the mirror as Daisy quickly buttoned a myriad of small buttons down her back.

Of course Gillian Pythian-Adams deserved a man like Rafe. He was sober now. And Gillian herself said that she meant to marry Rafe, didn't she?

She was a bit of a bluestocking. Wouldn't Rafe grow bored of talking about plays? She didn't even ride long distances, and when they went to the Roman ruins the year before, if Imogen remembered correctly, Gillian had caused a carriage to follow along, and she rode in it.

Even when Rafe was as drunk as the proverbial lord, he rode every day.

Perhaps she should speak to him. Lord knows, she was the survivor of a marriage in which the participants had few interests in common and little to talk about.

Daisy was shaping her hair into a long, elegant curl, but Imogen shook her head. "There's no need. It's just Rafe," she repeated.

Of course, Daisy didn't approve, any more than Josie had. To Daisy, Rafe was the duke, and everyone should be campaigning to marry him.

Well, she wasn't.

Imogen grabbed her riding crop and headed out the door, followed by a mumbled farewell from Josie.

Rafe was waiting at the bottom of the stairs, tapping his crop against his boots. He looked up as she came down and smiled that rueful smile of his. Imogen felt a rush of pleasure. He might not have the deliciousness of his brother, but Rafe was quite wonderful, in his own way. Especially now he wasn't drinking.

So she tucked her arm into his and smiled up at him.

"When you look at me like that," Rafe said, grinning back, "I know you want something. What is it?"

"Will you come with me over there?" She waved her hand.

"Over there?"

"Over . . . to Draven's house. Maitland House."

Rafe stopped and looked down at her, those beautiful shadowed eyes of his looking straight into her soul. "Are you sure you wish to?"

"Quite sure," she said, her voice coming out absolutely steady. The previous night had given her courage. Cheered her from the dreary grief of the past year. "I know that Lady Clarice would want her jewelry sent to various relatives," she said. "She only left the briefest of wills, you know, because she was so weak toward the end. She asked me to give things to the women of her family, and I have been sadly remiss in waiting a year."

Rafe touched her cheek for a moment. "She was lucky to have you as a daughter-in-law."

Imogen's smile wavered. "She wanted Miss Pythian-Adams to marry Draven because she would have kept Draven from the racetrack. I didn't succeed at that."

"It's not that you couldn't have, Imogen. You never chose to, did you?"

Her eyes searched his dark gray ones. "I should have."

"He was a man, and he lived as he wished to live. If I

hadn't wished to quit drinking, Imogen, you couldn't have nagged me to it. Though you might have driven me mad in the trying."

She smiled a little at that, and they kept walking.

Posy and Rafe's horse were tied up in the yard, nuzzling each other.

"They're the best of friends," Rafe told her. "I'm too heavy for Posy, but I had her taken out every day while you were in Scotland. And meanwhile, she and Hades had stalls next to each other."

"Come here, you beauty," Imogen said. Posy nickered and strained toward her and then she was cupping her dear, heavy nose in her hands and laughing as Posy blew whiskery, grass-smelling breath in her face.

"Up you go," Rafe said.

His hands came around her waist from behind and he threw her up on the horse. It was odd how similar he was to his brother. Imogen felt as if she knew those large hands from the night before, when Gabriel pulled her from the wine barrel as easily as if she weighed no more than a feather.

"What are you smiling at?" Rafe asked, as they began walking down the road leading to the west.

"A random thought," Imogen said. "So do you think that I should sell the manor? It does no good sitting there, after all."

"Would you ever wish to live there?"

"No."

"Are you absolutely sure?"

"Without question," Imogen said. "Look at that field, Rafe. Isn't it beautiful?"

"Dandelions," Rafe said. "Lots of thistle. I should have had it mown." It was pleasant to know that he would never neglect decisions of that nature again.

"Look at all those daisies. They're cornflower blue. We haven't any daisies like that in Scotland."

"They aren't daisies. That's chicory; some people eat it."

"We must stop and look more closely on the way home. I want to bring a bouquet to Josie."

"In that case, we'd better make haste. Chicory is an intelligent plant. It closes at midday, and doesn't open at all if it's raining."

"How on earth do you know these things?" Imogen asked, looking sideways at him.

"I love the country," he said simply. "There have been many years when I never bothered to go to London for the season."

"Who taught you that chicory closes at midday?"

"An old man named Henry lives in the hut down next to the willows," he said, pointing. "We've spent many an afternoon together."

"An unusual acquaintance for a duke," Imogen observed.

"Not for a pickled duke, as you used to say of me."

"You drank together?"

Just the faintest shade of reserve in her voice made him tumble into a defense of Henry. "Not that. But I'd be too restless to stay indoors . . . thinking of the drink, you see." He grimaced at her ruefully. "I'm afraid that one does tend to think of it most of the day."

"And now?" she asked curiously.

"I still do. But it feels completely different: as if it were losing its grip on me. I shan't go back to that."

Imogen stared at Rafe. He had the same dusting of black stubble that he always had by noon, but the skin of his cheeks was pink and healthy, and his eyes didn't have that half-awake, hooded look that he used to have. He shook back a fall of chestnut brown hair, smiling up at the blue sky.

No wonder Gillian wanted him. He was a beautiful man, even with those little lines around his eyes.

He looked over his shoulder and smiled at her lazily.

Imogen's heart was beating quickly, though why she couldn't explain.

"Would you like to race?" he asked. "I'll give you a lead."

As much to get away from her thoughts—almost sinful it felt, to think of *Rafe* that way—she didn't even answer, just pressed her knees against Posy's sides. She leaped forward with such a great spring that Imogen's clever little hat flew away before Posy's front hooves even touched the ground.

She bent low and shouted encouragement, feeling the wind whip her hair into a frenzy. They were going so fast that Rafe couldn't catch up, but he was, he was . . . Imogen gripped her knees harder and urged Posy on, and then Posy showed that great heart for racing that she always had. She switched into that other pace she had, the one where she almost floated above the ground; or that's how it felt.

Then Imogen knew that Rafe had no chance of winning. "Oh you beauty, you beauty," she crooned to Posy, and signaled her to the right, into the great driveway leading to Maitland House. Posy pulled a beautiful turn, gravel spraying out from her heels but never losing her stride. And then Imogen saw the great curved gates of the house appearing and she began easing up.

She'd won; she'd won fair and square.

If Rafe was only a whisker behind her, it was still the kind of whisker that costs a man a golden cup given out by a royal duke.

A second later Rafe raced past with a laugh, and they ended up tumbling through the open gates of Maitland House, Imogen with no bonnet, and Rafe whooping like one of those wild men of deepest Africa in the London circus.

Imogen leaned over Posy's neck, gasping. Rafe had already leaped off his horse. To her considerable annoyance, he wasn't even out of breath. In fact, she couldn't help noticing the way his old shirt pulled free of his trousers as he leaped. What happened to that gut that used to hang over his trousers? Could it have disappeared in a mere few weeks? Because now that body looked as lean and hard as his brother's . . . even more so, perhaps. After all, Rafe always rode, every morning. Whereas scholars, one would have to think, sat at a table. . . .

But Imogen pushed that thought away as disloyal. After all, Gabe was her . . . her something. She led Posy over to the mounting block, but Rafe was already at her side, arms outstretched.

She had a moment's qualm. He was framed in the sunlight, grinning up at her, all tumbled hair, the old linen shirt and a coat that was as old as the shirt. And then a second later she was on the ground and he was turning away, greeting the Maitland butler with a cheerful "How do you do," and a flurry of chatter.

Imogen knew exactly what Rafe was doing. He was giving her time to get her bearings.

After all, this was the courtyard to which Draven brought her as a new bride. This was the house where they lived as man and wife. It was from this house that her husband's body was carried forth to burial, a mere two weeks after they married.

The courtyard was lined with old stones, warm in the fall sunshine. Thistledown was blowing over one wall, filling the air as if gentle snow were falling, the kind that spins and dances in the air before landing in a hand and keeping its perfect shape for a second.

The butler, Hilton, positively tumbled down the stairs to greet her. "Lady Maitland!" he said, bowing.

She smiled at him. "It's a pleasure to see you again, Hilton."

"If we had known you were coming," he was saying, "we would be more prepared, we would have a tea for you and his lordship."

"I have no wish for tea," Imogen said, "but I would be dearly grateful for a drink of water, if I could trouble you so far."

His face brightened and he trotted back to the open door. Imogen followed him slowly. There were no ghosts in the bright courtyard, but in the house, perhaps?

Yet she walked in without hearing an echo from the querulous voice of her mother-in-law, Lady Clarice. Nor yet the rather bullish, boyish voice of Draven. The house felt like a place dreaming in the afternoon sun along with its courtyard . . . at peace, waiting.

She looked up at Rafe. "I do believe . . ." But she couldn't put it in words.

He took her hand, as if she were a child of five, and led her into the sitting room. It was a gay room, papered with cheerful sprays of flowers.

"Lady Clarice loved this room," she said softly, touching the little china cat on the mantelpiece. There was no dust.

Rafe stood in the middle of the rug, looking like a man of the outdoors rather than a duke. More like old Henry who lived in the field. "It's a good old house," he said, looking around. "Strong bones, as one says."

"Is it as old as your house?"

"No. My house goes back to the days of Henry VII, and if I remember rightly, this little manor was constructed in anticipation of one of Queen Elizabeth's progresses. She stayed at Holbrook Court, but her people spilled over here."

Lady Clarice's sewing basket sat next to her favorite chair, a scrap of white linen poking from the top. Imogen bent down and touched it, and for the first time since she entered the house, she felt a pang of true sadness.

"There's always work left unfinished," Rafe said, appearing at her shoulder. For a moment she felt him there, large, solid, and comforting. "Shall we go upstairs?"

So they headed upstairs, past the crimson flocked wallpaper to Lady Clarice's chamber. It was neat as a pin, clean, swept of dust. No ghosts here.

But her own chamber . . . did she really want to enter?

With Rafe, there was no allowance for cowardice. "Better to get it over with," he said over his shoulder, and before she knew it, there she was, looking at the great postered bed where she and Draven had spent all of ten days of married life before he died.

The room looked as if it had never had an occupant, as if it were waiting for those happy gentlefolk of Queen Elizabeth's to come traipsing down the road.

Rafe leaned against the closed door to the hallway. "I found Peter's bedchamber the hardest to manage," he said, not looking at her. "I was such a dunce about it."

"Tell me," she said, moving over to smooth the coverpane. "Please."

"I wouldn't let them change the sheets. I slept on a cot in his room, as if he would return any moment. Ridiculous. I wasn't a child, you know. Peter died when I was thirty-two."

She could feel the tears now. Her vision blurred a little, but she swallowed hard. "I did that too," she admitted. "And I slept with Draven's nightshirt for oh . . . ages."

"Then one day, I realized that Peter had gone," Rafe continued. "Somewhere . . . who knows where? But he was gone. Truly gone. And I tore the sheets off myself and walked out of his bedchamber. But I had the room repapered before I entered it again."

"Which chamber was it?" She wandered across the room and opened the wardrobe.

"The west chamber."

"So you put in that deep cherry stripe."

"Yes."

"I'm impressed," she said, smiling at him faintly over her shoulder. He walked toward her. "Maitland's clothing?" he said.

"Yes."

"Hilton will give them away."

But she was reaching out, soothing an embroidered vest that she remembered Draven wearing the very first night she met him on English soil. And so Rafe, without saying a word, helped her bring Draven's clothing to the bed, where they left it for Hilton to distribute to the poor. And if a salt tear or two stained some of the brilliant embroidery, Imogen trusted that no one would care or notice.

She took only one thing from the room, a tiny figure of a leaping horse chased in silver, small enough to fit in a pocket.

"Rather lovely," Rafe said, bending over her hand so that his hair brushed against her forearm, soft as silk.

"It was Draven's lucky piece."

"Was he wearing it when he died?"

"He always wore it," she said sadly. "I cursed it afterward, for having not lived up to what he expected."

"Well," Rafe said, "he was doubtless wearing it the day he met you, Imogen. Perhaps that was all the magic this poor little horse had to give."

She smiled at him, and then she couldn't stop smiling, and her fingers closed over the little horse and slipped it into the pocket of her riding costume.

A second later, Rafe took her hand again—vastly improper, that was—and they walked through Lady

Clarice's room and made fast work of dividing her jewelry into piles and instructing Mrs. Hilton to have them sent to her relatives.

They started home slowly. At one point Rafe leaped off his horse and snatched her tiny hat from a long rose thorn where it was hanging. And then he caught up a bunch of hogsweed for Josie because the chicory had indeed closed itself up.

Imogen got off Posy to take a closer look, because in Scotland what Rafe was calling hogsweed was termed yellow cow parsley, a prettier and certainly more descriptive name. And then they waded farther into the field, brushing past dandelion clocks and yellow willow spears blown from the willows between Rafe's land and Maitland land. The sun was warm and the afternoon sleepy, with not a sound in the field but the "tink tink tink" of blackbirds calling to each other in the trees.

Imogen turned around to find that Rafe had thrown himself onto the ground, and was lying in a great heap of rough yellow flowers, arms and legs all akilter, as if he were no duke, and had never heard the word "gentleman." He was chewing a long blade of grass, like a country laborer taking a rest after a day spent hoeing.

He smiled up at her, squinting against the sun, and reached out a hand. Before she knew what happened Imogen was lying next to him, feeling the heat of sun-warmed earth at her shoulder blades, and a tingling feeling in her hand.

She stared up at the sky, trying not to think about the long fingers curling around hers. Baby clouds were floating high up, looking as pale and ephemeral as the thistle-down blowing into the Maitland courtyard. Before she knew what was happening, the tears that she'd ordered away in Draven's bedchamber came sliding from her eyes. She closed them against the sun, at the same moment Rafe pulled her against his shoulder.

There weren't so many tears. Only a few, shed for that final good-bye to Draven, good-bye to the gaudy embroidered waistcoats he loved, good-bye to his loving, testy mama, good-bye to all the adoration she'd devoted to their marriage and to him, starting years before he even noticed she existed.

Rafe didn't say a word, just let her huddle into the warmth of his shoulder.

When she sat up, he handed her a large white handkerchief, rather threadworn, like everything Rafe owned. It made her smile.

"Draven would never have contemplated carrying something this old," she told him.

"I don't see any holes in it," Rafe said, lazy amusement in his voice.

"When we eloped, he brought four waistcoats with him. But because he wasn't bringing his valet, naturally—"

"So one doesn't bring a valet along on an elopement? That's a good rule to know."

She tapped him on the chin with a yellow daisy. "You have no need for such rules. But in fact, if you ever elope, do not bring your valet."

"Trevick would expire from shock if I invited him to accompany me anywhere," Rafe said, with the enjoyment of a man who hadn't paid much attention to his valet in years.

His eyes were half-lidded now, as they used to be when he was drinking. Her stomach felt hot and muddled, so Imogen said, lightly, "Draven brought four waistcoats, but he forgot to bring enough shirts to change in the evening. He became very annoyed after a few days."

"I am making notes. When contemplating an elopement, bring sufficient shirts. How many? Three a day?"

"One for riding, a second for dinner." She bobbled the daisy against his chin again. "A third for evening."

"Do you suppose that you'll ever stop mourning Draven?" he asked, not looking at her.

"Yes," she said, feeling a bit of heartbreak at the sound of her own voice. "Because, you see, I cry now for what our marriage *wasn't* as much as what it was."

"And what wasn't it?"

"It was my marriage," Imogen said, dropping the daisy and wrapping her arms around her knees. "It was all mine."

There was silence.

"Do you understand what I mean?" she asked.

"I frequently don't understand when women complain about their marriages," Rafe said. "I never understood my mother, for instance, although I admit that Gabe's existence gives me a great deal more sympathy for her."

"Draven and I only married because *I* loved him," Imogen said. "It's humiliating."

"Life has a way of routinely humiliating us," Rafe

said. "A passion for whiskey gave me many opportunities to experience it."

Imogen smiled a little at that. "When I think back, I can't remember anything between myself and Draven except my feelings for him. He didn't truly wish to marry me. We didn't talk about anything serious, and"—she swallowed—"I don't think our intimacies were enjoyable for either of us."

He reached out and took her hand without saying anything, and they just sat for a while. A blue-winged dragonfly skated over the flowers. Rafe's jaw was strong and as chiseled as his cheekbones. A shadow of beard gave him a rakish look . . . as if he were drinking.

But he wasn't. Those very things that had pointed directly to his moral rot, back when she used to watch him empty his glass over and over, now made her feel utterly different.

"Your brother is always clean-shaven," she said suddenly.

"If he shares my beard, he must retreat to his room to shave during the day."

"And you don't?"

"Sometimes before the evening meal. It's tiresome, allowing someone to drag a sharp steel across your face."

"Does a beard start growing immediately?" Imogen said.

"It's the family curse," Rafe said, closing his eyes. "We're a hairy, fertile lot."

The sun was hot on the back of her neck now. She picked a stalk of chicory, its petals tightly closed against the sun, and tapped it against his lower lip. His lip had an immoral curve to it. She twirled the chicory thoughtfully.

Then he turned his head slightly and opened his eyes again. It was immensely improper for her to brush the flower against his mouth. What on earth had she been thinking? He was grinning. Everything in that wicked grin was in his eyes as well: desire, mockery, and something she hardly dared guess about.

"Why is that flower unlike a woman?" he asked.

"I have no idea."

"Because chicory opens in the morning and shuts most close at night. As I'm sure you know, wenches do the contrary."

She dropped the flower as if it burned her hand, but his laughter made her giggle too. She couldn't look away, and then he reached out, slowly, giving her time to leap to her feet and declare in a flustered kind of way that it was time they returned to the house. Because Josie was there. Or any other excuse.

Except she didn't jump to her feet, but sat there staring into his eyes. It was just Rafe, her guardian, her drunken old guardian, her—

He pulled her closer, the amusement in his eyes warring with something else, something she'd never seen on Rafe's face before.

"What—" she asked breathlessly.

"This," he said. And he pulled her so that she toppled over on top of him. She fell flat onto his hips, and he brushed his mouth against hers.

Imogen caught herself opening her mouth. Of course, Rafe wouldn't think that she was a candidate for those hot, hungry kisses of his brother—Gabe!—what was she doing—

He brushed his mouth against hers again, and her mind blurred.

"I think I've forgotten how to kiss," he said, sounding thoughtful.

She gaped at him.

"You've had much more experience than I've had in the last ten years."

"Do you mean that you haven't kissed a woman in ten years?" Imogen could feel her eyes getting rounder.

"No, I don't mean that."

"Oh."

"I haven't kissed any ladies in ten years."

Imogen's eyes narrowed. Perhaps Cristobel had sung in Silchester before.

"Now you," Rafe continued lazily, "you have kissed any number of people. So perhaps you could put me back into the spirit of it, so to speak."

She just stared at him.

Rafe sighed. "Luckily, I begin to remember." Large hands cupped her head and pulled her face down to his.

It wasn't like kissing Gabe. That was an assault: a hot, hungry pursuit of her mouth. This was a Rafe-like kiss: brushing her lips so lightly that she shouldn't have even noticed. Certainly she shouldn't have felt all her senses spring to life, so that suddenly every inch of her skin was aware of the hard body under hers, of its ridges and curves, of the power of the hands cradling her face.

Gabe and Rafe even tasted different. Rafe tasted clean, like sun-warmed grass. Gabe tasted like mortal sin—not like the shadow he insisted he was, but like the wicked thoughts a woman only had in the dark of night, in the security of her own bed.

I would know instantly, Imogen thought, who is kissing me. Rafe kisses like a gentleman and Gabe like a devil. Oddly enough, both kinds of kisses made her ache, a muddled, treacherous heat low in her stomach.

Rafe's kisses were slower, less feverish, pulling away to nibble on her lip and then slide his way back into her mouth. He acted as if he had the world enough and time ... whereas Gabe's kisses had a kind of urgent hunger behind them.

"Rafe," she said, and her voice came out like a little gasp.

"Hmmm," he said, and then he was rolling her over, his big hands still cupping her face, and he bent back to her mouth.

"Rafe!" she said, stronger now. But he was kissing her again, and he must have remembered how to kiss. Because this kiss made all her thoughts flee, and she just slipped into the moment: the hard body lying next to hers, the fingers tangled in her hair, the smell and the taste of him.

Of course, it was scandalous to be kissing in a field. Scandalous. And even worse, a little voice inside Imogen insisted that what she really wanted was the feeling of that hard body on top of hers.

She didn't open her eyes immediately after his mouth left hers. "Imogen," he said. His voice sounded odd.

"Yes?" She kept her eyes closed. There was something extraordinarily embarrassing about kissing Rafe. She couldn't quite work it out. He was just Rafe—her guardian, the thorn in her side, the man who shook her on the dance floor, the man she called a pickled drunk . . .

"I'm not sure how to put this."

"What?"

"Oh, marriage. Kissing and marriage." His voice was deep, and casual for such an important topic.

"There's no need to put it any way at all," Imogen said, sitting up. "Where have I put my hat?"

"I left it with the horses. I'm asking you to marry me, rather awkwardly, but . . ."

She was aware of him watching her brush the grass from her skirts, and then he helped her to her feet. "Rafe," she said, "why are you doing this?"

"Because we kissed in a field."

She couldn't fault that logic. "It's just you and me," she said patiently. "I expect it must be quite interesting for you to kiss a lady after ten years." She met his eyes for the first time. "But you would never wish to be married to someone with my temper. Imagine if I were about the house all the time."

"I can imagine it quite easily. We both know that you primarily lost your temper over my drinking."

She started walking toward the horses, talking over her shoulder. "Go find another woman to kiss, Rafe. If it's practice you're wanting."

"You are suggesting," Rafe said, sounding as if he were entirely enjoying himself, "that after being deprived of the pleasures of the flesh for years, I am foolishly enslaved by base desires."

She stopped and looked at him. "Did you understand anything I told you about my marriage?"

"Of course," he said. "You and Draven had a marriage that was precisely like that of every other member of the *ton:* empty of conversation and passion."

It was surprisingly hard to hear it drawn up in such a neat package. "When I marry again," Imogen said, "I want to be the one pursued, Rafe. Pursued *madly.* I don't want to marry someone just because he kissed me, and that kiss was only because I happened to be there. That's how it was with Draven, you know. He kissed me, and then he said 'If we elope, it'll turn my mother into a raving bedlamite.' That was his proposal." She admitted it fiercely.

Rafe's eyes were sympathetic, but he said nothing.

"The proposal that I accept, *if* I ever accept one, will be planned. It will be formal. It will not follow an inappropriate kiss in a field or elsewhere, and there will be *no* mention of mothers!"

Rafe was grinning now.

"We should not be having this conversation," Imogen said, realizing that she had turned pink with the fury of it. "I'm not going to marry you," she added lamely.

"I understand completely."

"I'm certain you will find someone to marry."

"But I suspect that you're right, and I would make a terrible husband," Rafe said. "The truth is that I believe my ambitions lie in quite another direction."

Imogen looked at him before realizing that his eyes were dancing with laughter. "What would that be?" she asked cautiously.

"Something more carnal than spiritual."

"I cannot believe we are having this conversation," Imogen said crossly, beginning to hurry toward the road. "I can only suppose that you should marry with dispatch."

"Better to marry than to burn," Rafe said thoughtfully. "Or so Paul says. If you are averse to saving my soul, I shall find someone else."

"I am barely widowed," Imogen said, finally realizing that behind all this teasing was a rather obstinate view that a kiss was tantamount to an acceptance of marriage. "I do not wish to marry again so quickly, Rafe."

The sun was almost directly overhead now. Rafe's hair turned a golden brandy brown, falling over his eyes, his collar.

"You should have your hair cut!" she scolded, brushing it from his forehead.

He caught her wrist. "Do you refuse me because you are engaged in an illicit *affaire* with my brother?"

The words cut her to the heart. He knew . . . and he kissed her anyway. He must think her the veriest tart, the plaything of two brothers.

She swallowed hard. "I am not engaged in an *affaire* with your brother!" Her voice came out low and hard, harder than she would have liked. "I—I am not."

"I thought by the way you looked at him at the breakfast table that something had happened between the two of you."

"You insult me!" Imogen could feel the red flags in her cheeks. She tried desperately to think of a phrase that any honorable, affronted lady would utter. "You have no right to speak like that." To her ears the words sounded feeble.

"I didn't mean to insult you."

"Then how could you suggest such a thing?"

"That you would have an *affaire* with Gabe?"

"Of course!" she said shrilly.

"Because I imagine that if I were a young widow with no particular propensity to marry, I would find Gabriel a quite delightful prospect for a small dalliance."

"I would never do such a thing."

But he continued as if she hadn't spoken. "If you *were* to contemplate such an *affaire*, you might want to modulate the way you look at the gentleman in question, Imogen."

She just gaped at him.

"This morning, for instance, your emotions were written on your face."

Tears were pricking her eyes, from rage, she told herself. "I did not look at your brother in an inappropriate manner."

"I apologize," he said slowly. "I expect that I am merely piqued because you do not wish to marry me." He turned away and began untying her horse's reins from the fence.

"Will you insult the next woman who refuses to marry you?" Imogen asked tightly, hearing the little shake in her voice.

He didn't look back at her. "I think I had better make more certain of my companion's feelings, don't you?"

"Yes! Because I wouldn't think of marrying you." She snapped it, and then she was sorry because his hands stopped on the horse's tackle for a moment, and she actually entertained the thought that he cared—that he truly wished to marry her.

But he turned around, and there was the familiar laughter in his eyes. "Forgive me?" he asked. "You know I'm damnably protective of your reputation, Imogen. I seem to have taken to this guardianship business with a mite too much enthusiasm."

"Guardians are not required to propose marriage to their wards in order to save their reputations," she said severely. But she was starting to understand now. He'd caught her looking at Gabe in the morning—and just as surely as had Josie, he knew that she wanted his brother. And he'd also seen that his brother was uninterested in her. It was humiliating.

But Rafe was still talking easily. "I've made up my mind that the next time I ask someone to marry me, I shall know the answer beforehand."

"I'm sure you'll find many women who will make it all too clear that they would like to be your duchess," Imogen said, a touch acidly.

"Do you think that Gillian would care for the position?" came his voice from behind her.

"Who?"

"Miss Pythian-Adams."

"Do you wish to marry her?"

"I hadn't thought about it."

"You're not going off like a piece of meat," she remarked. "You could afford to wait for a bit before finding a wife."

And then before she realized what was happening,

strong arms came around her from the back and pulled her against his body. She stood, stock-still, trying not to melt into him and turn her mouth up to his.

"I like kissing you," he said. "It's a strange thought, admittedly, but true. I like the way you taste."

And then she did turn her head, just to see what the look was in his eyes, and this kiss was almost like one of Gabe's.

Then it was over, and he pulled a strand of grass from her hair. "Please note," he said, "that no proposal of marriage will follow this inappropriate kiss."

Imogen tried to think of something clever to say—something witty about being glad to offer him an experience such as he hadn't had in ten years—but nothing came to mind.

They walked over to her horse without another word. After he'd thrown her up onto her horse, there was just one thought that she couldn't brush away.

Both Gabe and Rafe made her weak at the knees with their kisses. It must be a family trait. Or if it wasn't their innate ability, it must be that she was particularly vulnerable to those kisses. More the fool she! Why, it was positively incestuous to be kissing the two brothers at once.

Why was she kissing Rafe? Why on earth would her guardian have kissed her at all?

He answered that. Rafe looked over and said: "Are you feeling better about your husband, then, Imogen?"

"Don't laugh about that!" she said, without thinking about it.

"I wasn't." He said it quietly, without a trace of that insouciant grin he had earlier.

She could tell he wasn't. And of course that explained the kiss. Of course it did. He was wiping away the tears, and the memory of Draven. Very kind of him.

There was only one problem with his plan.

She could remember Draven as clearly as ever. She remembered every kiss they shared in their brief two weeks of marriage (six), every act of love they shared in the same two weeks (seven), and every time he rolled her over in a bed of flowers and kissed her to make her stop crying (none).

Just at the end of the road, Rafe looked at her and then leaned over his horse, and they raced down the curve of the road leading to Holbrook Court. Alas, the bouquet of cow parsley—or hogweed—intended for Josie couldn't take the gale, and tumbled away on the wind, rough yellow petals streaming behind them.

24

The Virtues—or Lack Thereof—
of Creatures Such as Dorimant

Gillian Pythian-Adams was in a foul mood. She scowled at her own reflection, even though her mother had strong views about wrinkles being the inevitable result of bad temper. Then she stopped scowling and readjusted her elegant cottage bonnet.

It was pale sage green and made her hair look as red as a deep port. "Lovely hair," she said aloud, a little savage mockery in her voice. She might as well compliment herself, because at this rate no husband would say it to her.

Her walking costume was a slightly darker shade of the same green, and buttoned up the front with Spanish buttons that made her appear more generous in the bosom than she was in truth.

"Lovely . . ." But her voice died out.

It wasn't that she was in a frenzy to marry. She could see perfectly well that a woman's life was a great deal more comfortable once she married. But since her grandmother had been kind enough to leave her a dowry that converted to a personal estate if she was unmarried at age thirty, the case was not desperate.

It just seemed that the moment she turned her eyes on someone, an Essex sister was there before her. Not just any Essex sister either: Imogen.

She hadn't really wanted Draven Maitland, mind you. She could admit that the engagement was a huge mistake. She had learned her lesson: do not engage oneself to a fool because his mother holds the mortgage to the family's estate.

Although one had to admit that it was nice when she received the mortgage back after Draven fled with Imogen.

Of course she wanted nothing to do with the depraved brother of the duke, for all she had enjoyed his kiss. It served as a powerful example of why men were able to turn women's heads and make them do foolish things, like running away with a footman. She'd always wondered about that, but after kissing Mr. Spenser, she didn't wonder anymore.

Not that she had the option of running away with Mr. Spenser, because Imogen had scooped him up directly. If Gillian actually turned her eyes to a footman, obviously Imogen would beckon him with a crook of her little finger.

But she *had* thought that the duke was eligible for matrimony, now that he was sober. She and Imogen had even discussed that fact: a sort of dividing of territories conversation, now she thought about it. So why were the duke's eyes following Imogen around the room?

Because Imogen was a magnet for men who interested Gillian, that's why.

Gillian was clearly a failed magnet for those same men. She scowled again. Who cared about wrinkles when there was no one left to admire her?

Lady Ancilla poked her head into the room. "Are you ready to go, darling?"

"Of course, Mama," Gillian said. But she stayed another moment, staring at the mirror. She wasn't an antidote. True, some people didn't care for red hair. But in secret, she herself liked red hair. Hers was a nice strawberry color, and it curled just where she wanted it to. And she had everything else that seemed to add up to the package men wanted to marry: green eyes, dimples, and a large enough bosom. Even a dowry.

It wasn't that men didn't want to marry her. It was that they didn't want to marry her once they met Imogen Essex.

"Gillian!" her mother called from the corridor.

"Coming!" Gillian snatched up her gloves and ran into the corridor.

A moment later the two of them joined Lady Griselda in one of the duke's carriages. Gillian's mother was quite interested to hear that the housemaids had finished the theater curtain.

"I read *The Man of Mode* last night," Lady Griselda said, bracing herself against the side of the carriage as they turned onto another road.

"What did you think?" Gillian asked.

"An inspired choice, my dear. My only question would regard casting. For you have cast Rafe as Dorimant, have you not?"

"Yes."

"And his brother, Mr. Spenser, as Medley?"

"Dorimant is a rakelike creature, is he not?" Gillian's mother asked. "I'm ashamed to say that I keep trying to read the play and falling asleep. I thought Dorimant a very foolish fellow. Are you quite certain that the play is fit for representation, Griselda? It would seem to me to cast a dubious light on our host, if he plays a man who is dallying with three women, if I understood the plot correctly."

"Mama—" Gillian began.

But Lady Griselda interrupted her with a charming little wave of her hand. "Ancilla, dearest, your delicacy is much to be credited. These days what provokes innocent enjoyment in the theater is, on closer observation, rather warm indeed. But the truth of the matter is that you and I are creatures of another era." She gently waved an exquisitely embroidered handkerchief before her unlined face. "We must make way for the exuberancy of a new generation. What we might consider vulgar, *they* consider delightful."

Ancilla looked at her for a moment and then burst out laughing. "What a complete hand you are, Griselda! I've known you these twenty years—and may I remind you, my dear, that when I met you I was already married, and you no more than ten years old? But even at that age, you had all the hallmarks of a young lady who would get precisely what she wished. I take it that you like the play."

"I think it's funny," Griselda said, dropping the handkerchief and smiling at Ancilla. "I think it will be enjoyable to see Rafe playing Dorimant—as far as I know the duke hasn't had a rakish thought in years."

Gillian thought the look on Rafe's face when he looked at Imogen spoke volumes, but she kept quiet.

"Now if you needed another male, and you wished me to summon my brother . . ." Griselda said, looking at Gillian.

"Lord Mayne?" Ancilla said. "I'll thank you, no, Griselda. The last thing I need, with Gillian's current situation, is your brother on the premises." She turned to Gillian. "Mayne is certainly handsome, my dear, but I'm sure Griselda won't mind if I point out that he is famously set against marriage."

"All true," Griselda said. "But I have hopes for him. He's getting long in the tooth. Perhaps *you* might change his mind as regards the state of matrimony, Miss Pythian-Adams!"

"And perhaps he might dent her reputation," Ancilla said. "As he has done with so many other women."

"Never with those who are unmarried," Griselda said. "But admittedly, he has inspired his share of unrequited sighs. I have high hopes that this will be the season in which he takes a bride. He said as much to me, when we returned from Scotland."

"That will be interesting to watch," Ancilla said, making it absolutely clear that Mayne would throw out his lures toward Gillian over her dead body.

Gillian decided to intervene. "I have met Lord Mayne, Mama, and he showed no interest whatsoever in sullying my virtue. Lady Griselda, may I ask you to reconsider your refusal to play a role in *The Man of Mode*?"

Griselda looked as surprised as if she'd been asked to fly into a tree. "I? If I remember correctly, there is not a single part for a respectable woman in the play."

"I think you would play the role of Belinda with éclat," Gillian said.

"She is the one who tricks her best friend, steals the woman's lover, and then ends up losing him to the country miss in the end?"

Gillian nodded.

Lady Griselda drew herself up. "Surely you do not think that I would betray a female friend, or allow a man in whom I had interest to flee to a country miss!"

Gillian wasn't sure which of these options Griselda viewed with more horror, but she decided on the second. "The man you chose would have no interest in a rustic maiden. But I think you would enjoy playing Belinda, Lady Griselda."

When Griselda seemed unconvinced, she added: "She is, of course, a most beautiful woman."

"Irrelevant," Griselda said. "With the amount of rouge worn even in amateur performances, beauty is a matter of art rather than life."

"You know, Griselda, perhaps it is you who should be thinking of the marriage market," Ancilla said. "There's the Duke of Holbrook, for example. He is quite a catch, to put it vulgarly, now that he's given up whiskey."

Gillian suddenly realized that she'd forgotten to inform her mama of her own intentions toward the duke.

"Absolutely not," Griselda said with a small shudder. "While I view Rafe with great affection, he has been my brother's constant companion since their schooldays."

Ancilla raised an eyebrow.

Griselda opened her fan. "He calls me *Grissie*."

Ancilla's eyebrow dropped promptly back into place. "I see. What of another gentleman, my dear? You are still young."

"I am considering that possibility," Griselda said. "I shall reflect upon it further when the season opens."

Wonderful, Gillian thought gloomily. The few men not cornered by Imogen would be taken by Griselda.

25

In Which Vulgar Behavior is Noted, Judged . . .
and Punished

O f course, Imogen wasn't going to Silchester in the
evening. Why would she wish to rub shoulders
with women like Cristobel? The last excursion had sent
her back to her chamber stinking of rotgut wine and
tired to the bone, having made an exhibition of herself
before most of the male residents of the county.

That must be why she was brushing black circles
around her eyes with unsteady hands. Her mind kept
throwing up tiny bits of reassurance.

Why shouldn't she go? It wasn't as if Rafe's kiss that
afternoon meant anything. It didn't. It was a consola-
tory kiss, the kind of kiss anyone might bestow on an

available female who happens to be snuffling into your shoulder.

Although her traitorous body didn't seem to recognize that commonsensical view and kept giving a little thrum every time she thought about it.

During supper she had met Gabe's eyes a few times, but he looked so uninterested that it almost made her shiver. How could she have kissed someone like that, whose eyes were patently unresponsive? It's merely that he's a good actor, she reassured herself. He hadn't been unresponsive in the carriage. His eyes weren't dispassionate when he was kissing her.

Yet there was a detached note to his voice at dinner—

The door opened. "Im-o-gen!" her little sister shrieked, closing the door quickly behind her. "What on earth are you doing?"

"I'm going out," Imogen said irritably, wishing that Josie had stayed in Scotland. "And you really ought to send your maid ahead of you and request permission, Josie."

"Well, if I'd known that I might catch you in illicit activities, I would have. I can only assume that you are returning to Silchester. I should have known the moment that you told Griselda you had a headache."

"In truth, I am returning to Silchester. I enjoyed my previous excursion."

"Mr. Spenser is not interested in you," Josie said firmly.

"When did you become an expert in such matters?" Imogen said, patting so much rouge on her cheeks that she looked like a laundrywoman on boiling day.

"Since I began paying attention to them. And I can tell you, Imogen, that Mr. Spenser does not look at you with the appropriate level of appreciation. Certainly not an appropriate level for you to disregard prudence. Why risk ruining your reputation for someone who looks about as interested in you as a married vicar might?"

"In case it hasn't occurred to you," Imogen said with dignity, "Gabriel Spenser does not wear his heart on his sleeve precisely to protect my reputation."

"If he's that good an actor, one has to wonder how many of these little affairs he's conducted," Josie remarked. "For all he's a Doctor of Divinity."

Imogen had to admit the justice of that observation. Gabe ought have gone on the stage; never in a million years would she have known that he was the same man who had pulled her, laughing, from a wine cask. "As a widow, I can enjoy a gentleman's company for the evening without being chaperoned," she stated. "Why, if we were in London, he might well take me to the theater for the evening."

"Going to the theater to see a perfectly respectable play is not the same thing as sneaking off in a disguise to a disreputable location with—let's be frank, Imogen—a disreputable companion. A fact you know perfectly well, given that you informed everyone that you were retiring for the evening to your chamber."

"You just said he was a professor of divinity. I hardly call that disreputable."

"I wouldn't have called him such a thing, unless I happened to know that he had lured one of my sisters from the house and taken her to an inn where she sang a duet with a woman of ill repute." Josie picked up a scrap of rouge paper and idly rubbed color on her lips. "I think that description confirms him as disreputable, don't you?"

Imogen stared at herself in the mirror. Of course, Josie was right. And yet the previous night had turned her into a woman who didn't need color because she had a natural flush, high in her cheeks, who felt a little unsteady, and . . .

The worst was that if Gabe avoided her eyes during dinner, Rafe hadn't. It was almost as if he were torturing her. He sat at the head of the table, sprawled out just as if he were drunk, his long fingers wrapped around a glass of water. He showed no sign of missing the whiskey, or wanting the wine that Brinkley poured for the others.

She had refused wine herself. She never liked alcohol much, and couldn't see any reason to drink something that her host couldn't join her in. Rafe noticed. Something flashed in his eyes, though she didn't know what it was.

And there had been something else in his eyes that told her he was thinking about their kiss, that kept her shifting in her chair. And yet . . . did he say anything to her? Show by the slightest gesture or phrase that he wished to kiss her again, or—or anything? No.

Gillian was seated on his left, and herself on his right. Mostly they talked about the play. Gillian had spent the afternoon cutting lines out of the play, and Rafe seemed to have a comment on every one she mentioned.

After they finished battling over a line that Gillian labeled *insipid* and Rafe thought *necessary*—of course it was spoken by Dorimant—Imogen finally said: "I don't understand, Rafe. How on earth did you memorize all your lines so quickly?"

"Oh, I have that kind of memory," he had said lightly.

"What kind of memory?"

"The kind that doesn't allow me to forget even nauseating little details."

"What do you mean?" Gillian had asked, apparently fascinated. Imogen couldn't help noticing that almost everything Rafe said fascinated Gillian. She was always leaning toward him with those big green eyes and touching his sleeve.

"I remember senseless dates."

"Such as?"

"Your birthday, September 5. January 13, 1786, the day I got my first pony. February 2, 1800, the day I was sent down from Oxford. Again."

"How curious," Gillian had said. "Are you saying that you remembered the entire play after one read-through, Your Grace?"

He had smiled. "I loathe my title. May I possibly convince you to address me as Rafe?"

"I think not," Gillian had said, but her eyes were smiling. "It would be most improper. But I will try to curtail my use of your title, Your Grace." Imogen had to admit that Gillian Pythian-Adams was a truly beautiful woman. Her eyes were as clear green as sea glass. There were those, Imogen thought moodily, who likely thought that Gillian Pythian-Adams had a charming smile. Rafe was definitely one of them.

"So you are determined to go on a reckless excursion

to Silchester with Rafe's brother, although you know that the likelihood is that your reputation will be damaged if not destroyed, should you be discovered," Josie remarked, pulling Imogen's thoughts away from supper.

"I shall not be discovered," Imogen said calmly.

"Aren't you in the least worried by the possibility?"

"No." And she wasn't. She was afraid of something that she couldn't possibly mention to Josie: that she would succumb to Gabe's dark kisses, even though after the way he acted around her today, she knew that there was nothing between them of any lasting value.

"I have to admit," Josie said, looking pensive, "that I envy you."

Imogen snorted.

"You are unmoved by the prospect of social disgrace. You have effortlessly captured the attentions of our now-sober guardian—and don't pretend you haven't, Imogen, I'm not blind—and here you are, sailing forth on an excursion that can, at best, be labeled decadent. If not thoroughly debauched. With our guardian's brother. Why, it's positively biblical."

"You have such a lovely way of putting things." Imogen rose and pulled her opera cape around her shoulders. Due to the unfortunate encounter with the wine cask, Mrs. Loveit's gold dress was not available for the evening, but the dress intended for Belinda was equally gaudy and made a brilliant disguise. It was scarlet and dotted, most peculiarly, with black chenille. The girdle was black as well, and ornamented with a scroll pattern, also in scarlet, although one had to admit that, to all appearances, the girdle only existed so that it could act as a frame for a generous display of cleavage.

"It's a good thing that I can't be in the play," Josie observed. "I would never fit in one of those dresses."

"I almost don't myself," Imogen admitted, glancing down. Her breasts were precariously caught up in the crimson bodice, if you could call such a scrap of satin by that name.

"Please don't be discovered by anyone," Josie said, as Imogen was just leaving.

Imogen smiled at her. "I'm not worried. I am a widow, and there should be some advantages to the state."

"I know. I'm being very selfish."

There was a pang of misery in Josie's voice that made Imogen pay attention. "In what way?"

Josie's eyes looked a little watery. "I don't want you to make a scandal, because I'm going to have a hard enough time getting married. If people discovered you were carrying on an affair with Rafe's illegitimate brother, how will I ever find a man willing to take me on?"

Imogen had a flash of blinding guilt. "Oh darling, don't worry!" She ran over to give her a kiss. "I shan't go out with Mr. Spenser after this evening. You *mustn't* be so worried about next spring. Really you mustn't. You are a beautiful young woman."

"I am—" Josie stopped. "I'm tired of my own tedious thoughts on the subject."

"I shall be entirely circumspect," Imogen promised.

He was leaning against the orchard wall, waiting for her. And despite all her resolutions, despite the stern talking-to she had given herself on the way down the stairs, despite her flirtation with Rafe and her conversation with Josie . . . Imogen's heart was beating quickly.

Her conscience was keeping up a furious inner commentary. *You're acting no better than a trollop! You kiss one brother during the afternoon and then . . .*

He came forward to greet her, face shadowed by the twisting apple trees, and a hat pulled low. She couldn't see his eyes: were they expressionless, indifferent, as they had been at supper? But he spoke, and the slow scholar's tone of him melted her bones. "Lady Maitland. I feared you would not arrive."

"Punctuality is the prerogative of kings," Imogen said. "Not being royal, it would be presumptuous of me to be on time."

He bent to kiss her hand. "I am glad to see you. I feared that you had changed your mind."

"I almost did."

He held open the orchard gate.

"Where shall we go tonight?"

"I thought perhaps we should leave the fair folk of Silchester to their own devices. There is a pantomime in Mortimer."

"A pantomime! Isn't it early for a pantomime? Why, we are still in October."

Gabe handed her into the carriage. "In London pantomimes play every day for three months prior to Christmas. I admit to taking a childish pleasure in a panto."

Imogen seated herself, arranging her cloak in such a way that her breasts were not too naked in appearance.

The carriage took off with a jolt. She felt a thrum of panic: what if he expected to kiss her immediately? She tried to think of some sort of polite conversation. "Have you ever seen Joseph Grimaldi?"

"The clown? I saw a performance of his last year. I do believe that his rendition of 'Hot Codlins' could give you and the lovely Cristobel a run for your money."

Imogen couldn't think of anything else to say, and Gabe seemed to feel as little inclination to speak to her, although he also showed no propensity to leap across the carriage and kiss her. It was disconcerting. She and Rafe had talked so easily this afternoon: was the current silence because a man interested in an available woman has no reason for speech?

The thought was disquieting.

But she couldn't help but be cheered by the pantomime. "Will it be *Cinderella*?" she asked. "My sisters and I read about the play in *Ackerman*'s *Repository* when we were living in Scotland."

"Very likely," Gabe said. "It is the most popular panto, I believe. I saw it when it first appeared on Drury Lane . . . ten years ago that must have been."

"Do you enjoy theater other than pantomimes?"

"I am fond of it, although I have never acted myself. I admit that I am not particularly looking forward to playing a part."

"Mr. Medley seems respectable enough. Think of me: I have to play an innocent country miss."

"Who snares the biggest rake of them all," Gabe said. "You trounce the city ladies, Belinda, and Mrs. Loveit, and take home the prize."

"If Dorimant can be called a prize."

"My brother will play Dorimant well, don't you think?"

"Well, he's hardly a rake," Imogen said, feeling a queer pang of defensiveness.

Gabe laughed. "A lady of your propriety may not even recognize the hallmarks of a rake, Lady Maitland."

Imogen narrowed her eyes. "I can assure you," she said frostily, "that my longer acquaintance with your brother has led me to an understanding that he is *nothing* like Dorimant. Perhaps, sir, you ought to switch places with him and play Dorimant yourself."

He laughed, and it was uncanny how much he sounded like Rafe. "My brother would be pleased by your loyalty."

Imogen sniffed and walked into the Fortune Theater, sweeping past the boy holding open the door before he could do more than ogle at her chest. The anteroom of the Fortune was awash in swags of red velvet and opulent lighting.

"It seems they have gas lighting," Gabe observed.

"This is one of the most important theaters outside London," announced the concierge, who waited to escort them to their seats. "The best in the county attend our performances." He looked sideways at Imogen's crimson gown.

"I thought we might be too obvious if I took a box," Gabe said into her ear, as they walked down the central aisle. "But I didn't want us next to the stage."

"Why not?"

"I gather you have never seen a pantomime?" Gabe

said, guiding her to follow the attendant with a light touch on her back.

"No," Imogen admitted. "I know they traveled to Glasgow in the past few years since they became so popular in England, but my father was not fond of traveling." Because, she added silently, he would never have spent money that could have been spent on the track.

"In that case, I am honored to introduce you to the panto, and I assure you that we do not wish to have seats in close proximity to the stage."

Imogen sat down in a seat lined with red velvet. There were boxes to the sides, positively dripping with velvet and chains of paste pearls.

"Remarkably vulgar," he commented in a low voice.

"I like it," Imogen said. "It reminds me of a picture of a gilded chariot I saw once." Somehow she had formed the opinion that pantomimes were wild affairs, full of screaming people of the lowest caliber. But all those she could see around them were of the middling sort: honest burghers, butchers, and country squires.

Directly before them a worthy matron wearing a bonnet of purple cloth turned with velvet looked about, swept an imperious glance down their row, and then looked sharply away, her very bonnet trembling with indignation.

Imogen turned to Gabe, biting back a laugh. "My gown is remarkably suited to this particular theater. But apparently it is ruffling sensibilities."

"Don't worry," Gabe said in his deep, professor-like voice. "If you look at my costume, I am dressed as a sailor on leave. The costuming company erroneously thought there was a sailor in *The Man of Mode*. I do believe that I shall readily be taken as a sailor with his—shall we say—Whitefriars nun?"

"Whitefriars *nun*?"

"A popular pun. Whitefriars is a less than salubrious area of London, which used to house a monastery. Nuns are, of course, sworn to a life of chastity—"

"And the current occupants of that district do not adhere to ancient standards," Imogen said, giggling. "I feel positively wicked."

"Well, you are embellished with a remarkable amount of color," Gabe said. "Any impartial judgment must label you a bird of paradise or something equally colorful."

She smiled at him.

"I shall have to wash that off your lips before I kiss you."

The laughter died in Imogen's throat, leaving her staring into his almond-shaped eyes. They were not indifferent at the moment, not at all. He bent his head close to her face. "What a pity this is such a well-lit theater," he murmured.

"Yes," Imogen managed. He had one of her hands, where no one could see it. She could feel the calluses on his hands from gripping the reins of a hard-driving horse.

"Because I have to tell you, Lady Maitland, that I have thought of little all day but kissing you."

"You never showed—" she said, her voice a gasp.

"I would no more risk your reputation than I would rob a bank."

"Oh," Imogen said rather foolishly. And then: "You're a *very* good actor."

The theater was packed now, every seat filled with someone's bottom. The noise of voices kept crescendo-ing and fighting with the musical cacophony coming from the pit.

"They'll be starting soon." He was still holding her hand.

Had she really considered not coming to meet him? Imogen felt as if her blood were inflamed, shivers kept going down her spine, and her companion's decadent eyes knew precisely what he was doing to her.

Seducing her, that's what he was doing.

She'd known, Imogen realized suddenly. Of course, she'd known. Why had she taken a long bath? Dressed so carefully, if ostentatiously? Why else but that she could be seduced, and her companion allowed the liber-ties he would have had the night before if she hadn't fallen into a cask of wine?

What's more, she was going to allow it to happen. It was an adventure, a change from all the grief and sobri-ety of the last year.

One night, she told herself. One night and then she would return to being a sober widow, care for Josie, care for her reputation, and stop this wild adventure.

Meanwhile, he had started a slow massage of her hand.

"Mr. Spenser!" she gasped.

"Gabe," he said.

"Gabe," she repeated slowly.

He bent forward and whispered in her ear. "A Whitefriars nun is on intimate terms with her *friends* . . . Imogen."

She licked her lips nervously. The orchestra was actually playing in tune now. He smiled, and in his eyes were all manner of unholy things that a nun of any sort—nay, a proper lady—and certainly a divinity professor should know nothing of.

"I thought you studied the Bible," she said.

"People remind me of that all too frequently."

At that moment the boys standing beside the gaslights at the side of the theater doused them. There was a roar from the crowd. And Gabriel's lips took hers. There was none of Rafe's gentle approach, sweet humor, sideways proposal. This was a punishing kiss that pushed her head back and sent an instant wave of heat over her body. This was an erotic friction that had nothing to do with the taste of sun-warmed grass or gentle brushings: this was a deep merciless possession. And she—

The curtain snapped up as the boys standing at the gas lamps relit them.

Imogen found she had her hands clenched in his hair, holding him close. He eased away, smiling at her.

From the row before her she heard a scandalized, "Well, I never!" and guessed that the matron in the purple bonnet had ventured to turn around in her seat.

Two seconds later, the stage exploded with a group of whooping, screaming actors, and Imogen forgot about her offended neighbor.

Two minutes later, she leaned over and said, "Are *all* the women's parts played by men?"

"Oh no," he whispered into her ear, "the Principal Boy is generally played by a woman. See, there she is."

Imogen blinked at the stage. Sure enough, there was a young woman, scandalously dressed in breeches with her legs in tights that made them visible to everyone. "My goodness," she said. "I was sorry that I didn't bring Josie, but—"

"It's all nonsense." But his lips left a caress on her ear that had nothing to do with the nonsense on the stage.

Gradually the show became more and more boisterous. Imogen's favorite character was called Widow Trankey. She kept prancing onto the stage and commenting on Cinderella's terrible manners and her long nose (for in truth, one could not say in all honesty that the man playing Cinderella had precisely delicate features).

By the time Widow Trankey had decided that the ugly stepsisters were a terrible lot, and really ought to be disciplined—and she was the woman to do it, since Cinderella's stepmother had failed in the task—Imogen was laughing helplessly every time she opened her mouth.

Finally, Widow Trankey announced that the audience needed to hear about what happened to her the night before, a tale that she would sing to them. *"I went to the Alehouse as an honest Woman should—"* she sang.

And to Imogen's astonishment, the audience uniformly opened their mouths and roared "So you should!"

"And a Knave followed after, as you know Knaves would," she said, swishing her skirts in a flirtatious manner.

"So he would!" roared the audience, and Imogen shouted it too. She was acting precisely like the lightskirt she was pretending to be, screaming out the lines with abandon.

"*I went into my Bed as an honest Woman should,*" said Widow Trankey with many wagglings of her fingers and eyebrows.

"So you should!" roared the crowd, and now Imogen saw that the lady in the purple bonnet was crying out the refrain too and that almost, not quite, stopped Imogen from noticing something her companion was doing.

Because he—he—

"*And the Knave crept into it, as you know Knaves would,*" said the Widow.

"So he would," Imogen said, her voice dying. Because he was licking her ear. It felt hot, gliding against her skin. Teasing and slow.

She risked a look sideways. His laughter was husky and suggestive, not at all like the excited guffaws coming from the rest of the audience.

"Stop that!" she said, and turned back to the Widow, who was berating the wicked Stepmother for her unkindnesses.

But he didn't stop it. A few seconds later she actually felt his teeth nip her ear, and it felt so extraordinary that she found herself shifting in her chair, and once she gasped.

Not that anyone could have heard, because just then the Principal Boy snuck onto the stage and stolen all the pies that Widow Trankey meant to sell in the market.

She was squealing, he was running, and suddenly a pie flew across the stage.

Imogen screamed as the pie sailed across the stage. At the very last second, Widow Trankey ducked—but the pie hit one of the evil stepsisters!

The theater alternately screamed and moaned as pies flew about the stage. Most of them were adroitly caught by either the Widow, the thief, or (on occasion) Cinderella. Within a few minutes, their costumes, faces, and the stage were generously festooned with crumbs and splatters of pie.

"They're such good jugglers!" Imogen cried, turning to her companion.

Rafe had seen the panto a hundred times before, and had never seen Imogen Maitland like this . . . like a delicious cherry pie that he couldn't wait to eat. He took one look at her shining eyes and those beautiful, deep lips and couldn't wait anymore.

He swooped on her, swallowing her excitement and her joy, turning it in one spellbinding second to something else.

There could never be a thrill of dominion like the one he felt when Imogen tensed, startled in his arms, but a second later fell into the kiss, her eyes closed, her breathing labored. She was his, his for the evening, his for life, if only she knew it, and if only he could pull it off.

"Imogen," he growled at her.

"Yes," she said, her voice catching.

"I'll be taking you back to your chambers tonight."

Her eyes fluttered open, and she looked at him. "Yes," she whispered. "Oh—yes."

Rafe stared unseeing at the stage. He had the night to convince her that they were suited in the most important of ways. Then, after she was *his* in all the ways that counted, he could tell her who he was. A slow smile spread across his face. Rafe may not have had much practice in the last few years, but if there was one thing in his life that he had no doubt about, it was his ability to make a woman happy. Thinking about it, he reached out and pulled Imogen closer, as close as those red velvet chairs would allow.

Meanwhile, the panto continued unabated. Widow Trankey had most of her pies back now. She'd decided that since she no longer had enough to sell—and to her lamentation, they didn't look quite as fresh as they used to—she would use the rest to dispense with the wicked stepmother and her daughters. Because, as she announced, the prince was a bit on the slow side. The glass slipper had been sitting around the palace for a day or two, and the lummox didn't seem to have a plan. He should be out trundling around in a glass coach and finding Cinderella but—just like a man—he was slow. Slow!

Doesn't know what side his bed is buttered on, she said.

"Yes!" roared the crowd.

"Now if he were a man with a nobler . . . *flame*," Widow Trankey shouted.

"Yes!" roared the crowd. Rafe didn't even hear it. Imogen's mouth was so sweet, so soft, and so delicious that he could have stayed there all night.

"If he were a man who felt no *shame*," the Widow declared.

"Yes!" roared the crowd.

"He wouldn't need me to help him out, would he?"

"No!" cried the lady in the purple bonnet, and all her immediate neighbors.

And then, though neither Rafe or Imogen saw it, Widow Trankey's eye was caught by a pair in his audience: by a sailor and his moll, so taken up with each other that they really ought to be charging a peeper's fee.

Widow Trankey's real name was Tom, and he was a clown from a clowning family: a man whose clowning was part and parcel of his makeup and his inheritance. Mischief had been his middle name since he was a scrap of a lad and, besides, he knew a crowd pleaser when he saw it.

Indicating with the tiniest waggle of his eyebrows to his friend Carn (playing the evil stepmother for the evening) that he'd found a wonderful diversion, he changed the rhythm of the song a bit to suit the present circumstances.

"These days modesty has scarcely room to breathe," he bellowed.

The crowd happily followed along.

"Young girls are skilled in all sorts of debauches."

"Debauches!" roared the crowd.

"Even when they're supposed to be sitting in their Glass-Coaches."

The crowd affirmed his thought.

Slowly, slowly, he spun a finger around the room. "And the Widow must delouse the debauches wherever they may be . . ."

"Yes!" howled the crowd.

And that was when Tom let fly a very nice cream pie,

one of the very best he had left. He gave it a little spin, so that it wouldn't hurt anyone. Up, up, up it arched.

The crowd gasped and screamed (depending on their proximity to the pie).

Only Rafe and Imogen said nothing, noticed nothing, heard nothing.

The pie spun lazily, and then (Tom sighed in relief: he had had a moment's fear that the pie would land on a nasty-faced matron a row too short—she was the type to get him keelhauled) . . . it came to rest, almost gently, on top of the two embracing lovers.

In fact, on the very top of their heads, as if the pan were a special sort of roof.

Tom wasn't a man without mercy. Before the couple could recover their wits, he had three other pies spinning into the audience, enlivening the shrieking, delighted crowd.

26

Loving Fools are Created Every Day

Gabriel Spenser was in a restless frame of mind. He had gone up to the nursery to check on Mary and all was as it should be. She was lying facedown in her crib, with her round little bottom humped in the air.

"Won't that injure her neck?" he asked Mary's new nursemaid, as he tried to rearrange his daughter into a better sleeping position.

"Never has," Mrs. Blessams said, her knitting needles clicking in the quiet. She was everything that a nursemaid ought to be: cheerful, efficient, and all-knowing. "I've raised babies that slept on their faces, and those that slept on their little bums."

Gabe felt useless. He had enjoyed carrying Mary around in the crook of his arm, and she seemed to like it.

But today he'd come up twice to find her playing quietly on the floor, and although she instantly brightened and crawled over to him, he hardly felt that she needed him.

So he didn't bring her down to lunch, because likely Mrs. Blessams would think it was an odd thing to do. Everyone knew that fathers didn't belong in a nursery. Nor did they carry their daughters around the house. Children stayed in the nursery and made occasional, formal visits to the drawing room.

Of course, his mother had been different. He could only suppose it was because her position kept her isolated from society. She used to come to the nursery and read him books. He did remember a nurse, but what he mostly remembered was his mother.

He couldn't seem to pull himself away from Mary's crib. "Mrs. Blessams, you may fetch a cup of tea from the kitchen," he said, over his shoulder. "I'll wait here with Mary."

Mrs. Blessams blinked up at him. "That's very kind of you, Mr. Spenser, but that nice girl Bess will bring me a cup on the dot of ten, so there's no need to worry yourself."

The image of himself snatching Mary out of her crib and holding her faded from Gabe's mind.

She was damnably efficient, this Mrs. Blessams.

"Of course," Mrs. Blessams said, coming to her feet, "if you really wouldn't mind watching the babe for a matter of a few minutes, I would be grateful for a small respite."

"I'd be happy to," Gabe said.

The moment the door was closed, he picked up Mary as carefully as he could, making sure that all her little blankets came with her. Then he sat down before the fire and arranged her in the crook of his arm. She stirred a little and threw a tiny arm over her head. She was so beautiful that she made his heart ache.

Mrs. Blessams came back long before he wished to put Mary back in her bed.

"She'll be waking up for a bit of a feed soon," Mrs. Blessams said. She didn't flicker an eyelash at seeing him there with Mary, and Gabe was grateful for that. "I'll just wake her night nurse. That young woman sleeps as soundly as a log."

So he handed Mary over, still sleeping, and closed the door behind him. He didn't feel like sleeping. Rafe was out somewhere, festooned in a mustache and pretending to be him. One could suppose that therefore he, Gabe, should pretend to be the duke. In reality, he had retired to his room directly after the evening meal.

He wandered down the great staircase, wondering what it would have been like to have been born legitimately into the house of Holbrook. Gabriel Jourdain rather than Gabriel Spenser.

The great entryway was shadowy and empty, but for a dozing footman who jerked himself upright, and said, "Good evening, sir."

Gabriel nodded. Would his life feel different if the footman had said, Good Evening, *my lord*? He thought not.

There was a light showing under the library door, so he walked in. Rafe's library was of the ancient, tired, and slightly moldering type. The carpets were almost as threadworn as Rafe's own clothing. The books were expiring slowly into powdery heaps of dust that marked the fingers and collected in the corners of the book-shelves. There wasn't much of luxury about the room, and yet it spoke of years of Holbrook dukes, reading or not reading, sitting here smoking pipes and cheroots until the ceilings were blackened and the books smelled vaguely like wood fires.

She was seated at the library table, her head bent over a sheet of foolscap. His heart hiccuped. He'd made a promise to himself to stay away from this enticing and proper young lady. She was too cool, too out of reach, and entirely too beautiful for him.

"It's late, Miss Pythian-Adams," he said, breaking all his own promises.

She looked up and rubbed her eyes unself-consciously, as if she were a mere girl of five or six. Tendrils of bronze hair curled about her neck and temples, fallen from an elegant, winding arrangement on her head.

"I must send the actress taking the part of Mrs. Loveit her role. She seems quite anxious about it. Rafe gave me a note from her today."

"*Loretta* wrote Rafe a note?" Gabe asked without thinking.

Miss Pythian-Adams didn't miss anything. She glanced up at him, and then said: "Yes, Miss Hawes inquired about the play, so Rafe passed the letter on to me."

Gabe stared at her face. She had the chiseled perfection of a saint, the kind of clear beauty that one saw in statues—not lush Italian statues, but the ascetic northern saints. He'd forgotten that she knew that Loretta had once been his mistress.

"May I help with the copying?" he said, sitting down

without further ceremony. He was a degenerate man who was bringing a former mistress to the house of a nobleman. It could hardly be worse.

"Actually, I would be grateful for the help," she said, with a little, exhausted sigh.

"You read the lines, and I'll write them down."

She read, and he copied all the impertinent, silly lines of the hysterical Mrs. Loveit.

"He shall no more find me the loving fool," Miss Pythian-Adams said.

Gabe looked up to find that her eyes were on his face. Her mouth was set in a line of deliberate composure as if she would—she would what? Laugh?

"She was never my loving fool," Gabe said conversationally, blotting the foolscap. "We had a brief, if foolish, encounter. And I truly did knock her down with my coach, Miss Pythian-Adams."

"I have no need of these details, Mr. Spenser. Surely I would never ask you to clarify."

"I think those eyes of yours see many human foibles, do they not?"

"These are the only eyes I have, and there are certainly many foibles to be seen," Miss Pythian-Adams said with some dignity.

Gabe couldn't help it. He liked baiting her, this self-contained gentlewoman. "And what do you think of my foibles?"

She looked like a cat in the light of the candles on the table. "I think . . ." She closed her book. "I think you are a beautiful man, Mr. Spenser."

His mouth fell open.

"I expect that you use your beauty to make your way into delightful situations. If I understand the matter correctly, Miss Hawes is unlikely to have suffered by your attentions, be they ever so brief."

Gabe felt as if he had been struck to the ground by a large rock.

Miss Pythian-Adams composedly opened her book and read the line again: *"He shall no more find me the loving fool he has done."*

Gabe hadn't the faintest intention of picking up his pen.

"I regret if I overset you with my assessment," she said. "I greatly prefer clarity in conversation to social niceties."

"I am honored," Gabe murmured. He'd been a fool again. Miss Pythian-Adams's little smile revealed an original and interesting personality, and had nothing at all to do with being a member of polite society. "I have underestimated you."

"I was not aware that you were interested enough to make an assessment."

The little smile that curled on Gabriel Spenser's mouth was, if he but knew it, very close to that smile he admired but a moment before.

"I think one could describe my feelings as close to fascination."

"Indeed," she said, closing her book again. "In that case, perhaps I should retire, Mr. Spenser."

"We are unchaperoned."

"Yes." Unhurriedly, she rose. And he rose. "There is nothing fascinating about me," she said.

Gabe felt slow-witted around her, but even a fool can

understand an invitation of that nature when it is prof-
fered. He walked toward her, seeing her green eyes
widen, but didn't manage to enumerate her fascinations
before he had her in his arms.

She melted against him with all the urgency of Mrs.
Loveit, and he pulled her to him with all the flair of
Dorimant himself. But that kiss . . . a kiss that went on
far too long, that took them to a sofa in the corner, that
tousled his hair and turned her knees to jelly . . . that
was a kiss which had nothing of Loveit or Dorimant
in it.

But it had much in it of Gabriel Spenser, Doctor of Divinity, father of Mary, uncertain and desirous. And
much in it of Miss Gillian Pythian-Adams, who thought
never to meet a man who wasn't a fool.

She wasn't so much a fool that she could not admit her
own mistakes.

27

In Which Imogen Learns Something About Marriage Beds . . . and Other Beds

"**I** can't believe it," Imogen kept saying, shaking with laughter. "I just can't believe it."

"Mmmmm," Rafe said, hauling her out of the theater.

She half ran, half trotted after him, small specks of cream spinning from her garments.

"I can't go home like this!" she said, laughing.

"Nor get into my hackney like that either," said the driver, who was standing before his coach. "That's pie, that is."

Rafe fished out a sovereign.

The driver took it, but still shook his head. " 'Twill ruin my seats. Stink up the place, I shouldn't wonder. There's milk in that. Milk rots."

Rafe gave him another coin. "I'll take you as far as the Horse and Groom," the man said begrudgingly. "I'll not be taking you all the way past Silchester. You can wash at the pump in the back."

Imogen clung to his arm as they waited for the grumbling driver to spread out a horse blanket. Imogen had taken the brunt of the pie: it had slid down her left shoulder.

Rafe climbed in and then held out his arms. "You'll have to sit on my lap," he said.

Imogen hesitated for a moment and then climbed in. Of course, she would sit in his lap. Of course, he would visit her room later that night. It felt as inevitable, and right, and delicious as anything in her life.

A moment later she was nestled on his knees. He didn't say anything, so she said, "Where is the Horse and Groom?"

"I don't know."

"I've never washed at a pump, have you?" She couldn't stop the feeling of being about to laugh.

"Yes, I have. It will be quite chilly." He paused. "Of course, we could take a room."

"A room!"

His arms were tight around her. "Not for the night, of course. But you could have a bath, if you wished."

Her mind was reeling. "Gabriel?" Her voice came out soft and a little shaky.

He bent his head, and it was a moment or two before she could finish her sentence, and then she didn't remember how to phrase it.

But he saved her from embarrassment. "I could wash your hair," he said into her curls.

"No!" she said instinctively. She would never feel comfortable allowing a man to see her completely naked.

The carriage came to a halt, and the door sprang open. "Out of my carriage, you two!" the driver said, his tone nicely calibrated between disgust and appreciation for the sovereigns nestled in his pocket. "I'll wait for you, shall I?" He smirked.

"No." His voice was so chilly that Imogen almost shivered. "We'll find someone in a more liberal frame of mind."

The driver shrugged. The Horse and Groom was a sturdy little inn, the sort that catered to farmers coming to town year after year to sell their goods at the market. The door was so low that Imogen had the feeling that she should duck or she might strike her head on the lintel.

"My wife and I would like a room and a hot bath immediately. We suffered an event at the pantomime."

The innkeeper looked at the smeared cream in Imogen's dark hair and snapped into a bow. "I see that, sir. Right danger those pantomime players are. No respect for persons. Right this way, sir."

Two minutes later he deposited them in a pleasant, low-ceilinged room, with the promise of steaming water to follow directly.

Which was delivered, as promised, in a mere moment.

Imogen was thinking as hard as she could about Griselda, and those affairs that Griselda had had while no one, including her brother, had the slightest idea.

"Gabriel," she said, once a sturdy man had deposited the bathtub and poured quite a lot of steaming water inside.

"Imogen," he said, throwing her a teasing glance.

Their chamber roof was barely over his head, a line of massive beams. The little leaded-glass window squinted under the eves.

"This is my first affair of this nature—"

"And your last," he said, perfectly clearly.

Imogen started. "Well, that is as may be. I certainly do not plan on making—I do not—" she floundered to a stop. "I should like to take a bath now. Alone," she added. "Then I shall—" she stopped again.

"Why don't you take a brief rest?" he asked, for all the world like a courteous butler.

Imogen nodded jerkily.

And that was how she found herself wearing nothing more than a chemise, with a quantity of damp hair bound up in toweling.

Waiting to become an immoral woman.

One has to suppose that every bird of paradise had this moment in her life: a before and after. There must always be the hesitation before the first plunge into sin, the teetering at the river's edge before becoming a light woman, a lightskirt, a light-heeled maid.

He walked in quietly. Imogen was seated on the bed— not lying down; that reminded her unpleasantly of her wedding night. She was wrapped in a blanket. And she'd thrown her clothing to the side.

In for a penny, in for a pound.

No one could say that Imogen Maitland, once embarked on a life of sin, did so with maidenly docility or shyness.

Her companion walked across the room and snuffed one of the candles, using the little tin hat designed for that use.

Wasn't he in a hurry, the way she was? Imogen's heart was beating quickly.

Then he looked back at her, and there was something in his eyes, just glimpsed in the shadow, that gave her courage. He walked to the mantel and snuffed that candle, leaving only one lit, on the table by the window. Its small light played fitfully with the pale moonglow coming through the small leaded panes.

And then, after another glance at her, he put out the final candle. "If you'll forgive me my foolishness," he said in that slow scholar's voice of his. "Theatrical mustaches leave a red lip in their wake. I have my vanities, as you see."

Imogen couldn't help laughing: the idiotic, welcoming laugh of a fallen woman. She was aware that a moral conscience appeared to be missing in her character. She was positively thrumming with enjoyment. This meeting in a strange room in an inn with a beautiful, lean man who would lavish her with kisses wasn't raising a single qualm. Instead, joy and anticipation poured through her veins like molten fire.

The thought drifted through her mind that she was well and truly a fallen woman and floated away. She was more interested in the long line of male flank as he leaned over to pull off his boot. It was beautiful, all that hard-muscled leg.

The room was so dim now that she couldn't even make out his face. Imogen shook with the excitement of it. No wonder women made fools of themselves committing adultery: there was the pure liquid gold excitement of it. His second boot hit the ground and then his clothes followed. His body was just a shadow in the darkness, the body of a demon lover.

Rafe turned around, finally. Imogen was all shining white shoulders, the drab blanket slipping off. She'd let her hair down, and it fell like black water to one side.

"God, you're beautiful," he said, sitting on the bed to slip a hand by her cheek.

This was the moment that would make or break the evening: would she look at his face, mustache-free, and run shrieking from the room? But her eyes fell closed at the touch of his hand, so he just leaned closer and tasted her . . . a nip on her plump lip and then a fierce assault to answer her little pant. Somehow that moment when she was supposed to look at his face and recognize him was lost, because he kept kissing her as he pulled her blanket away.

There she was, as beautiful as he'd ever dreamed. Her eyelids flickered, so he gave her another fierce, open-mouthed kiss. Then he slowly let his body fall onto her soft one, telling himself to memorize this first time of feeling her, Imogen, under him. He felt dizzy with the raw pleasure of it.

But the sense—the dragging sense—that she would

open her eyes and realize who he was ... "Did you watch while you made love to Draven?" he asked. The sound of his voice growled in his ears. He used Maitland's first name deliberately.

And at the same time he ran a hand down, down the velvet sweep of her neck, over to the soft, unsteady weight of her breast, to the delicate curve of her ribs.

"I—" she gasped, turning her head.

"Did you make love in the darkness, under the covers?" he growled.

Her eyes were open, but he knew his face couldn't be seen because he was brushing his mouth back and forth against her breast.

"Yes," she choked.

"Then close your eyes," he said, his voice rough. "Close your eyes, Imogen. Stay still."

He began to stroke her breast with his tongue, and she fell back into the darkness, her hands reaching blindly for his hair, her body shuddering.

It was sometime later that Imogen realized that making love to a demon lover who won't let you open your eyes, who strips you naked in the night air, who bites you and licks you and nips you all over—

Has nothing in common with making love to a husband. Nothing. She kept trying to fill her lungs, kept trying to stop the little shudders, kept trying to ignore the sensations between her legs. Because he said—he said to keep her eyes closed. And not to move.

She was rolling her head back and forth. He was pulling her nipple into his mouth, driving her crazy, delirious. But along the sweeping waves of hot delirium came a swell of resentment. Draven and she had made love in the dark. Draven was the love of her life, the sweetheart of her youth, and she had longed more than anything else to make him happy. When he didn't seem to want her to move, she stayed as quiet as she could, making her body into a cradle for his, trying in every way possible to show him how much she loved and appreciated him. It was in the dark, under the covers, and she learned quickly that Draven didn't like it if she pushed against him. Once she had done it instinctively— her hips arched—and he said, "For God's sake, Imogen, let me do a man's business for once in my life, will you?"

But now she was in a hired room, and her companion was not her husband. She'd—she'd be *damned* if she was going to lie there like a compliant wife while he feasted on her body and she kept her eyes closed and her body still.

The moment that thought crystallized, Imogen was off the bed so quickly that she almost caught her companion in the crotch.

"What!" he said, coming to his knees.

For a moment she just looked at his body in the dim light. The bed was a large, old four-poster, made to survive the bouncing bouts of farmers and their wives on a holiday in town, as well as (most likely) loose women and their demon lovers. He was on his knees: one lean line of muscle from his chiseled shoulders through his chest, furred with slight hair that arrowed down . . . she took her time looking, and could feel her smile as if she were watching herself.

She hadn't been wrong, that time she glimpsed

Rafe's equipment. Apparently men came in all sizes, and these brothers must have been on the lucky side of the draw.

She couldn't stop thinking of Rafe's comment that he bet Draven made love under the covers and didn't show his equipment to a wife, only to loose women. Well, by God, she *was* a loose woman, and she wasn't going to cover her eyes for the pure shock of seeing it.

He was smiling. His face was in shadow, but she saw the gleam of white teeth, and then the lazy pleasure in his voice as he stretched, full of animal grace.

Imogen heard a little pant coming from her mouth. She snapped her mouth shut. She was standing naked in the center of a room, with a naked man before her. She pushed out one hip and put a hand on it.

"I don't wish to keep my eyes shut," she said, her tone accepting no question.

He nodded.

"We are not a married couple who has to hide under the sheets."

"May I beg you to return to bed, oh woman who is not my wife?"

She walked forward one step and stopped. "I have a few questions first." He laughed at that, a husky, full-of-enjoyment laugh that made her feel even more confident.

"What am I supposed to do when you're on top of me?"

"Whatever you like." He said it promptly enough, but it wasn't the answer Imogen wanted.

"How would a bird of paradise behave?"

"An old-fashioned term for one as sophisticated as

you," he said, sounding amused. "A bird of paradise would do precisely what would make her partner the happiest: and that would likely include a lively show of enthusiasm."

"Oh." It wasn't very specific.

"But perhaps you're more interested in a baggage than a bawd? Because a bold girl, a naughty girl, a woman who was in this bed for the pleasure not the profit, would make absolutely certain that she did precisely what she wanted to in order to increase her own pleasure."

"Oh . . ."

"She wouldn't give a damn about her partner. Let the man take care of himself."

Imogen smiled a little. Didn't she say that she wanted to have an affair in order to learn more about men? And yet it seemed that perhaps what she really meant was that she wanted to learn about herself.

"Well, you baggage," came his voice, slow syrup deep and sweet. "I'm thinking that Lady Maitland has just decided to turn herself from a lady to something quite different."

She could barely see him, just a gleam of all that rumpled brown hair. She climbed back onto the bed with a little swagger about her. In one swift movement, he pulled her against his body.

"I'm not a lady," she gasped.

It was like throwing a piece of paper into a fire, how quickly her body flamed at the sense of him, tight against her back, her bottom round against him. And his hands were on her breasts . . .

She let her head fall back against his shoulder, and he bent to her mouth, tasting the bad girl, baggage taste of her, Lady Maitland dancing into wildness.

"Do you like that?" he said, low and demanding, his hands on her breasts, doing things, touching her hard and then soothing, one then the other until her body was shaking.

"Yes," she said, and her voice didn't come out with bad girl sauce, but all slumberous and sleepy.

And then one hand started to slide its way down her stomach, and Imogen didn't even try to stop her body from moving. She was moving to a ballet that only she could hear, a seductive little twist that was saying *touch me, touch me*.

But he didn't seem to hear her because one hand kept tormenting her breast, and the other was kneading her stomach and then creeping to the soft skin of her thighs, and rubbing little teasing circles but not—

She arched her hips.

"Please!" It came out a growl.

"Imogen . . ." It came out like a sigh, a man sigh, the kind a man makes when he has his hands full of exactly what he likes best and is taking his time with it.

But Imogen sounded as if she were growing crotchety, so Rafe let his fingers walk over her skin, as soft as satin, and he couldn't wait to taste it there, and then into a tangle of the sweetest hair he'd ever had under his fingertips. She was whimpering now, and it sounded good. Better than the sound of whiskey pouring into a glass. Better than anything he'd ever heard in his life. So he gave it to her.

Because he was always going to give her exactly what she wanted, even if she didn't know that yet.

He took her mouth at the same moment that his fingers dipped deep, caught her cry in his mouth and he didn't let her down easy either. He kept her there, pulled back against his body so that he was tucked right into the soft curve of her ass, working magic with his hands, taking her mouth in the same wet, hot flurry that was driving her higher, and higher—

She was twisting against his hands now, and he turned her closer to him, tucked her face against his chest and set out to remind the world before he started drinking, Rafe Jourdain was a man who never let a woman go unpleasured.

To be frank, Imogen wasn't presenting a challenge.

It wasn't more than a moment before she cried out so loudly that he was pretty sure they heard her down in the sitting room. He'd have to take her out the back door because there wasn't a bit of face paint on her and anyone who saw a woman with a face this beautiful would never forget her.

She cried out against his chest, and a surge of pride took his mind off his own problems. To wit, was he going to sleep with Imogen before wedlock?

He eased her down, and didn't have to worry about whether she'd take a good look at his face because those eyes were closed now, and she looked as if she were just trying to get a good breath.

"First time?" he asked, kissing her shoulder. This was fun, but he was feeling like a man who hadn't been inside a woman in years. Not that it would have made any difference, because he wasn't stupid enough to think that there was any other woman in the world for him.

She woke up nicely. Her hands were in his hair now, pulling him down to her. But she hadn't answered, so he said it again, "Was that your first time?" Then he started kissing down the line of her collarbone, heading to the next step.

"For goodness sake," she said, sounding like she was about to laugh, "of course it wasn't, you dunce. Now come here."

And just like that, before Rafe could even wrap his mind around the fact that Draven apparently had had a trick or two up his sleeve, she had him rolled on his back and all that luscious black hair was stroking his body like fire . . . or maybe it was a sweet tongue.

He tried to pull her up, but she pushed him down and what she was doing felt so good . . .

"What *are* you doing?"

"I'm tasting you," she said. "Like all those other bold women you've been with. And Gabriel . . . You taste good."

He should tell her that bold women were usually only so bold, and that this particular sort of generosity was usually paid for, but he couldn't find the words, and she was saying breathy little things that were enormously flattering, and all of which he saved up so that he could work out a very nice comparison of himself and Maitland later.

At the moment, she'd trailed her mouth all the way below his belly, and she wasn't showing any signs of revulsion, but playing with him instead, so much that his hips were coming off the bed, and he was trying hard to remember that he was a man who never, ever lost control. Even when drinking. Why he'd been drunk as a wheelbarrow and still kept plowing ahead until the woman he was with found satisfaction. He'd never embarrassed himself—

But perhaps there are women who are more potent than whiskey.

It's a powerful lesson, one designed to put a man like the Duke of Holbrook in his place.

Because Imogen was playing with him, touching him, and then all of a sudden a warm, wet mouth came on him. And it wasn't some lady of night, but Imogen . . . touching him, looking at him with those beautiful eyes, touching him, her hair wild and her eyes wilder, and—

There are some women who are more powerful than whiskey, more potent than wine, who take a man's self-control and shred it to the winds.

28

In Which Delicate Decisions to Do With Class are Made

Loretta arrived in the evening at the back door of Holbrook Court, because that's where the hackney driver left her. It was a big house, bigger than a house had the right to be, and Loretta had to say that she didn't like the way there was nothing on either side. It looked naked, really, without other houses up against its walls.

She left her trunk where it was in the dust and walked up to the back step. Even the door was a great deal grander than anything Jack Hawes and his daughter had ever walked through before. She had a moment's qualm when it swung open and a footman stood there, dressed in a fancy costume with some braid, as fine as the captain's uniform that Blackbeard wore in that play written by a lady, the one she acted in last year.

But then she remembered that she was an actress, and all an actress ever needed was a role. Pretty Patsy would do. Pretty Patsy was the village maid who married a footman in *The Loving Thief*. It was a deplorably old-fashioned play, but a useful little role. She smiled up at the footman with Pretty Patsy's dimples. "Good evening. I'm here to see the Duke of Holbrook."

His eyebrows shot up so fast it was a wonder they stayed on his face. "Oh, so you wish to see the duke, do you?" he said. "And where are you from, then?"

Loretta wasn't worried anymore. "I'm nothing more than a maid from Larding," she said, dimpling at him and only just stopping herself from uttering Patsy's next line: "If you'll excuse me from begging your pardon."

He frowned again, and said, "Oh, that's what it's all about, is it? Follow me, miss."

Loretta sighed. Of course, the country was full of people who hadn't seen a play in a long time, perhaps even in months. But given that the *The Loving Thief* played for eighteen weeks—Loretta saw it fourteen times herself—she could have expected he would catch a line from it.

A moment later she found herself before a sturdy-looking individual who looked precisely like Harry Keysar when he was decked out as the butler of Buckingham Palace, and sure enough, that was precisely what this man was. Mr. Brinkley, butler of Holbrook Court.

It took a while to get everything straightened out, as

the footman had formed the opinion that she had come to take the place of one of the upstairs maids, who had apparently left in disgrace after stealing two silver spoons, but finally Loretta made it known that she was a guest of the duke.

Then Mr. Brinkley said that he'd heard something of an actress coming to help with the play and went to ask what to do with her.

When he returned, Loretta was cozily seated at the kitchen table with all the kitchen staff gathered around her. "And then the horses smelled all those sheepskins," she was saying. "All four of the horses threw up their heads and took off running. The driver fell between the horses and the coach . . ."

The cook, Mrs. Redfern, gave a great sigh and crossed herself hastily. "Dead, I'll warrant."

"Dead," Loretta agreed, her curls bobbing. "The coach hit a post. There were two outside and five inside passengers."

"All dead?" Mrs. Redfern cried.

"You weren't one of them, were you, miss?" cried one of the upstairs maids.

"No, indeed, or I wouldn't be here to tell you about it," Loretta said. "But I saw it happen. There was only one woman on the mail at all, and that was a Miss Pipps."

"What happened to her?" the maid cried with fearful pleasure.

"Well, when they took her out of the carriage, she threw her hand up to her head like this." Loretta sprang to her feet and threw her hand across her forehead.

"Then she sank down to her knees." Loretta sank, slowly and with trembling emphasis.

"And then she died, didn't she?" Mrs. Redfern said. Even Mr. Brinkley, who'd missed the first part of the story, was waiting to hear.

"She cried to her mother," Loretta said, looking up at the ceiling. " 'Mama, take me to your breast, Mama.' " The quiver in her voice made Mrs. Redfern suddenly start blinking rapidly.

"And she was dead," the footman said.

"Actually, she lingered twelve hours," Loretta said, briskly getting to her feet.

"The good Lord decides these things," Mrs. Redfern said heavily. "When it's time to go, it's time to go."

" 'Tis I who will decide about your time, if you don't go about your chores," Mr. Brinkley told an upstairs maid, who was looking agreeably terrified. "You know that Lady Griselda will be wanting a fresh cup of tea."

He sat down at the table. "Now, young lady, we must decide what to do with you. In the old days, that would be the days of the duchess as was, the actors stayed in the house proper, if you follow me."

Loretta didn't, but she nodded anyway.

"Anyone can tell that you're a true actress," Mrs. Redfern put in. She sat down just next to Loretta. "Mr. Brinkley, she doesn't belong in the house proper. Miss Loretta—if you'll forgive me taking the liberty—should stay here with us."

Loretta nodded.

"Don't you have ambitions to stay in the house

proper?" Mr. Brinkley said, watching her so closely that he could have been a constable sniffing out one of her pa's schemes.

"If I'm not in the house, do I have to stay over the stables?" Loretta asked.

Mr. Brinkley snorted. "I should hope not! We have good, clean quarters in the west wing of the house."

"If you're asking do I need a big chamber and someone to bring me my tea, then no, I do not."

Mr. Brinkley beamed at her. "Now, and you're a good girl, aren't you? I should have known the professor wouldn't kit us up with one of them actresses like that Mrs. Jordan. He's a divinity professor, after all."

"Who's Mrs. Jordan?" Mrs. Redfern asked.

"You do know it, Mrs. Redfern, that you do. She's the actress that's had children with the Duke of Clarence."

"Oooh, to be sure!"

"You see," Mr. Brinkley said, turning to Loretta, "I wasn't sure whether you was hoping that the Duke of Holbrook would be amenable to that sort of arrangement. I'm by way of the gatekeeper for the duke."

"He's had to be, the duke's been cup-shot for the past few years," Mrs. Redfern put in.

"That's gossip," Mr. Brinkley said to the cook. "His Grace doesn't drink a drop at the moment."

"I've no wish to have ten children with your drunken duke," Loretta said. And she meant it.

"Nay, and I can see in the shake of a lamb's tail that you're not that sort of girl," Mrs. Redfern said comfortably. "I think you'd do better here with us, love, rather than eating at the big table and having to worry about your manners and such. I expect you have a young man wanting your hand once you're done with this acting business."

"His name is Will," Loretta said, nodding. "We've exchanged rosemary."

"There, and isn't that nice that the old customs are being kept up," Mrs. Redfern said. "Why, Mr. Redfern and I exchanged rosemary not so many years ago ourselves. Perhaps thirty."

Loretta thought that sounded like an eternity.

"I'll speak to His Grace," Mr. Brinkley said. "I'm thinking you're right, Mrs. Redfern. Miss Loretta will do nicely with us. We'll keep her safe for her Will. One never knows when Lord Mayne will stop by."

"Not that the young man's ever said a rude word to one of my maids," Mrs. Redfern said comfortably. She had a lot more tolerance for the handsome earl than did Mr. Brinkley.

Loretta didn't care where she slept, nor who the Earl of Mayne was. "May I see the theater?" she asked.

"I'll take you tomorrow morning to meet the young lady who's in charge of the production. Miss Pythian-Adams, she is, and a very cultivated young lady indeed."

Mrs. Redfern leaned in, confidentially. "Her maid's quite convinced that His Grace will ask for her hand before the month is out."

Loretta unwittingly proved herself above reproach when she showed absolutely no interest in this fascinating nugget of information, but instead begged for the history of the theater.

29

In Which Various Improprieties Continue

As Rafe saw it, there were very good reasons for stopping this erotic play. Those reasons all had to do with honor and propriety, and included things like not anticipating one's wedding date.

Warring against propriety was a kind of hunger that he'd never experienced before. Imogen was lying beside him, looking pleased with herself, and his personal equipment didn't even seem to have noticed what had just happened. The only thing pounding in his head—and his groin, which at this moment was practically the same thing—was an insistence that he roll over and acquaint Lady Imogen Maitland with what it felt like to sleep with a man who wasn't underendowed by nature, as Draven Maitland almost certainly had been.

Then she opened her eyes and smiled at him, and he forgot for a moment that he didn't want her to have a good look at his face. She looked a little limp and a lot happy, and the dim golden light from the dying fire was enough to make it clear that Imogen Maitland had the most beautiful female curves that he'd seen in years. Probably in his whole life. They had to be touched, and tasted . . .

You have your whole life to do it in, argued his conscience.

Only once you truly convince her that your skills are such that she should take on a bad bargain, argued back his common sense.

Common sense won, backed as it was by a hefty dose of pure lust.

He began an exploration of the plump underside of her breast, an intimate investigation of every inch that almost—but not quite—took all his attention.

A gentlemen wouldn't take advantage of his future wife before the vows are spoken, pointed out his conscience.

I'll vow anything, the rest of him mumbled, teasing her nipple until she began making little gasps of pleasure. It would be most ungentlemanly to leave a lady in such a condition.

Imogen's whole body was damp, her breath shallow, her eyes languorous and unfocused. His lips drifted south. He had his hand there already, playing with her damp, warm flesh, making her jump and roll her hips. She had stopped making little squeaks and was uttering throaty moans.

He was having a little trouble breathing himself. Who

was he fooling? Of course he was going to make love to Imogen. He felt as if he'd been intending to make love to her since the first moment she strolled into his house, all passionate over Draven Maitland, so in love that she didn't even see him.

No, that wasn't true.

He can't have been base enough to lust after a woman in love with another man. The very thought made him roll over Imogen and pull her hips toward him.

She reached up her arms without opening her eyes, so he could lavish just as much time as he wanted kissing her eyes and her nose, her high forehead and her lush mouth.

And all the while another part of him was stroking her as well, making her gasp, strangled little sounds of pleasure wrenched from her chest until she snapped open her eyes, and said, "If you're planning to go somewhere, would you mind doing so now?"

"Tsk, tsk," he said, grinning down at her. "There's no point in hurrying these things, is there?"

He clenched his teeth and stopped himself, withdrawing. She clutched his arms so tightly that he almost winced. Then she arched up, following him, seeking him, *needing* him.

And suddenly he realized that those were the words he needed to hear . . . had to hear. The vow he kept thinking about.

"Imogen," he said, between clenched teeth, "do you need me?"

She followed him again, arching that beautiful lean body in the air, but he stopped halfway and didn't give it to her. She opened her mouth, panting a little, and said, "What?"

"What?"

"What are you doing?"

"Making love," he said reasonably. "Is there something wrong with the way I'm doing it?" He went a little deeper and then withdrew again.

"Yes," she said tightly.

"Do you need me to do something different?"

He managed an insouciant tone, even though every muscle in his body was vibrating like a spring wound too tight. Halfway, and halfway, and she was pushing against him, turning her head against the pillow, trying to catch him.

"Just tell me this, Imogen," he said between clenched teeth, "tell me you need me. You need—" His voice died, for her hands had slipped from his shoulders down his back, held onto his ass, and pulled.

And despite himself, he slipped an inch. A blissful inch, to judge by the low moan she gave.

"More," she said. And then: "Please. I beg you."

That was a vow. There are limits to what a man can put himself through when there's only one thought in his mind. So he pressed a kiss on her mouth that was his vow, silent but heartfelt, and then pulled her hips into just the angle he wanted.

And plunged.

She didn't moan this time; she screamed. Her fingers clenched, and he drove forward again, just that half centimeter until their bodies were as joined as possible . . . and after that, he didn't have the energy to think about vows or consciences or anything of the nature. He just concentrated on breathing, staying with her, plunging deeper and deeper, harder and harder, riding her as if the two of them were trying to reach some imaginary country of sweat and sobs and little cries.

And then—and then fire raced up his body and every muscle froze for a moment as if he'd died and gone to heaven. He managed to pull free just in time.

It must be because he hadn't made love to a lady in years. That must be it.

Because men didn't fall like a felled tree on the body of their female companion and find that their eyes were inexplicably damp, at the same time their lips were curling in a fool's grin.

Only a fool would think it was something sacred, making love in a hired room, with a widow who thought he was his own brother. But if the rightness of what just happened meant he was a fool . . .

She was lying in the crook of his arm (because he shifted his weight after a moment). He couldn't see her face, but he could hear her breathing, and then as he was holding her, her body shook with one final little tremor.

There hadn't been much to be proud of in the past few years. The only thing he'd done with passion was drink, and there were no prizes for that.

But the bone-deep satisfaction roared through his body. She was his, after this. He'd done it. He'd seduced Imogen Maitland, and now she was having an affair, and of course, he would tell her who he really was.

And then she'd marry him.

And then . . . he was grinning when a sweet, hot

thought had come to him. Who was he to think that Imogen was *definitely* won by that encounter? He couldn't resist, so he brushed his mouth over her nose: just that delicate little nose, and yet it made him swallow hard.

Her eyelashes fluttered, and he was tired of trying to stay out of her line of vision, never mind the fact that the room had grown as dark as the bottom of a scullery bucket.

One moment Imogen was lying in a comfortable dazed state, and the next broad hands had lifted her and before she had a moment to see what was happening, she was facedown in the pillow and those hands—those hands—

Her body arched up, and a powerful body reared behind her. For a moment she tried to pull away; the situation felt oddly vulnerable, for all she couldn't see his face. But those hands held her hips, and he was holding her, forcing her to yield, pulling her up so that . . .

And then her body decided of its own accord. She cried out, aloud, and didn't even register that it was her own voice. She was frantic, pushing back against his every stroke, and the only sound in the room was his groan of pleasure and her own soft pants in her ears. He was bent over her now, braced on muscled arms that came down beside hers, as sturdy as if those long, heated movements of his body weren't happening at all.

But they were, they were, and Imogen was greedy for them, aching. And then suddenly he straightened his back, and his hands caught her in the hips, and he began to thrust harder, high and deep, pounding.

It wasn't until later that she even felt the pressure of his ten fingers on her hips. It wasn't until later that she remembered hearing his hoarse voice, telling her—nay, commanding her—to *come*, and even though she had no idea what he meant, her whole body had clenched around him and then turned to heat, a sobbing, pulsing kind of heat that was like nothing she could have imagined.

Nothing.

30

It Doesn't Take Shakespeare for a Man to Make an Ass of Himself

Rafe woke the next morning, in his own bed, with a distinct sense of shame. It had been the most wonderful act of his life, and why on earth he'd let it pass without asking Imogen to marry him, he didn't know.

Except, as he stretched and started at the ceiling (the plaster really was starting to flake; he'd have to have that fixed before inviting a bride into his chambers), he knew why. He'd run scared. Coward that he was.

Imogen had been so laughingly dismissive after he kissed her in the field. What if—what if she'd said *yes, I'll marry you.* But she meant, *Yes, I'll marry Gabe?*

So then what if he'd said first, *I am Rafe,* and she'd been as indignant as she had every right to be?

He groaned. The fact of the matter was that he was a bad bargain. He was a half-pickled duke who was only just picking up the jumble of his affairs again. Thanks to God—and his old friend Felton, who had pretty much told his man in London what to do—the Holbrook estate seemed to have ballooned in the past few years. He could afford a wife. Hell, he was a duke. He could afford fifteen wives.

But he had never been any good at fooling himself. It all sounded good: a sober duke with a great deal of money and land to spare.

Peter had been true nobility, and if he'd lived, Imogen would likely . . . Except he, Rafe, would never have let Peter even take a look at Imogen. He'd have had to slay his own brother.

He got out of bed, buck naked, and walked to the window. The memory of the previous night was in every satisfied inch of his body. She had to acknowledge that.

A rich duke might sound good in a fairy tale, but he knew that Imogen saw him for precisely what he was: a man who no longer drank and never would be able to again. A man who had neglected his estate for years. A man who had no real passions in the world other than riding horses, watching yellow cow parsley bloom, and making love to his wife.

And the last was only true if somehow he managed to make Imogen into his wife.

Perhaps his own desire would be enough to persuade her. After all, by her own account that ass Maitland hadn't really wanted her, Gabe didn't, and, thank God, Mayne hadn't either, because Mayne was not a man a woman ever forgot. There was no one in Imogen's memory but himself.

He leaned against the window, looking again at the sweep of cobblestones and knowing that in truth, he only had one significant thing of value to offer her: last night. But even thinking of it made his breathing hitch. His breath fogged the panes, and he turned away.

Rafe tried not to look at Imogen during breakfast. She was involved in a long conversation with Miss Pythian-Adams about a scene that they had rehearsed the previous afternoon. She didn't glance at him; of course he noticed that. She looked briefly at Gabe, but apparently she had taken the scolding of the previous afternoon to heart. No one could have told from her glance that she thought she'd passed a delightful evening with him.

So Rafe ate eggs, and corners of toast, and whatever else Brinkley put before him, and tried to discipline himself. He would not stare at his ward like a lovesick calf.

Miss Pythian-Adams was planning a full-length rehearsal for the afternoon. "Miss Hawes arrived yesterday," she explained.

"Where is she?" Rafe asked, waking belatedly to the conversation.

Miss Pythian-Adams glanced at Gabe for a moment and then looked toward Rafe. "She will join us for the rehearsal. Apparently she finds Mrs. Redfern congenial company. She has chosen to stay belowstairs."

Rafe was stunned. He looked immediately at Gabe, only to see that his brother looked as poleaxed as he felt.

"Didn't Brinkley tell you that Miss Hawes feels she

would be more comfortable taking her meals below stairs?" Miss Pythian-Adams asked Gabriel.

"Of course," Gabe said, and closed his mouth like a trap. "I shall make certain that Miss Hawes is entirely comfortable."

"I'll come with you," Miss Pythian-Adams said, leaping from her chair. "I am most anxious to meet my Mrs. Loveit."

"Miss Hawes can be found in the theater," Brinkley announced.

"In that case I shall come as well," Griselda announced, adjusting her shawl. "I will admit to being quite curious about our guest."

Rafe raised an eyebrow. Apparently the entire household was desperate to meet the young actress who had so aroused Gabriel's sympathy. Of course, now he thought of it, he would quite like to meet Mary's mother as well.

He stood and saw that Imogen was finally looking at him, an eyebrow raised. Without thinking about it, he grinned at her. Her eyes were laughing, and she obviously agreed with him that the rush to the theater was ridiculous.

For her part, Imogen was in a state of what felt very like pure joy. She'd been there from the moment she woke up and stretched, feeling a delicious warmth all down her limbs. Life was . . . life was good.

It wasn't a thought she had entertained for years. Not, she thought, since the moment she saw Draven Maitland. Because the moment she saw his sweet, petulant face, and his sleek, yellow hair, she'd fallen into a muddled pit of longing and desire that had hardly been satisfied by marrying him. In truth, not satisfied at all.

She liked to tell herself that it might have been, had they years together. But she was beginning to wonder about that optimistic idea.

She'd woken this morning without feeling sharp longing for Draven, and without the anguish that replaced it when they married, and without the grief that replaced the anguish when he died.

In fact, she felt like laughing. All the time.

"Your mother loved theatrical productions, didn't she?" she asked Rafe, smiling up at him.

"I believe that 'obsessed' would not be too strong a word," he said reflectively. "She created the theater, of course. There used to be a supper room off the ballroom"—they were walking through that gracious, cavernous space now—"but she enlarged it into a theater shortly after marrying my father. Unfortunately, he showed no theatrical talent whatsoever, and less interest as the years passed."

The double doors at the end of the ballroom stood open. Imogen paused for a moment on the threshold. "It is beautiful," she said, awed.

"She had it fashioned after the theater at Blenheim," Rafe explained. The walls were entirely covered with vivid murals, bedecked with a frieze of laughing antique masks along the ceiling. The proscenium stage was faced by rows of chairs upholstered in a deep red stripe.

Just then a young girl with a face like an eager flame appeared from stage left. She ran toward them, calling an eager greeting. Then Miss Hawes—for surely it was Miss Hawes—dropped a very pretty curtsy to Griselda, who had just been introduced by Mr. Spenser. And now Miss Pythian-Adams and she were exchanging courtesies.

Rafe was staring at the actress intently. "She's no lady," he whispered to Imogen.

"No," Imogen replied. "She's so pretty." She was the prettiest girl Imogen had ever seen: from her shining curls, to her little triangular face, to her large eyes and trim figure. She seemed the essence of femininity, wearing pink the color of blush roses. It was a costume nicely calculated to be entrancing and yet not vulgar.

"Yes," Rafe said thoughtfully, "a fortunate attribute for an actress."

Miss Hawes was beaming at Miss Pythian-Adams and talking nine to a dozen about the part of Mrs. Loveit. She was apparently illustrating a point about the character she would play because suddenly she fell into a world-weary posture.

"Don't you think so?" she cried, dropping Mrs. Loveit as if it were a cloak she shrugged off.

Imogen blinked. It was the oddest thing she'd ever seen. One moment, Miss Hawes *was* a rather tiresome, petulant, desirous beauty who was on the verge of losing her delectable lover, and the next she stood before them as a fresh-faced young girl.

"Don't you agree?" she asked Miss Pythian-Adams, who seemed rather stunned by the energy that flowed from Miss Hawes.

"Of course," she said faintly. "You're absolutely right.

I'm afraid I have a small headache. Shall we resume this discussion when we begin rehearsal after luncheon?"

Miss Hawes beamed at her. "I am available whenever you would like me."

"Of course," Miss Pythian-Adams murmured.

"My mother," Rafe said to Imogen, "always stiffened up the amateurs with a good dose of professional actors. You can see why she did it. We will just fumble around and likely fall over ourselves, but Miss Hawes, young though she is, will straighten us out."

"Yes," Imogen said, "although I'm not certain that Miss Pythian-Adams likes being straightened out."

Then Gabe brought Miss Hawes over to them. Her curtsy was a beautifully calculated mixture of welcome and respectfulness.

Only Miss Pythian-Adams didn't seem to like Miss Hawes. Her tone was rather sharp as she ascertained that Miss Hawes knew her entire part. Her voice grew a little sharper when Miss Hawes said that, in fact, she knew the entire play and would be happy to act as a prompter, although—as she said—she had no doubt but what all the gentlemen and ladies knew their parts.

"Not I!" Griselda said cheerfully. "You'll have to help me, my dear." She had obviously realized that Miss Hawes was far from being akin to the kind of immoral actress who lured the Duke of Clarence into setting up an establishment and spawning near to a dozen illegitimate children.

Rafe drew Imogen away from a discussion of where the prompter might stand when she wasn't on the stage to show her the theatrical paintings that lined the walls. "My mother," he said, "was very fond of murals. In fact, she had the hunt of Diana painted in her bedchamber."

"Goodness," Imogen said, staring at a vivid rendering of Prince Hamlet on the battlements. At least she assumed it was Prince Hamlet because the man in question was clutching a shining skull and a dagger at once. "Is the painting still intact?"

"My father painted it over when she died," Rafe said cheerfully.

Imogen frowned. "Why?"

"The picture showed Acteon surprising Diana while bathing," Rafe said obligingly. "If you remember, Diana promptly turned Acteon into a stag, and his own hunting dogs brought him down."

"Your father—"

"Apparently felt that my mother was issuing a veiled warning."

"Your parents must have been interesting," Imogen said.

Since it was Imogen, he told her the truth. "My mother was in love with the theater, of course. But my father was, by all accounts, in love with Gabriel's mother."

She glanced up at him. "That must have been difficult for your mother."

"Holbrook was always stiff and cold," he said, remembering it. "I do believe that he disliked her . . . and us as well. Although perhaps he tolerated my brother Peter better than me."

"How remarkably selfish: to dislike your own children for coming from a marriage you regretted!"

"Yes," Rafe said slowly. "I'm afraid that my father was a rather selfish man, in many respects."

He led her to the next panel. A plump Bottom was looking around quizzically while Puck was in the very act of lowering an ass's head onto his shoulders.

"Who is this?" Imogen asked.

"Have you read *A Midsummer Night's Dream*?" Rafe asked.

"I suppose so . . . oh, that's the workman who is given a donkey's head."

"Only then does Bottom dare court the Queen of Fairies," Rafe said, feeling rather queer. "When he wears the ass's head. He has to be disguised because she's so beautiful." He looked down at Imogen. Her hair was shining, sleek, as if he had never rumpled it in his hands, drawn it across her breasts, and then replaced that caress with a rougher touch of his own. She was looking up at him, amused, her eyebrows arched.

Slowly the amusement faded from her face, and after a moment she wrenched her eyes away and fairly ran back to the group.

Rafe just stood there a moment. He could almost feel the weight of the ass's head on his shoulders.

31

In Which Several Parties Warn
of Ruined Reputations

Gillian marched out of the theater and straight into her bedchamber. She stood there for precisely one moment, her fists clenched. Then, solely because her chest was compressed and for some reason she couldn't even take a breath, she marched back out of her chamber and into the nursery.

Mary's new nurse was sitting comfortably by the fire, and Mary herself was lying on a blanket, kicking about and talking to herself.

The nurse launched herself to her feet and bobbed a curtsy with some creaking of knees. "It's Miss Pythian-Adams, isn't it? I'm Mrs. Blessams. I remember your name, of course, because it sounds just like a heroine in a novel. I don't suppose you read them, but I'm fair addicted to Minerva Press."

"Oh, I have read them," Gillian said, trying hard to shape her mouth into a smile. A heroine she wasn't. Because a heroine—

Even in the most degraded of situations, a heroine never found herself—

She knelt next to Mary. The baby gurgled and smiled and made a swipe at one of Gillian's curls. She was a darling. "Mamammmmmma," Mary sang.

Gillian had seen Mary's large eyes before and that delicate pointed chin.

The baby had just reached out again, when the face looking down at her suddenly disappeared. Mary's little face crinkled with rage, and she let out a shriek.

Gillian looked down at Mary, kicking her fat little legs in disapproval, as Mrs. Blessams hoisted herself out of her chair.

"She's that dramatic," Mrs. Blessams said. "As good as an angel, but if you cross her in the smallest way, you'd think she was being murdered. There you are, lovely. She likely just had enough time on the blanket. It's good for them, but of course they might take a chill." She said it importantly, and Gillian again tried to summon the kind of smile required: a complimentary smile. Then she walked out, closing the door quietly.

He was there, leaning against the wall, waiting for her.

She tried to walk past him, but he grabbed her arm.

So she looked, chin high. There was no point in pretending. "It's none of my business," she said.

He looked at her. "Mary is mine."

She just couldn't stop herself. "Yours and—and that—"

"*Mine.*" He said it fiercely.

She nodded and pulled her arm away. "Good afternoon, Mr. Spenser."

She walked most of the way down the corridor, but she could feel his eyes on her back, and so finally she looked back. He was looking after her, and there was something in his eyes that she—Gillian Pythian-Adams—had never seen in any man's eyes. So she turned around and walked back to him.

It was despair.

"I won't tell anyone," she said, gentling her voice. "It is irregular, but I respect the fact that you are raising Mary yourself."

He moved so fast that she didn't even see him, just pulled her shoulders to him and kissed her, hard and despairingly.

He was worse than Dorimant.

She should let him know in no uncertain terms that she, Gillian, was no woman to be manhandled by a rake.

But the flood of exhilaration that filled her chest had nothing to do with rakes.

"Are you having an illicit affair with Lady Maitland?" she asked, pulling back just far enough so that she could see his face.

He looked down at her, and the confused, bewildered man look of him made her smile deepen.

"No, you're not," she said to herself. "And you are not currently having a relationship with Mary's mother, are you?"

"I doubt you'll believe this, but such things are not in my normal course of life." He sounded so earnest that she almost giggled. "You think me a Dorimant, but I assure you that I'm tediously sober in my daily life. Although—" he said it haltingly—"I don't precisely regret that night with Loretta."

"Of course not, because Mary came of it."

This time it was she who drew his head down to hers. And she whose tongue touched his lips, in that daringly mad kiss that he had taught her.

"You must not," he said, after a few minutes.

She felt as if her heart would burst, hearing the pain in his voice. It was perverse, really, how much she felt like crowing with delight merely because—because—Mr. Gabriel Spenser was in love with her.

"I must," she said simply.

"No. I'm—"

"You're illegitimate. You're raising a child from an illicit liaison with an actress. You are Mr. Dorimant to the life," she said severely.

But he had caught something in her voice, or her eyes, now.

"No," he said suddenly. "I will not allow it."

"I will not allow anything else."

They stared at each other for a moment.

"You know nothing about me," he finally said hoarsely. "My mother—"

"I look forward to meeting her."

"You will *never* meet my mother. My mother was a kept mistress to the duke for years. And I am no secretly illegitimate child, as Mary will be. Everyone knows my parentage. You would be ruined to even—to even—"

"Yes," she said, smiling at him. "I suppose so."

"No!" he said again.

Men were so foolish. She'd always thought so, and thus she'd never been able to bring herself to feel any affection for one of the poor creatures. So how did it happen that she had fallen head over heels in love with this one, who was showing just as much blind stubbornness as the rest of his gender?

She put her palm to his cheek. It was an angular cheek, a strong sweep of slightly prickled beard under her fingers. He was everything she ever wanted: a true scholar, a person with whom she could talk for hours, a man who made her blood race.

"As far as I can see there is only one *no* about it," she told him, her fingers clinging to his cheek.

"I can see a hundred," he said harshly, obviously determined to hold his ground, like that silly bulldog her father had owned.

"You don't like Shakespeare," she said. "It's a grave fault."

"Don't play with me." He growled it.

"I'm not playing," she said, smiling more brilliantly than she had ever smiled before. "I'm taking you, Gabriel Spenser. I'm claiming you. I'm marrying you. I'm—"

But he broke into her thoroughly arrogant list by trying to leave, so she had to kiss him again. And then she found herself backed against the wall, and his fingers raked into her hair. A while later there was a smile in his somber eyes, and Gillian knew without asking that she was the only one in the world who had seen that particular smile.

"I shan't take you," he said, belying the smile.

"I'll build a willow cabin at your gate."

"My house is in Cambridge," he said, adding "more than a few people would see you. And they do not know Shakespeare as well as you do."

"Shakespeare's heroine threatens to sing love songs in the middle of the night. It will ruin your scholarly reputation." She said it with relish.

"I have no reputation."

"You have your own reputation," and she said it gently, because he so obviously needed to be told. "That of a brilliant scholar and a man of honor. A man who loves his daughter and will do anything for her, even going against his own instincts and introducing himself to a distant family member, a duke who knew nothing of his existence."

"Shakespeare's hero was not such a fool as I, to go where he should not have been welcomed."

She felt as if her smile were warming both of them from the inside out. "Rafe welcomed you."

"I took advantage of his hospitality to court you."

"Were you courting me?" she asked with some curiosity. "I thought you were merely passing time by kissing me."

"I most certainly was *not* courting you," he said, reversing himself. "I would never ruin your life in that fashion."

She put on a mournful face. "I suppose I will go back to my first plan."

"And that is?" he asked warily.

"To marry Rafe, of course. Why, Imogen and I planned it quite carefully: she is to have an *affaire* with you, and I am to marry your brother."

He made a sound in his throat that sounded dangerously like a growl.

"If I have your assessment correctly, you think that I should marry an appropriate aristocrat, no? Why not Rafe? After all—" and her voice stilled—"if I can't have you, Gabe, I don't suppose I will care very much. Rafe and I will have a wonderful time . . . do you suppose he has read Shakespeare?"

"At some point."

"Philosophers? Because I was very interested to read of the new manuscript of Plato's dialogues that the Bodleian Library just acquired."

"We are negotiating to acquire a twelfth-century manuscript of the *Discourses of Epictetus*."

"Do you suppose that Rafe knows that?"

He shook his head.

"Perhaps I can learn to talk about horses. Did you know that I'm afraid of riding?"

He shook his head again.

"I'm a paltry rider, and horses dislike me. Do you suppose that might impinge on Rafe's and my happiness once we were married?"

"You could learn," he said, feeling as a drowning man does when the water closes over his head.

"Yes," she said. Then she came closer, right up to his body, and looked up at his face, his dear face. "I will learn to kiss him . . . the way you taught me?"

He seemed to be struggling to say something, or perhaps to hold his tongue.

She didn't allow herself to smile. Instead, she ran her hands up the muscled planes of his chest. "I'll learn to enjoy talk of horses and stables; I'll forget that I was ever interested in Shakespeare and philosophy; I will learn to kiss Rafe the way you kiss me . . ." That last part trailed off in an aching whisper because his hands had closed on her waist.

"You'll be the death of me," he said. But he sounded resigned, and her heart sped up.

"Yes," she whispered, and then, her eyes on him, "no?"

"They call it a *petit mort*," he said, and his mouth came down on hers.

32

A Chapter for Which Brazen Jokes
About Holes Would Be Appropriate
(But Your Author Refrains)

Imogen was going to be late for rehearsal. She had fallen asleep after luncheon and had a delicious set of dreams in which masked men with huge mustaches did various delightful things to her, while she weakly said "no," and then, "yes."

All of which concluded with Imogen waking up and dressing, aware of a not uncomfortable but quite new feeling between her legs. It was a funny feeling. A rather—

She wrenched her mind away, ran down the stairs, and began to rush along the corridor toward the theater. But just as she neared the end, a deep voice suddenly said: "Imogen!"

She turned around. "Yes?" And then in a circle. There was no door from which someone could have spoken to her. And yet—she whirled back. One of the painted panels that lined the corridor was ajar. Apparently that was a door, a secret door.

No one emerged.

"Come here." It was unmistakably the grave, low voice of Mr. Spenser. Imogen bit back a grin. Suddenly she knew precisely why she was rushing toward the ballroom, and it had very little to do with whether she was at the rehearsal precisely on time.

"Yes?" she said, walking toward the wall cautiously.

Silence. But the painting was ajar.

She reached out and opened the slender panel, but she didn't have time to peer inside. His arms scooped her up and backwards, and his mouth was on hers. Her eyes fell shut, and she melted against him as if no time had passed between the night and this kiss. It was as if they had both been simmering all day and burst into flame at the same moment.

When she opened her eyes they were in thick, warm darkness. His mouth was tracing fire on her neck, his hands shaping her breast almost roughly, thumb rubbing across her nipple so that she gasped and forgot her own questions, which had to do with the dark—

But he knew. "It's the priest's hole," he said, his voice rasping.

She couldn't see anything, and neither one of them

wanted to. This was about feeling: the rasp of his beard across her skin, the silk of her hair on his fingers. The weight of her breast in his hand, and the way she squeaked when he suckled. The softness of her skin and the shaping of his fingers. The muscles in his legs when her hands dropped that low, and the way he trembled when she dropped kisses: bolder here, in the darkness, with the memory of the night before between them. The priest's hole was like the Horse and Groom inn, apart from the world.

By the time he poised himself over her, she was sobbing, pulling him closer with all her strength, wrapping her legs around his body. And when he came to her, she closed her eyes against even the dark, so that her whole body focused on the way he was surging into her, the way her body was melting around him, the way—

"Oh God!" she choked.

He bent his head to kiss her just at the moment when she almost blurted out something fantastical, something about love.

But he was kissing her, and the words got lost in her throat as her body clutched his, feeling him ride higher and harder, increasing her pleasure, driving her higher . . . until a groan burst from his lips, and he surged against her one last time.

And then he brought all his rough, silky hair into the curve of her shoulder, and she wound her arms around him.

33

A Chapter Including a Performance . . . or Two

It wasn't that Rafe strutted into the theater. He would never do such a thing, even after dispatching his future wife back to her bedchamber for a nap (and carefully waiting a good period of time before stepping out of the priest's hole himself, so that she didn't catch sight of him).

He'd done it. She was his, bought, signed, and paid for. She had sighed, there in the warm dark, after they lay together a few minutes, and said, "I never even thought." That was all, but it was enough.

She might not think to marry Rafe, but she was intoxicated by Gabe. Or by who she thought Gabe was. All he had to do was reveal his true self, and she would say yes.

The stage was teeming with people. Gillian Pythian-

Adams was darting everywhere at once. "There you are!" she cried, when she saw Rafe. "Where's Imogen?"

"Terrible headache," he said promptly. "She'll be here as soon as she can."

She hesitated for a moment, and then nodded, turning to answer a burly groundsman who wanted to know where to place the potted shrubs.

Rafe strolled onto the stage with a remarkable sense of well-being. All he had to do was get through the weekend's performance of *Man of Mode*, kick the guests out of his house, and then tell Imogen that she was marrying him.

I never . . . He could hear her soft voice in his mind, and the very memory made him stiff as a board.

"Mr. Dorimant, Mr. Medley," Miss Pythian-Adams said.

"Here!"

"We'll start now, if you please."

Rafe dropped into the seat before a dressing table taken from the old green chamber on the third floor. Miss Pythian-Adams was pushing Mr. Medley, otherwise known as Gabe, into place beside him. Rafe was to sit next to his dressing table, lazily leafing through a book, while his friend Mr. Medley sprawled in a chair.

Gabe wasn't much of a sprawler; Rafe could have told Miss Pythian-Adams that.

Two minutes later, he could have told the world that Gabe was a terrible actor as well. He sounded like a scholar, reciting the lines of a rake. It was almost humorous. Rafe amused himself by wondering if he could play Medley, as Gabe playing Medley. After all, he did a good job of stealing Gabe's voice.

"No, no," Miss Pythian-Adams said with anguish, for the fortieth time. "Mr. Spenser, you really must try to relax."

Rafe narrowed his eyes. Gabe was laughing at Miss Pythian-Adams . . . they . . . they couldn't! If Imogen caught the glance that just passed between those two, she would think Gabe was truly a Dorimant—sleeping with Belinda while he courted a young lady—or she would know instantly that he, Rafe, had tricked her.

And he wasn't ready to tell that yet.

Suddenly he realized that he had to make love to her . . . oh perhaps once or twice more. Enough so that he was absolutely *certain* that she wouldn't refuse him, once she found out who was under the mustache.

Miss Pythian-Adams ran off to talk to Griselda, who had a query about Act Three, instructing Rafe and Gabe over her shoulder to practice their lines. "Please, teach your brother how to relax," she told Rafe.

"Relax," Rafe growled, and then bent over, pulling Gabe by the sleeve. "What the devil are you doing, smiling at Miss Pythian-Adams like that?"

Gabe didn't pretend to misunderstand him. "I'm going to marry her," he said simply. "Even though I shouldn't—"

Rafe cut him off. "You can't go around looking at her like that! Imogen will see you."

Gabe looked at him.

"Yes, I am still wearing the mustache," Rafe hissed.

"And that means that *you*, dear brother, are engaged in an *affaire* at the same time that you are courting Miss Pythian-Adams! If you weren't such an appalling actor, I'd say you should be Dorimant, not I."

"Ah, but it is in fact *you* who are Dorimant," Gabe pointed out. "After all, *you* are having an *affaire*. And *you* are courting a young lady at the same time. If Imogen doesn't happen to know that she is the object of both kinds of attention, it would be hardly polite for me to point it out."

"Exactly! So you must stop looking at our stage manager in such a besotted fashion."

"I will do my best," Gabe said tranquilly. "Would you like to run through the rest of the scene?"

"No. I know the play, and no amount of practice is going to turn you into anything but a professor masquerading as a rake."

"Whereas you are a rake masquerading as a professor?"

Rafe scowled at him.

"When do you think to reveal the truth of your charade?"

Miss Pythian-Adams flitted back to them, and Rafe almost groaned aloud. So much for Gabe keeping his secrets to himself. His eyes said everything, and what's more, Miss Pythian-Adams got a little pink every time she looked at him.

"It's not a charade," he said the moment Miss Pythian-Adams was called away again. "I shall tell her—soon."

"Why not immediately?"

Rafe opened his mouth, and stopped. He couldn't tell

her. Didn't Gabe see that? She wasn't entranced enough yet, not enough to look over what he was . . . what he had been. "I'm not ready," he said shortly.

"Are you afraid that she will refuse to marry you?"

"Any sane woman would."

Gabe's eyebrow went up. "A duke with an estate and—"

"Imogen knows *me*. She's seen me drunk time and again. She knows precisely what a hopeless excuse of a duke I am."

Miss Pythian-Adams darted up, and somehow they found themselves launching into Act Two. They bumbled through the play. Rafe didn't fool himself that it was going to be a wonderful performance. That actress of Gabe's, Loretta Hawes, was brilliant. When she was on the stage, the play took flight.

After an hour or so, Imogen walked in, with apologies for her delay. A while later, Rafe had to say that the little barbed exchanges between Dorimant (himself) and the pert young lady he was courting (Imogen) went pretty well too.

Miss Pythian-Adams seemed happy. It was dark before they finished the rehearsal, and she looked flushed and exhausted, but triumphant.

Gabe turned to him, just as the cast was leaving the stage. "You're quite good at playing someone else. Anyone would think you were making a practice of it."

Rafe's eyes narrowed. He seemed to be thinking about fratricide quite often.

"It's quite wonderful," Miss Pythian-Adams's mother declared from the front row, where she had been knitting all afternoon. "You're far better than that mingle-mangle of a Shakespeare play Lady Bedfordshire put on last season."

Of course, Miss Pythian-Adams couldn't stop herself from smiling at Gabe when she heard this, but luckily Rafe nipped Imogen around and had her out of the room before she noticed.

The theater was bursting with guests who'd come from London and the surrounding counties. They sounded like a crowd of self-important bees, more curious about who didn't receive an invitation than the performance itself.

"This young actress," Lady Blechschmidt said to her companion, Mrs. Fulgens. "Is she that red-haired piece who made such a remarkable hash of Lady Macbeth at the Olympic Theater last year?"

"No, I believe she is quite new," Mrs. Fulgens said. "Everyone is saying that Holbrook *discovered* her, whatever that means." She said it with the clear hope that the discovery did not involve intimacy; Mrs. Fulgens was having a difficult time launching her only daughter into matrimony, and she was holding out hope for the newly sober duke. But if that duke was exhibiting his mistress to the *ton* in his family theater . . . well, even a desperate mother would reject him as a potential son-in-law.

"Is that Lord Pool over there?" Lady Blechschmidt said. "My goodness, his hair seems to have quite changed color: from gray to black. It must be from grief at his wife's passing."

"I heard he was acting like an old fool, but I can't see him," Mrs. Fulgens said, squinting. "Lady Godwin is in the way. Could she really be carrying another child?"

"It seems so," Lady Blechschmidt said with the severity of someone who was rather more pleased than not when no children graced her marriage. Just look at how much difficulty Mrs. Fulgens was having with Daisy. Of course, the girl's spots made the whole business of marriage thorny.

"They are remarkably devoted," Mrs. Fulgens said, watching Lord Godwin help his wife to her seat with the possessive air of a man whose wife has grown more dear to him with each day.

Lady Blechschmidt counted it as a sad failing in herself that she found Lord Godwin far more interesting when he had Russian dancers prancing on his dining room table. Happy marriages were so rare in the *ton* that one would think they should be fascinating, and yet they were remarkably tiresome to watch.

Just then there was a peal from a trumpet played by a footman.

"Finally!" Lady Blechschmidt said. "I must say that I am all agog to see dear Lady Griselda in costume. *I* would never do such a thing myself; so lowering to one's dignity."

The curtain rose and there was a collective sigh at the sight of the Duke of Holbrook, dressed like a Restoration rake and sprawled at the dressing table.

Daisy, on the other side of Mrs. Fulgens, pinched her mother rather sharply, which Mrs. Fulgens rightly took to mean that Daisy wholeheartedly agreed with the idea of marrying the duke.

A thrum of excitement careened through the room. For onto the stage strolled a man who must be the duke's illegitimate brother—the man who had been one of the foremost subjects of conversation amongst the *ton* for the past months. There was no mistaking the resemblance between the brothers: they had the same shadowed eyes and the same cheekbones.

"His brother is the very image of him," Lady Blechschmidt said with some delight. "Shocking, isn't it?"

"He actually looks like a professor, doesn't he? It's a pity he's ineligible."

A gentleman in front of them turned about and raised a sardonic eyebrow.

"Who's *that*?" Lady Blechschmidt said loudly.

"Lord Kerr. He's a shareholder in the Hyde Park Theater," Mrs. Fulgens murmured. "Cruikshank did a wicked drawing of those gypsy eyes. Hatchard's had it in their window for a month."

They watched the play in silence for some time. Lady Blechschmidt was rather appalled by the loose principles being demonstrated by all the characters. Really, Griselda was showing an altogether different side of her character in accepting the role of a would-be mistress to Dorimant.

"The duke is quite good, isn't he?" Mrs. Fulgens whispered, after a time.

The duke wasn't nearly as good as Miss Loretta Hawes. They could both see that, and presumably Lord

Kerr felt the same, because he leaned forward each time the girl came on the stage.

Finally, Mrs. Fulgens had to ask. "Do you think she is the duke's *chère amie*?"

Lady Blechschmidt had been watching the foibles of men and women for longer than she cared to admit, and she saw nothing loverlike in Dorimant's brisk exchanges with Mrs. Loveit. In fact, the duke cast off Mrs. Loveit with a thoroughly convincing lack of interest. "Absolutely not," she told Mrs. Fulgens.

That worthy matron lapsed into her chair and ceased to pay any attention to the play, lost in a happy dream in which her daughter, Daisy the Duchess, figured prominently.

But Lady Blechschmidt was caught up in the play, frivolous though the characters were. It was Dorimant's exchanges with Harriet, the country girl, that made her eyes narrow. In fact, she was so struck by them that by Act Four, she called Mrs. Fulgens's attention back to the stage.

Mrs. Fulgens watched the duke flirting with Imogen Maitland for five minutes and then discarded her dreams for Daisy.

34

Temptation Takes Many, and Varied, Forms

The evening after the play, Rafe leaned against the orchard wall with a pleasurable sense of exhilaration. He was thinking of the carriage. Perhaps they wouldn't even make it as far as Silchester. Then he heard the whisper of skirts coming through the fallen leaves. He straightened and wondered, just for a second, whether he would always greet Imogen with this blistering sense of anticipation.

But it wasn't Imogen; it was unmistakably Josie coming down the path. He drew farther back into the shadow of the old apple tree. It still flummoxed him that Imogen hadn't recognized him, even with the mustache, but Josie was sharp as a tack.

She stopped before him. "I'm to tell you that my sister

is not coming," she said without preamble. "She's very grateful for the adventure, sir, and thanks you for your company." She held out a note.

Rafe took it, feeling a creeping unease. "Is she feeling well?"

"Of course. She does not wish to go to Silchester. I believe she explained everything in her note."

Rafe shut his mouth. He could hardly ask Josie for the reasoning. A girl as young as Josie should have nothing to do with the "adventures" of a young widow. So he bowed, and watched Josie trot back up the path to Holbrook Court.

It was times like these that a brandy-soaked evening sounded appealing. Instead, he read Imogen's brief note (which said nothing), made his way back to his own bedchamber, and waited until the middle of the night, for the hours when the dark is as thick as velvet, and dawn seems an impossibility. Even the birds had stopped twittering, when he finally walked, mustache-clad, down the corridor.

Imogen slept on her stomach. He put his candle down on the bedside table and looked for a moment at her cheekbones. Her face looked different when her eyes were closed: as if it belonged to a more docile woman. He sat down next to her, and the bed tilted a bit, just enough so that she opened her eyes blearily.

"Hello there," he said.

"It's you," she replied, rather ungraciously. Then she rolled over and yawned.

Rafe watched her nightrail catch against her breasts and beat down a fiery impulse to drop on her like a stone from a great height.

"Why didn't you wish to go to Silchester?" he asked, his voice taking on Gabe's cadence as if it was his own. "I read your note, but it was hardly informative."

She leaned forward and patted him on the arm, for all the world as if he were a pensioner who'd asked for bread. "I am so grateful to you for your companionship, which I *tremendously* enjoyed, but I have decided to live a more celibate existence."

Rafe leaned forward to kiss her. She put a hand out to stop him, but he brushed his lips across hers. "Come, Imogen," he said. "You're too passionate to live a celibate existence. You can hardly join a convent. You are a widow, and there's nothing to stop you having a dalliance."

But she didn't melt into his arms; instead she pulled back and looked at him steadily. "It's true that I do not betray Draven by spending time with you . . . but I think that in some way, I betray myself."

Rafe opened his mouth, blinked, and shut his mouth again.

Imogen looked at the dim face of the man sitting on her bed and bit back a smile. Griselda had been absolutely right. The line about betraying oneself had silenced him.

He cleared his throat. "You're saying that you truly wish to stop our meetings?" He sounded stunned.

She nodded. "As I said, I'm grateful. It was—" she hesitated—"remarkably pleasurable. But I do not care to think of myself as someone who makes love in broom closets and carriages. This has been a valuable lesson."

"We don't have to make love in carriages!" he said, a note of hope entering his voice.

"I do not wish to continue having a surreptitious affair."

Silence. Then: "You appear to find it remarkably easy to forgo the pleasures we have shared."

"I enjoyed them," she said. "But if I were ever to embark on another affair, Gabriel, I shall not be the one to chase my partner."

"My feelings—" He said it through clenched teeth.

But she was smiling at him. "I can tell that your desire is genuine, and I am grateful for it." It was a dismissal.

"I see." He rose to his feet, thinking desperately that he ought to rip off the mustache. And yet . . . he was terrified. He was a paltry man to offer marriage to Imogen. Not much more than her benighted, foolish husband, if it came to that. Draven Maitland hadn't been a drinker, after all. She deserved better.

"Good-bye," she said.

"Imogen." He turned to go and then paused, back to her. "What will you do now? Do you plan to marry?"

"Not in the immediate future."

Rafe walked into the corridor feeling as if he had been struck about the head. Apparently his plan to prove himself an irresistible lover while pretending to be Gabe so that Imogen would have no recourse but to accept his hand was a failure.

He didn't feel heartbroken. What he felt was a tremendous, burning wish to take a drink. To retreat into the soft golden hue of forgetfulness that came along with whiskey. In the days when he was drinking, he didn't care that he wasn't a fit consort for a woman such as Imogen.

He found himself walking down the stairs. Moonlight filtered dimly into the great stairway that led to the floor below. The great stairs trod by so many dukes who actually—

But he stopped, hand on the door to his study. Like any drunk, he had whiskey hidden there, liquor from the days when he used to have a quiet nightcap, or two or three.

But were all those dukes so worthy of the great stairs? His father, with his second family and his coldness toward his legitimate sons? Peter, who though Rafe loved him dearly, was so hidebound that he didn't even bother to share the news that Rafe had a half brother? What he remembered of his grandfather was a cold, thin man with a cane and a permanent sneer. It was his grandfather who had arranged his father's marriage, when his son was a mere lad. Perhaps his father would have been a different man had he been allowed to marry as he wished.

Finally, Rafe did open the door.

He walked into the study, the inner sanctum of dukes, where Peter, and his father, and his grandfather had sat.

He stood for a long time, looking at the two crystal decanters, concealed behind paneling that swung open at his touch. Then somehow a decanter was in his hand, open. The sharp scent of the whiskey lured like a siren's smile. It was oblivion, that extra cape and mustache that he could wear from keeping the world from judging his impoverishment. His inability to be a proper duke. The whiskey seemed to call to him, promise him relief from the press of failure, from the sense that Imogen didn't need him.

Or perhaps it was the other way around, he suddenly thought. He didn't need Imogen, not for this. And perhaps she had need of him.

God knows, he needed her more than he needed a glass of whiskey.

A moment later he emptied the two decanters onto the courtyard stones, far below the window.

Then he sat down. He knew precisely what to do. He started to make a list. His solicitor, at the man's earliest convenience. Gabriel.

And Imogen.

35

*Raphael Jourdain, Duke of Holbrook,
Comes into His Title*

Gabriel Spenser was clearly in love with Miss Pythian-Adams, and when and how that had happened, Imogen didn't know. It was all one with the lump of dull misery that seemed to have permanently lodged itself behind her breastbone.

She hadn't even seen Rafe in days because he'd left for London without saying good-bye. Her maid told her that his valet was greatly excited because the duke had visited a tailor and had ordered a wardrobe "fit for a duke." Even presentation breeches, Daisy said, the morning Rafe was back at Holbrook Court. "And he saw his solicitor in London. Mr. Brinkley says it likely indicates that His Grace means to marry, once the season starts."

"I'm sure he does," Imogen said. Her smile felt strange on her face, like a wrinkle before its time.

"We all thought he was to marry Miss Pythian-Adams," Daisy continued. "But there, she's made her choice. Mr. Brinkley says that the duke only came back to Holbrook Court for a day or so. He's off to London again tomorrow perhaps, so Mr. Brinkley thinks he might be courting a young lady even now, before the season begins."

Imogen blinked away a dimness in her eyes. So Rafe meant to marry. And Gabriel meant to marry. Why, so did she. As soon as she found a man who wanted her for more than a casual kiss and a casual tumble at an inn.

And as soon as she could overcome a growing, desperate sense of grief and loss that threatened to match what she had felt when Draven died. It was a blasphemous thought, and had Imogen's throat close with tears at the shame of it.

Josie met her at the bottom of the stairs, glowing with excitement. "Rafe has seen Mayne in London, and you won't believe this, Imogen, but Mayne is getting married!"

Imogen took a deep breath. "Who is he marrying?"

"A Frenchwoman," Josie said, "with a delicious name that I forgot. She sounds like a heroine in one of my novels. Rafe has met her; he says that she's exquisite and will keep Mayne in line. Oh, you're wearing a riding habit. Are you taking Posy out before breakfast?"

In fact, Imogen had thought to ask if Rafe wished to accompany her, but she abruptly changed her mind. "Yes," she said. "I'm going to the stables now. I'm not hungry."

She didn't return until an hour later. She and Posy had galloped along country lanes, ducked under the willows between her land and Rafe's, ambled through the field where Rafe had asked her to marry him, even if it was only in jest. The mist was gone from her eyes, and her chin was up again.

She would go to London and find a husband who treasured her. Who thought she was interesting and funny, even in the daylight. Who didn't need to be seduced, but would want to seduce her. Who didn't need to sneak into her bedchamber, but would ask for her hand in marriage before she even thought he was interested. Who would say that he loved her.

Imogen strode into the entryway and handed her hat and crop to Brinkley. "His Grace would like to see you at your convenience in his study," Brinkley said. "Shall I inform him that you will join him in, perhaps, an hour?"

Imogen ran a hand over her hair. At one point her hat had almost blown free again, but she had snatched it just in time. Still, her hair was doubtless tangled. She probably smelled like leather and yellow parsley, because she'd lain down in the field for a moment and looked at the sky. "I'll stop in to see him now," she said, making up her mind. "I intend to take my sister to London tomorrow morning, Brinkley. We both are in desperate need of a new wardrobe."

"But—"

She pushed open the door to the study. It was a dim room, with large, comfortingly male, furniture. The walls were lined with books, and one had the odd feeling that they were leaning in at the top, as if the walls were bowed under their weight.

"Rafe?" she called. "Where are you?"

"We are here." She walked forward and then saw Rafe's hand go out in the dim light and turn up the Argand lamp.

She stopped short.

Rafe was wearing court dress. His suit was of red velvet, a suit created for an encounter with the king. Or the queen. He wore formal breeches, and a square vest of embroidered satin. He was magnificent. Every inch of him was ducal, from the beautiful fit of the velvet on his shoulders to the braided trim on his vest. His hair no longer fell around his shoulders but was tied back. The shoulders of his coat looked slightly strained, and yet he wore the elegant, tight-fitting garment with the ease of someone who pulls on a waistcoat embroidered with pearls every day.

"Rafe?" she gasped.

He bowed. It was the bow of a duke to a young widow, a bow that combined to a calculated degree a sense of both their positions—her beauty, his wealth.

Her eyes slid to the side, and there was Mr. Spenser, smiling with his customary scholarly gravitude. "Lady Maitland," he said, bowing.

Griselda stepped forward. She too was dressed as magnificently as if royalty were expected. "Darling," she said, kissing Imogen on the cheek.

"How extremely formal you are," Imogen said. "All of you."

"Gabriel will act as your guardian in this discussion," Rafe said.

"He will?"

"Under the circumstances," Mr. Spenser said. "Your guardian has received a request for your hand in marriage, Lady Maitland."

"But Rafe *is* my guardian."

"I hereby disavow the position," Rafe said. "I've asked Gabriel to help me with a great many of the ducal responsibilities. In fact, he is thinking of giving up his post at the university."

"Oh," Imogen said flatly. "I shall not accept that offer of marriage."

"Wouldn't you like to hear who offered it?" Mr. Spenser had both her hands, somehow, and he was smiling down at her with that gentle, lopsided smile that was somehow both his and Rafe's.

She didn't dare to answer, just looked at him.

"His Grace, the Duke of Holbrook, has requested the honor of your hand in marriage. As your guardian, I have advised him that since you are a widow, and not a dependent in anyone's household, you are free to make your own choice." Gabriel's face creased into a swift smile, and he picked up her right hand and kissed it. "I shall leave you to contemplate your decision."

Griselda took his arm. "I believe that widows may accept proposals without chaperonage, my dear." She smiled, and then the door closed quietly behind them.

Imogen turned slowly to Rafe. She felt as if she were in a dream: that it wasn't Rafe at all, but some glittering, aristocratic creature who stood before her.

And then, as she watched him, he sank onto his knee before her. He took her hands, and those *were* his hands, so large. They weren't a pampered duke's hands, but the calloused hands of a man who held the reins every day. He brought her palm to his lips, and her heart leaped.

"Lady Maitland, will you do me the honor of giving me your hand in marriage?"

The words hung in the air of the study.

She pulled at his hands, trying to raise him to his feet. But he stayed there, looking up at her. "I love you. If you don't marry me, Imogen, I shall never marry. There is no other woman for me in this world. I did not know it was possible to feel such emotion as I feel for you."

She sank onto her knees and held out her arms. "Oh, Rafe!"

"I am a slow man, and a careless one. There is, I suppose, a chance that at some point I will take up whiskey again. I can perhaps never be the man you would wish—"

She cried out, involuntarily, but he continued. "But I love you, Imogen." He had both her hands to his lips now. "I want you with a passion that will never leave me, not even when one of us sees the other into a grave, and by God, I hope it's at the same moment."

She was blinking away tears, but he wasn't done.

"I think I've loved you from the moment you walked into this house. God knows, I've never hated a man as much as I hated Draven Maitland, from the moment you mentioned his name, and your eyes shone. I know you likely will never feel the same for me, but—"

She tried to speak, but he stopped her again.

"I love you enough for both of us."

"There's no need to say that!" she said it through her

tears, through a brilliant smile, through the joy making her heart sing. "I love you . . . I love you too." She tried to pull him toward her, but his eyes were still dark, tormented almost.

"You might not when you realize what I've done to you, Imogen."

She stopped him by the simple method of capturing his face in her hands and pressing her lips to his. And when he still tried to say something, she kissed him into silence.

"I came to you under false pretenses," he said, sometime later. Some three hot, endless kisses later.

She was struggling with the buttons on his magnificently embroidered vest. "What are you doing?" he whispered into her ear. "Dukes don't make love on the floor of their study."

"This duke does," she whispered back.

"You're seducing me. I thought you would never make a bold advance to me again." He was laughing with the pure joy of it. "Didn't you tell me that in a properly ordered marriage . . . wasn't that what you meant?"

She was laughing too, laughing at him, laughing as she unbuttoned, as she trembled, as she wondered just how far Brinkley was from the door. "I was wrong," she said. "I was wrong."

"I have been wrong about so many things," Rafe said, stopping her hands so he could kiss them again. "You still don't understand, Imogen—"

"Don't I?"

"You don't." He said it desperately, because her hands were running over his chest, and he knew that his wife would always be like this, seducing him, taking him. Unless he stopped her. So he did. He eased her to the ground, rolled on top of her, and growled, "Imogen!"

She looked up at him, her eyes all languorous, and said, "I love you, Rafe."

He forgot for a few minutes what he meant to say, what he had to confess. He could tell her later. He wasn't even thinking of that when he'd finally gotten himself out of all that embroidery, and her out of her riding habit. All the thinking he did—and that briefly—was to wonder whether Brinkley was smart enough to stay away from the room (he decided yes).

So, finally, she said it for him.

"Do you think that you might put on the mustache sometimes?" she whispered, with a wicked smile that went straight to his heart. "It tickled, and I found it vastly . . . amusing."

Epilogue

December 23, 1828
Holbrook Court

The Christmas pantomime was running late again. The entire village and a good sprinkle of Londoners were lined up in the red velvet chairs of the theater. Of course, every one of the four Essex sisters was there; Christmas at Holbrook Court had become a tradition. But most of them weren't in the audience. One of the thoroughly original aspects of the Holbrook pantomime (one of the most coveted invitations in all England) was that the four Essex sisters took roles, even though most pantomimes were performed by men. And some years, the youngest had even played the prince.

This year, the prince was being played with undoubted gravity by Mr. Lucius Felton; his wife Tess would play Cinderella herself.

"Aunt Annabel plays the best wicked stepsister," Tess's sturdy son Phin told his cousin.

"I like watching Aunt Josie," the future Earl of Ardmore said disloyally, discounting his mother's performance. "Aunt Josie is always so *mean* to poor Cinderella."

"My mother says they're mean to her because she's the eldest," Phin said. "It's hard to be the eldest. My sisters are just as mean to me." He said it with feeling.

Everyone was in the theater waiting, from Lady Griselda to Lady Blechschmidt, and yet the Spensers hadn't even made their way from their house—the house that used to be called Maitland House—to Holbrook Court.

Finally, Imogen walked into the audience to tell everyone the performance was running a trifle late. "What a pleasure to see you, Your Grace!" Lady Blechschmidt crowed. "I was just telling dear Lady Griselda that I shall never forget the first play I saw in this delightful little theater. Did you see the *Midsummer Night's Dream* playing at Drury Lane? *She* was wonderful, wonderful as always!"

There was no need to clarify who was wonderful; the fact that Loretta Hawes began her triumphant career as an actress at Holbrook Court was known to every member of the theatergoing public from London to Paris.

"Rafe and I are particularly fond of that play," Imogen said, smiling at Griselda's handsome husband as she spoke. "We were there on opening night."

"Loretta," Griselda said with the delight of someone who enjoyed dropping the famous actress's first name, "will always shine in a tragic role. But she—"

Imogen was interrupted by a pull on her gown.

"Mama!" She turned around. Her firstborn child, Genevieve, was standing there, looking uncannily like her papa, barring her deep lower lip, inherited from Imogen. Genevieve lowered her voice in the important way of a seven-year-old who understands proprieties. "Miss Metta has had palpitations from excitement, and now Luke is running about with his pants below his knees!"

Imogen curtsied to Griselda and Lady Blechschmidt. "If you'll forgive me, ladies, I'm afraid there's a domestic crisis behind stage."

Two minutes later the pandemonium in the green room was doubled as the Spenser family burst into the room. One family member was laughing (Mary was one of the merriest girls for leagues, or so her papa said), one was crying (Mary's brother Richard was at an age where he felt terrible rage if he didn't achieve his own way,) and yet another was crowing (alas, Richard's twin brother Charles was devoting his third year of life to ensuring that Richard did not achieve his own way).

But in a half hour or so, the pies were in position, the actors were costumed, and the audience was applauding madly.

On the stage strolled Widow Trankey, her wild blond curls concealing a duchess's glowing hair. She had a hand on her hip and an insouciant smile for Professor Cheatley. He was played not by the duke's brother, as would have made sense, but by the duke himself. There hadn't been a year in which the entire audience hadn't screamed with delight every time Professor Cheatley opened his mouth and drawled a few slow, pedantic phrases in his brother's voice. Professor Cheatley spent most of the pantomime trying to pull Widow Trankey under the mistletoe, although she was most adroit at avoiding it, and him, and seemed to particularly delight in flinging pies in his direction.

But the star of the show, as it had been for the past three years, was the Principal Boy, played by Miss Mary Spenser in a pair of breeches that (her mother had made certain) were neither revealing nor indiscreet. In fact, she looked rather like a Dutch trader in great billowing breeches. But none of that mattered, for it was her face that made everyone break into gales of laughter: the way she darted under Widow Trankey's arm, avoiding a pie, the way her eyebrows shot up as she listened to the pedantic statements of Professor Cheatley, alias the Duke of Holbrook. It was the way she tore across the stage and hid behind her mother's skirts (playing the role of evil stepmother, naturally), and then danced silently behind her father (playing the king) to drop a pie on his head at just the right moment.

All in all, this Christmas pantomime was just as exuberant, delightful, and beloved as it had been the last six years.

The curtain fell, as it had for the last six years, when Professor Cheatley finally managed to grab the Widow Trankey and pull her under the sprig of mistletoe hanging from the center of stage front. The curtain fell on their kiss, and there wasn't a member of the audience who didn't sigh.

Well, perhaps Lady Blechschmidt wasn't quite as delighted. She felt that the duke and duchess's embrace was a trifle too passionate for her taste . . . the way the duke bent the duchess back over his arm . . . really!

They seemed to have quite forgotten their rank, not to mention the presence of their children.

In truth, the Duke of Holbrook often forgot his rank. Particularly when he was kissing his wife.

"Rafe, you must stop!" Imogen whispered, trying to push him away.

"That's not what you said yesterday afternoon in the Priest's Hole," he said in her ear.

"Oh *you*—" Imogen said, but he was grinning down at her, and he was so dear, so perfect, and so much her own Rafe that her eyes filled with tears.

He knew . . . he always knew what she was thinking. He said it so quietly that she almost didn't hear him. "I'm not planning on dying, Imogen, but I'm yours past that moment."

The curtain rose for bows, only to discover that the duke was still kissing his wife and Miss Mary Spenser was tiptoeing across the stage elaborately, her finger to her lips hushing the audience and her face alight with laughter.

A moment later a cream pie landed on top of the kissing couple, and the curtain fell again.

A Note on Drinking Whiskey and Editing Plays, Though Not at the Same Time

I's a difficult thing to make a hero of a man addicted to alcohol. And it's even harder to keep the story both accurate to the historical period and the process of drying out. Back in the 1800s, people did not think of alcoholism as an illness, and methods for overcoming addiction were not in the public vernacular. I am lucky enough to have friends who have survived the harrowing process of overcoming an addiction to alcohol; their descriptions were invaluable to me. One book that was a tremendous help in deciphering early English attitudes toward drink was John London's *Jack Barleycorn: Alcoholic Memoirs*, first published in 1913. The publication date falls a century after my period, but I found the book invaluable because it pre-dates our medicalized view of alcoholic addiction. I am prouder of Rafe than any of my other heroes: unlike the rakish gentlemen who populate so many historical novels, the problems Rafe faced were huge, if not insurmountable, and yet he managed to overcome them with a modicum of grace and a good deal of humor.

Some years ago when I was an assistant professor of English literature at Washington University in St. Louis, I was offered a truly magnificent sum to edit two plays, one of which was *The Man of Mode*. My edition of that play appeared in the 1998 *Longman Anthology of British Literature*. The work of editing *The Man of Mode* served the double purpose of helping to pay my student loans and causing me to fall thoroughly in love with George Etheridge's witty, caustic prose. It has been a true pleasure to include threads of that play here, especially the shadow of Etheridge's great hero Dorimant who has, like Rafe, "something of the angel yet undefaced in him."

The Taming of the Duke contains so many echoes of early English literature that I can't catalog them here. If you would like to know more about Cristobel's songs, Josie's quotations of Shakespeare, or Christmas pantomimes in the 1800s, please visit my website at *www.eloisajames.com*. The "Inside Take" section of the Bookshelf entry for *The Taming of the Duke* documents all these enticing bits of early modern prose.